FLORA'S FURY

Cierra Califa

YSABEAU S. WILCE

FLORA'S FURY

*How a Girl of Spirit
and a Red Dog Confound
Their Friends,
Astound Their Enemies,
and Learn the Importance
of Packing Light*

HOUGHTON MIFFLIN HARCOURT

Boston   New York

All rights reserved. Published in the United States by Graphia, an imprint of
Houghton Mifflin Harcourt Publishing Company. Originally published in
hardcover in the United States by Harcourt Children's Books, an imprint of
Houghton Mifflin Harcourt Publishing Company, 2012.

Graphia and the Graphia logo are trademarks of
Houghton Mifflin Harcourt Publishing Company.

For information about permission to reproduce selections from this book,
write to Permissions, Houghton Mifflin Harcourt Publishing Company,
215 Park Avenue South, New York, New York 10003.

www.hmhbooks.com

The Library of Congress has cataloged the hardcover edition as follows:
Wilce, Ysabeau S.
Flora's fury: how a girl of spirit and a red dog confound their friends, astound
their enemies, and learn the importance of packing light / Ysabeau S. Wilce.
p. cm.
Summary: Determined to find her true mother, Flora Fyrdraaca,
accompanied by her red dog, embarks on a journey filled with magical
encounters, pirate battles, and unexpected romance.
[1. Fantasy.] I. Title.
PZ7.W6438Fn 2012
[Fic]—dc23
2011027325

ISBN: 978-0-15-205409-0 hardcover
ISBN: 978-0-15-205415-1 paperback

Manufactured in the U.S.A
DOC 10 9 8 7 6 5 4 3 2
4500416217

To Sieur Stilskin:
Thanks for the lift in your balloon.

*The tygers of wrath are wiser
than the horses of instruction.*

—WILLIAM BLAKE

FLORA'S FURY

Statement of Intent
Magickal Working No. 9

by
Nyana Georgiana Brakespeare Haðraaða
ov Tyrdraaca
Written in Sub-Rosa Ranger
Scriptive Code

Dear ~~Mamma~~ ~~Butcher~~ ~~Brakespeare~~ ~~Azota~~ Tiny
Doom:

Everyone thinks the Birdies killed you, sacrificed you
to one of their gods, whose priests ate your body while he
ate your soul. Everyone thinks you are more than just
dead, that you've been erased from the Waking World
and Elsewhere, without a trace of your Anima surviving to
cross the Abyss. Even Paimon thinks this. *I am the denizen
of Bilskinir House,* he told me. *No member of the Haðraaða family can be unknown to me; if she escaped the Birdies and survived, I
would know it. But she didn't,* he said. *Tezcatlipoca took her and
she's Gone.*

I don't care what Paimon says, or what he thinks he
knows. He might be Bilskinir House's Butler, but I am the
Head of the Family and I know you are still alive. I am
your daughter, and I know.

1

I *know* it. In my heart and my head and my very gut.

And I'm really fiking furious about it.

Never leave a comrade behind, the great ranger Nini Mo said. Well, you not only left me behind, *Mamma,* but you left me in the lurch.

I'm sure you'd say that you were trying to protect me by getting Buck Fyrdraaca to pass me off as her own child, by getting Buck to lie to me all those years about being my mother. (And by the way—was it really fair to hide this knowledge from Poppy, too? He's my father. Didn't he deserve to know who my real mother is? He knows now, but finding out was a terrible shock. And believe me, after all the horrible things Poppy's been through, he did not need another terrible shock.) I know you were only trying to save me from the Birdies, who would kill me for no other reason than I was your daughter. But did you ever think about what this meant for me?

My entire life—my family, my name, even my birthday—is a lie.

I used to be so sure of myself. I used to know who I was: the youngest child of General Juliet "Buck" Fyrdraaca and her crazy husband, Hotspur. I used to have a home: Crackpot Hall, old and moldering and with a banished Butler, but a home nonetheless.

I used to have dreams: I'd be a ranger, like Nini Mo, stealthy and secret. I'd speak Gramatica, the Language of magick. I'd cross from the Waking World to Elsewhere as easily as crossing the street. I'd be clever, cunning, and shrewd, true to my own Will.

I used to have sand and grit, hope and a future. And now I have nothing. Now I have to skulk around in the shadows, trying to be small and unobtrusive, so our Birdie overlords won't notice me, won't discover who I really am.

I can't even use my real name. You named me Nyana, after the great ranger Nini Mo, but Buck changed my name to Flora, after her daughter who was lost to the Birdies when she was small and perfect. As far as everyone is concerned, I am just Flora Segunda, a pale shadow of the original.

Unless the Birdies catch me. Then I'll be Nyana Brakespeare ov Haðraaða. (As far as they are concerned, my Fyrdraaca half doesn't count.) Then the Birdies will take me to Anahautl City. They'll march me to the top of one of their black obsidian pyramids and rip out my heart with a slick black obsidian knife. Then they'll eat my heart and feed my Anima to Tezca-whatsit, the Lord of the Smoked Mirror. That will be *punto final* for me, the absolute end. I'll be done before I even got started.

Needless to say, I'm not so keen on that.

So, to avoid exactly that, I've spent the last eight months being anonymous. I've pretended to be a good little Fyrdraaca and have done everything a good little Fyrdraaca is expected to do. Like a good little Fyrdraaca, I went to Benica Barracks Military Academy. There, I was a good little cadet. I shined my shoes and dug latrines, calculated trajectories and marched eight miles with a fully loaded pack and an empty canteen. When, thanks to the Infanta Sylvanna, I was detached from the Barracks and sent to work in Buck's office as her junior aide-de-camp, I went with a smile, happy to settle in to a prison of paperwork. Now I spend all day copying reports and going to meetings and reviews and inspections and briefings, and baby-sitting Pow. If the Birdies don't get me, this will be the rest of my life.

And I can't spend the rest of my life this way. I just can't. Can't spend the rest of my life hiding, afraid and alone. Ignored and overlooked. Trapped in a lie. I'd almost rather the Birdies catch me and put me out of my misery.

No, that's not true. I want to live. As my true self.

Also, *Mamma* dear, I'd like to point out, it's not just me that you left in the lurch, but the entire Republic of Califa. Thanks to you, the war was lost. Thanks to you, the Birdies own us now. We are their lap dogs. The Infanta Sylvanna has lived with the Birdies most of her life. Basically, she *is* a Birdie. The Warlord is old and on his last legs. Once the Infanta is in charge, Califa will become a Birdie State. There'll be no chance for me to be free, and no chance for anyone else, either.

If Nini Mo were alive today, she would not stand by idly as Califa is sucked ever deeper into lap-doggery, as we

4

bow our heads ever lower to the Birdie yoke. *Free the oppressed!* Is that not the Ranger Motto? Nini Mo would never live as a slave, subject to another. She would be working tirelessly to overthrow Califa's Birdie overlords; she would do everything she could to undermine them.

Well, I can't start a revolution, Tiny Doom, but you could.

I know you weren't very popular when you were alive—hence the Butcher nickname—but now that everyone thinks you are dead, they love you. Azota, they call you now, the Whip, and they mean it as a compliment. They scrawl CIERRA AZOTA! on public buildings and sing heroic ballads about you—"Lo' She Wields Her Mighty Goad" is particularly popular right now—and wear shocking-pink ribbands in your honor. They make offerings to you and name their children after you. Somehow, I don't know exactly how or why, you have become a symbol of freedom.

But if you came back, you'd be more than a symbol; you'd be a leader. The people would flock to you, would rise up and kick the Birdies square in the teeth, right out of Califa. Califa would be free. I would be free. You owe us this freedom. It's your fault the war was lost to begin with. It's time for you to come back and make amends.

So where the fike are you?

The Waking World is a vast place. There are many places to hide: The Kulani Islands, Bexar, Espada, Ketchikan, Varanger, Porkopolis. How do you track someone whose tracks are fifteen years old? Who left those tracks a thousand miles away? Who hundreds of people saw die—*thought* they saw die. Who is able to hide from the denizen of her own house?

Not even Nini Mo could cut that sign.

Oh, I know that wherever you are, you think you are well hidden. No one has found you so far, so no one ever will.

We'll see about that.

How does one cut sign if there isn't any sign to cut? I've been puzzling over this for a long time. Then, on my dinner break a couple of days ago, I noticed one of the other clerks reading *Nini Mo, Coyote Queen vs. the Crab King of Krake Island.* In case you don't remember, it's the one where Nini Mo and the Macaroni Kid are trapped in the belly of the Crab King, and Nini Mo charges a drop of her own blood into an Erucate Sigil, which she then uses to blast them both out to freedom. Suddenly the answer was obvious.

I may not be a ranger and I may not be an adept, but I have an edge no one else can claim. I have a connection to you, the strongest connection two people can have.

Blood.

Blood calls to blood, Nini Mo said. It's the one bond that can never be erased. You can hide from the Birdies, Poppy, the Warlord, anyone. But you can't hide from me.

All I need is a simple Locative Sigil and a few drops

6

of blood, my blood, which is your blood, too. Blood, and the Will to do the Working. Of course, I have to be super careful not to do anything that might reveal me to the Birdies. Magick being number one on that list. But here's the clever part. Tomorrow night is Pirates' Parade, amateur magick night, when the Current is full of snapperheads playing at conjuring, sigils, and fortunetelling. The perfect camouflage. With all the other magickal hijinks going on, no one is going to notice me.

I know a Blood Working won't be easy. I may be in hiding, and my magickal studies may have been cut short, but I'm not some tyro. I stood up to Lord Axacaya, the City's greatest adept, when he tried to kill me. I've been to the very threshold of the Abyss and back. I helped birth a baby etheric egregore of the ninth order. I've parlayed with Springheel Jack and fought a Quetzal. I may not be a real ranger, but I've pulled off the Ultimate Ranger Dare. I am confident I can manage it. I have to. It may be my only chance.

I am going to track you down and make you come back to Califa. Not because I'm desperate for maternal affection or looking for some melodramatic reunion. But for Califa's sake. For my sake, too, but mostly for Califa.

SO THIS, THEN, is my Statement of Intent, the what, how, and why of the Working.

What: Calling upon the Sanguinary Link between One Member of a Family to Another, and by Following this Link thus Determining Her Whereabouts.

How: A map, a razor, the Current, the adept's own Will.

Why: Because it is my Will.

This is a paltry Statement, I know, but it's all I have time to write. It's already almost two in the morning and I still have to polish my buttons, shine my shoes, wash my gloves, and finish packing my gear before I can go to bed, and I have to be at the office by seven.

And, of course, I'm never actually going to show this to Tiny Doom. I'll burn it during the Working, and anyway, it's just a way to screw up my nerve. I know she doesn't care about me. If she did, she would have come back long ago. Well, she doesn't have to care. She just has to come back. I'm sure of that. The only thing I'm not sure of is how I will get to her once I locate her. But I'll worry about that later. I have to find her first.

And I will.

ONE

Paperwork.
Pow. Duty.

WHEN I GOT TO the Commanding General's Office at seven thirty-five, my desk was already piled high with papers. Either Buck had been working late or Lieutenant Sabre had been in early. Both, probably. I made coffee, and, as the other clerks trickled in, began to sort. At eight thirty, Poppy rushed in, hung Pow's cradleboard on the coat rack, and rushed out, saying he'd be back by lunchtime. I'd just finished stamping the incoming mail and begun to log it in the Correspondence Received Register when Pow woke up and began to howl. Even Private Hargrave's bunny imitation, normally a baby side-splitter, failed to distract him; you can't tell a five-month-old baby to wait for his chow. So I hefted the cradleboard over my shoulder and went in search of Buck.

I found her down at the cavalry stables, worrying over Sadie, who still hadn't foaled. While Buck sat on a hay bale and fed Pow, continuing her conversation with Dr. Mars, I ran over to the post bakery and got two dozen donuts and three cups of coffee. I returned to the stables and found that Buck and Pow had already gone.

So back to the office I went, balancing the coffee and donuts carefully so I wouldn't get anything messy on my uniform. The rain, which had been pouring down for the past week, was finally letting up a bit, but everything was soggy. The parade ground was too wet for drills and the roads were ankle-deep in mud. At Building 56, a sign had been hung by the main door reminding everyone to scrape their boots before coming inside, but the front porch and hallway were streaked with mud. A sorry-looking private with a wet mop was trying to keep the mess down, without much success.

Buck took a coffee and donut and put a finger to her lips: Pow was asleep again, so I was dismissed back to my correspondence. I finished logging and had begun on my endorsements when Buck realized she was late for a meeting with the Warlord and had left the Command Baton at the O Club.

I rushed to the Club, found the Baton in one of the lavs, and raced back to the CGO. There I discovered that Sergeant Carheña had gone to the quartermaster storehouse to get more paper and pen nibs, leaving Private Hargrave in charge, and Private Hargrave, who is what's commonly known in the Army as a coffee cooler, had disappeared into the sinks with the *Califa Police Gazette*. Flynn and Pow were alone in the office—Buck had left without the Baton—and while Pow was still sleeping peacefully in his pen, Flynn had eaten an entire box of donuts, fourteen in all.

So, back to Dr. Mars, with a puking dog slung over one shoulder and a sleeping baby slung over the other. Dr. Mars dosed Flynn with calomel and pronounced he'd live. Back again to the CGO, Flynn sluggish but no longer foaming, Pow awake and chirping happily. I stuffed Pow into his pen with a toy to chew on, and had no sooner sat down at my desk when Lieutenant Sabre popped out of his office and asked why I was taking so long with the mail.

I bit back a snappy reply. They are not big on snappy replies in the Army. While Lieutenant Sabre lectured me on time management, I glanced at the wall clock. Surely it was almost lunchtime.

It was only nine-thirty.

With the Infanta Sylvanna's arrival only three weeks away, the CGO was frenzied. The Infanta was traveling from the Huitzil Empire via a small flotilla of ships, which had to be protected from pirates, sea monsters, icebergs, typhoons, kelp forests, and goddess knows what else. Once she arrived in the City, she had to be protected from terrorists, overzealous admirers, assassins, and goddess knows who else. All this protection took a lot of organizing, which took a lot of paperwork, which took a lot of staff officers, which is why I'd been detached from the Barracks and sent to be Buck's slave.

From the fire into the flood, as Nini Mo said.

The duties of an ADC are tedious enough to make you weep. It's all meetings and reviews and inspections and briefings and endless errands. Buck may be my mother (sort of), but she treats me like any other member of her staff, for the most part, which means she works me like a servitor.

The one exception to the most part is Pow, or, to give him his full name, Powhatan Reverdy Florian Poligniac Fyrdraaca ov Fyrdraaca, a name that weighs more than he does (currently, fifteen pounds five ounces). If I had been an ordinary aide, Buck would never dare stick me with baby-watching. After all, Lieutenant Sabre isn't expected to change Pow's diapie or burp him or give him tummy time. When I pointed this out to Buck once, she gave me a sorrowful look and said that Pow was *my* brother, not Lieutenant Sabre's, and that Lieutenant Sabre actually had, on occasion, changed Pow's diapie and burped him without complaint, and how sad it was that I balked at helping her when she asked so little of me, really (ayah, right).

Buck is a genius when it comes to putting the screw in. That's what makes her a great general; people are compelled to follow her orders not just because she'll court-martial them if they don't, but because they will feel so terrible if they disobey her. I felt like the world's worst person for complaining even while I knew that she was gaming me, because Pow is only my half-brother. But Buck doesn't know I know that. She doesn't know I have discovered she's been lying to me all my life.

Lieutenant Sabre finished his lecture and returned to his office, taking the mail with him, and I went back to work. The morning crept by like mud until just before lunch, when Buck, long since returned from her meeting, came out of her office with Pow in his cradleboard slung over her shoulder and went off to an inspection, Lieutenant Sabre in tow.

As soon as they were out the door, everyone but me gave up any pretense of work and started to chatter about costumes and pirates and candy. The enlisteds didn't dare shirk off around Lieutenant Sabre—as the old Army saying goes, he's so regulation, he pisses at attention—but I was only a second lieutenant (provisional), so they weren't particularly worried about me. All they cared about was that tonight was Pirates' Parade, the holiday that commemorates the time long ago when pirates tried to plunder the City but were kicked back by resourceful citizens. Once a year, kids celebrate this event by dressing up as pirates and going door-to-door, demanding a candy tribute. Later, pirate effigies are burned in the old City Center zocolo. Since no one remembers the exact day the pirates came, the holiday now falls on the night of the year when the Current is at its highest. Hence, it's also magickal amateur night, which I intended to take full advantage of.

I ignored the chattering and continued to work. I couldn't leave until all my copying was done, and I intended to leave exactly on time, if not a minute or two early. Normally I hate copying, but today I welcomed it. The concentration kept me from feeling jittery about what I had planned for later that night.

"Hey, Lieutenant," Private Hargrave said.

"I'm working." I did not look up from my ledger.

"Are you going to see Califa's Lip Rouge tonight? They got a new lead singer, you know."

A sharp, sour feeling jabbed me in the liver. Califa's Lip Rouge did indeed have a new lead singer, and just the thought of him made me feel a weird combination of jealous and mean.

"No, I'm not going," I answered.

"I thought Udo Landaðon was your friend," Sergeant Carheña said. "He used to come in to the office with you all the time."

"That was a long time ago," I said. "He's a courtier now. He's busy. He's important."

"The Zu-Zu is so sweet," Hargrave said. "She plays a mean guitar. I'd like to—"

"That's the Infantina you are talking about, Private,"

Sergeant Carheña said sharply. "Be respectful of the War-lord's granddaughter!"

"I am being respectful!" Hargrave protested, wink-ing at me.

I did not wink back. Instead, I wiped my pen and put it on my pen rest, and went down to the lav. There I locked myself in a stall and spat up the Gramatica Word lodged in my throat. The Word was black and shiny, with wiggly antennae. I didn't recognize it, but when it landed in the toilet, the water roiled and bubbled pinkly, so I knew it was a hot one. Well, I'd known it was a hot one already; my throat felt like I'd been eating sandpaper.

I used to think you learned Gramatica. Now I know Gramatica learns you. I hadn't gotten far with my Gra-matica Vocabulary before I had to give up my studies, but the Words I had already learned still skitter around inside me like mice. I can feel them crawling through my veins and scrabbling in my brain.

Most of the time, I can control the Gramatica, keep it inside where it belongs. I know it's dangerous to let the Words out, but sometimes I just can't help it. It's either spit or explode. Literally, maybe.

BACK IN THE office, the clerks were now bent over their papers, silent and industrious. Lieutenant Sabre had re-turned. After lunch, Buck rushed in from her meeting in an absolute fury. Between the pirates and the Birdies and the Warlord and the budgets, she was almost always in a fury now. In a clipped voice, she told me not to disturb her unless there was a fire or a war, then shut herself and Pow in her office. Lieutenant Sabre dumped a rush copy job on my desk and went off to another meeting.

The afternoon crept by as slowly as the morning, the quiet of the office punctuated only by the scratching of our pens, Flynn's sleepy yawns, the hiss of the gas lamps, the click of the office clock. No sound at all came from behind Buck's door. I suspected she and Pow were napping. The closer it got to dismissal, the more excitement pricked at me. Finally, after all this time, tonight.

Finally.

At a quarter to nineteen, Sergeant Carheña picked up his bundle and said he had some papers to deliver. I doubted he was coming back. Hargrave was still copying away. With Lieutenant Sabre out of the office, I was in charge, and even though I'd finished the rush job, I couldn't leave until Hargrave was finished. So I took advantage of my rank and dismissed him, even though he wasn't done yet.

Private Hargrave did not wait for me to tell him twice. He threw down his pen, shoved his papers into a desk drawer, grabbed his sack coat and forage cap off the coat rack, and ran out the door, not even bothering to salute. I dumped my completed copies on Lieutenant

Sabre's desk and rushed back to the outer office to gather up my overcoat and hat. As the sounds of Retreat spilled in through the open window, Flynn sprang out of his snooze and ran to the door expectantly. We were now officially off-duty. I was pulling the office door closed behind me, when I heard Buck calling my name. I froze, hoping that if I didn't answer, she would think I had already left.

"I know you haven't left yet, Flora!"

Fike. Buck has catlike hearing. I sighed heavily, flung my overcoat on my chair, and answered Buck's call. She was sitting in her nursing chair, Pow curled in her lap like a pill bug, slurping noisily. The faint smell of apple pipe-weed lingered on the air, and I looked at Buck sharply. Had she taken up smoking again? Surely she wouldn't smoke around Pow.

Buck said, "Hotspur won't be here to pick up Pow for another half an hour; can you keep an eye on him until then? As soon as Tiny Man is done, I have to run over to the stables to check on Sadie. In the meantime, can you read me the officer-of-the-day report? It's too awkward to balance the logbook with one hand, and also could you make me some tea?"

"But I'm off-duty! I'm going to the Califa's Lip Rouge show!" I lied.

"It won't take very long, Flora. I know it's a big night," Buck said. In her lap, Pow's pink feet waved and kicked;

he is a very energetic eater. "Please. I really need your help here. You'll still be able to make the show. Don't cross me. I'm in a bad mood."

Thinking many sweary evil thoughts, I went to the stove to make the tea. Poppy had better be on time; I had a lot of prep work to do still. Buck leaned back in her chair, eyes closed. Pow was sleeping six hours at a stretch at night now, which Poppy said was pretty good for a five-month-old. But Buck had been back at her desk within forty-eight hours of Pow's birth, which had been a bit rough, and she'd never had a full chance to recover.

Well, I didn't have any sympathy. No one made her have a baby at her age, and no one made her do all the extra work. She took it all upon herself, and she should know her limits. Not very charitable, I know, but it was hard for me to think charitably about Buck at all—not after my discovery of how she had let me believe for all those years that she was my mother. Just because my true heritage had to be a secret from our Birdie overlords didn't mean that it should be a secret from me. Buck could have trusted me with the truth. She had not. And I had suffered.

"Here's your tea." I carried the cup over to her and put it on the arm of her nursing chair. Buck jerked awake and handed Pow over to me. Wobbly with fullness, he was soft and pliable like a doll, and he smelled warm and cozy. I balanced him against my shoulder; he wrapped his pudgy hands around my dangling aiguillettes and almost strangled me. He was a Fyrdraaca, no doubt about that.

Buck said, "Thanks. I needed that. Pigface, I wish this day were over. Can you read me that logbook, please?"

I disengaged Pow from my aiguillettes, put him down in his pen, and gave him a stuffed horse to strangle while I dug the logbook out of the mess on Buck's desk. Three tedious pages later, a tapping interrupted me. A pigeon had alighted on the windowsill and was gently rapping at the glass with its beak. When I opened the window, the bird glided across the room and took up perch on the carrier stand on Buck's desk.

"Pigface, I hope this is good news. I deserve some," Buck said, putting down her cup. The pigeon extended one dainty pink foot and she unclipped the message cylinder from it, withdrawing the tiny message roll. I hoped for good news, too, but all the news I would consider good (that Lord Axacaya was dead, that the Birdies were withdrawing from Califa, that Udo had broken up with the Zu-Zu) was pretty unlikely.

"Pigface!" Buck said. "Hotspur's stuck across the Bay. He won't make it back until tomorrow morning. And I have to go to the Pirates' Parade party at Saeta House. You'll have to sit with Pow tonight."

19

"But I have plans, remember?" I said desperately. It had to be tonight.

"I'm sorry, Flora, but I can't take Pow with me. You'll have to watch him. I'll try not to be too late."

"I haven't had a full night off in weeks. Lieutenant Sabre authorized my leave and you endorsed his authorization."

"I'm sorry, Flora. Someone has to watch the Tiny Man."

Buck has lots of nicknames for Pow: Powser, Powie, Chubblet, and Scratchy, but Tiny Man is her favorite. Buck has nicknames for Poppy and my sister Idden both (Glorious Boy and Pudgie). She even has even a nickname for Lieutenant Sabre. But she never calls me anything but Flora.

"Can't Lieutenant Sabre do it? I've been looking forward to the show forever," I pleaded. "It's Udo's big debut."

"Lieutenant Sabre has gone on sick leave. He's got the ague, so I sent him home. Besides, I thought you and Udo were no longer friends."

"We made up," I lied hastily. "Can't you take Pow with you? He went with you to lunch with the Mayor of Millos last week."

Buck switched from mother to commanding general. "I don't understand why you are arguing with me, Lieutenant. Shall I make it an order?"

I could play this game, too. "The Articles of War, section twelve, paragraph fifty-two, forbid any superior officer from asking a subordinate to do personal work."

"Why don't you prefer charges against me, then, *Lieutenant*?" Buck said. At her tone, Pow burst into a frightened howl. Sighing heavily, Buck scooped him up and over her shoulder, where he began to gum her shoulder board. "Can't you just help me out, Flora? Please?"

A nasty Gramatica Word was making my blood tingle, my head pound. "I don't see how I have a choice."

Buck bounced Pow and kissed his head, making hushy noises. "You don't. But you could be gracious about it. I count on you, Flora. You are the only person I can rely on. You are all I've got. Also, can you file this letter before you leave? It got mixed up in my mail this morning."

My jaw clenched tight enough to bite silver, I took the letter from her. If I was all that Buck had, she was in sorry shape indeed.

And now, so was I.

TWO

Rain.
Offerings. Resolution.

I WALKED BACK to my quarters, depressed and furious. I had to do the Working tonight, when the Current was at full flood and I could hide amid all the other magickal noise. It would be a full year before the Current was this high again. I couldn't wait that long.

Where there's a Will, Nini Mo said, *there's a way.* I had the Will, and while I was changing out of my dress uniform into my civvies, I thought of a way.

When I got to the Commanding Officer's Quarters, Buck was waiting impatiently, a soggy Pow wailing in his pen. She kissed him, saluted me, and disappeared into her carriage in a flurry of black skirts and flapping wig. As soon as the carriage was gone, I changed Pow's diaper, bundled him into his sleepy-suit, and stuffed him into his cradleboard. Five minutes after that, we were on our way to the stables.

Buck had ordered me to watch Pow, but she hadn't said a thing about where that watching should take place.

The night was clear and chill, and despite the hour, there was a lot of activity on the post. The barracks buildings on the north side of the parade ground blazed with light; in addition to the party at the Social Club, each of the regiments was hosting its own Pirates' Parade party. The sidewalks were thick with soldiers, making their way from one punch bowl to the next. The guardhouse was going to be very full in the morning.

At the stables, a private sat in the tack room, reading the CPG and splashing tobacco juice haphazardly into a grain bucket. Sieur Caballo leaned over his stall door and huffed reproachfully. After the rousted private saddled Sieur Caballo, I strapped the cradleboard securely to the saddle and we set off. At the Lobos Gate, the guards waved jauntily and bent down to fawn over Flynn, but they didn't ask where I was going or if I had a pass or remind me to be back before curfew. Oh, the privileges of rank.

Flynn darting ahead like a furry hummingbird, I rode down the Battery Road, the soggy corduroy drumming beneath Sieur Caballo's feet. Above, the stars were washed out by a brilliant full moon. As we crested Bannock Hill, I could see, to the east, the lights of Lone Pine Hospital. To the south, a bright blue star burned high above the dark swell of the Pacifica Ocean: Bilskinir House, seat of the Haðraaða family, my true home. Of the six great houses in the City, Bilskinir is the greatest. Its Butler, Paimon, is the most powerful denizen in Califa. As the last living Haðraaða, I'm the Head of the House and Paimon is *my* Butler, subject to *my* Will. Yet I dared not go near it or him. If the Birdies saw me there and guessed why . . . The thought made my blood curdle.

I turned Sieur Caballo onto Bannock Ridge Road, and we rode past the post cemetery. Though we were now outside the Presidio wall, we were still technically within the military reservation; the cemetery had been located well away from the main post for health reasons. In the bright moonlight, the small white headstones glowed like a long line of regimented ghosts. How nice it would be to someday lie among the peaceful dead, quiet and still. Forlorn hope. When I died, I would lie in the Antechamber of Eternity at Bilskinir House with the other chatty Haðraaða dead, my Anima added to the engine that keeps Paimon going. I'd be as much a slave in death as I was in life. *That day, that sorrow,* said Nini Mo. I didn't aim to die for a long, long time.

As we passed the cemetery gates, I thought I saw movement out of the corner of my eye; when I turned to look back, the cemetery was full of ghost lights. The Current was rising and the line between the Waking World and Elsewhere was blurring. I put a heel to Sieur Caballo's side and hurried him up. Not all ghosts are harmless.

At the Califa's Grotto trailhead, I drew Sieur Caballo

to a halt. The path to the Grotto goes through a tangle of live oaks too thick to take a horse through, so I dismounted. Lulled by Sieur Caballo's gentle amble, Pow had fallen asleep. Carefully, so as not to wake him, I unhitched the cradleboard from the saddle and slung it over my shoulders, then shoved my dispatch case under my arm. I left Sieur Caballo ripping at some bushes and headed down the trail. Thanks to the recent rains, the mulchy path was wet and sucking, clogged with debris, broken sticks, and wet clumps of leaves. I had to go slowly, each slip sparking a sick fear of falling and dumping Pow into the mud. Flynn had already disappeared into the darkness ahead of me, even though I kept whistling for him to wait up. Coyotes lived in these woods, and while Flynnie was probably a bit scrawny for their taste, why chance it?

The trees closed in overhead and blotted out the moonlight. Ankle deep in mud, I stopped, took a deep breath to quell my jittery tum, and conjured up an ignis light. The pink glow was dim, but it was enough to show me where to put my feet. I was glad I had remembered to put the hood on the cradleboard and had swaddled Pow up extra tight. He should be nice and dry. Now he wiggled a bit and squeaked once, but when I jiggled back and forth, he quieted.

Ahead, Snapperdog stood in a suck of mud. He waited, bogged down, tail wagging anxiously, until I reached him and wrenched him free, and then carried him in front of me until we were out of the worst of it. Once, the combined weight of Pow and Flynn would have seemed pretty heavy, but after six months of marching around with a forty-pound pack, the load seemed like nothing. A forty-pound pack doesn't lick your ear, though, or give out occasional sleepy snorts.

After what seemed like a very long slog, I saw flickering lights ahead. Fike! I had hoped that the wet, combined with the festivities elsewhere, would ensure I had the shrine to myself. My Working required privacy. I extinguished my ignis light, but when I reached the edge of the glade, I saw that it was empty and completely underwater. The spring had overflowed its catch basin and turned the clearing into a small lake, a round stillness pinpricked with stars like eggshell candle boats. The smell of apple tobacco and rose incense mingled with the odor of wet mud and moldering leaves.

This serene image was ruined when Flynn flung himself forward with a splash. The water wasn't deep, so, thanking the Goddess that my boots were waterproofed, I followed him. Long ago, this spring had been the City's water source—and its source of Current. Back then, the City had a Governor, a praterhuman guardian, somewhat like a denizen only much more powerful, and the spring was the locus of the Governor's power. No one has seen the Governor in a long time, and she is forgotten in all but name—Califa, of course—but the spring and the Current remain.

The spring has been channeled into a fountain; in the center of the catch basin, a marble statue of Califa stands on a plinth. The statue shows the Goddess as a hunter, a sturdy woman dressed in buckskin with a rifle slung over her shoulder, a powder horn clipped to her belt, and a limp marble fox dangling from her outstretched hand. A hound dog crouches at her feet, looking up at her with a panting grin. Of all the shrines to the Goddess, this one has long been the most neglected, due to its remoteness to the City.

But in the last few months, Califa's Grotto had become less obscure. The statue had been altered with paint and ribbands, the white marble hair stained red, the blank marble eyes colored deep blue, scars painted on the white marble cheeks. A shocking pink ribband fluttered from the end of the white marble rifle, and the limp fox hanging in her grip was splattered with black and gold spots, jaguarlike, adorned with gold and jade-green ribbands: Birdie colors. The dog had been painted the same red hue as the statue's hair. On the bottom of the plinth, someone had splashed white paint over the inscription CALIFA and written in red AZOTA.

The statue had become a shrine to my dear supposedly dead mamma, now called by her admirers Azota the

Whip. The candles that flickered in the darkness were offerings to her, and so were the garlands of flowers hanging from the bushes surrounding the Grotto. I had never seen anyone else at the Grotto, but clearly the statue got many visitors, bearing with them many gifts, for the plinth was covered with things: a box of candies, a bottle of gin, a small silver ukulele, a clay statue of a rabbit, several gilt bells, one silver engraved spur, and tiny redheaded clothespin dolls.

I waded over to a low-hanging branch and hung up Pow's cradleboard, then checked to make sure he was dry and sleeping—yes to both. After unpacking the equipment I needed for the Working, I hung my dispatch case next to him. A small picnic table stood, islandlike, beside the catch basin. It, too, was covered with offerings: a half-eaten chicken (now, that's a cheap offering!), more pillar candles, a furry coat, and a pair of black boots. I pushed this stuff aside to make room for my Working and lay the equipment out.

The water in the catch basin felt warm and oily. My finger, as it curved across the surface, left behind a faint pink trace: the Current. The pinkness swirled in the darkness but did not dissolve. The Current wouldn't crest for another twenty minutes or so. Pow was still sleeping peacefully, so I clambered up onto the rim of the catch basin, grabbing at one of the stone dog's legs and pulling myself up. I hung there for a moment, balancing on my tum, and then I pushed my feet against the side of the plinth and hauled myself up the last little way.

The plinth was narrow, but carefully I managed to inch myself into a standing position, keeping a firm grip on the statue until I was standing face-to-face with her. The marble was chilly and slightly damp. But when I closed my eyes, I could pretend for a second or two that the figure I clung to was warm, was real.

I tried to conjure up some memory of Tiny Doom. Once, I'd met her in Bilskinir's past; then she'd been young, like me, and sour, but also fearless and loyal. But that wasn't what I wanted to remember. Once, I had been a baby and she had held me, rocked me, and kissed me. Surely, deep in the recesses of my mind, I must remember that. But no matter how hard I tried, I did not.

And no matter how hard I tried to pretend the cold marble was warm flesh, it remained icy beneath my cheek.

Still, I clung to the statue, waiting for the Current to crest, and then, despite myself, I found my mind drifting away from the Working and toward the last person in the world I wanted to waste a thought on: Udo Landaðon, my former best friend. On the other side of the City, he was gallivanting across a stage, being adored by his fans—and by the Zu-Zu, the Warlord's horrific granddaughter. Well, fike him. He'd made the wrong choice and someday he would realize it. Let him play at his fun, play at being a singer, play at being a courtier. I had work to do.

Below me, thick curls of coldfire fog were beginning to wisp up from the surface of the pool. Time to focus.

I swung down from the statue, filled my silver collapsible cup with icy-cold Current, and waded over to the picnic table. Pow made a hiccupy snore but stayed asleep. Spreading the map out on the table, I anchored the corners with four of the offering candles. I had stolen the map from the CGO; it was the largest map of the world I could find. On top of the map, I lay the Statement of Intent that outlined my goals for the Working. Then I took a deep, calming breath, to quell the nervous flutter in my stomach. I closed my eyes and lifted the silver cup of spring water, which glowed an unearthly pink. The cup was as cold as ice, and when I placed the rim against my lips, the metal stuck to my skin, burning.

Dare, win, or disappear.

I drank.

The Map.
Interruption. Retreat.

THE CURRENT FIZZED in my mouth, bubbly as soda water, and when I pulled the cup away, it took with it the skin from my lips. But the pain was nothing compared to the buzz that was surging into my head, making my ears ring and my vision go shadowy. A huge pressure built up behind my ears. Then, just as I thought my head might explode, the pressure popped and a great glorious feeling washed over me. I felt fine. I felt marvelous. I felt strong as sulfur, tall as a thundercloud. All my fear and anger dropped away and was replaced by a firm, hard certainty.

My Banishing was loud and authoritative, hitting high notes I'd never managed before. I held the last tone a full minute, my lungs going flat and wheezy with effort, and when I was done, the Grotto was flooded with a brilliant pink light, the Aethyr shorn of all negative energy. Now the meat of the Working, the Invocation.

I stood before the statue and made my Courtesy (Supplication and Humble Request), then folded my hands into the Gesture of Respect and spoke the Invocation, being super careful to conjugate the verbs in the vocative case. The Gramatica Words began small and pebbly in my mouth but grew enormous and choking, and as they fell from my lips, the sounds became twists of light that curled and rolled around each other, braiding together into a lash that surrounded me in a glowing lariat-like circle.

I held up the Statement of Intent and set it alight with a Gramatica Command. The paper hung in the air, fluttering like a bird on fire, and then its ashes blew into the darkness. Rolling up my sleeve, I hunkered down in the glowing circle. I had found the razor in Tiny Doom's Catorcena trunk at Bilskinir; its handle was made of polished jade, poisonous green. Now it left a thin red line across my wrist, a silver stripe of pain that felt marvelous. I flexed my fist and the line thickened, oozed, blood as black as ink in the flaring candlelight. I flexed my fist again until the blood was flowing freely, dripping down my wrist. The cut had been thin but deep.

"𝍈 𝍈𝍈 𝍈𝍈 𝍈𝍈 𝍈𝍈 𝍈!" I commanded, and flicked my hand out. Blood drops splattered on the map. Thrusting the razor into my pocket, I bent down to examine where the drops had fallen, and as I watched, the smaller flecks began to fade from red to brown, from brown to beige, and then they were gone, leaving one stain behind.

The contours of the map had changed, grown unfamiliar. I looked closer, trying to make out the topographical markings. A gust of wind blew through the Grotto and extinguished all the candles at once, flooding the glade with bright silver moonlight. The underbrush on the left side of the Grotto was rustling violently. Flynn, messing about in the woods, I hoped. He'd run off while I was banishing, trailing some scent. The swaying of the bushes was accompanied by a heavy growling, much too low and rumbly to be Snapperdog. The Grotto was filled with the rank, rich odor of rotting blood mixed with wet fur.

The City is full of wildlife: rabbits and squirrels, coyotes and badgers, skunks and opossums. I had never seen any animals during my previous visits to the Grotto, but that didn't mean they weren't out there. Whatever was making that sound in the bushes was definitely big.

The growling grew louder and the bushes cracked and snapped. My heart boomed in my chest like a drum. I jumped to my feet, took three splashy steps, and clambered up onto the rim of the catch basin, my dispatch case banging painfully into my kidneys. Just as I swung up onto the plinth, the Current giving me lift, a dark shape burst out of the underbrush. It loped across the Grotto, hoisted itself over the edge of the basin, lowered its shaggy head, and slurped up Current. Fortunately, it didn't see me, frozen a few feet above its head. I looked down at the shaggy bulk that was not a coyote, or a badger, or a feral pig. It was a bear.

I clutched at the statue's cold marble legs, my insides turning to goo. Not five feet away from the bear, Pow's cradleboard dangled, and surely there are few things in this world more delicious to a bear than a chubby milk-fed boy. Since I was off-duty, I was unarmed. I didn't even have Pig with me; I'd left him at home, at Crackpot Hall, as it wasn't very becoming for an army officer to carry around a pink plushy toy, even if that pink plushy toy was actually a protection egregore. Now I bitterly regretted being so concerned with appearances.

Stay asleep, stay asleep, stay asleep, Pow, stay asleep.

I clutched the statue with ice-cold hands, trying not to breathe. The bear sat on its haunches for a moment, chewing on its paw. Its head was as large as Pow and the moonlight gleamed off claws as long as my fingers. Even hunched over, it was enormous, and I was horrifically aware that my perch on the plinth was no security from those long arms. Drops of Current clung to its fur, dappling the dark brown with pink. I swallowed hard, trying not to gag or cough; the smell of wet fur and blood was overwhelming.

The bear leaned over and plunged a paw into the Current; the water churned and a fish flipped upward. The bear caught the fish with its other paw and crammed it into its enormous gaping maw. With one crunch, the carp was gone. I had a sudden awful vision of a fat baby going the same way.

Stay asleep, stay asleep, stay asleep, Pow, stay asleep.

The bear fished another carp out of the spring and shoved it down, heedless of bones. Moistly, I continued to cling to the statue, my shins burning. The bear gobbled down one more fish, then dropped back onto all fours. It splashed over to the picnic table, sniffed at the candles, then at the map, drawn, I realized sickeningly, by the smell of my blood. The bear nosed the map, then reared back on its haunches, peering studiously at it. At least this interest was keeping it from noticing the tastier snack dangling just a few feet away.

Stay asleep, stay asleep, stay asleep, Pow, stay asleep.

Abruptly, the bear ambled back over to the spring and lumbered up onto the edge of the basin. It lowered itself into the water, the same way a human might lower herself into a pool, first one leg, then the other, and then sliding all the way in. The Current surged up and over the rim. The basin wasn't big enough for the bear to do anything except splash around, but this it did quite energetically.

I took advantage of the bear's distraction to reach into my pocket for the handle of the straight razor. It was a paltry weapon and probably useless against a bear, but better than nothing. A gravelly Word was rolling around in my tum; if worse came to worst, I could spit that at the bear. I wasn't sure what the Word would do, but I was willing to bet it would provide enough distraction for me to grab Pow and escape.

The bear seemed to enjoy its bath. It heaved and rolled, grunted and snorted, like a man singing in the tub. I glanced in Pow's direction. He wasn't making any noise, but I could see by the moonlight that his eyes had popped open.

Don't cry, don't cry, don't cry, Pow, don't cry.

The bear sank down into the water and submerged. A squeak came from the cradleboard. A second squeak turned into a grumble. The water in the catch basin was roiling and bubbling, but the bear did not come up for air. Pow, however, had plenty of air; he let out a howl that could probably be heard in Arivaipa Territory.

Desperately, I flung myself from the plinth, jumping across the roiling water, and landed with a bright wrench of pain. Stumbling into a run, fumbling in my other pocket for his soother, I got to Pow and shoved the soother into his mouth just as the bear began to surface. I snatched up the cradleboard and dove into the bushes. There I crouched, clutching the cradleboard in one hand, the razor in the other. The sound of Pow's sucking seemed thunderous. How well could bears hear? Hopefully, not well at all.

The bear climbed out of the catch basin, shaking itself, spraying drops of Current. It seemed shrunken and smaller, only slightly spangled with pink. The Current was fading. The full moon had slipped beyond the edge of the trees, so the Grotto no longer glowed with silver light, but a few shafts of moonlight penetrated the foliage. As the bear, now upright and not nearly as tall as I expected, passed through the moonlight, I saw that it was no longer a bear.

It was a man.

Oh, fiking hell. A skinwalker. A wer-bear.

I had read about skinwalkers in *The Eschatanomicon*. Some are magicians. Some have had geases placed upon them. Some have been infected with shape-shifting by other shape-shifters. (Nini Mo herself was said to be a skinwalker who could turn herself into a coyote.) But all skinwalkers have one thing in common: under Birdie law, they are outlaws.

The Birdies also have skinwalkers; they are priests, called nahuals, who can change themselves into the totem animal of the god they are dedicated to. The nahuals are even more horrible than the Flayed Priests; in addition to their shape-shifting, they eat only human flesh and drink human blood, and only they are allowed to shape-shift. It's strictly forbidden for anyone other than a nahual to transmogrify into an animal. The Birdies didn't impose all their laws upon us when they became our overlords, but the law against skinwalking they insisted upon. There was no way this skinwalker could be a Birdie priest, for there is no Birdie god whose totem animal is a bear. That meant he was an outlaw.

The wer-bear shook himself and stretched, reaching his arms over his head. He had his back to me, so I couldn't see his face. But there was just enough light for me to see that his dark hair hung over his shoulders in a tangle of curls. His back was dappled in markings—tattoos of some kind, though I couldn't make out the patterns.

I had to admit that it was a very nice rear view.

Done stretching, the wer-bear walked over to the picnic table and the remnants of my Working. He pulled on the furry coat I had pushed aside, and—fike!—picked up my map, examined it briefly, and then, after folding it up, shoved it inside his coat. Next to me, the cradleboard began to shake; Pow had spat out his soother and begun to hiccup. The sound seemed explosive. The wer-bear was pulling on his boots and he didn't seem to hear the hiccups, but he certainly heard Flynn barking, for at the approaching sound, he lifted his head.

Snapperdog was going to lead him right to us. Now that the bear was a man, I had more confidence I could handle him with the razor, no Gramatica Curse needed. But putting up a fight meant Pow would be in danger, and that I did not dare. I hated like fike to leave that map, but I had no choice. So as quietly as I could, I crept through the brush to the trail. Once out of the trees, I slung the cradleboard over my shoulder and lumbered through the muck. I knew I was leaving a trail as obvious as the moon in the sky, but I couldn't help that. I hoped very hard that Sieur Caballo had not already encountered the bear.

But Sieur Caballo was exactly where I had left him, head drooped in a snooze. I was frantically strapping the cradleboard to the saddle when Snapperdog burst out of the woods with a dead rabbit in his jaws. I wrestled the rabbit out of his mouth, flung him over the front of the saddle, mounted up, and then rode like fike back to the safety of the post, Pow on my back howling the whole way.

FOUR

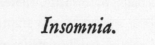

Insomnia.
Bad Dreams. Poppy.

*I*F BUCK HAD had her way, I'd be living in the Commanding Officer's Quarters with her. But as a second lieutenant, I was entitled to my own quarters. With Poppy, for once, taking my side, Buck had agreed to let me live in the Unmarried Officers' Quarters, or UOQ for short. My room there wasn't luxurious, but after Crackpot's moldering grandeur and the Barracks' cells, it seemed wonderful to me It was all mine. I didn't have to worry about nosy denizens, or nosy fathers, or nosy mothers, or nosy sisters, or nosy roommates, or nosy proctors.

Never had I been more grateful for this privacy than when I got back to the UOQ still upset by the events at the Grotto. Upon our return to the COQ a pot of blueberry mush had put an end to Pow's howls; I had put him to bed and awaited Buck's return. But once home, I couldn't stop shaking. I had faced a lot of fearful dangers in my time—a kakodæmon, Buck in a bad mood, oblivion, Axacaya's Quetzal guards, having to recite the Califa Declaration of Sovereignty in front of all of Sanctuary School—but somehow none of those dangers had engendered quite the same visceral reaction that the wer-bear had.

No, it wasn't the wer-bear himself—it was the knowledge that I had almost gotten Pow eaten. Chubby little Pow with his double chins and pea-green eyes. His tongue might hang out in a wormy fashion sometimes and his screeches could cut glass, but I did not want him to be eaten by a bear, wer or not.

Added to this fright was the awful fact that I had lost the map before I'd even had a good look at it. The Working had been a success, and yet I was still clueless, with no idea where Tiny Doom was. I didn't dare try the Working again. The Current was already falling, and without the noise of the Pirates' Parade revelers, anything magickal I did would stick out like a sore thumb.

There was one recourse: Somehow I had to find that wer-bear and get the map back. Fast.

Tonight I was too wrung out to come up with a plan; I'd think of something tomorrow, when I was fresh. But despite my exhaustion, it took me a long time to fall asleep. And when I did, my dreams were full of roars and slavering jaws, as the bear and I raced for Pow, but the bear got there first . . .

I woke up in a cold sweat. I staggered to the washstand and rinsed my mouth out, then drank most of the carafe of water. The cut on my wrist throbbed with a fiery pulse and my head pounded as though a percussion dæmon were playing a tattoo upon my skull. My watch said it was four a.m. The room felt stifling hot and my nightgown was sticking to me unpleasantly. I slid the window open a crack, letting in a rill of cool, moist air that smelled of the bay. The other buildings were dark except for the Convalescent House, which had a light burning on the second floor. A solitary figure walked slowly down Officers' Row; at first I thought it was a guard, but then I recognized the slightly limpy gait: Poppy.

I slid on my boots and put my greatcoat over my nightgown. As I went across the front hall, I heard the squeaky sounds of heavy footsteps coming up the steps and across the porch. Though the entry window, I caught a glimpse of dark red, but when I opened the door, the porch was empty. A heavy smell of roses lingered in the air. The dæmon didn't like the fresh air or the smell of roses, for the pounding in my skull began to ease.

"You are up late," Poppy said when I caught up with him in front of the Visiting Officers' Quarters. "Or up early. Which is it?"

"Both, I guess." I fell into step with him. "At first I couldn't sleep. I finally did, but then I woke up and couldn't go back to sleep."

"Insomnia runs in the family. That's why we are out

here, too," Poppy said as he lifted one side of his greatcoat, displaying Pow nestled in a sling underneath. "He woke up and wouldn't stop crying, even after Buck fed him. I think he might be teething, poor soul. I've been walking up and down Officers' Row for the last two hours. Every time I stop he starts up again. I am getting my exercise. Ah, well, I don't sleep much myself anymore, so it's all right."

I wondered guiltily if the wer-bear had anything to do with Pow's crying. Surely he was too young to know the danger he had been in, wasn't he? He probably just had a bad tummy from too much blueberry mush, that's all.

I changed the subject. "I thought you were across the Bay and couldn't get back tonight."

"I was, and I thought so, too, but then I hitched a ride with a produce schooner, and so here I am. I picked up some really good tomatoes and a couple pounds of lettuce. I'll make a nice salad for lunch."

Since Poppy had sobered up, he seemed almost ordinary. He'd been letting his hair grow, and now the ends brushed the tops of his shoulders, almost long enough for a queue. This was a great improvement over the razor-short cut he'd had before, which had made his head look skull-like; now his hair, a foxlike silvery red, softened his face. Now that he no longer traced the Alacrán scars on his cheeks with black paint, they were almost invisible. After Pow was born, he'd cut back on smoking and started eating more, so he no longer looked emaciated. People don't cross to the other side of the street when they see him coming now. But he is still dangerous.

"What were you doing in the East Bay?" I asked.

"Meeting Idden," Poppy said. "She says to tell you ave."

Sourness twanged inside me. My sister had always done exactly what she was supposed to—went to the Barracks, went into the Army, got mentioned in reports—until, out of nowhere, she deserted and joined Firemonkey and his crew of radical chaoists. Now she sneaks around painting slogans and trying to incite violence against the Birdies. This doesn't accomplish much, but I guess it's fun.

"Is she coming back to the City?" A couple of weeks ago, Firemonkey had distributed a joke book in which the Birdie Ambassador was always the punch line. The police caught up with the printer, who, under questioning, admitted he knew where his clients lived (sloppy!), and Firemonkey and his crew, Idden included, had left the City one step ahead of the law.

"No. They are still lying low. Anyway, never you mind about that. So tell me what's going on at the office these days. Anything interesting?"

"No." I gave him a rundown on the latest in paperwork and meetings. Poppy had asked me to keep him apprised of everything that went on in Buck's office, and so

I do. But I don't know what he does with any of the information I give him. As far as I can tell—nothing.

When I was done reporting, he said, "Listen, have you seen any special couriers at HQ recently?"

"No, why?"

We reached the end of Officers' Row and turned around, stepping up onto the wooden sidewalk to avoid being run over by the milk wagon. A small girl on a pony rode by, whizzing a newspaper over our heads. The darkness was beginning to fade, and so, too, the still of night, as the birds began to sing. Reveille was not far off.

"I heard a rumor that an express agent was in town, and that he had a delivery for Buck."

"An express agent? You mean like an estafette?"

"No, I mean a secret agent for the Pacifica Mail and Freight Company."

"I didn't know that the Pacifica Mail had secret agents. I thought they just delivered packages and stuff, mail and freight."

"Exactly, and some of the things they transport require absolute secrecy. Express agents are very reliable and very discreet, highly trained. Sneaky as fike, and expensive. But trustworthy and completely nonpartisan. They'll deliver anything anywhere, for a price. Not many people know about them. They like to keep their services private."

"How come you do?"

"Because that's how I got back to Califa after the war. Buck hired an express agent to bring me out of Birdieland. As I said, they deliver things that require discretion."

Well, now, this was interesting. I glanced up at Poppy's face. It did not invite further inquiry. He never talks about his time in the Birdie prison, when he was tortured and when Flora Primera, just a little kid, was taken from him, never to be seen again. For years, Poppy buried those memories in drink. Now he's sober, but he still never talks about that time.

The loss of Flora Primera remains our great family tragedy. I never knew her, of course, and I have never heard Buck speak her name, but Idden has told me all about Flora's glories. She was golden-haired and cute as a shiny diva. I might be named after her, Flora Segunda, but I am neither golden-haired nor cute. I know that when Buck and Poppy look at me, they see second best.

Squeaks came from inside Poppy's greatcoat. He jiggled up and down and the squeaks subsided. We reached the other end of Officers' Row. A truck was parked by the Convalescent Home, and an orderly was loading bundles of laundry into its wagon bed. He paused to salute us. We saluted back, then turned around.

So I said, "I haven't seen any secret couriers. Or any couriers at all. Nothing out of the ordinary, or I would have told you."

"Hmmm," Poppy said. "Any correspondence from Arivaipa?"

Arivaipa is one of Califa's territories. It's a miserable desert, hotter than the dæmon Choronzon's temper, full of wild tribes and outlaws. But it acts as a buffer between Califa and the Huitzil Empire, which is why, I guess, the Warlord went to the trouble of conquering it.

I remembered the letter Buck had given me to file, the one she said had been mixed in with her mail. "There was a letter yesterday, from some fort in Arivaipa requesting an extra detail of soldiers to help deal with a chupacabra. Fort Sandy, I think it was."

"Good luck to them," Poppy said. "Chupacabras are pretty nasty. I saw one once, when I was stationed at Fort Mohave. Even dead it was the ugliest thing I've ever seen, like a coyote crossed with a lamprey. Those teeth! It caught the son of our chief of scouts, sucked his flesh and bones right out of his skin, left him looking like an empty balloon—" He broke off his description and jiggled Pow. "Anyway, it was nasty."

"Well, that's all I've seen, other than monthly reports. If you told me what I was looking for, I'd probably be able to find it easier."

"I don't know exactly," Poppy said. "And even if I did, it's better you didn't. Maintain deniability."

"You can trust me, you know, Poppy."

"I know I can, Flora, but it's for your own good. I

hated when people used to tell me that, and here I am telling you. I'm sorry. You've been a real trooper, honey. I know it's terribly hard to sit and stew like this, to feel powerless. But it won't be forever, I promise you that."

"The Infanta will be here in just a few weeks. She's been totally Birdie-ized. When she's in charge, it will be too late. The Birdie grip will be too tight. That sounds like forever to me. And Buck isn't doing anything," I complained.

"There's nothing she can do, Flora."

"There is! The Army would follow her—" I kept my voice low, but he cut me off.

"Shush!" Poppy said, looking about. "Don't say such things, not where anyone can hear them, not even me. And anyway, it takes more than just that. Your mother is doing the best she can—"

"She's not—"

"Shush!" he said again. "Ears. Walls."

"There are no walls here, Poppy," I said. "And no place for anyone to loiter."

"You never can tell," he said. "No more of that, Flora. Please trust me." He was almost pleading, and guilt panged me again.

"I'm sorry, Poppy."

"It's the hardest thing in the world to do, I think," he said sadly.

"What is?"

"To wait. I've done a lot of hard things in my time, but waiting was the worst. It makes you feel powerless and hopeless. I waited once for two years, and those two years seemed like an eternity. I think a little part of me is waiting still. Will wait forever."

I knew he was referring to the two years he'd spent with the Birdies, not sure if they would kill him or release him. Guilt changed to shame. I might be waiting, but I was hardly powerless or hopeless. Nor was I waiting to see if I would live or die, wondering if I would ever see my family or my home again. What did I have to complain about?

"I'm proud of you, you know," Poppy said. "You are being a real trooper. Waiting without a complaint. No whining."

The shame grew. If only Poppy knew how much of a whiner I was inside. I changed the subject before I started bawling.

"Poppy, have you ever met a skinwalker?"

"Back in the day, ayah, but recently, of course not. No skinwalker would dare show his face anywhere the Birdies might see him. They do not look kindly on those who usurp their gods' powers. Why?"

"Oh, I was just reading a Nini Mo beedle and I wondered."

Again we reached the end of Officers' Row. Now there were signs of life on the parade ground. At the northern end, a troop was forming up, horses jostling into ranks while a mounted sergeant rode along the line, shouting. Some captain trying to get extra practice in before the Grand Review. The sky was mostly light now, with just the western horizon still dark and star-studded. Soon the honor guard would march out to raise the colors; the post bugler would sound Reveille and another day would begin.

Another day, and my goal was clear. I had to find that wer-bear and get my map back.

FIVE

On Duty.
Sylphs. A Lucky Encounter.

I HATE ACCOMPANYING Buck to official functions. You stand around for hours, feet throbbing, while Buck hobnobs with bigwigs and notables who don't pay the slightest bit of attention to you because you are just some lowly aide. Delicious food is served, but you don't get any. Ice-cold drinks are quaffed, while you perish with thirst. By the end of the evening, you are bored, hungry, thirsty, and your feet hurt.

But there is one thing worse than accompanying Buck to official functions: going alone.

Then you are the one on display, representing your country and your Army, trying to be witty and polite and well-mannered. Trying not to spill wine on your gloves, whack someone with your saber scabbard, or knock your wig crooked. If you do any of these things as an aide, no one notices. If you are the official representative, they notice. Oh, do they notice.

In my mind, the Zu-Zu's birthday party hardly qualified as an official function. Who cares if she's the Warlord's granddaughter, the Warlord's *only* granddaughter? She's a skinny stuck-up arrogant stick. If left to my own desires, I wouldn't have gone to her birthday party if she had begged me on her knees to attend. Not that that would ever happen, since she likes me even less than I like her.

But I didn't have any choice. The invitation had been official, addressed to me as an officer in the Army of Califa, not as a private citizen, and so it wasn't so much an invitation as an order. *You are going,* Buck told me. *Answer yes politely and enthusiastically, and be there bell-sharp, and do your commanding officer—me!—proud.*

So that's how, three days after Pirates' Parade, I found myself emerging from Buck's carriage in front of Saeta House, ready to do my commanding officer proud. I was bell-sharp, but I was not enthusiastic. In fact, I was in a pretty foul mood. I had made no inroads into finding Sieur Wer-bear. Not because I hadn't tried. Oh, I had tried every avenue I could think of.

I had checked the Officer of the Day register to see if anyone had reported any sightings of a particularly large hairy animal, i.e., a bear, but no one had. I had asked Private Hargrave if he'd heard of any recent bear sightings;

he is an incurable gossip and knows everything that happens on the post. He hadn't heard a thing.

I'd sent fake official-sounding inquiries regarding wild animal sightings in the City to both the Califa Police Department and the Califa Game Warden. They had reports of skunks, possums, coyotes, a great white shark, an eight-point buck, and an alligator, but no bears. I checked all the newspapers, even the *Warlord's Wear Daily* and *A Child's Own Newsie*. Nothing.

Sieur Wer-bear was remarkably—and annoyingly—discreet.

I'd even returned to the Grotto during a lunch break to see if the wer-bear had left any clues behind. I found more offerings to Azota, but nothing at all to indicate the recent presence of a bear. The water had receded from the glade, leaving a churn of mud, but no obvious bear tracks.

Maybe he was already gone from the City, taking my map with him.

That was too depressing to contemplate. He *was* in the City and I *would* find him. Flynn's not much of a tracker, but maybe I could borrow Sergeant Carheña's beagle, take her back to the Grotto, and see what she could sniff out. She's won Best Scent Hound in Califa three years in a row. It was worth a try.

But first I had to give the Zu-Zu honor that she didn't deserve. As I stood at the foot of the stairs leading up to the palace's portico, trying to gather the enthusiasm to trudge upward, a gaggle of green-faced ghouls wafted by me, followed by the Man in Pink Bloomers arm-in-arm with a person in a furry cat suit crusted with fake blood. The Zu-Zu's birthday party was a fancy-dress affair, with guests requested (ordered) to come as someone or something dead. (The Zu-Zu is very into doom and gloom.) My carriage had already rumbled away, and another vehicle now took its place: a huge black coach with the arms of the Huitzil Empire on its side, drawn by four heavy black horses and escorted by two more.

As the coach's outriders dismounted, I stepped back into the shadow of one of the shark statues that framed the base of the steps. The outriders wore Birdie Army uniforms: dark green kilts and capes made of blue and gold feathers, gleaming iridescently in the torch light, their faces covered with leather masks. Another figure was climbing down from the guard's seat on the back of the coach: a Quetzal, half eagle, half human, all horrible creepiness. I shrank back further. Last year I'd accidentally killed a Quetzal; I didn't know if the others would hold a grudge against me, and I didn't really didn't want to find out.

While one officer held the horses, the other flipped down the coach's steps and opened the door. Out stepped the Birdie Ambassador. The torch light flickering off the smoothness of his mask made the jade features seem briefly animated: lips curling, eyes blinking.

The Birdie Ambassador is a Flayed Priest; having long

ago given up his own skin to his Hummingbird god, he now wears the skins of the poor snapperheads he forces to make the same sacrifice. Unlike the Ambassador, these poor people don't survive their stripping. Tonight, no sign of a borrowed skin was visible; he was swathed *cap-à pied* in a cloak made of black feathers, the cape furled so tightly around his body that he looked cocooned.

The Ambassador went up the stairs with small delicate steps, the Quetzal following close behind. Even after the Ambassador disappeared through the portico, I stayed in the shadows and contemplated scarpering. Surely the Zu-Zu wouldn't care if I showed or not. But if someone else noticed I was missing and that got back to Buck, I'd really be in deep. A demerit, maybe even charges. Best go, make an appearance, be tiny and insignificant and then leave. No one said I had to stay long, just that I had to show up.

At the top of the stairs, the portico was draped with funeral wreaths, white lilies woven with black ribbands. A smoldering burner of funeral incense sent up clouds of stenchy smoke. I followed a line of red luminaries away from Saeta House's main entrance and down a narrow covered walkway. I seemed to be the last to arrive; there was no one behind me. The walkway wandered through a garden filled with skeletal trees and dead rosebushes. Cackling shadows wheeled overhead, blotting out the cloudy sky. The air smelled like overblown roses and rotting meat. Ahead, a small marble building gleamed in the moonlight. The heavy iron door to the crypt was ajar.

Sighing heavily, I squeezed inside and found myself in a dark, narrow room lined with shelves full of marble jars: not a crypt, a columbarium. At the far end, light flickered. Sighing even more heavily, I followed the light down a flight of worn stone stairs, terminating at a small dock jutting over a rushing stream. Furfur, Saeta House's denizen, stood morosely on the dock, holding up an ignis light. A small boat was tied to the dock, bobbing in the swift black water.

"Do you wish to pay homage to enter the realm of the dead?" he shouted over the roar of the water.

Not really, I thought, but I answered, "I do, sieur." I flung my hell-diva at him. He caught the coin and said dolefully, "Then embark."

I looked at that tiny boat floating on water as slick and black as oil and suddenly wished I had scarpered. If Furfur hadn't been watching, I might have turned and gone back—but that would be silly. After kakodæmons, ghouls, and all the other horrible things that had tried to kill or eat me before, what the fike was a little boat ride?

There's no way out but through, Nini Mo said. Resigned to the fact that I was going to get wet, I took Furfur's damp hand and stepped down into the boat.

"Where will it take me?" I asked. The boat jumped

and jiggled, and I sat down quickly before I fell into the drink.

"To your death, of course," Furfur said dramatically, and then paused. A latecomer was careening down the steps. He—a man, I thought, although it was hard to tell in the dim light—jumped into the boat, sending it heaving. I grabbed at the side of the boat to keep from being thrown out. The boat rocketed forward and the man sat down heavily, almost squashing me.

"Sorry," he grunted.

Within seconds we were enveloped in absolute darkness. Wind blew hard against my face; I let go of my death grip on the boat long enough to mash my hat down on my head so it wouldn't fly away. The darkness around echoed with screams and shrieks, mixing with the roar of rushing air. We were not the only ones on Zu-Zu's little joy ride.

The boat bounced like a wild mustang, turning dizzily, whirling my tum into a nauseous spin. My grip started to slide, and as I began to slip to the bottom of the boat, an iron hand fastened on me. I fell against my companion, and his arm snaked around my shoulders, holding me in place. He smelled of wet dog and sweetish pipeweed, oddly familiar. His arm felt reassuringly strong.

The boat picked up speed and swept along a series of sharp curves, flinging us against each other. He was big and squashy, and every time he fell into me, I could hardly breathe. My organs sloshed inside my chest, my brain pinged in my skull, my vision glittered with white stars. The boat did a complete turnaround—my hat flew off—and then we were hurtling backward so quickly, I could barely suck any air into my lungs.

The boat revolved again and the darkness began to lighten. The water took on a sickly glow and wispy figures rose from its surface, sinuous boneless women with writhing hair: sylphs. They reached for us with talonlike fingers, their mouths gaping to reveal razor-sharp teeth, long tentacle-like tongues. The boat had slowed and now I could get air to scream. As a tentacle-tongue snapped toward me, I let out a yelp, the sound tearing at my throat, and then realized in horror that I had just screamed a Gramatica Command. The Command hit the sylphs and exploded. They howled and danced as they caught fire. We shot through the flames with a roar. Beneath my head, I felt my companion's chest rumble with laughter.

The boat picked up speed and left the burning sylphs behind, but we weren't out of it yet. Directly ahead, a shape loomed out of the water, large and slimy. Enormous jaws hinged open, revealing a dull red cavern, a writhing black eellike tongue, glittering pointy teeth as big as plowshares. The boat was hurtling directly into the gaping maw of Choronzon, Dæmon of Dispersion.

I shrieked again, and my companion bellowed, his chest heaving beneath me. He pushed my face away from the horrible sight, and like a coward, I shut my eyes, burying my head in the rough wet fur of his jacket. A blast of hot air scalded the back of my neck, and I cringed, already feeling the sharp shear of teeth on my tender flesh. A deluge of water hit me, and the shock of the cold drove me, for a second, into darkness.

Then I realized the roaring was gone, replaced with the rapid thump of a heartbeat. My cheek was pressed against warm, bare flesh, and the boat was barely moving. I jerked away, sitting up, and my companion relinquished his grip on me, yanking his jacket closed. Of course, Choronzon had been an illusion; we had rocketed right through the apparition and come out its other side, uneaten but soaked. Very funny, ha, ha, ha.

Now the boat drifted placidly through a small tunnel. Above us, a ribbed stone roof; around us, walls glowing green with mold. It wasn't nearly as dark now, so when I turned to look at my companion, I could see him clearly.

And although I had never seen his face, I recognized him instantly.

"You are that bear!" I blurted, then cursed myself for being such an openmouthed fool.

"Bear? What bear?" he said sharply. He had a faint accent I couldn't quite place.

"You know what I mean."

"I assure you, madama, I do not," he countered.

"I saw you in Califa's Grotto."

He shook his head, water drops flying. "I don't think so."

"Yes, I did. And you took my map!'

"What map?"

He looked so sincerely bewildered that for a moment I wavered. Maybe I was wrong—maybe I was crazy—but then, as he turned toward the roaring sound just ahead, a deep red light flared in the lenses of his eyes and I knew I was not.

"You know what map I mean," I said, pitching my voice over the roaring, which had been getting louder as our boat drifted on. The walls of the cavern had narrowed; the ceiling was now so low that the wer-bear had to bend his head. He ignored me, looking straight ahead, his brow furrowed.

"Hey!"

He answered my call for attention by whipping around and catching me up in a bear hug. I flailed, but he had my arms pinned.

"Let me go!" I wheezed.

"Hold on!" he shouted in my ear. The roar became deafening. I couldn't move, but I could see over his shoulder. Ahead of us, the water churned and foamed into the torrent of a waterfall.

"Hold on!" the wer-bear repeated. He braced his legs against the bottom of the boat. At that moment, Choronzon himself could not have pried me out of his arms.

SIX

Lost.
Found. Cake.

Bᴜᴛ ʟɪᴋᴇ ᴛʜᴇ ᴇᴀʀʟɪᴇʀ apparition of Choronzon, the waterfall was an illusion. We jetted through the foam and slid down an incline that had just enough drop to generate another giant splash. The wer-bear got soaked but I was relatively dry, for his bulk had shielded me from the worst of the surge. We ended up in the bottom of the boat, where we lay, breathless and tangled. The hilt of my pistol was pressing painfully into my kidney, but he felt warm and solid and oddly comforting. And he smelled so good, of apple tobacco and the faint furry smell of dog. These days Udo smells like a bagnio. The fur jacket began to quiver and shake, and I realized he was laughing again.

"What's so funny?" I demanded, feeling a bit foolish for the tightness of my grip.

"That we did not drown," the wer-bear said. "And that we almost pissed our drawers!"

"I didn't almost piss my drawers!" I said hotly, trying to untangle my legs from his. He raised himself back up onto the seat, still smiling. The spray had sprung his hair into fat coils so dense it was hard to tell where they stopped and his jacket began. He wasn't handsome, but he had beautiful eyes, slate gray with a bluish tinge to the iris. They reminded me of the glacier water that runs down from Mount Astar, cool and tingly, and they were all the more vivid in contrast to the darkness of his skin.

"Didn't you?" he countered, still smiling.

"No!"

"Liar!"

"Fike you!" My curse sparked pink with Current. The wer-bear's laughter turned sour, and he glared at me, eyes icy. With a hard jolt, the boat came to an abrupt stop against a set of stairs. The wer-bear jumped up and out, his sudden exit almost ditching me into the water.

I followed, determined not to let him get away, but his long legs quickly outpaced me. By the time I reached the top of the stairs, puffing heavily, he was long gone.

Still, I hurried after him, through a mazelike series of rooms, each one with a lovely special surprise. In a blood-splattered morgue, I ran a gauntlet of chittering cadavers, trailing sheets and entrails. In a dusty ossuary, I was menaced by a clacking gaggle of skeletons wielding their own bones like swords. I waded through a swampy garden lit by foxfire, where a reanimated alligator snapped its jaws at me until I kicked it in the nose. And on and on and on. The Zu-Zu's Horror House was never-ending.

By the distant shrieks I heard as I made my way through the maze, I could tell others were finding the horror house happily scary. I wasn't impressed, just irritated. If the Zu-Zu had ever faced a real danger in her life, then maybe she wouldn't be so hot on facing imaginary ones now.

Finally, after descending a flight of slimy stone stairs, I came to a dungeon. Next to an iron maiden, a small child sat on a bloodstained block, crying piteously. Another one of the Zu-Zu's ghastly little gags, probably. Figuring he'd go at me with an ax or something if I got too close, I gave him a wide berth as I crossed the room. But as I was ducking under a gibbet, the kid gave an anguished cry.

"I want to go home!"

"You me and both, kid," I said, realizing that he was another guest. And he was as fed up as I was.

"Take me home!" the kid demanded. He stood up, hands on hips. Now that he had my attention, the piteousness had dissolved into cockiness. And he certainly wasn't lacking in flash. He wore a dark purple coat, with puffed and slashed sleeves, puffy purple trunk hose, bright gold stockings, red-toed bootees, and a high-brimmed, buckled hat topped off with a quiff of golden plumes. A small sword hung from the golden buckler slung across his small chest. His face, however, was dirty and streaky with tears and one of his stockings was falling down.

"What's your name?" I asked him.

"Don Baltasar Villaviciosa Ixtlilxóchitl Viana y Xipe Totec, Conde de Xolo," the boy said imperiously. He doffed his hat and bent one knee in a Courtesy: To Those Lower Than Me. "But tonight I am the Dainty Pirate!"

Are you now, puggie? I thought. The Dainty Pirate wasn't dead, but of course this kid had no way of knowing that. Then his name sank in.

"Did you say your name was Xipe Totec? Like the Birdie, I mean, like the Huitzil Ambassador?"

"My papi is His Excellency the Don Nxal Alejandro Villaviciosa Ixtlilxóchitl y Xipe Totec, Duque de Xipe Totec, Her Holiness the Vicereina of Huitzil's ambassador to Califa. I demand that you take me to him immediately."

Oh fiking hell, just what I needed. The Birdie Ambassador's son. The real topper to an already glorious night.

"Where's your bodyguard?" I asked.

"We were attacked by a man with an ax. My duenna got so scared, she ran off," the kid said. "I did not run—I stayed to fight and struck that man with my sword and he vanished into smoke. Now I cannot find my duenna, or the way out. I demand you help me."

"A please would go a long way to making me feel like helping you, kid." I had no desire to have anything to do with any Birdie, even a small and dirty-faced one.

64

In response, the kid stuck his nose in the air. "I am a diplomat in your country. You owe me the respect of following my orders."

"Ayah so?" I turned on my heel. I had had enough snotty attitudes tonight. He could find his own way back to his nasty skin-ripping papi. Lightning fast, he was following me, crying, "Please, madama, please! Don't leave me."

The kid was a snot-nosed monster, but he was persistent; I had to give him that. Sighing heavily, I halted again.

"How old are you, Conde?"

"Five," he sniveled.

Oh, fike it all. I couldn't leave a five-year-old kid, snotty as he might be, Birdie as he might be, sitting alone in the middle of the Zu-Zu's Horror House. I was pretty sure most of the dangers were vapors, conjured by Furfur for the fun of it all, but what if they weren't? Those sylphs we had escaped had looked mighty real, and the alligator had certainly *smelled* real. I dug out my hankie and wiped the Conde's face, though he tried to squirm out of my grasp. How on earth had the Birdie Ambassador produced such a cute kid? Maybe the Conde was adopted. For his mamma's sake, I sure hoped so.

"All right, you can come with me. But if you see the Man in Pink Bloomers, you must protect me from him with your sword, ayah?"

"Ayah, madama," he said. "If I see the Man in Pink Bloomers, I will cut his head off and feed his eyes to the crows. I will cut out his heart and feed it to my dog!"

Nope, probably not adopted.

So on we went, the Conde sticking to me like jam, chattering about how he was going to whip his duenna for leaving him, not that it mattered, as he was too big for a duenna, anyway, and how his papi had promised him a monkey with a jeweled collar, who would carry his books to school and then sharpen his pencils (I was skeptical); and how soon his mamma would come with the Infanta, and wouldn't she be surprised to see him so tall and brave, and not once had he eaten any spinach although his duenna had said no boy would grow big or strong without eating spinach, and see, what did she know, the old crank-face, but I was nice, maybe I could be his duenna, that would be fun, he'd ask his papi, and what did I think about spinach?

"I eat it three times a day," I said. "Everyone should, I think."

The Conde gave me a sour look and, blessedly, shut his yip.

We hiked up another long flight of stairs, dark and rickety, and went through a wispy black curtain into—at last!—Saeta House's ballroom. There, the doom-and-gloom theme continued, leavened with moldering glamour. The walls were draped in black and silver cloth; more black and silver cloth muffled the chandeliers. Bare trees, their branches looking like skeletal white fingers, encircled the dance floor. A white fog drifted through the ballroom, and in the dome above, crows and bats wheeled and screeched. In the minstrel gallery, a band dressed like ghouls played wild music while the party guests danced the tarantella with much stamping of feet and flinging of arms. For a group of supposedly dead people, the guests were pretty lively.

"My papi will thank you for helping me," the Conde said happily. A servitor bearing a tray full of champagne glasses drifted by; the kid reached out and grabbed one.

"There's no need for thanks," I answered, taking the glass from him. He started to protest and I cut him off. "You go find your papi, and I'll see you later." I did not want to get anywhere near the Birdie Ambassador. The Conde was close enough.

"I see him, there! Come! Come!" The Conde pointed through the swirl of dancers to the far side of the room where the Birdie Ambassador stood next to the last person in the world I ever wanted to see again (Udo aside): Lord Axacaya.

Every time I thought about Axacaya, I felt like a total nitwit of a fool for having been captured so easily by his sweet words and the charming curve of his lips, not to mention his butter yellow hair and his marvelously sculpted muscles, which were always so well displayed by the skimpiness of his clothes. What an utter cow-headed moron I had been to fall for such prettiness. He had been kind and sweet to me, fattening me up on lies so I would be tender to his knife, ripe for slaughter. Well, I wasn't slaughtered. And I wanted nothing to do with him.

I wrenched out of the Conde's grip and, ignoring his protests, headed in the opposite direction. Behind a large statue of Archangel Bob, Avatar of Death, I found a sweet spot where I had a good view of the crowd. There was no sign of the wer-bear. But he had to be here somewhere. I wasn't leaving until I found him.

"Well, look who it is! A dog of war!" A mocking voice said behind me.

I turned around and there stood the Birthday Girl. As usual, the Zu-Zu was accompanied by her entourage, a gaggle of vapid pale-faced Boy Toys, all jockeying for the privilege of escorting her. Today that privilege had been bestowed upon a boy got up in a style that the *Warlord's Wear Daily* had dubbed à la *cabeza de la muerte,* or Death's Head. He stood at her right hand, languidly waving a fan made of black angel feathers.

With an awful shock, I realized that this apparition was Udo.

He looked like a freshly disinterred corpse. He wore a tattered green frock coat and a big wide-brimmed leather hat. Matted blond hair hung around his face; red powder made his eye sockets look hollow and livid; his lips were a black gash against his pallid white skin. Red sparkly boots glittered on his feet. For one horrible moment, I thought he was wearing Springheel Jack's boots, but then I realized, thankfully, that these boots were copies. Thank the Goddess, Udo was not that dumb.

The Zu-Zu herself wore a sangyn uniform with batwing sleeves and a crimson red wig, the uniform of the Alacrán Regiment. Black scars were painted on her cheeks. As I realized she was dressed as Tiny Doom—my mother!—a Gramatica fury began to roil in my stomach. How dare she! How dare she dress up as Tiny Doom! She wasn't fit to kiss Tiny Doom's spur.

"Happy Birthday, Infantina," I said through tight teeth.

"So sorry you missed our Pirates' Parade show," the Zu-Zu said. "Udo was brilliant. He set the stage on fire."

"That must have been fun for the fire brigade," I answered. "I am sorry I missed the show as well, but I had to work. Some of us do work, you know, Your Grace."

The Zu-Zu's lip curled. "What are you dressed as, Private Fyrdraaca? A dead muleskinner?"

Before I could answer with a snappy comeback, Udo said. "Now, Your Grace, not until midnight can we reveal who we are. Until then, we must allow others their guesses."

The Zu-Zu pouted. "It's my party and my rule, so why should I not break it?"

Udo answered, "Because then you would lose the fun of the game, Zu."

"Well, then, let's guess," the Zu-Zu said. "I look at that nasty buckskin jacket, all ragged and stained, and say dead muleskinner. Am I right?"

"No," I answered through even tighter teeth.

"That awful plaid kilt and scruffy boots," said a Boy Toy wrapped in a bedraggled red satin suit embroidered with dragons, the musician Nicky O, I supposed. "Must be Mag Hagbun, Queen of the Ear Chewers."

The other Toys roared at the guess. Then they all had to have a crack, trying to outdo one another in cleverness. Of course their guesses were highly uncomplimentary and—to themselves, at least—hilarious. I stood there, trying to act nonchalant, while the Gramatica boiled in me like an inferno. I bit my lip until I felt the skin give way.

"What about you, Sieur Wraathmyr?" the Zu-Zu said, when they had all had a turn, even Udo (who had guessed I was a vampire, even though I knew full well he knew exactly who I was). The Boy Toys parted and there stood Sieur Wer-bear at the back of the pack, smoking a little ivory pipe and looking bored.

He barely glanced at me. "Nini Mo, the Coyote Queen, of course."

"I think he's right," Udo said, the coward. "I now recognize the outfit."

The Zu-Zu looked disappointed. Then she smiled and said maliciously, "You have guessed right, Sieur Wraathmyr. Claim your prize!"

The wer-bear looked blank. "I cry your pardon, madama, but I do not know your customs."

"A kiss," one of the Boy Toys said. "Zu has proclaimed that a correct guess gets a kiss. Sometimes it is better to be wrong, eh?"

The Toys looked at me and giggled, Udo among them, and for a tiny second, I was tempted to open my mouth and let the Gramatica Curse fulminating in my mouth fly—let's see how hard they'd be laughing then, writhing on the ground with their livers turned to mush. But as sweet as the short term would be, the long term of being caught with magick would be rather sour. So, although my teeth were starting to ache, I kept my mouth shut.

Sieur Wraathmyr looked at me as though he'd rather kiss a scorpion. I curved my tingly lips into what I hoped was a scornful *Try to impress me, puggie,* smile.

"Kiss her!" the Zu-Zu demanded, and the Toys began to chant the command. Sieur Wraathmyr didn't hesitate. He stepped forward, grabbed me in his arms, and dipped me down, off balance, turning his back to the Zu-Zu and her cronies. If I struggled, I risked falling or looking like a fool. So I tried to neither tense up nor go limp, but to remain nonchalant, as though people swept me off my feet all the time. Sieur Wraathmyr bent his head down to mine, hair falling across my face. Goddess, even though he was a snapperhead, he did smell wonderful.

"Why do you dog me?" he whispered. I couldn't answer, at risk of letting the Word out. I tried to swallow it, but it stuck in my throat like a piece of sticky toffee.

"Leave me—" But he didn't complete his sentence, for I felt my feet slip, and as I let out an involuntary squeak of alarm, the Word flew out of my mouth into his.

Sieur Wraathmyr jerked back as though I'd stung him. I thought he would drop me, but he recovered quickly, and in another smooth movement, stood me on my feet.

The Toys were whooping, and applause splattered around us. I didn't recognize the taste of the Word, but it was bitter, like very dark chocolate, with a little kick of spice. Surely at any moment Sieur Wraathmyr would explode into jelly or dissolve into flames, or transmogrify into a six-headed coyote. Instead, he turned back to the Zu-Zu and sketched an insolent Courtesy. Udo, I noticed joyfully, was scowling. Standing in contrast to Sieur Wraathmyr, Udo suddenly looked raw, green, just another pretty boy. Sieur Wraathmyr hadn't even noticed him.

"Very nice, Sieur Wraathmyr," the Zu-Zu said, fluttering her fan at him. "I like your technique. Perhaps I shall have a go at guessing your costume."

Sieur Wraathmyr said, "I cry your pardon, Your Grace,

but I fear I do not have a costume. Your Grace's invitation came to me so late that I had not time to prepare an outfit."

"Then you must pay me a forfeit," the Zu-Zu answered. Before she could name the forfeit—and by the way she was now looking at him, I had a feeling I knew what it would be—Denizen Furfur manifested next to her and said mournfully, "The cake is ready to be brought in, Your Grace. The Warlord wishes to see it cut so that he may retire."

"My cake!" Grabbing Udo's arm, the Zu-Zu rushed away, the Toys jockeying for position behind her.

I did not rush to follow them, and neither did Sieur Wraathmyr. He brushed by me without a second glance. And I thought the Zu-Zu was arrogant! Well, he could be snobby all he wanted. I wanted my map, and I'd better get it, too, before he exploded, or worse.

I followed Sieur Wraathmyr as he skirted the dance floor, trying to catch up with him but being thwarted by the dancers, now cavorting to a very loud falandio. The dance ended with a fanfare, and the dancers scattered; I weaved in and out of the throng, gaining on him. I almost had him cornered near one of the punch bowls when I heard a voice at my heels.

Ah, fike, not now.

"Ave, Flora!" Udo said, breathlessly. I pretended not to

hear him, and dodged around a man done up to look like a dissected cadaver. But Udo was persistent, and reached out to grab my arm.

"Shouldn't you be with the Zu-Zu?" I turned around to face him.

"Zu is getting ready to receive her cake; she won't miss me." Udo looked at me expectantly, and when I didn't say anything, he said, "I was surprised to see you here."

"I was invited. It was my duty to come." I scanned the crowd, but Sieur Wraathmyr had vanished. Thanks, Udo.

"Mine, too."

"Is being the Zu-Zu's lap dog part of this duty?"

"It is, actually," he said, grinning. "I've been promoted. I'm second gentleman in the Warlord's bedchamber now. I get to hold his mirror while he is shaving. And I have to bark whenever Zu requires it."

"How nice for you." If my tone was a bit nastier than I had intended, well, too fiking bad. "And her costume! How dare she!"

Udo looked a bit abashed, as well he should. "Ayah. I didn't think you'd like that much. But you know the Zu-Zu is a huge fan of Azota. She hates the Birdies, too—"

"She grew up among the Birdies," I said. The Zu-Zu had gone to school in Anahuatl City, as a "guest" of the Birdies, and had only been allowed to return to the City last year.

"That's why she hates them. The Birdie Ambassador

is not pleased with her outfit. She's making a political statement."

I had no desire to hear about the Zu-Zu's political leanings, or anything else about her. She might be the Warlord's fourth heir, but I was the Head of the House Haðraaða, so I trumped her, even if I couldn't admit it yet. I made a move to squeeze by Udo, but he was immovable.

He said, "I like your outfit, Flora. You make a good Nini Mo."

"Thank you." I didn't return the compliment because Udo didn't look good; he looked like a fool. A bootlicking slavering toady of a fool.

Alas, no, he didn't. Even made up like the corpse of an outlaw, Udo looked gorgeous. But I was never going to let him know I thought that. I said, "Who was that man, that Sieur Wraathmyr? I've never seen him around before."

"Oh, just a traveling salesman. He works for Madama Twanky, I think. He was at Saeta House, showing Zu some ribbands or something, and she invited him to the party. He's a bit common, don't you think?"

"He acts like he's Choronzon, King of All Creation," I said savagely.

"You seemed to enjoy his kiss, though." Udo sounded accusing.

"If I did, what's it to you?"

"What's it to me?" Udo asked incredulously. "How can you say that?"

"You'd better get back to the Zu-Zu. She's going to miss you."

Udo made no move to get back to the Zu-Zu. "You never answered my letter."

"I didn't?" I knew full well I had not. Every time I had sat down to try, I hadn't known what to say. So, in the end, it was easiest to say nothing.

"You know you did not. Flora, can't we—" He made a movement as though to touch me, but I flinched away.

"Excuse me, madama." Sieur Wraathmyr had popped up from behind the punch bowl. He bowed stiffly at Udo, then said to me, "I believe this is yours."

For one heart-leaping moment, I thought he was offering me my map. Then I realized he was holding out a wadded napkin. I took it from him, and with another stiff bow, he walked away. Something moved inside the napkin and I almost dropped it.

"What is that?" Udo asked.

I peeked inside the napkin and saw a ladybug nestled in its folds. But it wasn't a ladybug. It was my Gramatica Word, which I now embarrassingly recognized as the verb *ardor*.

I quickly closed my hand, crushing the Word in my fist.

"Nothing," I said.

SEVEN

Orders.
Bad News. Confession.

THE SINGING OF THE Zu-Zu's birthday hymn saved me from further conversation with Udo, but in the hoopla surrounding the cutting of the cake, Sieur Wraathmyr escaped me. I never did see him again at the party, but now that I knew my quarry's name and profession, he would not be that hard to find. I went back to the UOQ filled with vigorous hope and, after a late-night snack of apple pie, slept like a dead alligator.

Among the many pieces of paper Buck's office receives each day are copies of the manifests of all ships and coaches entering and exiting the City. The first thing I did when I got to the CGO the next morning was to pull these lists, and thus I discovered that Sieur Wraathmyr had arrived in the City the morning of Pirates' Parade, on the steamer *Pantico*. His profession was listed as drummer, or traveling salesman, his point of origin Cuilihuacan, and his nationality Varanger, which explained the accent. The Varangers live in the far north, where the summer days are very long and the winter days are very short. Not much grows up there, so they are mostly traders and raiders and are notorious for being quarrelsome, arrogant, and vain. That explained everything else.

And in the day before's *Alta Califa,* I found the following notice: *Newly arrived on the steamer* Pantico, *Sieur T. N. Wraathmyr, representative for Madama Twanky's fine luxury goods. Sieur Wraathmyr carries with him a fine array of exquisite linens from Seneg; sweet perfumes from the Huitzil Empire; the choicest fruits from the Kulani Islands; beaver hats, both fancy and plain; lace goods of all persuasions; Bradstock bootees; linen brollies; ETC. He will be staying at the Palace Hotel, for those who wish to peruse his samples and place orders.*

Well, I did not wish to peruse Sieur Wraathmyr's items or place an order, but he could bet his Bradstock bootees that I would be paying him a visit at the Palace Hotel as soon as I was dismissed. But first a day of tedious duty punctuated by only one joy: accompanying Buck to the Embarcadero, where we joined a huge throng and the Califa National Band in waving goodbye to the Infantina. The Zu-Zu, her Boy Toys (including Udo), and an enormous amount of luggage were to sail down the coast and meet up with the Infanta at Angeles and then travel back to Califa in the Infanta's convoy.

The sendoff was a big event, with the band playing,

cannons firing, and the Warlord sniveling into his hankie, as though the Zu-Zu were going to be gone for a year instead of only a few weeks. I saw Udo from an extreme distance. Or, rather, I saw Udo's hairstyle from an extreme distance: He'd swept his hair up into a giant pouf and perched a small wooden boat upon its wave. Judging from the admiring noises I heard from the crowd, he was about to start a trend.

I hoped the Zu-Zu and Udo had a very nice voyage to Angeles. I hoped the sea was rough, and their ship was leaky, and maybe even that there would be sharks or a pirate or two. *Hope is free,* Nini Mo said. *You can have all you want.* I had to admit one thing: Sieur Wraathmyr might be arrogant, but he wasn't a bootlicker. It was very hard for me to imagine him as anyone's lap dog. Or wearing his hair in a giant pouf, either.

That evening, I had to work late and then accompany Buck to dinner at the O Club with a bunch of yaller dogs, but as soon as I was dismissed, I hightailed it down to the Palace Hotel. Sieur Wraathmyr wasn't there. According to the bellhop, he'd gone to Sacto and would return by the end of the week. I had no choice but to wait until he returned.

So on to an excruciating week, filled with frantic days full of frantic preparation for the Infanta's arrival, and frantic nights when I lay in bed and imagined what would happen if I didn't get the map back. Four times I went down to the Palace Hotel to see if Sieur Wraathmyr had returned, just in case. He hadn't, and by my third visit, the bellhops were nudging each other and winking when they saw me. Clearly they thought I had something other than Bradstock bootees in mind. Which was true, but not at all what they were thinking.

Not at all.

Never.

As the week dragged on and on, my mood grew fouler and more desperate. I considered asking for leave and sneaking up to Sacto to confront Sieur Wraathmyr there. But Lieutenant Sabre had gone on sick leave, and I didn't dare ask Buck. I even considered telling Poppy what I had done, sending him after Sieur Wraathmyr. Let's see Sieur Wer-bear tell Hotspur to jump into the Bay! But I didn't dare that, either.

First, Poppy would kill me if he knew I had gone against our agreement that I stay out of the Current. And second, he didn't know that Tiny Doom was still alive, and I wasn't sure what he would do when he found out. Scream? Howl? Revert back to the crazy Poppy of old? Of course, he would find out eventually, but I'd just as soon put that day off.

Time was slipping away, and with it my future; the Infanta would arrive in a few weeks and that would be it. It would be all be over. Califa would be fully Birdie-ized and my hopes of reclaiming my family heritage would be *punto final.* I'd be trapped in duty and paperwork, forever powerless.

If my mood was foul, Buck's was even fouler. Pow was on a poo strike and hadn't produced all week. His grunting and wailing was keeping them both up, and so she was even less inclined to put up with budget overruns, missing returns, and squabbles over who was supposed to be in charge of painting over the anti-Birdie slogans that kept appearing on the wall of the Birdie Ambassador's house. No one had seen or heard of the Dainty Pirate in over a year, but other pirates, equally ruthless and far less mannered, had taken his place, and their antics up and down the coast were giving her fits.

Without Lieutenant Sabre to protect us, everyone in the office was feeling Buck's teeth. She sent Private Hargrave to the stockade for spending too much time in the loo; she complained about Sergeant Carheña's handwriting; she had a huge blowout with the quartermaster about how much money he had spent on flowers for the Infanta's welcome-home parade. She even banished the dogs, Flynn included, for barking at a courier and waking Pow from his nap. The other clerks and I hunkered down at our desks and hoped to stay away from her bite, and we were not always successful.

Then, on Friday afternoon, while I was at my desk working on yet another giant pile of paperwork with my forebrain and worrying about the wer-bear with my back brain, Buck called me into her office. Obeying her summons, I found her bent over her settee, changing Pow's diaper.

"Reporting as requested, sir," I said. She handed me the soggy diaper and I threw it in the pail.

"Have a seat, Flora, I need to talk to you."

For a moment I could hardly breathe. All the things that Buck could want to talk to me about ran through my head—the list was long and quite punitive.

Buck sat down in her nursing chair, settling Pow in for a feed. Trying to act innocent and casual, although my insides were quivering, I plunked down on the settee.

"I was at Saeta House just now, where I saw the Birdie Ambassador."

"Hmmmm?" I tried to sound noncommittal.

"Did you meet his son, the Conde, at the Infantina's birthday party?"

"Well, ayah, yes."

She said, exasperated, "And you didn't think to mention this to me?"

"I didn't think it was that important, really. The kid was lost in the Zu-Zu's haunted house. I just helped him get un-lost. That's all. It was nothing."

Buck sighed. "Well, it was something. It was something to the Duque. Apparently he was so taken with your kindness toward his son that now he's asking you to do him a favor."

"A favor?" I asked in horror. Surely the Conde hadn't stuck to his desire to have me as his nanny. Pow was bad enough, but to be duenna to a Birdie? And the Birdie Ambassador's son to boot? *No good deed goes unpunished,* Nini Mo said. I should have left that kid to wander the haunted house until he turned twenty-five or the reanimated alligators ate him, whichever came first.

"The Duquesa de Xipe Totec, the Ambassador's wife, was traveling to Califa with the Infanta. She took sick in Cuilihuacan and had to stay behind when the Infanta's convoy moved on. Now she's better, but she needs to be escorted from Cuilihuacan to rejoin the convoy. The Ambassador asked a favor of me. Well, he couched it as a favor, but it wasn't really. It was an order. They say things so sweetly, the damn Birdies, as though you have a choice, but you never do. So you'll have to go to Cuilihuacan and escort her back."

It took a moment for Buck's words to sink in, and when they did, they sank all the way to the bottom of my boots, along with my heart and all my courage.

Cuilihuacan!

Cuilihuacan is in the Huitzil Empire. Buck was sending me into Birdieland. My body went stiff with panic. The Birdie Ambassador knew who I really was. He had to. Someone had betrayed me and now the Birdie Ambassador was tricking Buck into sending me within the Empire, where I'd be arrested and sent to Anahuatl City to be sacrificed to the Lord of the Smoked Mirror.

"Don't look so green, Flora. It's a ruse, of course. Xipe Totec just wants to use you as leverage against me. He figures if you are within his control, I'll have to behave, and he is most eager for me to behave right now. He's the one who advocated that the Infanta be allowed to return to Califa, that we no longer needed such strong oversight, that we were well pacified. So it would look very bad on him if there were to be, shall we say, trouble. And as long as there is no trouble, you'll be perfectly safe, Flora. And there will be no trouble." But Buck sounded as though she was trying to convince herself as well as me.

"Can't you get me out of it some way, Mamma?" I pleaded.

"I can't refuse, Flora. I would if I could, but I can't. But I promise you, you'll be safe." Pow had fallen asleep, and she rocked him gently. "Xipe Totec may figure that if he has you, he also has the goods on me. But I've got goods on him, too, as he knows full well, so he'll be careful."

"But what if they try to sacrifice me?"

"Don't be hysterical, Flora. They wouldn't dare. You'll be fine."

"Mamma . . ."

"Don't give me that look, Lieutenant. This is not a request. It's an order." Then Buck started babbling about politics and diplomacy, and my fear turned to anger that flared higher and higher. Did she think I was an idiot? I knew she'd give me over in a minute if it meant keeping the peace in Califa. After Idden had deserted, hadn't Buck issued a warrant for her arrest? Hadn't she ordered the Dainty Pirate, Califa's last great hero, executed? Hadn't she forced Poppy to drop his suit for slander against the Birdie Ambassador? She was nothing but a Birdie lap dog, and now she was throwing me to them.

"You'll be fine," she said again.

I said furiously, "No, I won't. You don't have to pretend anymore. I know the truth. I know you are not my real mother. I know who my real mother is. I know why the Birdies want me."

As soon as the words were said, I regretted them. But it was too late to take them back.

Buck stared at me, her face as white as her shirt. Without a word, she stood up and, cradling Pow against her shoulder, locked the door. She cranked the transom down, closed and locked the office window, and snapped the shutters shut.

She turned back to me and said very quietly, "How did you find out?"

"Lord Axacaya told me," I mumbled.

"Axacaya knows? Ah, fike. Fike. FIKE!" The last was a furious whisper. I had never heard Buck swear before, and although it was stupid to feel shock, I did. She collapsed into the nursing chair, clutching Pow.

"Then it is a trap. It is a trap. Ah, fike. Why didn't I kill him when I had the chance? Oh, blessed Califa. Shite. Fike. Piss." Buck closed her eyes for a moment, then opened them. "How long have you known?"

"A few months." I was glad she hadn't asked me why Axacaya had told me or why I had been talking to him in the first place. "You lied to me! All these years you've lied to me!"

"To save your life, Flora."

"You owe me the truth!"

Buck sighed heavily. "I suppose I do."

But she didn't say anything else. She just sat there, twiddling one of Pow's ensocked feet. I twisted my fingers tightly. The silence grew longer and emptier, and then, just as I was thinking she wasn't going to say anything at all, she spoke. "The Birdies are not monumental in their philosophy, you know, Flora. There were some who were opposed to the War, and some who were opposed to breaking treaties, and, some who were sympathetic to the Califan cause. Anyway, through various machinations, which don't much matter now, your mother and Sorrel—"

"Udo's father."

"Ayah, Udo's father. They escaped."

"What about Poppy and Flora Primera?"

"Hotspur was being held in another part of the City. Flora was already gone. Your mother hoped that once she and Sorrel were free, they'd figure out how to rescue Hotspur, they'd find Flora. But before any of that could happen, she realized she was pregnant with you. The Birdies were on their track. She didn't want them to catch you, too. So we came up with a plan: We'd keep the Birdies at bay until you were born and could be whisked away, far from Birdie discovery. Then, she'd allow herself to be captured. The Birdies would be satisfied and would never know there were any other Haðraaðas left. You'd be safe from them. As soon as you were born, she gave you to someone who brought you to me. Then she and Sorrel gave up."

"But you weren't even pregnant. Why would anyone believe I was your baby?"

"It was winter; coats were more voluminous back then. I was in the middle of a campaign—I told the press I hadn't wanted to distract from the campaign, so I had kept the pregnancy under wraps. They swallowed the story whole. The only hitch was Valefor. He would know, of course, that you were not a full Fyrdraaca. I wasn't sure if he would accept you, so I abrogated him."

Poor Valefor, the denizen of Crackpot Hall, banished through no fault of his own. When he found out I was the cause, he was going to be pretty fiking pissed at me, and I couldn't say that I blamed him one bit.

"But why didn't you tell me this before?"

"It's a hard thing to pretend to be someone you are not. I thought it would be safer for you both if you didn't have to fake it."

"Poppy deserved to know, too."

"I know. I know." She sighed heavily. "But Hotspur was in such bad shape when he got back, I didn't want to burden him further. I thought I should wait for a good time, but that good time never came." She paused and then asked warily, "Did you tell him?"

She saw the answer on my face. "Oh, pigface. Was he pissed?"

"He wasn't very happy."

"I'm sorry, Flora. I should have told you before. I should have told you both."

In my imagining of this scene, I was always full of righteous fury. Sometimes Buck was defiant and accusing—*I took you in and saved your life and now you give me shite?* Sometimes she was high-hatted—*I am the head of this family and know what is best; do you dare to question me?* In my daydreams, none of these attitudes dimmed my righteous fury, only sparked it. Now I found that my righteous fury was not standing very furiously in the face of Buck's explanation. In fact, it was dying down into a giant sick-making guilt. What did I have to be angry about? Buck had saved my life.

She continued, "But I hope you don't believe that this means I do not love you as much as if you came from my own body. I could not love you any more if you had. You are the child of my heart, Flora. I know it's been hard on you, and I have been so severe, but that's why; I didn't want you to bring attention to yourself. I didn't want you to do anything that would make the Birdies suspicious. I'm sorry."

Now I was crying, and feeling like a complete pigheaded jackass. To my horror, I realized that Buck was crying, too. This sight knifed me to my very core. I had never seen Buck cry over anything before—not Poppy at his worst, not when Idden ran away, not when Bronzer, her favorite stallion, had to be put down when the infection in his knee wouldn't heal. She wiped her nose on her sleeve.

"I'm sorry, Flora. I'm truly sorry."

"It's all right, Mamma," I answered, sniffily. Should I tell her I knew that Tiny Doom was still alive? She must not know; if she did, she would tell me now. But I didn't tell her. A nasty little demon inside of me said, *Don't do it. She didn't trust you. Return her favor.*

"I don't want to hide from the Birdies forever," I said instead.

"You won't, I promise you. You won't have to. Besides your father, did you tell anyone else about all this?"

"Udo," I admitted.

"I think we can trust Udo."

"And Idden knows, too."

"Califa, why didn't you take out an advert in the CPG?"

Buck said in exasperation. I guess our tender little moment was over. "Don't tell anyone else, all right? Let's keep it—"

A knock at the door interrupted her. She hollered, "Come back later!"

"I'm sorry, General, but it's important," Sergeant Carheña answered.

"Come back later, Sergeant!"

"Very, very important."

"Hold your thoughts, Flora. We are not done. Open the door."

I got up and unlocked the door. Sergeant Carheña held a piece of paper in his hand. He looked upset and worried.

"What is it, Sergeant?" Buck said impatiently. "I'm really not in the mood—"

"A courier just brought a dispatch from Saeta House. The *Warlord's Delight* was waylaid by the pirate ship *Nada* yesterday afternoon. Everyone was taken prisoner and the *Delight* impounded. The Warlord just got a ransom demand for the Infantina. He asks that you attend upon him immediately, sir."

"Give me the dispatch," Buck ordered, and Sergeant Carheña handed it over. She tore it open, began to read.

"Udo!" I cried. "He was on that ship, too! What about Udo?"

Pow stirred, and Buck looked up from the note. "Shush—lower your voice. There's no mention of Udo, Flora. But I'm sure he's fine. No one will pay for damaged goods. The pirates are usually careful about how they treat their prisoners."

"What about the *Happy Rabbit*? The *Nada* keelhauled all its passengers." No one seemed to know who the pirates of the *Nada* were, but their treatment of the crews they captured made the Dainty Pirate and his sailors seem flamboyantly harmless in comparison.

"Only when the ransom wasn't paid. This ransom will be paid, no fear."

"Udo's family can't afford a ransom!"

"But I can, Flora," Buck said soothingly. "It's just a business transaction with them. Money for prisoners. Trust me, it will be fine. Sergeant, call for my carriage and send a courier telling the Warlord I'll be there as soon as possible."

Sergeant Carheña saluted and exited. Buck handed Pow to me and I took him, feeling sick—and guilty. Hadn't I kind of wished that maybe pirates would get them? Surely my wish had nothing to do with the pirates actually getting them, but still, I felt terribly bad now.

Buck pulled her boots back on and buttoned up her frock coat. "Don't worry, Flora. I promise you, Udo will be fine. I've got to get down to the Warlord. You're dismissed for the day. Go home and pack. You'll travel south on the *Pato de Oro*. It leaves with the tide tomorrow morning. We'll finish our talk when you return."

Return? Did Buck still expect me to go to Cuilihuacan? "But I thought you said it was a trap! How can I still go if it's a trap?"

"It would be awfully suspicious if I yanked you now. I'll think of something, don't worry. Here, I'll take Pow with me."

I lay Pow on his cradleboard. My hands were shaking so hard, I could barely get it laced up. "But what will I do? They'll kill me!" I said in a very wobbly voice.

"Trust me," Buck said firmly. "I'm not going to let that happen."

"But you won't be there!" I cried.

There was a tap-tap-tapping on the office door, and Sergeant Carheña's voice said, "The carriage is ready, General."

"I have to go. Trust me, Flora. You and Udo both will be just fine. I promise." And with those hollow words, Buck picked up Pow's cradleboard and rushed out the door, leaving her hat, coat, gloves, and the Command Baton behind.

My knees gave out; I was about to start bawling, although with fear or anger, I wasn't sure. I sat down on the settee and buried my face in my hands. I was as good as dead.

And Buck didn't seem to care.

EIGHT

Departure.
Chickens. The Oro Gate.

*T*HE EMBARCADERO WAS a madhouse. The steamer from Porkopolis had been sighted off Land's End, and hordes of people had descended upon the waterfront, eager for their mail and freight. I hoped that the crowds would delay us and I'd be too late, but alas, no such luck. Buck sent her outriders ahead to clear the way and I made it to *El Pato de Oro*'s berth just in time. The Warlord had decided to keep the news of the Zu-Zu's capture under wraps for the time being, so the mood on the docks was bright.

I was bleary-eyed and exhausted. I'd hardly slept a wink the night before. After Buck left, I'd gone in search of Poppy. Surely he could talk some sense into her. At the COQ, his striker told me that he'd gone into the City; I left a message for him to come to my quarters as soon as he returned, and then went to pack. Poppy never showed.

When I finished packing, I took the last horsecar into the City and went to the Palace Hotel. But Sieur Wraathmyr still hadn't returned, and thus my last chance to get my map was gone.

Not that knowing where Tiny Doom was would matter much to me after I was dead.

I had then considered fleeing to my true family home. No one could get to me at Bilskinir House; Paimon could protect me forever. But I'd be trapped, unable to ever leave the House for fear of Birdie capture, and I would have exposed myself to the world as a Haðraaða, which in turn would expose Buck's deception. She and Poppy would be at the Birdies' mercy. Despite Buck's perfidy, I couldn't leave her and Poppy—and Pow—in the lurch like that.

The rest of the night, I had paced my room, alternating between visions of Udo being tortured by pirates, and me being sacrificed by the Birdies. And, of course, my brain now boiled over with new questions: Why had Major Sorrel, Udo's father, gone back to Birdieland with Tiny Doom, gone back to his own death? How had Tiny Doom gotten word to Buck that she had escaped? Who had delivered me to Buck? How had Tiny Doom escaped in the first place? I would probably never know now.

At dawn, a buckboard wagon had appeared at the front door of the UOQ to haul my trunk away. A few minutes later, Buck and Poppy had showed up in her carriage to pick me up. If Poppy had tried to talk any sense into Buck, he had failed, yet he was strangely cheerful about the whole thing. Maybe I had overestimated how much he cared as well.

The captain of El Pato, Captain Ziyi, was a tall solemn-looking man in a black frock coat and a wide-awake hat, his eyes hidden behind a pair of sunshades, his skin tanned to leather by years of salt spray and sun. He met us at the foot of the gangplank, after we had forced our way through the throngs waiting before the steamer slip. He didn't look particularly thrilled to have me onboard, but he was gracious and accepted my introduction and Buck's thanks with a slight nod. Then he strode off to do whatever it is that captains do before their ships set sail.

While the stevedore lugged my boxes onto El Pato, Poppy and Buck peppered me with advice: Expect poison from standing water; always shine my boots right before bed; keep my saber close at hand; never pass up a chance to potty; don't camp in a wash; keep the chamber under the hammer empty; never share towels, et cetera, et cetera.

Only Pow was advice-free. When I kissed him good-bye, he gurgled and blew a giant milk bubble that I managed to deflect with a burp cloth before it ruined my nice clean frock coat. Then he tried to claw my nose off. Poppy removed him from my arms before he could do any more damage. I had to admit that I would miss the little monster. When he looked at you with those big green amazed eyes, it was hard not to be sweet on him. If I never returned, he would not remember me. This thought panged me greatly.

"Are you sure you have everything, Flora?" Poppy asked. The wind tousled his hair, whipped the tails of his frock coat. Before we'd left the UOQ, he had given me his own hat to replace the one that I had lost at the Zu-Zu's birthday party. It was a bit too big, but he had stuffed some paper in the crown, just enough to make it fit. Still, I kept a firm grip on its brim.

"I don't see how she could have forgotten a thing," Buck said. "She's got enough luggage for six people. And she's only going to be gone a week."

"You are a fine one to talk, Buck," Poppy said. "It took a string of mules to haul your campaign gear around."

"I have a reputation to uphold." She smiled at him. He smiled back and then called to Flynn, who was leaning dangerously over the edge of the dock, barking crazily at the sea lions nosing around the underside of the pier.

Buck said jovially, "The portmaster says you should have clear weather. That's good—I know you can't stand rough water. Remember that time we took the ferry to Dogtown and you were sick the whole way—"

"I'll be fine," I said hastily. I was not a child anymore and I was not going to get seasick. The bottle of Madama Twanky's Salty Dog Sea Leg Tonick in my trunk would ensure that. Anyway, it seemed silly for her to be worried that I might get seasick when she was sending me to certain death.

"Go up top, on deck, and stare at the horizon, Flora—" A shrill blast interrupted Poppy and inspired Pow to howl. He was almost louder than the whistle.

The purser was waving frantically at me, and two sailors stood by the gangplank, ready to swing it back. I hastily kissed the howling red-faced Tiny Man, who quit his howling and grabbed at my aiguillettes. Disengaging his paws, I turned to salute Buck, who, against regulations, snatched me up into a squeezy hug. I clung to her for a moment, feeling the butt of her revolver press against me, the thump of her heart, the mingled smell of horse and milk, the cold metal of her gorget pressing against my cheek.

She whispered, "I promised her I would never let anything happen to you and I will keep that promise. Trust me." My throat choked as a thousand thoughts raced through my head, but before I could blurt any of them, my hat fell off and Buck released me.

Poppy swept me up into another hug, murmuring, "Don't worry, honey. You'll be fine. Trust your mother. And here's a stash, just in case." I took the fat roll of divas and slipped it in my pocket. The whistle blew again. I kissed Tiny Man on his chubby pink cheeks one last time, and would have kissed Flynn, too, but Snapperdog had disappeared and there was no time to look for him. The first mate was hollering at me; at the prow of the ship they were already cranking up the anchor. Poppy shoved my hat at me and I ran up the gangplank, just as the sailors started to cast aside the lines.

The deck of *El Pato* was crowded with crates and boxes. I squeezed through them, the schooner's movement already making me unsteady, and leaned against the railing. We were twenty feet from the dock and moving away quickly. Buck had taken Pow from Poppy and was holding him up, pointing at me and waving. They looked like the perfect little family. They would do just fine without me. And if I never returned, well, they still had Pow. They could start over.

Trust me, Buck had said. How could I trust her when she had never trusted me?

And Udo, oh Udo.

The figures on the dock were very small now, dwindling. I turned away, lurching through the crates of lettuce and asparagus piled high on the deck.

I'd never been on a schooner like *El Pato de Oro*. The ferry to Benica Barracks is large and lumbering, wallowing along at a steady clip to the *thump, thump, thump* of its paddle wheel and the distant hum of the coal servitors deep within its bowels. *El Pato de Oro* was a three-masted ship, and she glided lightly through the water. Over my head, sailors scampered from line to line, calling to each other. They seemed completely at home among the rigging, balancing like birds on the lines. After a brief glance, I looked away, feeling queasy at the heights.

From a sailor's point of view, I guess, it was a good day to be underway. The wind was billowing the sails. A thin veil of fog was winding through the Oro Gate and the sky above the City was gray and overcast, but streaks of blue shone above Mt. Tam and beyond Goat Island and the Tiburon peninsula. When the schooner passed Black Point and I knew that the Embarcadero would be out of sight, I went back to the port side. This might be the last time I'd ever see my home. The City looked like a child's diorama of tiny houses spread out over a series of small hills. The spire on Saeta House gleamed like a small gold needle, and on Crackpot Hill, I could just make out the top of Poppy's Eyrie tower poking up above the trees.

I leaned on the railing and watched the red roofs and white walls of Fort Black Rock slide by, then the curving green line of Cow Hollow Cove, the laundry lines flapping like banners in the wind; the Presidio, with the green swell of the Parade Ground, its summit surmounted by the pink adobe sprawl of the O club. Next, the batteries perched along the Scott Cliffs, and at the base of the cliff, the looming red brick hulk of Fort Hawkins, guarding the Gate.

And beyond the Gate, the open sea.

I couldn't enjoy the scenery. This might be the last time I saw the City. And Udo—Udo might already be dead. Or sold, or taken far away. Even if somehow I returned to Califa, I might never see him again. Ayah, recently he'd been acting like a snapperhead, but maybe I'd been acting a bit like a snapperhead, too. He had tried to apologize, and caught up in my own self-righteous anger, I had ignored it.

And now it was too late. Too late for the both of us.

Fort Hawkins's gun ports were open, ominous black cannons protruding from each little window, but the muzzles on the Fort's upper deck were pointed slightly up, signifying they were not on highest alert. A small figure was perched on an enormous siege howitzer nicknamed the Warlord's Hammer, the biggest of the guns. (The Redlegs called it something a little less respectable.) The muzzle stuck out from the walls of the Fort over open water, but that didn't appear to fret the figure sitting on it. It waved a tiny black hat at me.

I was waving back when I heard an all too familiar frantic yipping. I dashed toward the barking, or at least wobbled my way toward it, for we were nearing the Gate, where the water is very rough by design. Behind a stack of crates, I found Flynnie being hoisted by his collar and shaken by none other than my maddeningly elusive werbear quarry, Sieur Wraathmyr.

"Hey—let him go!" I shouted. Sieur Wraathmyr dropped Flynn, who skittered over to me. "What the fike are you doing?"

A scowl darkened Sieur Wraathmyr's face. "Are you following me?"

"Of course I'm not! What you are doing to my dog?" Flynn pressed against my legs, and I bent down to soothe him.

"He was menacing the chickens." Sieur Wraathmyr pointed to the coop, where the chickens were fluttering and squawking. In a cage next to the coop, a pig peered quizzically at us.

"Flynn's afraid of chickens! If anyone was being menaced, it was him!"

"I have never heard of a dog that is afraid of chickens," Sieur Wraathmyr said scornfully.

As I started to defend Flynn, the ship heaved, sending me careening into the chicken coop and upsetting the chickens even more. The ship jerked again, this time flinging me toward Sieur Wraathmyr, but I managed to catch myself before I hurtled into him, and landed against the pig cage instead. The pig oinked in annoyance.

"You'll end up overboard if you don't hold on," Sieur Wraathmyr said. "You should go below. And tie up your dog, or you will lose him for sure." With that prediction, Sieur Wraathmyr turned and disappeared into the maze of crates.

I unwound my sash and tied it to Flynn's collar as a makeshift lead.

"Flynn, you moron," I said. "Now they are going to get

you, too." But I was glad to see him. Whatever fate awaited me, I would not face it alone.

And suddenly I felt a dart of hope. I had thought that leaving the City meant I had lost any chance at getting the map back. But now the Goddess had given me a second chance, and I intended to make the most of it. That map wouldn't save me from the Birdies, but at least I'd go to my grave knowing where Tiny Doom was, that my Working had been successful. *Take what you can get,* said Nini Mo.

The water was now churning as the two currents, bay and ocean, met in a violent froth. We were entering the Oro Gate. The Warlord had once sailed through the Gate to conquer the City and was determined that no one would ever repeat his feat. Even on a calm day, entering and exiting the Gate is dangerous. The rush of the water trying to enter the Bay meets with the rush of water trying to exit, creating waves and riptides and dangerous currents. Many a ship had been wrecked on one of the hidden rocks or tossed up against the cliffs.

But just in case nature is not a strong enough barrier, at the Warlord's bidding, Axacaya has used his magick to churn the water into a deadly maelstrom. Only a ship carrying a Charm of Passage authorized by Axacaya can safely navigate these watery defenses. We were in for a bumpy ride, but I knew we'd make it through all right.

As the ship bounced, my stomach bounced with it. I should have taken a preventive dose of Madama Twanky's

Salty Dog Sea Leg Tonick before I had boarded. The Tonick was in my trunk below. Hauling Flynn behind me, I staggered down the narrow stairs into the captain's parlor. Since the schooner wasn't set up for passengers, it didn't have any real staterooms, but the captain had kindly moved his children into his own cabin and given me theirs. The children were playing cards at the parlor table, unconcerned with the swaying and jolting of the room, or the swinging parlor lamp throwing wild shafts of light on the polished wooden walls.

Down here, without the fresh air and the salt spray, the motion seemed much worse and my head began to spin. Holding on to various bits of furniture, I wobbled my way to my cabin door, Flynn scrabbling behind me. I thought I'd better dose him with Madama Twanky's, too. His tum is very delicate and there are few things more annoying than a retching dog.

"Don't worry, the water will be calmer when we have passed through the Gate," the girl called to me as I threw my cabin door open. On the sideboard, the glasses and bottles tinkled alarmingly. "Axacaya keeps the Gate rough so no one can get in that he doesn't like."

"Lord Axacaya," the boy corrected. "Show some respect, Elodie."

"He's a Birdie, Theo," Elodie said. "I don't have to respect him. Hey, your dog is puking."

Alas, so Flynnie was, and when I saw him, then I

couldn't help but do it myself. Leaving Flynn to Elodie's ministrations, I staggered to the washbasin in my room. Then, adios sourdough pancakes, adios. The boat bounced and heaved; I retched and spat—and cursed Axacaya, the cause of my suffering. After a long while, my tum was empty and the ship's violent heaving began to ebb, until finally the only motion was a slightly rocking glide. I let go of the washbasin and straightened up. My head was still feeling a little spinny, but my stomach was starting to calm down.

At least it was until I turned around to open a porthole, and saw that there was a corpse lying in my berth.

NINE

A Ghost.
Dinner. A Deal.

NOT A CORPSE, I realized after that first panicky moment. The ghost of Hardhands, my long-dead step-father, lounging on my narrow bed and licking something red off his long white fingers. Now that my nose was not full of the smell of puke, I realized my cabin was filled with another, more noxious smell: a mixture of roses, funeral incense, and decay.

"What are you doing here?" I demanded.

Hardhands laughed and crossed his legs, which were muscular, bare, and streaked with mud. I had first met Hardhands—or at least his Anima—at Bilskinir House, when Udo and I had gone to reclaim Springheel Jack's boots. Then, he had been breathtakingly glorious. Now, he looked a wreck. He wore what appeared to be the filthy remnants of a sangyn Alacrán Regiment uniform, the kilt tattered and bloodstained, weskit torn and stained, shirt white no longer. The cravat around his neck looked more like a bandage, and his hair hung in dirty straggles around his face, which was also streaked with dirt and blood.

He looked, in other words, like a corpse that had just been carried off a battlefield. But his eyes were clear blue glints of wintery sky.

"We took a poll, we Haðraaðas, and clearly you could not be sent into the jaguar's den alone, unaided, with no bodyguard, despite the fact that your dear second-mamma seemed to think you should be."

"How did you know I was going to Birdieland?" I interrupted him.

"I have very good hearing. One of us must go as a representative of all of us; you are the last hope of our family, thus, all our eggs are in your basket. I being the most recent Haðraaða dead—barring one, of course—and thus strongest, was deemed to be your comrade-in-arms. So here I am, to nurture and shelter you, to give you succor and aid, and to make sure you don't do anything catastrophically stupid that will doom us all."

Oh fikety-fike-fike. The last thing I needed was a drippy ghost hanging around me, offering me obnoxious advice.

"Does Paimon know you have left Bilskinir?"

"Of course, my dove," he said, but I didn't believe that for a minute.

"Go home. I don't need your help."

"No, but you need a weapon, and I am that weapon: your sword and your shield. Have I not already long been watching over you? Not that you noticed, of course, which is very lax of you."

Now I recalled that flash of red on the UOQ porch the night of Pirates' Parade, the heavy stench of roses. Hardhands must have used the Current's high tide to escape Paimon and Bilskinir.

"Nor do I need your supervision," I said firmly. "You can go back home to where you belong. I can summon Pig if I need to. He's all the protection I need."

"Pig! You'd pick Pig over me?" the ghost said scornfully. He picked at his teeth with a long black fingernail, and at that gesture, I couldn't stifle the tickle of revulsion that ran up my spine.

"He's cleaner. He's a Protection egregore. You are just a ghost." Pigface, the smell was awful! If I didn't get rid of him soon, I was going to puke again.

"Just a ghost? I am the Anima of Califa's greatest heroes, a military genius, and an excellent musician, not to mention handsome as hell."

Not anymore, I thought. "Well, maybe all that once, but you are dead now. I don't need you. You can either go back to Bilskinir on your own, or I will banish you back there. Your choice."

The ghost grimaced at me. "You have no respect for your elders, Nyana Haðraaða."

"I respect those who have earned my respect," I answered, quoting Nini Mo.

"I doubt you can banish me, girl. I was an adept when your mother was still in her mother's womb. I know such tricks as you can hardly even imagine. And," the ghost said cunningly, "you must quit playing in the Current or you'll doom us all. Remember?"

Alas, I remembered. Before I could issue another threat (that is, before I could think of a threat that did not involve magick), the door to my berth began to creep open. Hardhands vanished, leaving behind muddy sheets and a moldy smell. A curly head poked inside. "I cleaned up the doggie puke. I gave him some medicine and now he's better. Do you have any candy?"

"No." I flung myself over the muddy bed and opened the porthole, gulping in large lovely breaths of moist air. I'd have to brush my teeth to get the taste of puke and the smell of death out of my mouth.

"It stinks in here," Elodie said, "and there is dirt in your bed. Why is there dirt in your bed?"

"I spilled my flowers. Do you think I can get fresh sheets?"

"I don't see any flowers." Elodie squeezed her way into the cabin and poked at my dispatch case.

"I threw them out the window."

"Oh. Poor drowned flowers. I like chocolate best, but

108

I would take swizzlers. I deserve something for cleaning up the dog puke."

Well, I couldn't argue with her there, plus I wanted her out of my cabin as quickly as possible. So I gave her one of my bars of Madama Twanky chocolate, and asked if she would like to help me take Flynn for a walk. After I had a long swig of Madama Twanky's Tonick, we went back up top, Elodie scampering like a monkey up the swaying stairs and hauling Flynn by my sash, me following slowly behind. Even the faint motion was making me feel slightly queasy. I hoped the Tonick would kick in soon, or it was going to be a very long trip. I did not want to spend what were possibly my last few days alive puking.

Up top the weather had improved mightily. Now that we were outside the Oro Gate, the fog had vanished into the bluish haze. The schooner skimmed through the water like a swallow, swooping and speedy.

With the wind and sun on my face, I felt much better. We perambulated around the deck, dodging sailors and cargo. Elodie was a chatterbox, which was good. I needed information, and she was only too happy to provide it. She was six; her favorite color was purple; she had been born on *El Pato*; she was going to be an actress when she grew up; her pet monkey had fallen overboard on the last trip, et cetera, et cetera.

Eventually I managed to turn the conversation to the

subject that interested me most: Sieur Wraathmyr. Elodie didn't know much about him, but what she knew, she was happy to share. He was only going as far as Cambria. He had a lot of luggage in the hold, cases of stuff he was selling, she supposed. He wasn't very nice. He didn't have any candy.

We were supposed to dock at Cambria tomorrow morning. That gave me the rest of the afternoon and the evening. Now, we were both trapped on the ship; he would not escape me. It occurred to me, also, that my certain Birdie doom afforded me some freedom. I no longer cared much if he tried to expose my magickal dealings. Buck could hardly court-martial me for illegal magick if I were dead.

Alas for me, as we rounded Crescent Bay, the ocean became rough again, no match for the Madama Twanky's. Leaving Flynn, who seemed to have found his sea legs, with Elodie, I was forced to take to my berth. I lay for hours upon the clean sheets Elodie found for me and stared fixedly at the ceiling, trying very hard not to think about food. Or the Birdies. Or anything else that might make me puke.

Eventually, Elodie appeared at my cabin door with a giant cup of hot chocolate, which she insisted that I drink. The chocolate was thick, mudlike, and not very sweet, with a dark orange undertone. Within a minute of finishing it, I felt fine. Elodie refused to tell me what was in the drink, only ordered me to get dressed for dinner. Fifteen minutes earlier, I had thought I would never eat again. Now I was ravenous.

My dress uniform was a bit creased, but again I was grateful for it. The uniform is one aspect of being a Blackcoat that I actually enjoy. I never have to worry about being in fashion. No matter how bad my hair looks, the wig covers the sin. No matter how pallid my cheeks, regulation rouge makes them rosy. Ayah, there are a lot of silver buttons to polish and the aiguillettes can be somewhat strangling, but it's worth it to always have something cool to wear.

The cabin was so tiny that winding my red sash the mandated three times around my waist proved to be a bit of a challenge. I left off my saber sling; it kept whacking against the furniture. The mirror above the washstand was small; tarnished and dark, it showed a narrow slice of my face. By craning my neck and leaning against the edge of the basin, I was able to get my left eye into the reflection. The eyeliner is liquid and easy to smear, but the line came out perfectly. I shifted over, and this time my hand was not so steady. The brush slipped and I ended up with black liner trailing down my cheek. I scrubbed the black off and leaned in again.

And froze.

There was something off about my reflection. The eye in the mirror was green, not blue. It was already smeared with thick smudges of kohl. And the pupil was a catlike slit.

I took one step back and was blocked from further retreat by my trunk. The eye stared at me, unblinking. I held the liner brush like a weapon; the brush was shaking. The eye closed, revealing a second golden eye painted on the lid. The golden eye gazed at me, and the force of the gaze nailed me to my place. The eyelid flickered and there was the green eye again. It receded and a nose appeared in the mirror, sharp and with a golden ring through its septum, and then another eye, equally green. Angular cheekbones and wisps of long black hair. Thin lips opened to reveal black teeth, a crimson tongue—the mouth pursed in a Word—and suddenly I was flung sideways onto the bed. Hardhands slammed his fist into the mirror. The glass spidered and shattered, spraying the cabin with knife-sharp shards.

"Well, now," the ghost said.

I lumbered to my feet. There was broken glass everywhere. The mirror frame gaped emptily. "What the fike was that?"

"You were being scried, Almost Daughter," Hardhands said. Mirror shards glittered in his matted hair. Flecks of glass sparkled on his cheeks.

"Scried? By who?"

"Do you not know?"

"No! I have no fiking idea. Fike." I sat down on the

bed. I still had the liner brush in my hand; I threw it away. Fike. My heart was walloping against my rib cage. I took a deep steadying breath but that didn't help.

"It was a small mirror," Hardhands said. "I don't think he saw you very clearly. Let's hope not."

"Didn't I tell you to go home?" I snapped.

"And well it was that I did not. You standing there like a gaper. If I hadn't broken the mirror, he'd have seen you for sure. And that Word he was about to speak was a hot one, I could tell—"

There was a quick knock at the door, Elodie hollering, "It's dinnertime, Flora!"

Hardhands evaporated. I opened the door and told Elodie I'd fallen against the washstand and broken the mirror. She helped me sweep the mess up and we went to dinner. Dogs, Elodie explained, were not allowed in the parlor during mealtimes, so she'd left Flynn in the galley. Apparently he had been a real hit with the cook.

The rearrangement of the furniture had transformed the parlor into a dining room. Captain Ziyi and Sieur Wraathmyr were already drinking sherry. Captain Ziyi greeted me politely, but Sieur Wraathmyr bid me ave in a voice that could have frozen boiling hot tea, and received my own cold hello with a slightly raised eyebrow. Udo had more manners in one strand of his golden hair than Sieur Wraathmyr had in his entire body.

Dinner was brought to the table by the cook, and then

served by the captain, who took our passed plates, filled them, and passed them back. As you would expect on a ship with a full cargo of vegetables, the menu was comprised mostly of salad and asparagus, with one of the chickens from the coop as the centerpiece.

The captain led the conversation, and while I did my best to be charming and witty, Sieur Wraathmyr spoke only when directly addressed, otherwise remaining aloof and disengaged. You would think that someone who earns his living selling things would be amiable, but Sieur Wraathmyr did not seem the slightest bit concerned with being nice. He even seemed immune to Elodie's charm, and that girl could have given Udo a run for his money.

Oh, Udo! I hoped that charm had bought him something with those pirates.

The captain had changed into a black wool coat with golden frogging, Elodie wore a poison-green satin frock, Theo had exchanged his linen smock for a smart red jacket, and I, of course, was in my uniform. Sieur Wraathmyr had not bothered to get gussied up. He still wore that furry jacket (although today he did seem to be wearing a shirt underneath) and his curly hair still needed a good brushing.

The combination of the shaggy hair and the shaggy jacket really did make him seem bearlike. If I were a werbear, I would probably have tried to downplay any ursine qualities I might have, but Sieur Wraathmyr seemed unconcerned with his bearishness. Or his boorishness, for that matter. After about the third attempt to include him in the conversation, Captain Ziyi gave up, and the talk went around him while he continued to sullenly stir his soup.

"Sieur Wraathmyr," I said sweetly, when Theo finished telling us about the telescope he was building, "I am so pleased to find you onboard."

Sieur Wraathmyr looked up from his soup warily and made a sound that might have been an acknowledgment.

I continued. "I saw your advert in the *CPG*, and had been so hoping to visit you and see some of your wares. But before I could do so, I was ordered on this journey, and I thought I had missed my chance. You can imagine my happiness when I saw you onboard and realized I might be in luck after all."

"I am sorry, madama," he said. "But my cargo is all packed below."

"Oh, dear. How disappointing. I was very much interested in obtaining a bottle or two of Madama Twanky's Bear Oil Hair Oil. I have found nothing better for an unruly hairdo than Madama Twanky's Bear Oil Hair Oil."

Sieur Wraathmyr stared at me with a glinty blue-gray gaze. "I'm sorry, madama, but I am out of bear oil."

"Oh, boo. Well, it's lucky I have a bottle to see me through, then," I said. "How about maps? I am most particularly looking for a good map. I'd much rather have the map than the bear oil."

"I will look through my manifest, madama, and see what I have in stock, but I fear that my map supply is rather low at this moment. I cry your pardon, Captain. Will you please excuse me? I find that the motion of the water has cured my appetite. " And with that rudeness, he was gone. But I was pretty sure he had gotten my point.

After dessert, the table was cleared and folded back into the wall. We were treated to a recital of sea shanties sung by Elodie, and then a recitation of *The Warlord Stood On the Burning Deck* by Theo. Finally, the captain went up to the bridge, and Elodie and Theo went to bed. I retrieved Flynn from the galley and took him back to my berth, took off my wig, and went up on deck determined to corner Sieur Wraathmyr and settle the map matter once and for all.

The night was dark and moonless, but the stars above were as thick as clover on a grassy field, and the water glowed phosphorescently as it churned away from the ship. A snatch of song flew by on the wind: the sailor in the rigging high above. I followed the sweetish smell of apple tobacco to a corner of the poop deck, where I found Sieur Wraathmyr sitting on a hay bale, smoking his stubby little pipe and watching the dark coastline slide by our port side. I had the feeling he had been waiting for me.

"Why are you on this boat?" he demanded. "Did you follow me?"

"No. Just luck, that's all."

"Luck! No such thing," he said bitterly. "There is fate, but there is no luck. What do you want of me, madama, that you so insistently keep popping up wherever I go?"

I could have pointed out that *he* had been popping up wherever I went, but I let the comment slide and said, "Look, I just want my map back. I saw you take it from the Grotto, and I need it."

This time he didn't bother with protests. "That map was part of a magickal Working. Are not officers in your army forbidden from magickal practices, upon pain of death?"

"I don't see how that matters to you, sieur. But you do admit, then, that you were at the Grotto?"

"Since you admit it, I will, too. But you didn't answer my question. If you say that I am against the law, it seems to me that you are, as well."

He glared at me, the pipe clenched in his teeth. I glared back. I'd been stared down by experts, and while his stare was fierce, it wasn't even in my top ten.

"You are right that it is against *The Articles of War* for a soldier to perform any magickal act," I said. "I'd be in serious trouble if anyone knew. So let us trade silences. Give me the map and I shall be silent as to what I saw in the Grotto, and shall expect you to keep silent as well."

"Why should I take your word," he asked, "when I could take your life?"

I didn't see it coming. One second he was sitting on the hay bale; the next, he was looming over me, pressing me into the sharp edge of a crate. His breath was apple-scented, and his hand was soft on my neck, but very firm.

"I could crush your throat in an instant, and toss you overboard so you could tell your secret to the sharks. Everyone would think you stumbled and fell. It happens, and you have admitted you have no sea legs." His hand tightened in a not-so-soft squeeze. I had no doubt he could toss me over the side with very little effort.

"You could," I wheezed. "But I don't need a voice to tell your secret. I left it in a letter addressed to my mamma, which she will find when she goes through my things after I am gone. I don't think you want to mess with my mamma."

"Your mamma? Why do I care about your mamma?" The grip tightened, and I was finding it hard to breathe, pressure building in my skull. "Who is this mamma?"

"Juliet Fyrdraaca, Buck Fyrdraaca," I wheezed. The grip loosened slightly and I knocked his hand away from my throat. He let me do so, and then said, "Your mamma is General Fyrdraaca?"

"Ayah."

"That letter trick," he scoffed. "I don't believe you."

"Take the chance and see." I hoped he wouldn't, because, of course, there was no letter. He was still pressed up against me, and now that he wasn't choking the life out of me, I had to admit the sensation was not entirely unpleasant. I gave him a good shove, and he moved away.

"And also, I am not without my own magickal defenses," I said. "I could turn you inside out with just one Word."

"I saw an example of your vocabulary at the Infantina's birthday party," he said jeeringly.

My cheeks were turning warm. I said quickly, "I was using the Word in its truest sense: *to burn.* I've seen things explode into flames when that Word was conjugated."

I returned his skeptical look with a glare of my own. He said, "Lucky for me, then, that I am not cinders. I will take your promise. But not until we reach Cambria. I wish to be off this ship first. I will leave the map with the captain and instruct him to give it to you once I have disembarked. Then, even if you betray me, I will be out of your reach. Do we have a deal?"

He held out his hand, and I took it. As our palms touched, a little thrill went through me. But I shook off the feeling and said, businesslike, "Deal."

TEN

Regrets.
Boarded. A Pirate.

ALTHOUGH I HAD LEFT my porthole open, my cabin was stifling hot. But at least there was no sign of Hardhands. I put on my nightgown and crawled into the narrow berth, Flynn settling down at my feet. The air coming in through the porthole was damp and my sheets felt sticky. Elodie's potion had cured my tum but had done nothing for my nerves, which were now working overtime. I lay in my berth, listening to the creak of the hull, the snap of the sails, and bony Flynn, snoring on my feet. My busy brain careened from one thought to another. Pow and Poppy. The map and my Working. My last conversation with Buck. The wer-bear. The ghost of Hardhands. The eye in the mirror.

And Udo.

Mostly, I thought of Udo.

Once before, I had believed I had lost Udo, lost him

to the Jack Boots, those malicious avatars of the outlaw Springheel Jack. After I saved him from the Jack Boots, I had sworn I would never underappreciate Udo again. But then he acted like a total jackass, and I was a bit of a jackass myself, and so we had parted. Let him do his Udo thing, hang with the Zu-Zu if he preferred her over me; well, that was just fine. Who needed Udo, anyway? And now he was gone, and unlike before, this time there was nothing I could do about it.

You never realize how much someone matters to you until it's too late. So Udo was stuck-up and bossy? He was also loyal and kind. He'd saved my life, twice really, and I had given him the high hat. No one knew me better than Udo; he was my best friend, and how had I repaid him? I had been mean and slighting; I'd never taken him seriously.

I imagined Udo beaten and tortured, forced to walk the plank or keelhauled. Or what if Udo was redeemed, only to return home ruined, like Poppy? Or what if the pirates had already killed him? I didn't care so much if the Birdies killed me, as long as Udo still lived. Eventually I gave up trying to sleep and lit my lamp. I had a copy of the yellowback *Nini Mo in the Panopticon* in my trunk. I'd read it before, but it was still distracting.

Hours later, I ran out of Nini Mo and drifted into a dismal sleep, only to be woken up when a sudden roll of the ship almost tossed me out of bed. As I tried to sit up, the ship rolled even more violently and I hit the floor with a thump, Flynn landing on top of me, paws scrabbling painfully against my back. I shoved him off as the door to my cabin popped open and there stood Elodie, a little white-nightgowned ghost, holding a lantern.

"What happened? Did we hit something?" I asked groggily.

"No! Daddy is trying to outrun them!"

"Outrun who?"

"The pirates! He said to tell you to hide in case we are caught!"

Elodie disappeared. The ship was heaving and bucking, but I managed to hoist myself up on the bed, after banging my knee hard against the washstand. I peered out the port-hole and saw only darkness and the spray of water, but I could tell that we were moving much faster than before. Could we outrun a pirate ship? I hoped, hoped, hoped so.

Footsteps pounded overhead, and the ship rolled so hard that Flynn and I were flung onto the floor again. My trunk slid, slamming against the door. For one sickening second, I thought the ship would roll right over and cap-size. Water splashed in through my porthole. But with a screeching groan of wood, the ship righted itself. Flynn and I, and everything in the cabin not nailed down, slid again. I clambered to my feet and slammed the porthole cover closed. For the next twenty minutes or so, the ship leaped and rolled while Flynn and I huddled in our soggy berth. But eventually, the ship began to slow.

We had not outrun the pirates.

I stumbled off the berth and pawed through my trunk for my gun belt. Elodie had said to hide; that sounded like an excellent idea, but if they found me, I wanted to be armed. As I was pulling my boots on, my cabin filled with a sickly white glow: the ghost of Hardhands.

"Yum, pirates," Hardhands said jovially. He was rubbing his skeletal hands together and licking his bloody lips. Flynn stared at Hardhands with wary eyes, a low growl buzzing out of his throat. "Aren't you glad I stayed now, honey pie?"

"Quit it, Flynn! Thanks, but I can take care of myself." The queasy feeling in my stomach told me that I hardly believed that statement myself. I went into the parlor, dragging Flynn behind me, Hardhands following. Elodie and Theo had vanished, probably into the bowels of the ship, where I hoped no pirates would ever find them. Good idea, but the only way out of the captain's quarters led up to the deck. Footsteps thudded overhead, mingled with the clang of steel and a lot of screaming and shouting. It did not seem like a good idea to go topside, but the parlor was sadly bereft of places to hide. The furniture was too low for me to squeeze under, and there were no closets.

"Don't worry, sweetie girl," Hardhands said. "I won't let them get you."

Voices came from the stairs, loud angry voices, loud angry *pirate* voices. I ran back into my cabin, Flynn scrambling behind me, and slammed the door shut and locked it. This time, Hardhands did not follow.

I stuffed Flynn under the berth and was ready to squeeze in after him when the door rattled. *Rangers fight,* Nini Mo said, and if the pirates were going to get me, well, they could bleed a little first. The room was too small for gunfire, so I excavated my saber from my trunk. The words of Captain Bothwell, my saber instructor, raced through my head: *Strike as hard as you can—and don't forget the bite!*

The door jumped, as though someone had just slammed a giant boot against it. Flynn barked and I shushed him.

Someone sang out happily, "Come out, come out, little mouse!"

"What did you find?" another voice said. The door jumped again.

"I was here first, so it's my spoils," the first someone said.

"You got the last one. This one's mine."

The pounding stopped and was replaced by the sound of slapping. Let them fight; maybe they'd kill each other and I could escape over their dead bodies. No such luck. A muffled *oof,* another smack, and then the second voice said, "I forgot. Sorry. Course it's your turn."

The assault on my door resumed. The door vibrated on its hinges. The pirates shouted extremely nasty things. Flynn wormed out from under the bed and flung himself at the door, yipping frantically. I pulled on the sash, trying to yank him back. I couldn't swing at pirates with him in the way. At the next blow, surely the hinges would give way.

But there was no next blow. I heard, "What the fike? Don't fike with me, Petey—" The voice choked off into a horrible gurgling sound. The other pirate began to wail like a siren. Flynn howled in sympathy. The siren scream abruptly cut off, leaving Flynn's howl to fill the silence. I clamped my hand hard over his muzzle and leaned forward, pressing my ear to the door. All I could hear was a faint slurpy sound. The lock on the door snapped up and the door began to open. I jumped back, swung my saber, felt it chop through empty air. Or, rather, through Hardhands, who stood in the doorway, licking something gooey off his long fingers.

"I told you that you needed my help, sweetling," he said.

Behind him, the parlor was empty of pirates, but the wreckage of the room was festooned with red gooey *something*. A soggy red pile of clothes lay on the floor.

"What happened to the pirates?"

"Gone." Hardhands giggled. He licked his fingers again. Flynn squirmed past me and eagerly nudged at one of the soggy piles. Squeezing by Hardhands, I pulled Flynn away from the gory pile.

"But they left their duds behind?" I kicked at the soggy clothes with a boot toe and then immediately wished I hadn't.

"They didn't need them anymore," Hardhands said. "Want a taste? Bitter, but piquant. Very ripe."

I shuddered. "Thanks, but no thanks." Hardhands laughed as I dragged Flynn back to the cabin. He did not want to go; he wanted to stay and lick the blood off the walls. Too fiking bad. The immediate pirates might be taken care of, but I had no doubt there were more. I didn't want to be wearing my nightgown when I faced them, so I quickly finished dressing. Since I was on duty, technically I was supposed to be in uniform all the time, but it seemed best not to advertise my military status, so I threw on a kilt and old jumper, and pulled the buckskin jacket over. I was buckling on my gun belt when Hardhands opened the door and announced, "Captain Ziyi has surrendered. They've rounded everyone up and are going through the ship's manifesto. I daresay soon enough they will realize who is missing. And then they'll come looking for you."

I had studied a lot of tactics in the Barracks, but none of these tactics had covered retaking a ship from pirates. I was one person, with one gun and one saber. Nini Mo might have been able to take out that many pirates by herself (or maybe not, as her accounts of her adventures were apparently extremely exaggerated), but I sure as fike couldn't do it. Not alone. But maybe with a little corpsey help . . .

"How many pirates can you eat?" I asked Hardhands.

"A lot, but not that many," he admitted. "My appetite is not what it used to be, and pirates are a bit gamy for my taste."

That left the Big Gun, which was not a gun at all. I could summon Pig. I had seen him take out the Quetzals and a kakodæmon. He could handle some pirates. But Paimon and Poppy had been adamant I save him for when All Else Failed. If his signature appeared in the Current, it would be an instant red flag that a Haðraaða was still around. I had used Pig before I'd known that, but Paimon had been able to cover my tracks. He might not be able to this time. All Else had not yet Failed. I should take my own chances.

Maybe the best thing to do was to surrender and hope for the best. Buck had said that the pirates were more interested in ransom than in murder, and that people wouldn't pay for damaged relations. I hoped she was right. Just in case, I transferred all my valuables, including the wad of cash from Poppy and my toothbrush, to my dispatch case and then shoved it as far under my berth as it would go. But what to do with Snapperdog? Leave him and risk him barking up a storm and antagonizing the pirates? Or take him and still risk him antagonizing the pirates? Snapperdog made the decision for me by flinging himself into a frantic yipping dance when I tried to slide out the door without him. Surely I could persuade the pirates he was worth a fortune, too.

"Flora?" A voice drifted down the stairwell. I froze, a trill of hope ribboning through me. I would know that voice anywhere, and it wasn't the voice of a pirate.

"Flora, are you here?" Flynn burst from my grip and dissolved into an ecstasy of barking and spraying, flinging himself at the figure tromping down the stairs. This figure was blindingly garish even in the dim swaying lamplight: banana-yellow frock coat, shiny purple boots, yellow kilt, and vivid purple weskit. An enormous yellow and purple tricorn perched upon the long rolls of yellow ringlets, as fat as sausages. A rapier swung from the black leather buckler he wore across his chest, and his cravat and cuffs were as frilly as one of Pow's diaper covers.

Udo himself.

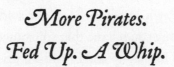

ELEVEN

More Pirates.
Fed Up. A Whip.

I FELL UPON UDO, not sure if I was beating on his chest in relief or anger, or a bit of both. His buckler cut into my chin, his lace cravat tickled my nose, his curls were slick with bear oil, and he smelled like a bagnio. But I didn't care. He was overdressed, but he was safe and alive. Udo lifted me up, squeezing me breathless, saying, "Pigface, you don't know how good it is to see you, Flora."

"How did you escape?" I twisted my head away from his attempt to kiss me. "Put me down!"

"Well," he said, and set me down, then bent to attend to Flynn's insistent head-butting. "I didn't exactly escape."

"What do you mean?"

"I kinda joined them," he said, looking rather sheepish.

"Udo!" I shrieked, and this time there was no doubt I was beating on his chest in anger. He staggered back against my blows and his hat fell off. I hit the middle of his buckler, almost breaking my fist, and the pain only made me more furious.

"I thought you might be dead, or sold as a slave, or worse—and now you tell me that you joined the *pirates*?"

He picked his hat up and brushed it off, protesting, "I would have sent you a message if I could have—but how could I? And why are you so surprised? You know I always wanted to be a pirate!"

"I thought you'd given up that childish dream. The way you were cavorting with the Zu-Zu, I figured you'd forgotten all about it. Forgotten about everything but her."

"Pigface, Flora! I had to make nice to her. It's part of my job! I was undercover. Did you think I was serious?"

"You sure as hell sounded serious when you dumped me, Udo!"

"Dumped you! You dumped me! You said, since you were going to the Barracks and I was going to Saeta House, there was no point in pretending that we might have a future. You said that, not me!" As usual, Udo was twisting my words around. I hadn't meant it the way he made it sound.

"But you agreed with me!"

"Only after you insisted! And then you sent all my letters back, so I figured what was the point? Why throw myself at someone who didn't want me? The Zu-Zu may be stuck-up, but at least she's honest. And she likes me the way I am; she's not always sniping at me or trying to improve me—"

"What the fike does that mean, Udo Landaðon?" Before he could answer, another familiar voice—and this one not nearly as musical to my ears—called Udo's name.

Like Udo, the Zu-Zu was now dressed à la piratical, though she wasn't nearly as garish. Still, with the tricorn balanced rakishly over one eye, the flouncy black kilt, the knee-high black boots, and the spill of black lace at her throat, she looked fabulous. The smug look on her face showed that she knew it. In one hand, she carried an unsheathed rapier, and this she now flicked at me dismissively.

"What's the holdup? We're in a hurry, remember?"

Udo answered, "We're just coming. Get your stuff, Flora."

"What? Are you a pirate, too, now?" I asked the Zu-Zu scornfully.

She grinned at me. "It's a fike lot more fun than being a hostage, let me tell you."

"The Zu is on our side, Flora," Udo said. "Remember, I told you? She hates the Birdies, too."

"What happened to your Boy Toys?" I asked her.

"Oh, we fed them to the sharks," she said airily. I doubted she was joking.

"Come on, Flora, get what you need and let's go," Udo ordered.

"I'm not going anywhere with either of you!"

"You can walk or I can carry you," Udo threatened. "You pick."

"You wouldn't dare." But I could tell by the look on his face that he would. The Zu-Zu kept grinning. I wasn't going to give her the satisfaction. When the moment was right, Udo was going to get it. But for now, *Stay cool, play cool,* Nini Mo said. I fished my dispatch case out from under my berth and went up top, with the Zu-Zu ahead and Udo behind, Flynn scrambling next to me.

The deck was swarming with pirates. In the flaring torch light, I saw some tossing baskets of produce into the drink, while others supervised *El Pato* crew members as they carried boxes up from the hold. The pirate ship loomed just off the portside bow; the boxes from the *Pato* were being transferred to the pirate ship via a rope and a giant net.

"I'd think that pirates could do better than steal boxes of ladies' underwear and cowhides," I said as they marched me toward the quarterdeck. Flynn was so close to my legs that I could hardly avoid tripping over him.

"Oh, we can, we can," the Zu-Zu answered. "I guess you didn't know that the *Pato* is carrying a shipment of jade for the Califa National Bank in Angeles."

"Shut up, Zu," Udo ordered, and she actually did, but

she gave me a little tongue poke. When I got through with Udo, she'd pay for that.

The crew members who weren't being worked by the pirates had been tied up near the anchor. Thanks to our hustle, I got nothing more than a quick look as we passed by, but I didn't think I saw Sieur Wraathmyr, or Elodie or Theo, for that matter. I was glad that the children had not been discovered, but too bad about Sieur Wraathmyr. His temperament would probably be improved by a good thumping.

On the bridge, a pirate held Captain Ziyi at gunpoint, while another was going through a sheaf of papers that I assumed was the ship's manifest. The captain had a black eye and blood on his mouth, but his eyes were as sharp and flat as diamonds, and he was staring at the pirate with the gun as fixedly as a snake stares at its prey.

Udo hustled me past this scene and into the ready room. He shoved Flynn after me, and slammed the door shut on us. That fiking snapperhead! Here I'd thought Udo was dead—or worse—yet he'd been swashbuckling around the Pacifica with the Zu-Zu, with not a care in the world for all the pain and sorrow he'd caused those he'd left behind. And then he had the gall to say that I had dumped him! My blood boiled with Gramatica; I didn't dare let the Words out, so I picked the nearest object— a coffee cup—and threw it. It smashed very satisfyingly against the wall.

"You snapperhead!" I shouted, and kicked the captain's chair. The chair skidded across the floor and Flynn barked and jumped.

The door to the ready room began to swing open. I grabbed wildly—a compass—and threw it with all my might toward the man coming through the doorway. He lifted an arm to ward off the blow, but my second projectile—a book—knocked his hat off.

"Holy fike, Flora!" the Dainty Pirate said. "Let up the volley. You've crushed my feather!"

His command came too late to stop my next throw, but my aim went wide and the bottle crashed harmlessly into the wall, knocking a painting of a frigate askew. I didn't stop throwing things because he had told me to; I stopped because I'd strained my arm, and now it fiking hurt. Flynn let out another howl and made as though to rush at the Dainty Pirate, but I grabbed his collar and held him, both of us panting with exertion.

The last time I had seen Boy Hansgen, the last true ranger, also known as the Dainty Pirate, he had just spent a month sitting at the bottom of an oubliette and hadn't looked—or smelled—particularly fresh. Now he was clean as a kite, and decked out in full Dainty Pirate glory. In fact, he made Udo the Popinjay Pirate look slightly underdressed. His doublet was encrusted with silver lace frogging, and his trunk hose looked like giant puffy cinnamon rolls. The queue of his silver wig was stuffed into a heavily embroidered queue bag. Silver and green boots with high stacked silver heels completed the outfit. The only thing unfrivolous about him was the plain silver buckler he wore across his chest, from which hung a very long saber and two very large pistols.

"Well, my dear, so we meet again," the Dainty Pirate said jovially. Cautiously, he came all the way into the room; Udo, the coward, was hiding behind him. "Welcome to the *Nada*."

"Is the *Nada* your ship?" I asked, incredulous. During his heyday the Dainty Pirate had been known for his exquisite clothes and the exquisitely mannered way he treated those he pillaged. The Dainty Pirate was a ranger and had been Nini Mo's sidekick. Surely he could not condone the brutal treatment that the crew of the *Nada* dished out.

"Ayah so. I have turned over a new leaf."

"Keelhauling innocent people is a new leaf?"

"In case you did not notice, my dear, Califa is preparing for a revolution. I cannot afford to be Dainty anymore—"

"Ha—"

"Hold your high horses, Flora," Udo interjected. "We are saving your skin here."

"Saving my skin? My skin don't need saving from

anyone but you! If there were no pirates around, I'd be safe as houses."

"Oh yeah, you think you are going to be safe as houses in Cuilihuacan—"

"How do you know I'm going to Cuilihuacan?" I countered.

Udo flushed and his mouth snapped shut. The Dainty Pirate shot him a look and said, "Hush, Udo. Hush. We are on the same side here. No use fighting. We don't have the luxury for it. As soon as the cargo is transferred, we must be underway."

"And by cargo, I guess you mean the jade, not the lettuce," I said.

"Ayah, the jade." The Dainty Pirate grinned.

"Buck's never going to let you get away with this!"

He laughed. "Buck? Honey, I'm acting on her orders!"

Her orders? The Dainty Pirate and Buck weren't on the same side. If I hadn't sprung him from Zoo Battery last year, he'd have been hanged on her orders. Did he think I was a total idiot?

I retorted, "As if I would believe that! The last thing I heard, Buck was going to hang you. I rescued you from that, remember?"

"Hang me! Ah, she never would have hung so pretty a man as me. And as I recall, you didn't rescue me at all, darling. I recall being torn apart by Quetzals, or some such."

"Which was a ruse, Axacaya said."

"Did he, now?" the Dainty Pirate said. "Did he say that?"

"If it wasn't a ruse, you'd be dead."

"Perhaps, maybe so, but anyway, believe it. Your dear mamma and I have been quite the compatriots these last few months."

Udo said, "Dainty and Buck are working together, gathering funds to help the revolution against the Birdies. You may call it piracy, Flora, but it's for a great cause."

Could this be true? Buck and the Dainty Pirate in league with each other? Why should I believe it? Buck would never dare cross the Birdies, and she and the Dainty Pirate had always been adversaries. It had been by her orders that the Ranger Corps had been disbanded and the Dainty Pirate had been outlawed to begin with.

"I do not have the time to be persuasive, Flora," the Dainty Pirate said. "The longer the ships stay hooked together, the more danger that we'll collide. We can talk about this all later. At leisure."

"What do you mean 'we'?" I demanded.

"You are coming, of course. Buck sent a message telling me to take you with us."

"I don't believe you!"

"Come on, girl, have some common sense. How would I know that you were on your way to Cuilihuacan to meet with the Duquesa de Xipe Totec if Buck hadn't sent me a message telling me so?" the Dainty Pirate said, exasperated. "Look, it don't matter to me if you believe me or not. What matters is that you are coming with us, chop-chop."

"Flora, don't be a snapperhead," Udo said. "You don't want to go to Cuilihuacan, do you? To the Birdies?"

My fury, slightly tamped after my lobbing spree, was beginning to flare again. First, Buck was going to hand me off to the Birdies. Now she was handing me over to pirates. And if Buck was in cahoots with the Dainty Pirate, then she had known Udo had never been in any danger at all. When she had gotten the Warlord's message, her reaction had been a total act. She had let me get onto the *Pato* believing that Udo might be dead, or worse. *Trust me*, she had said, but she still hadn't trusted me, not one bit. No one had: not Buck, not Udo, not even the Dainty Pirate, for whom I had risked everything to save.

Well, fike them all.

"I'm not going with you," I said. "I'm staying onboard the *Pato*. You can be pirates without me."

"I thought you were my ally, Flora," the Dainty Pirate said sorrowfully. "Buck told me I could rely on you, that you were afire for our cause. We are on the same side."

Nice try, but if I could withstand the Expert Guilter (Buck), then he could have no effect on me.

"No, we aren't. I'm not on the side of someone who can treat innocent people like he treated the passengers of the *Happy Rabbit,* like he is treating Captain Ziyi—"

"Flora—" Udo tried to hush me, but I ignored him.

"You have no right or good reason to treat the captain that way," I said furiously. "No reason to treat the crew like that—"

The Dainty Pirate said softly, "You think this is a game, girlie?" The sorrow had been replaced by a steely edge that sent a little shiver down my spine. "This is the real world, honey, not some Nini Mo novel. This is war, not a tea party. This is what a ranger does. A ranger gets the job done. By any means necessary. You are either with us or against us. Choose."

No longer was the Dainty Pirate amiable. He stared at me grimly, his hand on his sword hilt, and I had no doubt that he would spear me through the liver if I didn't go his way. I was outnumbered. I said, deflated, "You are right, sieur. I cry your pardon. Of course I am with you, always."

"Good choice. Go with her, Udo. And be snappy."

"Aye-aye, sieur. Come on, Flora."

Halfway to the door, I saw my chance and took it. I pretended to stumble over Flynn. Flynn yipped and twisted, and Udo yelped and tripped. As he started to go down, I shoved him, knocking his hat over his eyes, then grabbed the oil slicker hanging on the door and threw it over him. While he thrashed about, I snatched the whip off the whip rack, glad that Captain Ziyi liked to enforce discipline the old-fashioned way. Udo was trying to clamber to his feet, but Flynn was jumping all over him, yelping with glee, trying to play. The Dainty Pirate lunged at me, saying, "Don't be a fool, Flora!"

"Hit him," the ghost of Hardhands said, materializing behind the Dainty Pirate. "Hit him hard. Go for the eyes—"

I snapped the whip. The lash curled outward and caught the Dainty Pirate hard on the shoulder. The force of the blow juddered through the handle of the whip, and I stepped back to absorb the recoil, the lash curling behind me.

"Fiking hell!" the Dainty Pirate howled. He staggered back. I flicked the lash again; it undulated through the air with a hiss and landed on his other shoulder. The Dainty Pirate let out a holler that was half yelp, half laugh. Udo was clambering to his feet. As I ran by him, I gave him a good kick in the middle of his back and he went down again.

"⟨✶⟩!" shouted the Dainty Pirate. The Word missed me, but not by much; I felt it scorch my head as it whirled by. With a loud splat, it blew a hole in the cabin door.

At the door, I turned and lashed out at the Dainty Pirate one last time, barely missing his eye. Blood sprayed from the cut on his head, blinding him. I flung the door open and ran, Flynn at my heels, past the pirates who were rushing toward the Dainty Pirate's roars. They tried to grab me, but I dodged them.

The deck was a melee of sailors and pirates, flying lettuce and asparagus, random gunfire and fog. The crew must have rebelled. Good timing. I weaved my way through the confusion, shoving and pushing, Flynnie snapping and growling behind me, and dashed behind the chicken coop, where the poultry were shrieking and fluttering. A pirate lurched for me, but I kicked her in the shin. Ahead of me, a dark figure swirled out of the confusion, bare rapier in her hand: the Zu-Zu.

"Come and get it, Nini Mo," she said mockingly.

Oh, ayah, this was going to be sweet. I didn't bother to hold in the Gramatica Curse. While she was reeling from its impact, I charged at her, whip snapping, and knocked the rapier out of her hand. I was almost upon her when my foot came down on slippery liquid. I did a sudden painful split and hit the deck. The Zu-Zu crowed and bore down on me as I struggled to get my footing, and something small and dark plummeted from the rigging above and landed on top of her.

TWELVE

Jumping Ship. Rowing. A Beach.

I SCRAMBLED TO MY FEET, leg throbbing. The Zu-Zu was trying to stand, but Elodie was pummeling her so mercilessly that she couldn't get up. Elodie was small, but fike, she was tough. I whistled Flynn away from the downed pirate he was licking—he's a bloodsucker, all right—grabbed a fire bucket, hauled Elodie away, and dumped the bucket over the Zu-Zu. Oops, it wasn't a fire bucket. It was the pig's slop bucket. The Zu-Zu howled. Wait until she saw what my Curse had done to her; then she would really howl. Her hair was now a sickly glowing green, visible even under the slop.

"Come on! Hide!" Elodie shouted. I followed her as she darted between boxes, Flynn skittering behind me, until she stopped so suddenly, I almost ran into her. Ahead, the way was blocked by a very large pirate with a revolver in his hand.

I pushed Elodie behind me, and told him, "Take another step and I'll blow you both to the Abyss."

"With what, lovely? You ain't got a gun."

"I got this whip!" I hoped the pirate wouldn't realize he was out of its range. He did and laughed. Reinforcing my decision not to throw in with the Dainty Pirate's crew, he then made an extremely rude suggestion that I hoped Elodie did not understand. Alas, she did, and yelled her own rude suggestion back, adding a comment about the pirate's mother for good measure.

"Shut up, Elodie!" I hissed. With a roar of rage, the pirate raised his pistol. I hoped he had terribly bad aim or that his powder was wet or that it wouldn't hurt too much and that he would hit me and not Elodie and—

The pirate crumpled to the deck as though he'd been hit by an anvil. Sieur Wraathmyr stepped over him and said, "I'm leaving. You can come if you want." As far as I could see, the only weapon he had was his bare hands, but apparently he had a punch like a mule kick.

"Leaving? How?"

"The lifeboat," he said impatiently. "Now."

"Let's go!" I turned to Elodie, but she was already climbing the rigging. High above, Theo dangled, shouting encouragement.

"We can't leave her!" I followed Sieur Wraathmyr. "We can't leave her and Theo to the pirates!"

"Get the dog," he ordered, tossing something heavy

and ropy over the side. I hoisted Flynn up, and then Sieur Wraathmyr picked me up and threw me over his shoulder.

"Hey! Hey . . . *Hey!*"

"Hold on." He climbed over the railing and down the rope ladder that was banging and twisting against the ship. With one hand, I clutched his furry shoulder; with the other, I kept a death grip on Snapperdog, who had, fortunately, gone limp with fear. Salt spray blinded me and I closed my eyes, buried my face in Sieur Wraathmyr's furry jacket, and tried not to think about what would happen if he missed his footing. The ship would probably squash us before we could drown. Very little consolation.

Sieur Wraathmyr dropped into the little boat, then dumped me on a seat. I kept the death grip on Flynn, now trying to crawl into my lap, and grabbed the side of the boat with my other hand. The boat was heaving and bouncing in a very wet, sick-making way.

"What about Elodie and Theo?"

Sieur Wraathmyr cut a rope, then reached out an oar and pushed away from the *Pato*. "The pirates are retreating now that they have what they came for. I'm pretty sure those kids can take care of themselves. Can you row?"

"Not really." At the Barracks, I had considered joining the rowing team, but two practices had convinced me that yanking on two giant paddles was not my idea of fun. Now I rather wished that I had stuck with it.

"Move to the bow."

I crawled to the bow, hauling Flynn with me, and Sieur Wraathmyr took the oars and began to row. The *Pato* vanished into the dark night, and the sounds of pirate havoc dampened and then faded away completely. Now we were surrounded by darkness and water, swelling, rolling water. It suddenly occurred to me that maybe this was worse than pirates. "We aren't going to drift further out to sea, are we?"

"No."

"How do you know?"

"I have been to sea before," Sieur Wraathmyr said shortly. Well, Varangers were supposed to be famous for their seafaring ability. I hoped Sieur Wraathmyr was true to form. Otherwise, we were shark bait.

The oars looked heavy, but he didn't seem to have any trouble pulling them. The sea was not rough but the waves were high, and despite the stiff breeze and salt spray, my head began to lurch in time to the ocean's swells. Flynn huddled on my lap, shivering and hacking.

Sieur Wraathmyr didn't say anything, just rowed and rowed. My rage was wearing off, replaced by a horrible queasiness. I had made a hasty decision to jump ship and now I was sitting in a rickety boat in the middle of the ocean with a wer-bear, who had good reason to want me dead, and a puking dog.

Well, too late, that sorrow, Nini Mo said.

Anyway, better a wer-bear and a puking dog than faithless Udo and his equally conniving pirate friends. And Buck! Yet another betrayal. From here on I would trust no one but myself. And Flynn, of course.

Sieur Wraathmyr rowed, never tiring, never flagging. Neither of us spoke. His face was closed in concentration and my tum was too queasy for talk. Flynn subsided into a shivering, panting dog; he was bony, but at least he was warm. Eventually, the stars began to fade and the darkness took on a white tinge. Then one edge of the horizon turned pinky yellow, the colors slowly spreading until the bowl of the sky was filled with dawn.

"What's that noise?" I asked Sieur Wraathmyr.

It took a moment for his concentration to break. "Surf."

I turned around and craned my neck. Ahead of us a line of white frothy waves was emerging from the early morning fog. It was another half hour before we landed, a half hour in which I thought any moment I'd be swimming, Flynn beside me, tempting the sharks. The boat pitched over the breakers, nose so high at times that I could barely keep from being tossed out. But Sieur Wraathmyr kept pulling at the oars and we made it through. I was never so glad in my life when the hull of the lifeboat scraped ground.

Sieur Wraathmyr picked me and Flynn up and swung us out of the boat, then carried us through the surf and up onto the beach. He set us gently on the damp sand, which seemed to heave and swell beneath me. Snapperdog scrambled to his feet, shook himself, and ran over to piss on a piece of driftwood. That reminded me that I needed to do the same. I staggered to my feet, muscles stiff and cold, and staggered behind the driftwood, which luckily was rather large. My hankie was already damp but I didn't care.

When I came back, I found that Sieur Wraathmyr had beached the boat and pulled it far up onto the sand. Pig-face, he must be strong. The morning sun was burning the fog off; above us, wisps of blue began to emerge through the white tatters. Landscape was also emerging from the fog. We were in a curved bay about a quarter of a mile long. The beach swept upward, sand turning to rocks, rocks terminating in a fringe of scrubby deformed cypress trees. Except for us and a few darting birds running along the water line, the cove was empty of life.

Sieur Wraathmyr had climbed back into the boat; now he tossed one of the emergency kits onto the sand and jumped after it. He offered me my dispatch case, which I took, asking, "What now?"

"Rest."

He hoisted the kit and set off across the beach, away from the water. Flynn and I followed. Halfway up the hillside, just below the rocks and in the lee of an enormous driftwood log, he threw the kit down and began to scrabble a shallow impression in the sand.

"Take off your boots and socks," he ordered.

"Why?"

"You should never go to sleep with wet feet."

I glanced down and realized that his feet and legs, below the knee length of his kilt, were bare. I took my boots and socks off, rubbing my cold white toes. Sieur Wraathmyr unpacked the emergency bag from the lifeboat and lined the impression with a blanket. I lay down, Flynn squirming at my feet. Before I could protest, Sieur Wraathmyr lay down next to me and pulled the other blanket over both of us.

The sand was hard, my back ached, my tummy surged. But I was asleep in seconds.

THIRTEEN

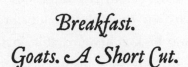

Breakfast.
Goats. A Short Cut.

I WOKE UP WITH FLYNN snuffling my neck. The space beside me was empty. The sky shone a brilliant blue, and the sun was warm on my face. My hands still burned, my back still ached, and my tummy was still empty. But the awful heaving seasick feeling was gone. I closed my eyes again, drowsily listening to the distant rumble of the waves, the thin whistle of the wind. But eventually my bladder became too insistent to ignore.

A scrim of fog still drifted over the trees on the cliffs above the beach. From the angle of the sun, it was mid-morning. I felt as though I'd slept for a week, but it had probably been only two or three hours. The surf was now very high, waves smashing thunderously onto the beach. Thank the Goddess we weren't trying to make landfall through that thunder; we never would have made it.

A few yards away, a small fire burned in a sandpit, but there was no sign of Sieur Wraathmyr himself. My bladder was getting painful, so I headed toward the edge of the beach, where a stunted cypress tree provided a potty screen. Then I washed my face and hands in the stream that wended its way across the beach before it vanished into the ocean. Back at the fire, still no sign of Sieur Wraathmyr, but there were his furry jacket, boots, and satchel, and also my socks, propped up on two sticks before the flames. While I put them on—nice and toasty—and then my boots, I looked at Sieur Wraathmyr's coat, so tempting, and at the satchel, even more tempting. My map had to be in one or the other. It's not nice to go through other people's belongings; it's even less nice to steal. But it had been my map to begin with, and you can't steal your own property.

Just as I was about to reach for the jacket, I heard furious barking. Flynn, who had wandered off while I was pottying, was bounding toward me, tongue lolling. Sieur Wraathmyr strode behind him, a writhing crab in each hand. Flynn flung himself on me. He was wet and smelled of salt.

"What are those crabs for?" I asked, pushing Flynn down.

"Breakfast," Sieur Wraathmyr answered. He wore only his knee-length kilt, made out of a dark blue-and-red checked fabric. No shirt, no weskit, no stockings, nothing but his own skin. But what skin! Almost every inch of Sieur Wraathmyr that I could see—and that was a lot—was covered in an intricate web of black lines. Dark crosshatching covered his shoulders and sides, and a series of rings encircled his arms. A diamond pattern was etched on his chest. More crosshatching marched down his legs. Only his face and the backs of his hands were bare. I've seen a lot of tattoos, but none like these. They were geometric, almost mathematical in their precision. I couldn't help but wonder if the parts of Sieur Wraathmyr that I could not see were also inked, and at that thought, I felt oddly spoony. I switched my gaze to the crabs.

"Where did you get those?"

Sieur Wraathmyr looked at me as though I was an idiot. "It's easy enough to get crabs. The rocks are full of them." He dropped one of the crabs onto the sand, unsheathed the very large knife thrust into the waistband of his kilt, and plunged it into the crab he still held. The crab wiggled one last time, sadly, and was still. The other crab scrabbled through the sand, making a break for freedom, but it got the knife, too, and then both were wrapped in seaweed and set on the fire to roast. A can of condensed milk was already half-buried in the coals; Sieur Wraathmyr fished out the hot can with the edge of his kilt and offered it to me.

"There's no coffee," he said. I drank and offered the can back, but he shook his head. As I finished the warm milk, Sieur Wraathmyr snatched the crabs off the fire and dropped one in front of me. He dismembered the other and fed it to eager Flynn.

"Aren't you eating?"

"I have already eaten," he answered.

I almost made a snappy comment about being as hungry as a bear, then decided to keep my trap shut until I had the map back. And until I had a chance to make sure my revolver and rounds were dry. We were alone on a beach, and no one knew where I was. Sieur Wraathmyr could easily get rid of me here. So best be sweet—and on guard—until I knew his intentions.

"Thanks for the chow."

"You are welcome." Sieur Wraathmyr tossed the last bit of crab to Flynn. He pulled his pipe out of a pocket of his furry jacket and tried to light it, but the wind was strong and kept blowing the match out. I threw my crab carcass into the fire and scrubbed my hands in the sand.

"Here, cup your hands around the bowl," I said, digging my match safe out of my pocket. He sheltered the pipe as I had instructed, leaning toward me. I struck the match on the sole of my boot and quickly brought it up to the bowl of the pipe, cupping my hand around his. His hands were warm, his palms heavily callused. He'd pulled oars before. He puffed on the pipe stem and the tobacco flared and caught.

"Thank you."

"You are welcome."

Sieur Wraathmyr stared off into the blue horizon, puffing on his pipe. Clearly, he wasn't going to make any conversation, so I said, "Where do you think we are?"

"The ship was just off the coast of Moros when we were boarded," Sieur Wraathmyr said. "Factoring in the tides and the drift, I would say we are a few miles south of there now. That puts us about fifteen miles north of Cambria. Angeles and Cuilihuacan are another sixty miles south."

I asked, "Why did you leave the *Pato*? The pirates were leaving. You'd have been fine once they were gone."

"The *Pato* will have to dock at Moros and make a report, and there will be hearings and newspapers and inspections, and much commotion. I have no time to waste on commotion."

I suspected that Sieur Wraathmyr did not wish to bring himself to the attention of the authorities; considering his true nature, I did not blame him. "What are you going to do now?"

"Go south to Cambria," he said, "to file a claim with my insurance company. You can catch a boat back to the City from there. I am assuming, since you abandoned the *Pato*, that you are not eager to get back onboard her."

I had no intention of either going on to Cuilihuacan or returning to the City. But my plans were none of Sieur Wraathmyr's business. Our only business was my map.

Now, more than ever, I wanted it back. And when I got it back, I would know where I was going.

"I hope you remembered to bring my map with you when you jumped ship," I said.

"Our deal has not changed. Only the details. When we get to Cambria, I shall give it to the postmaster there, with instructions to hand it over to you once I am gone."

"Why don't you give it to me now and we can go our separate ways? I will trouble you no more. You have my word on it. And I will accept your word for the same."

He puffed on his pipe, considering, and then shook his head. "No. We had a deal and I like to stick to my deals."

And with that I had to be satisfied, for, even armed, I wasn't sure I could take the map by force. He was big and he had a punch like a hammer blow.

I stood up, saying, "Then let's quit lollygagging and get a move on it."

While Sieur Wraathmyr kicked out the fire and buried its embers, I made a big show of checking my revolver, making sure that my rounds were dry. He watched me with a vague tinge of amusement, as though he was thinking I'd never have the nerve to shoot him. Well, let him try me. *Me or you,* Nini Mo said. *If it comes down to it, I'm gonna choose me, every time.*

At the edge of the beach, we found a narrow trail through the blackberry bushes and sea grass. Hidden in the brush to the left of us was a creek; I could hear the water. The foliage gradually closed in overhead, and the warmth of the sun faded into a moist chill. The grade up the hill was steep and rocky. But compared to marching up and down the Barracks' parade ground with a forty-pound knapsack and a twenty-pound rifle, trying to chant the quickstep cadence without puking, this was nothing but a stroll.

Sieur Wraathmyr took the lead and I took the middle, leaving Snapperdog to close up the file. We didn't talk, just marched, and this silence gave the previous night's events plenty of room to roll around unhappily in my head. Despite what the Dainty Pirate had said, I couldn't believe that Nini Mo would ever have endorsed his actions. She never hurt the innocent. He was a pirate, not a ranger, and I wanted no part of piracy. If that made me against him, well, so be it. I would always be against cruelty and violence. I hoped that Captain Ziyi, Theo and Elodie, and their sailors had managed to retake the *Pato* and had kicked the Dainty Pirate into the ocean to drown.

And Udo. After all those years of friendship, after I had risked my life for his, saved him from Springheel Jack, done his homework for him, he had let me believe he had become a fancy boy, let me believe he had been captured by pirates, let me believe he might be dead. When actually he was swooning around with the Zu-Zu, pretending to be the great hero, having a good ol' time. Well, fike him. I was done with Udo Landaðon for good. Let him be a pirate laddie, dally with the Zu-Zu, and good luck to them both.

And Buck. Here she had been planning for revolution all along, in league with the Dainty Pirate, but she hadn't trusted me enough to tell me. Even though it mattered as much to me as to anyone, she had let me believe I was trapped in secrecy forever, had let me believe that Udo might be dead. She had lied to me again. Betrayed me again.

No, actually, she'd done me a favor. Officially I had been captured by pirates. She would not dare advertise otherwise; she would not dare search for me. To do so meant admitting she was in league with the pirates. Her plan had backfired. Instead of handing me over to another keeper, she had set me free.

I was on my own. No parents to tell me what to do. No drill sergeants or company commanders full of orders. No pushy butlers or high-hatted best friends. No scheming adepts or nosy fathers. No one in the world, except Flynn and Sieur Wraathmyr, knew where I was or what I was doing. At long last, I was me myself alone.

I knew exactly what to do. As soon as I had that map, I would know where Tiny Doom was. And wherever she was, that's where I was going.

After an hour or so on the trail, we came to the top of the ridge, and there we stopped for a potty break and a short rest. With an ominous warning about snakes, Sieur

Wraathmyr disappeared into the brush on the left side of the trail, and I took the right side, nosy Flynn trailing behind me. I found a sheltered spot and once again was glad I had my hankie.

"You are an impetuous girl, aren't you, Nini? Just like your mamma—both of them, actually!"

I almost fell out of my squat. "Pigface Califa—do you mind?" I said, scrambling to my feet.

The ghost of Hardhands loitered behind me, grinning. "Oh, I don't mind. And you shouldn't, either, not if you are going to be a campaigner. There's no privacy on the trail."

"Get out of here! Go home!"

"Home is where the heart is, honey, and you are the heart of the House Haðraaða, so I am home."

"You know what I mean. Go back to Bilskinir," I said, exasperated.

"Now that you have run off with that boy, you need my protection more than ever, I think. I wouldn't dream of abandoning you now."

"I haven't run off with Sieur Wraathmyr. And I don't need your protection."

"Well, you have run off and you both seem to be going in the same direction. I daren't let you run alone. If it hadn't been for me, the pirates would have gotten you—"

"Are you all right, Lieutenant?" Sieur Wraathmyr hollered from the path.

Flynn left off sniffing at Hardhands's bloody white feet and scrambled back up toward the trail.

"I'm coming—" I hollered back. Then, to Hardhands, "Look, I appreciate what you did for me, I really do. But the last thing I need is a bloody corpse following me around."

The ghost was unimpressed. "Don't try to teach me bitchy, Almost Daughter. I am the king of bitch. After your impetuous actions of last night, it is abundantly clear that you do need my help. Ah, the Fyrdraaca temper! Also, look, that scrying the other day."

The horrible green eye in my mirror. I remembered with a shudder.

"What about it? Did you find out who it was?"

"No, I'm still working on it; my sources are rusty. But look, someone's looking for you, and it's best they not find you. I'm not sure if it's the magick they smell or the Haðraaða or both, being as they are somewhat linked together. You'd better cut with the magick. Swallow those Words down, no matter how they burn."

"I try," I said. "I really do try, but sometimes they just pop out."

"Control yourself, my girl, or the Gramatica will control you. And that is a very, very bad thing. Understand?"

"Are you sure you are all right?" Sieur Wraathmyr's call interrupted the lecture, for which I was grateful. I didn't need Hardhands to tell me what I needed to do.

"You go—right now!" I hissed to the ghost, and climbed back up to where Sieur Wraathmyr, actually looking slightly anxious, was waiting with Flynn.

"There's a panther in the area," he said. "We should stay together."

"A panther!" I reflexively looked up into the trees. "How can you tell?"

"I can smell it, but the smell is not too strong. It is not close by. I will be on guard, and surely the dog will set up the alarm if he catches a whiff of cat." The only smell Flynn ever set up an alarm for was the smell of frying bacon, but I didn't embarrass Flynn by pointing that out.

The track soon joined a wider road that followed the edge of a cliff; a long way below lay the foamy surge of the ocean. I thought we were out in the middle of nowhere, but the trail turned out to be as heavily trafficked as the Slot. We passed two farmers hauling hay, their burros almost invisible under their grassy loads. A small girl with a long stick herded a gaggle of geese, and then, not long after, two black-and-white collies herded a flock of sheep, no human beings in sight. Flynn ran forward to greet the dogs, the sheep scattering in fright. I whistled him back, and the collies regrouped their charges, ignoring Flynn completely, and continued on their way.

I had to admit that Sieur Wraathmyr was a pleasant traveling companion. He kept up a steady pace and never once complained about getting too much sun like Udo would have. Two years ago Buck had taken Udo and me on a School of the Soldier encampment; Udo had spent the entire time worrying about bug bites and fretting because he couldn't wash his hair. Sieur Wraathmyr was refreshingly free of such vanities.

Once, we heard the jingle of tack and the sound of approaching horses, and before I could protest, Sieur Wraathmyr pulled us into the brush. Two riders, rough-looking and well armed, rode past our hiding spot, and I was glad for Sieur Wraathmyr's caution. *There's no point in looking for trouble,* said Nini Mo. *It will find you eventually, anyway.*

Toward midafternoon the track turned inland, meandering through a twilit grove of cypress trees. We forded a rocky stream by balancing on a fallen log and then scrambled back up into the brilliant sunshine. We found ourselves traversing a grassy hillside, where small goats rushed toward us, bleating and pawing. As soon as they saw Flynn, they rushed away, and we continued on the track unmolested until we came to a long, low adobe building with a sign painted in bright red paint: THE SEQUOIA GOAT CHEESE COMPANY.

A weather-beaten lady in an apron and high muck-splashed boots came out of the barn and sold us a pound of goat cheese, a quart of goat's milk, a loaf of bread, and a basket of figs. I wanted to sit and eat, rest for a while. But Sieur Wraathmyr fussed over the delay. Afraid he (and my map) would leave us behind, Flynn and I gobbled our lunch while the goat lady gave Sieur Wraathmyr directions to Cambria.

"How long will it take to get there?" I asked when she was done.

"A day, depending on how fast you can walk," the lady answered.

"Some of us do not walk fast," Sieur Wraathmyr said pointedly.

"Some of us have short legs," I said. "Is there a place around here where we can hire some horses?"

"I do not ride," Sieur Wraathmyr interjected. "Is there any other way? A shortcut, perhaps?" He really was in a hurry to get rid of me. Well, the feeling was mutual.

The goat lady said, "There is. It's more a track, not a real road. But on foot, you should be fine. Here, I shall tell you the way." We listened carefully and when she had finished with the directions, she added, "Even that way, though, you shall not make Cambria tonight. But you may spend the night at the Valdosta Lodge. It was built as a hunting lodge for the Valdosta family, when they held all this as a land grant. Now the grant is split, and the only Valdosta left is Cecily, who runs the lodge as a hostel. It is plush."

"I could use some plush," Sieur Wraathmyr said. "I'm too old to sleep rough; my bones ache."

"Too old!" the goat lady scoffed. "And you less than

twenty, I'll wager. Wait, kiddo, until you are my age and then you'll know what aching is!"

I glanced at Sieur Wraathmyr, surprised. His attitude had been so aloof and his face so scowly that he had seemed to me middle-aged. Thirty, at least, maybe more. Now, with a smile still hovering around the edges of those glinty gray eyes, I saw that he was probably not much older than me. Well, so what? That didn't make him any less of a disagreeable snapperhead.

We thanked the goat lady for her directions and set off. The walk was no longer pleasant. The track was steep and slippery with rocks. The air grew chill and the sunlight vanished, hidden behind the tangle of branches. The brush was thick with spider webs and probably crawling with ticks. My feet were beginning to burn and my back ached. Sieur Wraathmyr, if he was tired, didn't show it. I guess bears have a lot of stamina, even when they are part human. Well, if he could keep pace, so could I. I marched on.

In the late afternoon, we came down into a valley where the air was so thick with moisture, it felt like walking through soup. The trees here were so tall that their tops were hidden in the mist high above; their trunks were enormous, some as wide around as a small house. Redwoods, the tallest trees in Califa, maybe the world.

The redwood grove was majestic, awe-inspiring, and . . . wet. Drops drummed on my hat brim, and the path beneath our feet squelched. My clothes felt clammy; my waterproof boots didn't stop the chill. The trees blocked out most of the sky, but I could tell that somewhere high above was twilight. The path was vanishing into the murk. I was about ready to give out, and Flynn already had. He flopped onto the mud and lay there, wagging his tail apologetically.

Sieur Wraathmyr bent down and scooped him up, slinging him over his shoulder like a side of beef. "Shall I carry you, too?"

"I can manage," I said. "But thanks for hauling Flynn."

"He doesn't weigh much. I can carry you, too. It is no trouble." In the gloom, with his hair wild from the wetness, his face in shadow, Sieur Wraathmyr seemed even more bearlike. I had no doubt he could carry me. And eat me, if it came to that. No one would ever know. A thrill of fear ran through me, along with a line from an old nursery rhyme: *It isn't very good in the dark, dark wood* . . .

"I'm fine, really." I hastily stepped back.

He frowned, then shrugged and went on. I trudged behind him through the wet dusk, wishing for hot coffee, wishing for dry socks, wishing for a very long nap. Once, I stumbled on a root, twisting my ankle and almost falling headfirst into the creek. Sieur Wraathmyr didn't look back. The murk faded into the gloom, and the gloom was rapidly becoming night when up ahead I saw the twinkle of yellow lights. We crossed a narrow wooden bridge over a stream and came to a little yellow house with three pointy gables and a second-floor balcony over the front door. The lights in its windows were cheerful and warm.

We had arrived at the Valdosta Lodge.

FOURTEEN

Plush Lodgings.
Rain. Confessions.

AT THE FRONT DOOR of the lodge, a small, round, cheerful old lady introduced herself as Cecily Valdosta, cooed over our bedraggled condition, and divested us of our soggy outerwear and boots. While we registered—I gave my name as Nyana Romney, just in case Buck was already looking for me—she poured us hot ginger toddies and rubbed Flynn dry with a towel. Then we followed her down a narrow low-ceilinged hallway and up a narrow flight of stairs. As we went, Madama Valdosta kept up a welcoming patter, but I was too tired to focus on her words.

"Here you are, my dear Nyana," Madama Valdosta said, opening a door. "I hope you will be nice and cozy. Don't hesitate to give me a ring if you should want anything. It is my pleasure to serve. Sieur Wraathmyr, you'll be right down the hallway. Come, dear, come." Sieur Wraathmyr gave me a quick look that I couldn't quite interpret and followed Madama Valdosta.

The cozy room was dominated by a giant bed, piled high with pillows and quilts, with bedposts of rough-hewn tree trunks. Low lights threw friendly shadows on the paneled walls and the carpet was lush beneath my feet. A leather sofa—already claimed by Flynn—stood before the fireplace; a small door next to it led to an immaculate bathroom.

I dumped my wet clothes on the floor by the bed. The ceramic stove in the corner of the bathroom gave off a gentle heat, and the water, when it gushed into the tub, was boiling hot. Lavender bath salts and two kinds of toothpaste (one mint, one apple) were arrayed by the sink. The tub was positioned so you could lie in the bath and stare out the window at the white mist drifting through the redwoods. I had a nice long soak, and when I finally, reluctantly, climbed out of the tub and enveloped myself in a fluffy robe, I felt wrinkled and relaxed and clean. Furiously hungry, too.

"At least the water is hot," a voice said.

I turned back from the sink, toothbrush in hand. The ghost of Hardhands had usurped the tub, and now leaned over the edge, staring at me. He was a lot cleaner than the last time I had seen him, but the dirt, at least, had covered up the worst of the wounds. Now the trauma of death was all too obvious. His bare arms were covered in long red welts and scratches, and slick white tendons showed through the arrow gash in his neck. "But the rest of this place is quite the dump, eh? Still, beggars can't be choosers, eh?"

"Did I tell you to go home?" I snapped.

"You did. But I did not." The ghost leaned back in the tub. He elevated one long leg and began to scrub. I averted my eyes. I had seen all that I cared to see. "Listen, your friend, the Varanger, he says he's a Varanger, anyway, though he's covered with Kulani tattoos—"

"Kulani?" I said sharply. "He's a Varangian."

"Oh, so he says. He's from the Kulani Islands, I'll bet my hat on it."

The Kulani Islands lie far to the west of Califa, out in the Pacifica Ocean. No one knows much about them, as they don't allow outsiders to set foot on the islands, and the only islanders that ever sail beyond the chain of islands are raiders.

Hardhands continued, "It's true that Wraathmyr is no Kulani name—they love their vowels, you know—but he's covered with Kulani markings. If he ain't a Kulani, and a high-ranking one, too, I'll eat your dog. There's something shifty about him—"

"He's a wer-bear. That's what's shifty about him."

"No, of course I know that. Something else. He's hiding something."

"I don't care a bit about him, so why would it matter to me?"

"You say this heatedly enough that I know that cannot be true."

I hastily changed the subject. "Did you find out anything about whoever is scrying me?"

"I'm still working on it." Hardhands soaped another bloody calf.

"Well, go work on it," I said. "And leave me be."

"So you can work on Wraathmyr? He is rather dark and brooding, and I know the young ladies like that."

"Shut up!" I said hotly.

"A murderous romantic—you have your mamma's taste! She always did like them with blood on their hands, like your dear papa—"

"⚖ ⟫⟩ ⌇ ⎘ ⧫!" I screeched. Oh fike, not again. The Command hit Hardhands in his bruised chest. His mouth opened in surprise and he began to quiver and shake. With a ripping sound, like cardboard shredding, he vanished and there was a large splash. I peered into the tub. A red shape the size of a housecat was eddying in the water, eight tentacles undulating. It shot from one end of the tub to the other, and then attached itself to the side and began to climb.

Oh fike. I had turned Hardhands into an octopus. And I had shown myself on the Current again. Control the Gramatica, Hardhands had said, or it will control you.

I took a deep breath. Next time, I would bite my own tongue off before I let a Gramatica Word pass my lips. The octopus reached the edge of the tub and waved its tentacles at me, pulsing a deep angry sangyn.

"I told you to keep it shut," I said. I went back to the bedroom and found the chamber pot under the bed. In the bathroom, I filled the pot with water, dropped my wet towel over Hardhands—Octohands now, really—and gingerly gathered up the bulging, wiggly towel. When I shook it out over the pot, Octohands fell out in a snarl of tentacles. Before he could escape, I slammed the lid on the pot and draped the towel over it. I had no idea how to reverse my Gramatica Command, and even if I had, I wouldn't have dared do it now. It wouldn't hurt Hardhands to spend some time as a cephalopod. Better that than a bossy, stenchy corpse. At least he couldn't talk now.

While I had been in the bathroom, Madama Valdosta had replaced my wet clothes with dry ones. The chemise was made of white lawn, the stockings had no holes in them, and the stays were embroidered with small pink flowers. The kilt was a bit longer than I was used to, but the dark blue knitted jersey was as soft as a cloud. I stuffed my feet back into the warm slippers and went to find Sieur Wraathmyr.

His room was next to mine; the door was ajar. I peered around the door jamb. Sieur Wraathmyr was lying fully dressed on the bed, on his side, his legs drawn up to his chest, arms folded around himself, his hands balled up into fists. He was fast asleep. A weird sharp pain cut through me. Sleeping, he didn't look arrogant or aloof. He looked tired and very young.

I stepped back into the darkness of the hallway, my heart racing, my breath shallow. He was just sleeping. So what? He was an arrogant, stuck-up snapperhead, and he could sleep until the Abyss froze over, for all I cared. I was going down to dinner.

Hardhands was wrong, I thought, as I went downstairs. My type is not dark and brooding. Nor do I care for romantics with blood on their hands. If I had a type—which I don't—it would be sunny and amusing and sure of himself. Someone who knew what to do and did it without dithering. Udo was sunny and amusing, all right, and sure of himself, but in a bad way: so sure he was right when he was not. He was also vain and silly. If I was looking for someone—which I'm not, of course; I haven't got time for spoony stuff—I would look for someone who was honorable and loyal and who would take me seriously. I certainly wouldn't go gaga over a stuck-up arrogant werbear. As far as I was concerned, Sieur Wraathmyr could stuff it.

In the dining room, dim underwater mirrors reflected the candlelight, playing off the silver plates and cups lining the china-hutch shelves. The long, polished wood table was set with gold-rimmed dishes and covered with bowls and platters of delicious-smelling food. I sat down in a heavily carved wooden chair, and Madama Valdosta introduced me to the other guests seated at the table: a writer on retreat and a couple on their honeymoon.

During dinner, the writer didn't say much—being sunk, I guess, into creative thought—and the couple was too spoony to care about anyone else. I was too tired for conversation and happy to concentrate on the chow. Every dish that came my way was yummy, even the braised cauliflower, and normally I hate cauliflower.

Midway through the soup course, Sieur Wraathmyr, still dressed in his damp clothes but looking a whole lot cleaner, appeared and gave his apologies for his late arrival. After dinner, Madama Valdosta tried to tempt us into joining a game of poker in the parlor, but Sieur Wraathmyr and I declined. We wanted to make an early start in the morning. Madama Valdosta gave us each a hot brick to warm our sheets and a basket of ginger drops, just in case we got hungry in the middle of the night.

In my room Flynn waited impatiently by the door, his supper untouched. At my urging, he raced down the stairs and outside into the rain, but then he wouldn't come back inside. I had to drag him in and upstairs by the collar. Snapperdog!

My bed had been turned down and the lamps extinguished, so the room was lit only by the glow of the fire. A flannel nightgown hung nearby on a warming rack. The towel over Octohands's chamber pot was undisturbed; I'd figure out what to do about him later. Right now I just wanted to sleep. Ignoring Flynn's whining, I heaved myself into the comforter, sinking into feathery wonderfulness. I was asleep in seconds.

The next morning, I woke to the gentle patter of rain on the roof. When I peered out the window, I saw that the trees were hidden behind a drifting fog and the rain was coming down quite heavily. Not a very good day to travel. A few more minutes of rest wouldn't hurt, surely? I closed my eyes again, just for a moment.

When I opened them again, it was much later and the delicious smell of pancakes hovered on the air. My clean, dry clothes hung on the rack by the fire. I got dressed and went to find breakfast, anxious Flynn trailing behind me. Sieur Wraathmyr already sat at the dining room table, devouring pancakes as though he were in a contest. Or a prison. There was no sign of the other guests.

"It's a pity you must travel in such miserable weather," Madama Valdosta said. "Perhaps you should stay another day." She refilled my coffee cup. Under the table, Flynn was draped over my feet.

Sieur Wraathmyr answered, "I wish we could, madama. Your hospitality has been very gracious. But we must go on."

"Such a pity."

I agreed with her. The thought of leaving the snug

little lodge and trudging through the cold wetness was not a happy one. My umbrella and my gum boots were still onboard the *Pato,* and so was Flynn's raincoat. He was liable to catch a chill, which would not be helpful at all. There's nothing more pathetic than a dog with a cold.

By the time we were done eating, the shimmery rain had turned into a fearsome drubbing, and the stream, barely visible through the silvery sheeting, was already over its banks. Sieur Wraathmyr went to investigate. When he returned a few minutes later, wet despite the umbrella Madama Valdosta had given him, he reported that the footbridge was already submerged. Until the rain stopped and the water went down, we were staying at the Valdosta Lodge.

I returned to my deliciously soft comfy bed and had another long lie-down, and after that, another wonderful soak. Then it was time for lunch: hot beef sandwies with cheese sauce, hashed herbed potatoes, and cherry trifle. Afterward, Madama Valdosta showed me to the library, which was wall-to-wall, floor-to-ceiling, with books. There I found the entire run of Red-top Rev, Vigilante Prince, the beedle dime novel series based loosely (very loosely) on Poppy. I settled blissfully into a vast leather armchair, a stack of yellowbacks at one hand and a pot of tea at the other.

After weeks of late nights, paperwork, and orders, and before that, months of marching, drilling, studying, and crappy food, just lying around was blissful. No one harassed me about missing mail or ordered me to change a nasty diaper or wondered why I hadn't finished my copying yet. I could do what I liked when I liked it, and if that meant eating only donuts for breakfast or spending three hours soaking in the tub, well, so what?

Sieur Wraathmyr, however, could not relax. He kept going to the window and looking outside, and once, he suggested we leave anyway, giving me a very scornful look when I told him I wasn't interested in getting drenched.

But slowly the charm of the Valdosta Lodge worked its magick on Sieur Wraathmyr and he began to unwind. He took long naps. He combed his hair. He ate Madama Valdosta's delicious chow with gusto. And once, when I asked him to pass the salt, he did so with a smile. That smile cracked his arrogance and made him seem almost handsome. Maybe I had been wrong about him. Maybe he'd just been tired and stressed and needed a break, too. The next time he smiled at me, I smiled back.

Only Flynn was unhappy; homesick, I guessed. He scratched on the door of whatever room we were in, but kept refusing to go out. He'd just stand in the doorway, looking anxious. He poked at me over and over with his shiv nose until I petted him, but as soon as I stopped, he'd start shiving again. He wouldn't go out into the rain to do his business unless I went with him, and then he'd run into the bushes and hide and I would have to drag him inside again. He skulked under my feet, tangling me up, and after I almost broke my neck, I left him in my bathroom, where he howled for a good hour before shutting up.

AFTER DINNER ON the third or fourth day—I'd lost track—Sieur Wraathmyr fired up his delicious-smelling pipe and asked me if I wanted to play backgammon. As we played, he became downright chatty. Eventually we abandoned the game and just talked, mostly about his travels. As a salesman for Madama Twanky's, Sieur Wraathmyr had been almost everywhere.

He told me about Bexar, where the men wear high-heeled boots, love their horses as their children, and will not walk even five feet if they can ride. He told me about Varanger, where in the winter the sun never rises, and in the summer, never sets, where the forests stretch for miles, full of moose, wolves, elk—and bears. There are no cities in Varanger; the people live in longhouses scattered among the forest, each house self-sustaining.

He had been to Arivaipa, where even the flowers have thorns and it rains only a few times a year. He had been to the Longhouse Nations and seen the sachems with their feathered headdresses and black-painted faces. He had crossed the Great Plains, where not a single tree grows for a thousand miles, and traveled up the Great River, which is so wide that at times you can't see its opposite bank.

He had even been to Porkopolis, which sits on the edge of a lake as big as a small ocean. The buildings in Porkopolis are fifteen stories high, the horsecars run on an invisible galvanic current, and airships drift out over the lake.

Udo acted like the Lord of Creation but he'd never really been anywhere or seen anything. And I'd like to see him in Arivaipa or the Longhouse Nations, worrying about the dust or if someone was going to scalp him.

"You are very lucky," I said. "I wish I had your job. You can go anywhere and do anything. You get to travel the world and be your own boss."

"Hardly. Madama Twanky is my boss. I have to go where she sends me. And sometimes the job is no fun at all. I have to travel through rain and snow. Customers can be a real pain in the ass. And sometimes I get attacked by pirates." We both laughed.

"Ayah, but you can quit if you want to," I pointed out.

"What else would I do? Where would I go? I have no family, no home."

"What happened to your family?"

I was lying on the sofa; he was sitting on the fire rug, legs crossed. Now he turned away from me and stared into the fire.

"I am only Varanger on my mother's side," he aswered.

"My father was a Kulani. My mother was a trader; a storm blew her ship up on a reef near my father's home island. He helped rescue her and the other survivors. They fell in love, married. When I was six, my mother died of an infection, and my father drowned in a surfing accident not too long after. They said it was an accident, but I wonder. He was a famous waterman, and very skilled with the board. I think he just didn't want to live without her. He still had me, but I wasn't enough. I wasn't her."

"That's awful," I said. He was still looking into the fire. I reached down and touched his shoulder gently.

"It is what happened. I grew up in my uncle's house, but he took me out of duty, not love. I wasn't a true Kulani, as my blood was tainted by my mother's."

"But your father was a Kulani!" I protested. "Doesn't that make you a Kulani?"

"Only half of one. And to the Kulanis, that's not enough. I never really fit in, and then . . ." He trailed away and was silent so long, I thought perhaps he wouldn't start talking again, but he did eventually. "My mother died without telling me about the bear strain that ran through her family. I didn't know until I changed for the first time, when I was fourteen." He paused, and I patted his shoulder encouragingly. He reached up and took my hand, squeezed it hard.

He went on. "I can control the change now, but I couldn't then. It would just happen—when I was angry, when I was hungry—when, well, at other times. They said I was dangerous, and I probably was. And there are no bears on the Kulani Islands, so this was just more proof I wasn't a real Kulani, that my Varanger blood was stronger than my Kulani blood. That I didn't belong there. I couldn't stay."

"They kicked you out?" I asked, incredulous.

"They are very pragmatic people, the Kulanis," Sieur Wraathmyr said dryly. "My uncle had fed and sheltered me for eight years. Such things are given freely to members of the family, but I was not really one of them. I owed my uncle compensation, but I had no way to repay him. So he sold me to an Imperial galley." He turned, pushed up his sleeve, and showed the galley brand on his forearm. I touched it gently; the scar was rough beneath my fingertips.

"Fike them!" I said hotly. "How could they do such a thing?"

"Apparently very easily. The first time I turned, my captain was delighted. He'd thought he just bought a scrawny kid, good for a few months at the oar and then into the drink. But a bear has a lot of stamina and can provide entertainment as well. I think he would have been happy if I remained a bear all the time."

"Could that happen? Could you change and not change back?"

"I don't know. I have always changed back. Anyway, I

was on the galley for a little over a year, and then the captain was killed in a drunken brawl. We got a new captain, and this one liked me enough to pull me off the oars and into his cabin staff. He was good to me, in his own way, but then he got an offer he couldn't refuse. Mostly the ship moved freight, but sometimes we took passengers. We picked up a Birdie priest, a nahual—you know what they are?"

"They are skinwalker priests."

"Ayah, and they think they are holy and special, that their god has chosen them. They don't take kindly to other skinwalkers. They call us abominations. This nahual found out what I was; there's no secret like that on a galley, and he offered to buy me from the captain. I guess he thought he could kill two birds with one stone: rid the world of a skinwalker by sacrificing it to his bloody god. My captain was fond of me, it's true, but he was more fond of money. He sold me to the Birdie."

This was so horrible, I didn't know what to say. I wrapped my arms around his shoulders and hugged him. He did not flinch from my embrace.

He laughed hollowly. "Well, it worked out, in the end. I was tired of being on that ship but hadn't found a way to get off it. Now I had my chance. Before we could get back to Anahautl City, the nahual had an accident."

"I hope it was a fatal one."

"Oh yes. It was extremely fatal. Then I bummed

around, doing this and that, and eventually met Oddvar Wraathmyr. He took me in, helped me get a job with Madama Twanky, and so I have been a salesman ever since."

He turned, and then pulled me down next to him on the hearth rug. He slipped an arm around me and I leaned against him, comforted by his warmth and the sweet smell of apple pipeweed.

We were in the same boat, Sieur Wraathmyr and I. We both had to hide who we really were, both faced rejection by our families, both risked death if our true natures were discovered. I had totally misjudged him. He wasn't sullen or closed because he was mean but because he was afraid, like me, afraid he would be found out, caught. Never before had I met anyone who understood exactly what I was going through, who shared my fear so exactly.

I asked, "Do you ever think of paying them back, the Kulanis that sold you, I mean?"

"I did, once. But revenge is a dish that will sour your stomach. It will eat you alive if you let it. I escaped the prison they made for my body; I will not live in a prison of the mind, Nini. But I do envy you. You have parents who care about you, and a home—"

"I wish that were true, but it's not!" I answered. "My whole life is a lie!"

And then, like a flood, it all came out. I was babbling, the whole horrible story of my miserable life pouring out of me in one long, wretched spiel. I told him everything:

my dreams of being a ranger and how those dreams had been quashed, and the long-gone namesake sister whose wonderfulness I could never live up to. I told him how the woman I had thought was my mother had lied to me all my life, and that my real mother had been condemned by the Birdies, who would condemn me as well if they discovered me. Like him, I had to hide in the shadows. I told him about Buck, and Poppy, and how Axacaya had almost killed him. I told him things I had never told anyone, not even Flynn.

When I finally fell silent, exhausted with relief, I leaned against him and closed my eyes, listening to the pump of his heart. For the first time in a long time, I felt safe.

"It's awful to hide all the time," he said eventually. "Sometimes I feel as though I am alone in the world."

"I feel that way, too. But you aren't alone. I'm here."

"You are." He twined his fingers in my hair. "I'm glad."

We lapsed into silence, staring at the coals glowing in the grate. The room had become chilly, but Sieur Wraathmyr's embrace was warm and snuggy, and I wasn't in a hurry to go anywhere. So I lay against him, feeling wrung out and sleepy, and hoped I never had to move again.

"Do you want the last ginger drop, Nini?" Sieur Wraathmyr asked finally. Now that he mentioned it, I did want the last ginger drop, but I wanted something else more. I pulled his face to mine and kissed him.

FIFTEEN

Snapperdog.
Eavesdropping. A Transformation.

LATER, I WENT UPSTAIRS half-hoping Sieur Wraath-myr would follow me. I was not exactly sure what I would do if he did, but my imagination was full of possibilities. When I opened my bedroom door, Flynn jumped on me. I'd left him locked in the bathroom during dinner, but somehow he had escaped. In the flickering lamplight, the room looked cozy and romantic. But the bed was a mess: covered in dog hair, the bedclothes muddled into a doggy nest.

I pushed Flynn down, swearing. "Back to the bathroom, Snapperdog."

Flynn twisted as I dragged him to the bathroom, tossed him inside, and slammed the door. A rapid-fire yapping began. Hopefully he would stop before Sieur Wraathmyr came up. I brushed the dog hair off the bed as well as I could, straightened the bedclothes, and tidied my wet towels away. Yawning, I lay on the bed to wait and drifted away on delicious thoughts of Sieur Wraathmyr's expert lips, his broad chest, the steady thump of his heart beneath my head—A yipping thud jerked me out of my happy fantasy.

All right. It was thumping time. Let's see if that would improve Snapperdog's mood.

When I opened the bathroom door, Yippy charged out, bouncing like a rubber ball. I reached out to grab him, and, snarling, he turned on me, teeth snapping. I snatched my hand back from a sharp bright pain. Snapperdog had bitten me!

Pissed, I whacked him across the head, and with a yelp, he ran behind the armchair. I stared in stunned amazement at my throbbing hand, now dripping blood. What the fike? Flynn had never even snapped at anyone before.

I bent down to look behind the armchair. Flynn was crouched low, looking chagrined.

"You are a bad, bad dog!" I scolded. He wagged his tail once, nervously.

"Get out from behind there. *Now!*" Flynn wormed into the carpet, his tail whisking back and forth, but he didn't come out.

"Get over here now, or I swear to the Goddess, I will thump you into the middle of next week, Flynn!" I didn't dare try hauling him out and risk another bite. I stood up and looked around for something long enough to poke him with. My head was whirling, the room wavering and wobbling, my vision blurring. For a second, all I saw was a swirl of gray sparkles. Then the sparkles faded.

Everything was different.

The charming little bedroom had turned sour. The wooden floors were splintery, the carpet torn and ragged, the walls green with mold. A peaty fire smoldered in the grate, and the glass in the windows was cracked, letting in tendrils of cold, wet air. The wonderful soft bed was revealed to be a sprung-out horsehair mattress, piled high with moldering wool blankets. I felt grubby, that horrible sticky feeling you get when you haven't changed your clothes in several days and have been sweating like a pig in damp air.

"What the fike?" I said, and Flynn whimpered nervously in response.

A very nasty smell drifted out of the bathroom, now a fetid dark hole. Green liquid bubbled in the bath and the potty—well, my dinner exited in a gush. I coughed and puked till my stomach was empty and a thin sour taste coated the inside of my mouth. Flynn had crawled out from behind the chair, and now he pressed against my legs apologetically, licking my throbbing hand.

What the fike was going on? The answer hit me like a hundred-pound weight. Madama Valdosta was not a genial host; she was an enchanter who preyed on travelers unlucky enough to fall into her grasp. Sieur Wraathmyr and I had been lulled into a sleepy security, fattened up for slaughter.

And I had let down my guard, given into spoonyness. I had blabbed all my secrets—my family's secrets, Tiny Doom's secrets. I had told Sieur Wraathmyr things that could get me arrested, get Poppy arrested, get Buck arrested. Things that could get us all killed. I had told him things I had never told another living soul, not even Udo. Not even Flynn. And then I had kissed him. I buried my face deeper into Flynn's coat, feeling sick.

Flynn licked my hand again, an aura of *I told you so* hanging around him. If he hadn't bitten me and broken the enchantment, I'd probably be ensorcelled still. After that, dead—or worse. I had rewarded his loyalty with a boot in the ribs.

"I'm sorry, Flynnie, oh, I'm so sorry." I kissed his ears, and he, blessed boy, licked my face, holding no grudge. In that he was very un-Fyrdraaca-like. "You are a good boy, a very good boy. I promise you I'll get you your very own pound of bacon, but first we have to get the fike out of here."

Flynn squirmed from my grip and ran to the door eagerly. My buckskin jacket and boots were still in the wardrobe, but my dispatch case and my gun belt were gone. I dressed quickly, and then, after steeling myself, went back into the bathroom. The chamber pot was empty. Octohands was gone, too.

I tore the room apart, which didn't take long, and revealed several other things—one desiccated, the other slimy—that I wished had stayed hidden, but I didn't find Octohands anywhere. Well, he might be an octopus, but he was also a magician and a soldier. Surely he could take care of himself.

I peeked out into the hallway. All clear. I scuttled into Sieur Wraathmyr's room, which was a nasty mirror image of mine. His satchel was gone, but his furry jacket lay on the moldering bed; I rifled its pockets quickly and found a match safe, a penknife, a memo book filled with spidery lettering too hard to read quickly, a leather bag of apple pipeweed, a small ivory pipe with its stem well chewed, and a little wooden carving of a monkey hanging on a gold chain. No map.

Fike. I crept down the rickety stairs, Flynn pressed tightly against my legs, the carpet squelching. The downstairs hall was dark with shadows. As I approached the kitchen, I heard the murmur of voices inside. Motioning for Flynn to stay quiet, I put my ear to the door.

An unfamiliar voice was saying, "... a fortune. His liver alone is worth at least six hundred divas."

Madama Valdosta answered happily, "And his skin, oh, my donut. Think of what that will bring! A thousand divas just as it is, not even cured. I shall be rich!"

"You shall be very rich. Such parts are not often available. All in all it's a rare opportunity."

"I have heard that wer-bear liver pâté is a great delicacy in Porkopolis."

"You have heard correctly."

"Oh, so rich! And a wer-bear skin—they say that a wer-bear-skin coat will make you invisible."

"I cannot speak of that, but perhaps it is true."

With a jolt of horror, I realized they were talking about Sieur Wraathmyr.

"All is going according to plan?" the other voice said.

"Oh, yes, dearie. They are well and true enchanted, cooing like turtledoves, much too bedazzled to notice anything else. Ginger drop?"

"No, thank you."

"I shall keep his teeth, I think, and make myself a pretty necklace. And I shall keep his tongue; there is nothing more delicious than a bear-tongue sandwie."

"You will send word to me when he has changed?"

"I will. It should be any time now. Oh, I am so excited! I'll feed the dog to the pigs, and the girl, well, she's not good for much, but I can get a nice price for her clothes. This will be my best haul ever."

"Congratulations. I will return later tonight."

"Of course! Of course! I thank you, kind sieur, for allowing me this opportunity . . ."

At the sound of chairs being pushed back, I retreated down the hallway, cursing to myself.

My plan to scarper and leave Sieur Wraathmyr to fend

for himself sputtered and died. It was one thing to leave him to be robbed, another to be killed and dismembered— even though, a tiny evil voice deep in my brain said, my secrets would then be safe forever.

I shoved a spittoon into the middle of the hallway so that if Madama Valdosta came that way, she'd trip and we'd have a warning. I pushed Flynn inside the parlor and shut the door behind us, whispering urgently, "Sieur Wraath-myr, we have to get out of here right this minute—"

Flynn strained against my legs, growling softly. I turned and my warning strangled into silence.

An enormous bear lay asleep in front of the fire.

I stood frozen in the doorway, afraid to move. If Sieur Wraathmyr woke up now, would he know who I was? Or was he now a bear inside and out? Would he understand me if I tried to explain what had happened, or would he just tear me limb from limb? The pain of Flynn's bite had snapped me out of the enchantment, but I didn't relish the thought of causing a five-hundred-pound bear any pain. He had told me he always changed back into his human form, but who knew when that would be. Did I dare wait?

I didn't.

His kilt and his shirt lay tossed on the sofa. I oh-so-quietly crept across the room and picked the clothes up, shook them. They were still warm and smelled of his apple pipeweed. The shirt had no pockets, but something stiff was sewn into the inside waistband of the kilt. With my teeth and fingernails, I unstitched the lining and found a small packet made of oilcloth. Inside was my map. I shoved the packet between my corset and my chemise.

On the hearth rug, the bear continued to sputter and snore.

I crept back to the door and looked out to see if the coast was clear. It was, but to get out the front door, I'd have to go past the kitchen door, which was now open. I could hear Madama Valdosta inside, humming. I glanced back toward the parlor window; it wasn't a very long drop. I could make my escape that way, Flynn draped over my shoulders, and get as far away from the Valdosta Lodge as fast as possible. Ayah, it was still raining, but better to take my chances and be drowned than the alternative. I glanced back at Sieur Wraathmyr. He could take care of himself. And if he didn't, well then, I wouldn't have to worry about him betraying me. Like Nini Mo said, *Me, every time.* What else could I do?

But even as these thoughts raced through my head, they hit the brick wall of my conscience. I had left a comrade behind once before, and though she had escaped unscathed—no thanks to me—I just couldn't do it again. I couldn't leave a man I had kissed—several times—to be killed, chopped up for parts, and sold. Plus, after hearing

Sieur Wraathmyr's story, I couldn't add myself to the list of people who had betrayed him. Oh, fiking hell . . .

Pigface, he was enormous. I could have ridden him like a horse and he would never notice my weight. His head alone was as big as Flynn, and even lying down, his shoulder was almost as high as my throat. Each leg was as thick as both of mine put together, and his paws were the size of dinner plates.

I imagined hitting him, sticking him with a pin, causing a spark of pain to break the enchantment. Then my inner eye saw him start up with a roar, huge paw swiping, me flying through the air, hitting the wall, my brains smashing like tapioca pudding . . .

Ayah, then, no scarpering. I would have to stand and fight, get rid of Madama Valdosta, and then hope that Sieur Wraathmyr turned back to himself before her friend arrived. If he didn't, then I'd have to take care of the friend, too.

If you must fight, Nini Mo said, *make your own odds.* My odds said that Madama Valdosta didn't know I had copped to her gig. At least I had the element of surprise. My odds said it was better to tackle the enemies one at a time, so best get done with Madama Valdosta first.

From the hallway came a thudding clank and a curse; Madama Valdosta had tripped on the spittoon. I took a flying leap across the room, flung myself down on the nasty sofa, hissed Flynn over, clutched him, and closed my eyes. The smell coming from the rotting upholstery was awful—how could I have not noticed it before?—but I tried to breathe into the crook of my arm, where the fabric still smelled faintly of Sieur Wraathmyr's pipe. The door creaked open and footsteps tiptoed inside, accompanied by humming. Flynn, suddenly, thankfully, had become quiet. I lay there, trying not to quiver.

"Ah, good." Madama Valdosta sounded pleased. I heard her rustling about the room, and then felt a hand on my foot. I bit back a shriek. Flynn growled.

"Oh, you go ahead and growl, skinny dog," Madama Valdosta said "I'll warrant the pigs will do you just fine." She shook my foot and dropped it, satisfied that I was asleep. The door closed, but I lay still for a long while, ears straining. All I could hear was the snuffle of Sieur Wraathmyr's breathing and my own rapid-fire heartbeat. Then something brushed against the back of my neck. The touch was feathery and delicate, slightly sticky on my bare skin.

A familiar voice spoke, the words echoing not in my ears, but in my mind. *I told you this place was a dump. How you disbelieved me, Almost Daughter.*

I opened my eyes and there was Octohands, perched on the back of the sofa. A tentacle reached for me; I allowed it to wrap around my wrist. I said, "What the fike are you doing in my head?"

Not so loud, or the old sow will hear you!

What are you doing in my head? I thought.

Communicating with you, honey pie. As long as we are in physical contact with each other, we can share thoughts.

I don't want to share thoughts with you!

The feeling is mutual. I fear your imagination is a swamp. But since your little magickal trick went awry, this is our only choice.

And how did you get out of the chamber pot?

I do have eight arms now, madama, eight sticky arms, and I can climb. I was bored and decided to have a little look-see around. There are four more corpses in the basement and Madama Valdosta has been sharpening knives all afternoon.

I know. I overheard her talking to some guy in the kitchen. We've been set up. He's coming back later to kill us. We have to get out of here, but I can't leave Sieur Wraathmyr. Madama Valdosta is going to chop him up, sell him for parts. I can't let her do that. Never leave a comrade behind. Isn't that what Nini Mo said?

I loved the woman but she was an idealistic nitwit sometimes. She didn't have the sense the Goddess gave a duck. You can't afford to be a nitwit; you are the last of your line—and that reminds me, since you seem to have a habit of putting yourself in life-or-death situations, I think it's time you bred, gave us an heir, a little cushion—

"You want me to have a baby?" I said incredulously.

Shush! Not so loud. Ayah, the sooner the better. Pick your man, the bear, that pirate lad, take out an advert in the paper, I don't care, but you can't play so loose and fancy without securing the family line.

We'll discuss this later. I'm not going without Sieur Wraathmyr, so if you are so concerned with my survival, then you need to contribute to its continuation.

She's a cheap enchanter. If I were myself, in my heyday, I could have broken her neck with one word. Alas, that I am entrapped in the body of a helpless invertebrate. Oh, woe.

I could try to do a sigil.

No! I told you not to mess with the Current! Shoot her.

She took my revolver. If you have any other bright fiking ideas, then give them.

People always said I was poisonous and had quite a bite. Well, lucky for you, Almost Daughter, now that I'm an octopus, it's true. I have a plan.

SIXTEEN

Hot Soup.
Cold Calculations. A Biting Plan.

LEAVING SIEUR WRAATHMYR sleeping on the hearth rug, Flynn and I, with Octohands perched on my shoulder, crept back up to my dark and nasty room. Five minutes later, I came back downstairs, lugging the now-quite-heavy chamber pot, Flynn trailing gamely behind me. The dining room was not the handsome room I remembered. Now it was dark and dingy, with torn carpet and water dripping from the ceiling. The animal heads mounted on the walls were balding and eyeless, antlers covered in glowing green moss. Three figures sat stiffly at the table, which was made of a few boards laid across two trestles. I saw why the other guests hadn't been very friendly. They were very dead. The wizened black corpses had been propped up in chairs, plates set in front of them, but their eyes were dull filmy marbles, and their jaws dangled open on ropy-looking sinews, displaying mulelike teeth.

I dragged a rickety empty chair away from the table and stood on it, awkwardly, trying to balance the chamber pot in one hand and hold on to the wall with the other. Not for the first time, I wished I wasn't so fiking short. The pot was heavy, but I managed to leverage it up over my head and into position. I rang the bell, and then sat down on another rickety chair and waited, staring at the door. Under the table, Flynn sat down on my feet.

"Oh, yes, my dear, can I serve you? I thought you were sleeping!"

My liver nearly levitated up and out my throat. Instead of coming through the door in front of me, Madama Valdosta had appeared behind me; it took me a second to realize how she had done so, but then I saw the outline of a door in the wall. It had been wallpapered to match the walls and I hadn't noticed it before.

"Oh, yes, madama, I was sleeping. But now I am awake and very hungry. I was wondering if I might have a snack."

"Oh my dear, what luck. I have just finished a batch of beautiful soup. I shall bring some immediately." She vanished the same way she had come. Fike. I had to get her to go through the other door.

When she reappeared, she carried a soup tureen; she set it on the table and ladled soup into my bowl.

"And here is your spoon," she said brightly.

I looked down at the soup. It was bright red, thick as blood, and bubbled slightly.

"What kind of soup is this?"

"Beet rhubarb. Made from my own garden." Madama Valdosta leaned over me with a smile. "So rich and nourishing. It will take all your cares away."

"It smells delicious," I lied. It smelled like baby poo. When I lifted the spoon out of the liquid, it was full of red worms, like swollen noodles. Wiggling swollen noodles. I thought back on the other meals Valdosta had served us. What had they been, really? Maybe it was better not to wonder.

"Oh madama, it looks wonderful. But I wonder if you might do me a favor."

Madama Valdosta bowed. "Anything you desire, madama. You would like a crouton, perhaps? A little garnish?"

"No, no," I said hastily, imagining moldy bread floating in the bloody soup. "Could you fetch my jacket from the parlor? I am a bit chilled."

"I will build up the fire—"

"No, really. My jacket is all that I need. Please, madama?"

"Of course, madama." Madama Valdosta's smile never faltered, but she seemed a bit impatient for me to eat the soup, which probably meant it was not a good idea to eat the soup. *Well, we'll see who gets who, you shifty witch.*

Madama Valdosta strode to the door and pulled it open with a flourish. The chamber pot tumbled down, spilling out a writhing crimson blob: Octohands. As he landed on her head, she let out a shocked squeal and staggered against the door, hands slapping. To no avail; Octohands had a good grip.

Madama Valdosta danced back into the room, falling against the furniture, against the wall, her squealing transformed into a high-pitched gurgle by the tentacle snaking around her neck. I jumped out of the way as she hit the table, which disintegrated into a heap of splintery wood. She writhed through the wreckage and over one of the mummies, which collapsed into a puff of black grit and a fetid smell. Madama Valdosta's face, barely visible through the strangling tentacles, was almost as red as Octohands. Flynn jumped out of my grip, snarling and snapping at her.

"Bite her!" I shouted to Octohands. "Bite her!"

Madama Valdosta let out a muffled wheezy shriek and flung Octohands from her.

"It bit me!" she screamed. Madama Valdosta struggled to her feet, shouting, kicking at Flynn. She mumbled something and a glittery Gramatica Word, sharp as a razor, whirled toward me; I dodged it, and it hit the molding bison head mounted on the wall. The head exploded into a ball of flaring coldfire. Flynn sank his teeth into one of her fat ankles, and she picked up a piece of broken chair and began to whack at him.

"Don't touch him!" I grabbed the soup ladle and ran

toward them, swinging wildly. With a bellow, Madama Valdosta managed to wrench away from Flynn and half hobbled, half ran from the room, shrieking like a teakettle. Flynn followed, nipping at her heels. I ran over to Octohands, who lay motionless where he had fallen. When I picked him up, a tentacle slowly unwound itself and attached to my wrist. *Uh, she tasted terrible. But I got her good. She won't get far.*

I thought she was just going to drop dead when you bit her. What if she wakes up Sieur Wraathmyr with all that screaming?

He's good and enchanted. He's not going to—

The high-pitched keening in the hallway was replaced by a high-pitched screaming. Flynn barreled back into the dining room, tail between his legs. Still holding Octohands, I rushed to the doorway to see Madama Valdosta cowering before the enormous shaggy figure looming at the end of the hallway.

Oh dear. Tactical error. Octohands sounded almost amused.

Sieur Wraathmyr reared up, his head brushing the ceiling, and roared. Madama Valdosta wasn't able to dodge the swipe of that enormous paw; she went flying. As she tried to get up, her feet scrabbling for traction, Sieur Wraathmyr dropped to all fours and charged after her. But Octohands's poisonous bite was beginning to affect her; her movements were wobbly and unsteady and her screams had diminished to a low squeaking.

I turned and ran, Flynn pushing against my legs, both of us tearing through the dining room and into the kitchen. There was no back door—fike, we were trapped. Horrible noises came from the hallway. Frantic for a hiding place, we ran back to the dining room and dove into the closet. Flynn wormed his way onto my lap and Octohands wound around my neck, uncharacteristically silent of snappy comments. I was sitting on something lumpy; I reached behind and found my gun belt. My revolver was only a .32 caliber, which wouldn't do much against an angry bear, but it felt reassuring and heavy in my hand.

We huddled behind the rotting clothes, listening to howling, screaming, moaning, groaning, roaring, ripping. I closed my eyes and buried my face in Flynn's neck. I had no doubt that once Sieur Wraathmyr was through with Madama Valdosta, he'd smell me, and crunchy Flynn, and chewy Octohands, and we'd be next on his menu. I had tried to save Sieur Wraathmyr, and for my trouble, I was going to get eaten.

I hope you are not too spoony to shoot him, Almost Daughter.

I doubt that this caliber will do much other than make him mad.

I once killed a buffalo with a .22. Aim for his eye.

Shut up.

After a while, the screaming stopped. All was quiet. But I didn't move. It was nice and dark in the closet. The rotting smell, now that I was used to it, wasn't so very bad. I strained my ears, but I could hear only my own labored breathing, Flynn's occasional snort. Octohands was stroking my neck with one tentacle. The sensation was both annoying and soothing.

Are we going to sit here forever? Octohands asked finally.

Ayah. Suddenly I was very tired. If I hadn't given in to a stupid bout of conscience, Flynn and I would have been miles away by now, with map in hand. Instead, here I was about to be eaten by the very snapperhead I had just tried to save. *Oh, the irony,* Nini Mo said, *don't it just make your teeth sing?*

A crack of light shone in the shadows. Flynn growled and I put my hand on his head.

"Nini? Are you all right?"

My eyes adjusted to the light, and standing before me was not a bear, but a man. Sieur Wraathmyr's face was a mask of blood; he was dripping red from head to toe.

"Nini?" Even his teeth were red.

I pointed my revolver at him. "If you take another step toward me, I'll shoot you."

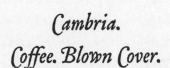

Cambria.
Coffee. Blown Cover.

$\mathcal{W}$HEN HE SAW that I was all right, Sieur Wraathmyr turned and walked away. I came out of the closet. The hallway walls were sprayed with blood, and more blood trailed toward the front door, but there was no sign of Madama Valdosta. I have to admit that I didn't look too hard for her.

Or what was left of her.

During his explorations, Octohands had found Madama Valdosta's stash room. Now he directed me there. The room was stuffed full of booty. Trunks, portmanteaus, valises, carpetbags. One cabinet held a jumble of silver: spurs, pitchers, plates. Clothes were sorted into baskets: jackets, socks, shoes. There were a *lot* of shoes. A small strongbox was stuffed with Califa divas, Birdie quetzals, Porkopolis hocks, and other currencies I didn't even recognize.

We should help ourselves. Octohands was riding on my shoulder, like a squishy parrot. *I think we deserve it.*

I shuddered at the thought of taking anything from the Valdosta Lodge. Surely the booty must be cursed.

You are too dainty. Someday you will be out of tosh and think back to all you left behind and be sorry you did not heed me.

"That day, that sorrow," I answered. I found my dispatch case and Sieur Wraathmyr's satchel and left everything else.

I did not check out the cellar, where Octohands said he had seen the bodies. Instead, I followed Sieur Wraathmyr's bloody footprints back down the hall and out the front door. Of course the rain had been an enchantment; outside, it was overcast but perfectly dry. Sieur Wraathmyr was standing in the stream, washing the blood off. I laid his gear on the bank and then retreated to the other side of the bridge to wait.

Octohands's weight on my neck was giving me a bit of a headache; after an intense argument, he agreed to ride inside my dispatch case. Apparently magickal octopuses do not need constant access to water. This was good, because I did not relish carrying the chamber pot all the way to Cambria.

Sieur Wraathmyr eventually joined me, hair wet, face as forbidding as the façade of the Califa Reformatory. Neither of us said anything as we climbed out of the valley. Since Sieur Wraathmyr's legs were much longer than mine, he soon outpaced me. That was fine with me; I'd rather have him where I could see him. I had buckled my gun belt on over my buckskin jacket, just in case.

But Sieur Wraathmyr didn't even acknowledge I was puffing along behind him. He marched on, shoulders hunched. From the back, with that fuzzy coat, he looked distressingly bearlike, though his human body, for all its bulk, was much smaller than his bear form. I had no idea what he was thinking, but I had a strong feeling his thoughts were not good ones. I *knew* that my thoughts were bad. I had been an utter fool, taken in by a cheap enchantment. I couldn't think of my behavior the night before without squirming. Enchantment or not, what a moron I had been. Never let down your guard, wasn't that the first rule of rangering? I had spilled all my secrets to a man who wouldn't even look at me now. Had I learned nothing from Axacaya?

Well, now that I had my map, I didn't need Sieur Wraathmyr anymore. Once we were in Cambria, good riddance to him. I was dying to peek at the map, but I didn't want to do so with him nearby. He'd seen and heard enough about me already. It could wait until I got to Cambria and privacy.

Ahead, a tree had fallen across the path, blocking our way. Sieur Wraathmyr halted, waiting for me to catch up. When I did, he offered me his hand.

"I don't need any help," I said, giving Snapperdog a boost over.

Sieur Wraathmyr made no move to climb over the tree. I waited for him to go on, but instead he said, "It's the oldest trick in the book, the honey pot. I can't believe I didn't see it."

"I fell for it, too."

"Ayah, so," he answered bitterly. "But that I am equally foolish hardly excuses either of us. I am well traveled. I should have known better." There was a streak of dry blood on his left temple. I resisted the urge to reach up and wipe it away.

"Madama Valdosta was an enchanter," I said. "How were we supposed to know that?"

Sieur Wraathmyr gave me a look that clearly expressed his thoughts, and scornful thoughts they were indeed: *You might be silly enough to be caught by an enchanter, but I should be above all that.*

Well, you weren't, now, were you, puggie? I thought, but I said, "Well, excuse me for saving your bacon. If it hadn't been for me, you'd be back there right now on Madama Valdosta's butcher block."

"If it hadn't been for you, madama, I wouldn't have been in that situation at all."

"How do you figure that?"

Flynn, on the other side of the tree, gave a *Hurry it up* yap.

"If you hadn't been such a slow walker, and so feeble you couldn't keep up, I would not have had to stop for

204

the night to begin with. I would long since be in Cambria by now."

"Well, I'm sorry I've turned out to be such a difficult traveling companion," I said sarcastically. "But you were the one so in a hurry to get to Cambria that you wanted to take the shortcut."

"And I am in a hurry now and not in the mood for chitchat," he said, ignoring the fact that he had started it. I started to retort as much, but he had turned away. He easily leaped over the tree, the snapperhead, and continued down the track. I launched myself at the tree trunk and managed to scramble over, getting wet and muddy in the process, but achieving the other side on my own.

WE HAD LEFT Valdosta Lodge just after dawn; we arrived at our destination midafternoon, footsore, damp, and hungry. Or at least Flynn and I were. Sieur Wraathmyr seemed impervious to the stresses of travel. Cambria was a conglomeration of scruffy buildings, well scoured by salt and fog, huddled around a rickety dock. A large black rock loomed in the middle of the bay; beyond it lay a fringe of breakers and the calm blue line of the open sea.

At the edge of town, Sieur Wraathmyr stopped abruptly. "I am sorry. But I cannot honor our agreement regarding the map. Still, you have my word that your secret will be safe with me. I hope you will extend the same courtesy to me."

"I thought we had a deal." I worked a tone of outrage into my voice. I was going to enjoy watching him squirm.

He had put his hands in his pockets; now he jiggled nervously. "I have lost the map, along with several other valuable papers. Madama Valdosta must have found them when she searched my things. I looked throughout her establishment before we left, but I did not find the papers anywhere."

I wasn't enjoying the squirming as much as I had thought I would. He looked so miserable. I said, "I found the map."

Relief washed over his face. "Thank the Goddess. Where did you find it? Were there other documents with it?"

I did not want him to know that I had rolled him while he was helpless. Before, it had seemed to serve him right. Now I felt rather ashamed. "I found it in Valdosta's trophy room," I lied. "I didn't see any other papers with it." That, at least, was true.

Sieur Wraathmyr exhaled heavily. "About last night—"

I did not want to talk about last night. "We were enchanted by Valdosta," I said quickly. "People do weird things when they are enchanted, imagine all sorts of things. I don't know what you think happened last night, but I promise you none of it was real. Your habits are your own, sieur, and I feel no need to describe them to anyone else. I think the best thing is for us to pretend we never met, ayah?"

I had no idea what I would do if he didn't agree. This man knew everything about me. It wasn't much of a consolation that I knew everything about him. I could keep my mouth shut. Could he?

He regarded me, and I put my hand on my pistol, just in case. Then he nodded and said stiffly, "I am glad you got your map back. Good luck to you. Goodbye."

Have a nice life, I thought. *And you're welcome for saving your skin, Sieur Arrogance.* As I watched him walk away, I should have felt relieved. Oddly, I did not.

Downtown Cambria consisted of one narrow sloping corduroy street terminating at a narrow dock, which continued into the expansive Cambria Bay. The upper part of the street was lined with small houses; the middle part with small businesses. Sieur Wraathmyr and his long legs had already disappeared.

My tum was flapping against my spine; Goddess knows what Valdosta's delicious chow had really been. At the Cambria Café, Flynn and I devoured an enormous breakfast and then went on to the Cambria Hotel, where I again checked in as Nyana Romney, just in case.

The room was small, but it had a real bed with clean sheets. I filled the washbasin with water and dumped Octohands in it; he refused the sandwie I offered him, moaning about a terrible headache, so I left him alone. Leaving Flynn to guard the room, I went down the hall to the bathroom and scrubbed the noisome feeling of the

Valdosta Lodge off. Alas, I could not do anything about the rankness of my clothes, but maybe later I could run out and buy some drawers and a new shirt.

I was fed; I was clean; I was private.

It was time to look at the map.

Back in the room, Flynn lay sprawled and snoring on the floor. Octohands's sandwie had disappeared and he eddied peacefully in the washbasin. I climbed up on the bed and settled back on the pillows. My hands were shaking slightly as I opened the oilcloth packet Sieur Wraathmyr had enclosed the map in; how nice of him to keep it so safe. When I pulled the map out, another paper fell onto the bed. I picked it up, a small vellum envelope, heavy and smooth, closed with a familiar red blot of wax, Buck's official seal. And on the front, in Buck's familiar scrawl:

To Our Beloved Friends
the King and Queen of the Kulani Islands.

I stared at the envelope, bewildered. How had he gotten a dispatch with Buck's writing on it? Then I remembered the lingering smell of apple pipeweed in her office the night of Pirates' Parade. The apple pipeweed that clung to Sieur Wraathmyr's hair, his furry jacket, his clothes. His desire not to get taken by pirates. His rush to get to Cambria. The important papers he thought he'd lost at Valdosta Lodge.

Sieur Wraathmyr wasn't a salesman for Madama Twanky. He was an express agent for the Pacifica Mail and Freight Company.

EIGHTEEN

Alliances.
The Map. Captured.

*W*HEN SIEUR WRAATHMYR had been pouring his guts out to me, he sure as fike had forgotten to pour out that little fact. I felt a stab of something—irritation—hurt, maybe. I'd told him everything and I thought he had told me everything as well. No wonder he hadn't wanted to be taken by pirates. He was just a courier; he probably had no idea that the Dainty Pirate and Buck were in league with each other. And no wonder he had looked upset when I told him I hadn't found any documents with the map; he'd thought the dispatch was gone for good.

And it must be an awfully important dispatch for Buck to send it via an express agent, rather than a regular military courier.

But why would Buck be sending a dispatch to the King and Queen of the Kulani Islands to begin with? The Kulanis have no diplomatic ties with Califa; they are aloof and removed and don't really have diplomatic ties with anyone. They limit their contact with the outside world. They send out trading ships and raiding ships, which return to their islands. Sieur Wraathmyr's story was one example of just how insular they can be.

The seal on the dispatch was unbroken, but that would be no trouble to me. In my time at the CGO, I'd lifted hundreds of seals and put them right back again, so no one ever knew the difference. It only takes a hot knife and patience. For a moment, I hesitated. Then, remembering all that Buck had done to me, I got my knife out of my dispatch case, lit the bedside lamp, and got to work.

The paper had been folded to make its own envelope. I carefully unfolded it and saw more of Buck's familiar handwriting. Normally she dictates her letters; sometimes she scrawls an addendum in her own hand. This was no addendum. It was a solid page of text, written in High Protocol, the grandiose language of diplomacy, in which everything is couched in delicate and fancy phrasings and nothing is said in one word that can't be said splendidly in ten.

Lucky for me, I'd been halfway through an introductory course in High Protocol before I was pulled from the Barracks to serve as Buck's slave. I couldn't translate the entire document, but I could get the gist.

And when I was done reading, I felt like the world's biggest fool. Here I had thought all this time that Buck had been bowing her head meekly before the Birdies. Even the Dainty Pirate's claims hadn't persuaded me otherwise. Now I realized her lap-doggery had been a pose, a ruse, a lie. While she'd been pretending to be meek and mild, all along she'd been quietly plotting and scheming, searching for allies.

And in the Kulanis she had found what she was looking for. This dispatch was clearly the latest in a long line of communications, because it agreed to previously discussed Kulani terms. Buck would provide the Kulanis with enough hardwood timber to build fifteen raiding ships, four hundred head of breeding cattle, one ton of iron ore, and a thousand pounds of jade. In return, Kulani raiders would blockade the Birdie ports, disrupt Birdie shipping, and support Califa's freedom.

I flopped back on the pillows, lousy with guilt. I had misjudged Buck as much as I had misjudged Sieur Wraath-myr. But why hadn't she trusted me? Why had she let me live on in such despair? She could have at least hinted that things were afoot. Poppy had hinted—is this what he was talking about? Were they in it together? Did everyone know but me?

But I couldn't afford to wallow in my private sorrows about how Buck had treated me. If this dispatch wasn't delivered to the Kulanis—or if it fell into the wrong hands—the Alliance would fall apart, as would Buck's plans and Califa's rebellion. I had to get the dispatch back on track, which meant I had to find Sieur Wraathmyr and make sure he delivered it safely.

I quickly folded and resealed the dispatch and stuck it in the inside pocket of my buckskin jacket. Redressed in my nasty dirty clothes, I shoved all my gear back into my dispatch case—everything but the map. I'd waited for it long enough; I wasn't waiting a minute longer. A quick glance would take no time at all.

When I had stolen the map from Buck's map case, it had shown the whole world. Now, when I unfolded it and cast it over the bed, I saw that the contours of the map had become unfamiliar. Califa had vanished; the Pacifica Ocean vanished. Tiny rows of triangles marked out mountain ranges I had never heard of: the Hierophants, the Dragons, the Verdes. Red lines traced out unfamiliar roads: Banastre Road, Hell's Track. Blue lines delineated unknown rivers: Sandy, Acre's Creek, Blue Wash. Where the fike was Calo Res? Or Hooker's Ranch? Or Camp Kumquat? A dotted line was drawn on the eastern side of the map, the only straight line on the entire piece of linen. To the right of this line, the map was utterly blank except for a small notation in block letters: BRONCOS.

That's when I realized I was looking at a map of Arivaipa Territory. The dotted line was the Bronco Proclamation Line, drawn up at the end of the Bronco Wars, when the Califa Army, under Hardhands, had fought the natives of Arivaipa. Under the terms of the final peace, all territory to the west of the line was ceded to Califa and became Arivaipa Territory. All land to the east was left to the Broncos, as the natives are called. No Califan was allowed across the Proclamation Line except on pain of death—a very long and protractedly painful death, enforced by the Broncos themselves.

Arivaipa Territory. A few years ago a song about Arivaipa had been very popular; every band in the City played it, and you couldn't go anywhere without hearing someone whistling it, humming it, or belting it out at the top of his or her lungs. The chorus went:

Old Arivaipa again,
full of outlaws and bad bad men.
They don't do the Califa dip,
but they shoot you from the hip,
out in old Arivaipa again, again.

But where was my blood mark? It was very hard to find, but I did, finally. The tiny splotch had landed near an equally small dot. I had to squint to read the label— Fort Sandy.

What did I know about Fort Sandy? There isn't much military presence in Arivaipa, just a couple of posts scattered along the Line, making sure it stays secure. Fort Sandy was the southernmost of these forts; there were two companies stationed there. I remembered the letter I had filed for Buck right before I left Califa—Fort Sandy had a chupacabra problem.

What in Califa's name was Tiny Doom doing in Arivaipa Territory? Buck had been posted there when she first graduated from the Barracks, and she had nothing good to say about the place. It only rained a few times a year and everything there was dangerous: the plants, the insects, the snakes, the animals, the people. It's so dry that you think your blood has turned to dust, so hot that you think your skin might burn away, so bright that you think you might go blind.

And Arivaipa shares a southern border with the Huitzil Empire. If I were Tiny Doom, I'd want to get as far from the Birdies as possible, instead of hiding out right on their doorstep. Granted, very few people cross this southern border, because it's a pitiless dry desert, but that would still be too close for comfort for me. Well, I guessed I'd find out her reasons when I got there. Arivaipa was only a hundred miles east of where I was now. With a little bit of luck, I could be there in less than a week.

But first things first. Sieur Wraathmyr and the dispatch.

When I poked Octohands, he grabbed at my hand. *You've got to go after him! Don't let him get away! Hurry!*

I am hurrying! With no prompting, Octohands crawled into the towel I held out and then allowed me to stow him in my dispatch case. Flynn wanted to stay in bed, but I rousted him and made him follow me. It seemed best if we all stuck together.

Downstairs, the innkeeper disavowed all knowledge of Sieur Wraathmyr; whatever he was up to now, he wasn't staying here. Outside, the weather had turned gray. A chill wind blew off the water. I pulled my jacket closed, and hurried.

The Pacifica Mail did not have an office in Cambria, so I went to the General Store and, using the excuse of purchasing new undergarments, asked the clerk if his Twanky rep had been in recently. The clerk said they were expecting a visit from their salesman but he was overdue, and anyway his name wasn't Wraathmyr, it was Jones, and he was a she. I checked the blacksmith's; Toby's Coffee Shack; the *Cambria Elixir*'s office; the dentist/barber's; the Purple Pig Saloon; the cooper's; and the wharf office. Sieur Wraathmyr was at none of these locations and they were it; Cambria was not a big place.

Fike. Had he left town? He couldn't possibly be gone already. The livery clerk at the stage stop informed me there had been no stage today, nor had anyone hired a horse. But then hadn't Sieur Wraathmyr said he didn't ride? Maybe he'd gone back to Valdosta's to try to find the missing dispatch. I did not relish the idea of following him back there.

What if I couldn't find him? I could try to deliver the dispatch myself, but I wasn't sure where it was going. Surely he wasn't taking it all the way to the Kulani Islands; they were several weeks' journey, even by fast clipper ship, and the dispatch had made the timeline sound urgent.

I walked down Main Street again, trying to swallow my panic. A thin rain was beginning to fall. The streets looked muddy and gray, hopeless. Flynn nudged my knee; he was damp and starting to shiver. I ducked into Toby's Coffee Shack. Toby, the coffee jerk, hadn't seen Sieur Wraathmyr, either. *When you need to think, drink more coffee,* Nini Mo said.

I was waiting for Toby to finish making my mocha when I heard a commotion outside. I looked out the window and saw a crowd gathering, their excited murmurs loud enough to be heard through the glass. The door flung open and a girl rushed in.

"Hey, Toby. You gotta come quick. The sheriff's caught an outlaw!"

"What kind of an outlaw?" Toby squirted a giant pile of whip on my mocha and pushed it across the counter toward me. He didn't look terribly excited, although considering all the fuss, this could not be an everyday occurrence.

"A big one!" the girl said.

"The last time Cletie said she caught a big outlaw," Toby said, "he turned out to be nothing but an egg thief. Where I come from, an egg thief don't qualify as a big outlaw. Twenty-two glories."

I handed Toby the money and dropped five glories in

his tip jar. He nodded at me and went over to the sandwich board, where he began to slice bread.

"Naw, this one is really big. I saw the poster myself!" An old lady had followed the girl in. Her hat was shaped exactly like a plush toy horse. In fact, it was a plush toy horse. The horse's mournful face flopped over the lady's forehead, and a plush hoof dangled over each ear. She said, hooves bobbing with excitement, "Wanted for larceny, thievery, and cupidity!"

"That's a busy outlaw." Toby continued with his sandwich-making.

"Aren't larceny and thievery the same thing?" I asked.

The old lady peered at me suspiciously, the horse-hat quivering. "It ain't funny, girl. He's a dangerous outlaw!" She waved a piece of paper: a WANTED sign. I had vaguely noticed the WANTED signs hanging outside the sheriff's as I had passed by, but I hadn't looked at them closely. Now I took the sign, and as I read it, all the air rushed out of my lungs.

WANTED: T. N. WRAATHMYR! Wanted for larceny, thievery, and cupidity: FIFTEEN-HUNDRED DIVAS IN JADE. DEAD OR ALIVE. Offered by the Sheriff of Pudding Pie, Califa. The drawing illustrating the poster was rough, but clearly Sieur Wraathmyr. The artist had caught his stuck-up attitude perfectly.

Pigface! How many people were looking for Sieur Wraathmyr, anyway? First the guy at the lodge, now the sheriff. He was more popular than the Man in Pink Bloomers. I could imagine Sieur Wraathmyr doing many illegal things, but larceny and thievery were not among them, and I wasn't even sure what cupidity was, but I doubted that, too. It must be a set-up.

I abandoned my mocha on the counter and followed the horse lady outside. The crowd in front of the jail was swelling with people eager to see the big outlaw. I pushed my way forward, ignoring the dirty looks that the liberal use of my pointy elbows got me.

Inside the jail, the sheriff sat with her feet propped up on her desk, a rancid-smelling seegar in her mouth, telling her admiring audience how she had captured such a terribly dangerous criminal. ". . . recognized his shifty face immediately. I said, 'Throw-down, Mug,' and he reached for his gun, but I reached faster and buffaloed him good!"

The crowd was hanging on her every lie; I knew that Sieur Wraathmyr did not carry a gun. Even the drunk in the first cell was quiet, leaning on the iron bars, staring in wobbly-eyed admiration. In the second cell, Sieur Wraathmyr was sitting on the edge of the iron cot, looking bearishly angry. His left eye was swollen almost shut. My exclamation of dismay must have been pretty loud, because suddenly everyone, including Sieur Wraathmyr, was looking at me.

The sheriff glared at my interruption. "Can I help you, citizen?"

"Uh, ah—" I stuttered.

"You got something to say?" The sheriff stood up. She was a very large woman, at least a foot taller than me and a foot wider.

"Uh—" Flynn saved me. He had wiggled through the crowd with me and was now sniffing around the spittoon. Out the corner of my eye, I saw his leg lift, and I gave a shout. Flynn dropped his leg and flashed over to me, hiding behind my legs.

"Sorry," I said. "I was yelling at the dog."

"Get that dog out of here!" the sheriff roared. "Before I arrest you both."

That dog and I retreated to Toby's, where I reclaimed my abandoned mocha and tried desperately—and quickly —to think of a plan. Regardless of the merits of the sheriff of Pudding Pie's accusations, I had to spring Sieur Wraathmyr somehow. Buck's dispatch had to be delivered, pronto. And, with a shiver, I remembered Valdosta's friend. At some point he would return to the lodge and find us gone. If he tracked Sieur Wraathmyr to Cambria and told the sheriff that Sieur Wraathmyr was a wer-bear . . . I had a sudden vision of Sieur Wraathmyr, a noose around his neck, being harried to a tree by a lynch mob waving torches.

This was not a pleasant vision.

My dispatch case was squirming and heaving.

"Do you have a bathroom?" I asked Toby hurriedly,

clutching the case to my chest, hoping no one would notice its squirms. He pointed toward the back. The bathroom was tiny and dark, but it was clean. I pushed Flynn in ahead of me and shut and locked the door. A plan was beginning to come together in my head, but I was going to need Octohands's help.

As soon as I unlatched the dispatch case, a tentacle whipped out and fastened on my wrist. *You can't let them take him, girlie!*

I thought you thought he was bad news.

Ayah, I did, but that was before I saw him in action. He's magnificent! Wonderful! As your almost father, I say that I heartily approve. What a shot to the bloodline he'll give! We've never had a skinwalker, except for Great Uncle Peter, but he was just a wer-flamingo, pretty but totally useless in a fight. Think of the little Haðraaða bear cubs! You couldn't have made a better choice!

I realized what he was saying and almost choked. *No! It's nothing like that at all! Oh Pigface, no! Goddess, are you insane?*

Don't be coy with me, madama, I can read your every thought, remember. Protest all you want, but I know the truth—

We'll discuss this later, I answered hastily. *Now, this is what we are going to do . . .*

NINETEEN

Keys.
Confusion. Escape.

YOU AGAIN!" the sheriff said when I arrived back at the jail a little while later. She and the deputy were sitting comfortably in front of the stove, drinking hot toddies. "Did you think of what you wanted to say? Keep that dog away from my spittoon!"

"Sit, Flynn," I ordered, and Flynn obediently sat. "I would like to see the prisoner, please." As I spoke, I glanced around. The door to the first cell stood open; the drunk was gone. A large ring of keys lay in a pile on the sheriff's desk, next to a half-eaten sandwie. Very sloppy, but good for me.

"That so? Well, he's being held in-communi-cado," the sheriff said with a sneer.

"But he's right there, looking at us. Ave!"

"Ave," Sieur Wraathmyr said, somewhat warily. He had been lying on the cot. Now he got up and stood against the bars. He still looked mighty pissed, though whether it was at his circumstances or my arrival, I couldn't tell.

"How can he be incommunicado if he's standing right there?" I asked.

"If you can't talk to him, he's incommunicado," the sheriff said triumphantly.

"But I can talk to him. I brought you a cinnamon roll, honey." I walked toward the cell, bag in hand. As I passed the sheriff's desk, I dropped my dispatch case. When I leaned over to pick it up, Octohands slithered out and undulated under the desk, out of sight. "I know you love cinnamon rolls!"

Sieur Wraathmyr looked bewildered, but he said, "Thank you!"

"Hey, now, one minute. You can't just waltz in here and give my prisoner a cinnamon roll," the sheriff protested. "Who are you?"

"I'm his lawyer. Did you feed him?"

"Well, no, but—"

I handed Sieur Wraathmyr the cinnamon roll through the bars. "Under Califa law, you have to feed a prisoner. You can't just lock him in a cell and throw away the keys. A prisoner has rights, you know. You can't let him starve."

"He's only been my prisoner for two hours. And dinner won't be here until six—"

"I don't see any water, either. Did she give you any water?" I asked Sieur Wraathmyr.

"Not a drop," he answered. Out the corner of my eye, I saw a flash of red movement: Octohands had made it up to the surface of the desk and was now creeping across it.

I said quickly, to keep the sheriff's and deputy's attention, "Under Califa Penal Code, Section 15, Paragraph 12, water, or a comparable liquid, must be made available to all prisoners at all times and may only be withheld by a judge's order. Do you have a judge's order to withhold water from this prisoner?"

"Well, no, but—" Now I had the sheriff good and flustered. I pressed my advantage by complaining about the lack of a window in Sieur Wraathmyr's cell, the fact that he had been given no blanket, and that he had a black eye. All those court-martial reports I had copied were coming in handy. I knew more about the law than the sheriff did.

While I blabbered and the sheriff blinked in confusion, Octohands grabbed the keys with one tentacle and the sandwie in another, then disappeared back under the desk. Under my barrage of complaints, the sheriff completely wilted. Finally I pulled out my trump card. "And how do you know this man is indeed Sieur Wraathmyr?"

"I recognized his picture. Here, see—" The sheriff flourished the WANTED poster at me. I made a great show of looking at it and then looking at Sieur Wraathmyr—back and forth, back and forth. Then I looked at the deputy. Octohands was scuttling across the floor behind the deputy's boot, but the deputy was staring at me in too much slack-jawed befuddlement to notice.

"Seems to me that your poster looks more like this man here." With a sneer of disdain, I let the poster waft to the floor. The sheriff picked it up and looked at it again—then looked at Sieur Wraathmyr and back at the deputy.

"Me? I'm not full of cupidity!" the deputy protested. "You know that, Cletie. I'm married to your mother!"

I said quickly, "You can't prove this man is T. N. Wraathmyr." *Or at least I hope you can't,* I thought. "And I am here to tell you that this man is not T. N. Wraathmyr."

"He did say he weren't this Sieur Wraathmyr," the deputy said. "I mean, I ain't him either, but he said he weren't, too."

"But if he isn't this Wraathmyr, who is he?" the sheriff asked.

"I told you," Sieur Wraathmyr rattled the bars in indignation. We all turned toward him. There was no sign now of Octohands or the keys. "My name is Oddvar Huenca! I've never heard of this T. N. Wraathmyr fellow!"

"Who is Oddvar Huenca?" the deputy asked.

"He's my fiancé!" I said triumphantly. "He thought he could run off and leave me, after making all sorts of promises, but I tracked him down. I'll bet he thought he escaped me, pretending to be this Wraathmyr, so as to be arrested, thinking he can hide behind bars—" The sheriff and the deputy were staring at me, mesmerized. Octo-hands slithered into the cell, and Sieur Wraathmyr bent down and grabbed the keys from him.

"I thought you said you was his lawyer," the sheriff said in bewilderment.

"I am, and his fiancée, too! And I'm gonna sue him for breach of promise!"

Sieur Wraathmyr said to the sheriff, "I swear that lady is crazy—I've never seen her before in my life!"

"You just try that, Oddvar! You think you can get away from me, but you cannot. You made a promise and you are going to keep it, if I have to have you locked up to do it! Sheriff, I demand that you release this man so that he may honor his obligations to me!"

"I am T. N. Wraathmyr!" Sieur Wraathmyr said fran-tically. "And I'll take my medicine—"

"You'll take *my* medicine and like it, too!" I turned to the sheriff. "Under the Califa Penal Code, Section 56, Paragraph 91, if you can't show due cause for detaining a prisoner, then you must release him. I demand to know what charges you are holding him under."

"If he is this Wraathmyr fella—" the sheriff began.

"I am! I am!"

I turned on Sieur Wraathmyr in a fury. "I swear, Odd-var, I'm going to boot you into the middle of next week.

How could you do this to me? After all I've done for you? Saved you from the gutter and lent you a hundred divas—"

"Now, wait one fiking minute," the sheriff protested. "You can't be his girl and his lawyer. That's a conflict of interest."

I turned on her. "How dare you slander me in such a way? I'll sue you for harassing my good name! If you don't want to make matters worse for yourself, I suggest you retract that accusation. And since you have no proof that this man is T. N. Wraathmyr, I demand that you release him to me."

"I swear I'm T. N. Wraathmyr," Sieur Wraathmyr said desperately. "I swear I am. Don't give me over to this crazy lady."

"Can you prove it?" the sheriff asked.

"Well, no, but you have my word."

"You'd take his word over mine?" I demanded. "A criminal over a solid citizen! You can keep him, then! I don't care if he rots in that cell forever!"

The sheriff took a large handkerchief out of her pocket and mopped up the sheen of sweat that had sprung out on her temples. "You know what? I don't care if you are T. N. Wraathmyr, or are not T. N. Wraathmyr, or are even the dæmon Choronzon himself. You can sit in that jail and rot, and you, madama, can sit with him. You are under arrest, and the fiking dog, too—"

She advanced upon me, but Sieur Wraathmyr swung the cell door open and charged through, hitting her like a sack of bricks. Down she went. The deputy stood gaping, and was still gaping when I picked up the truncheon from the sheriff's desk and bashed him on the head with it. He went down, too. Flynn, who'd sprawled out by the stove during our conversation, sprang to his feet and barked in triumph.

We dragged the two lawdogs into the cell, laid each out on a bunk, and locked them in, dropping the cell key into the spittoon, where it would take a long time for any potential rescuers to find it. And then we skedaddled, as fast we could skedaddle, pausing only long enough for me to scoop up Octohands and settle him on my shoulder and for Sieur Wraathmyr to reclaim his satchel. Out the back door, into the driving rain, past the privy, down the alley, and the fike out of Cambria.

We didn't pause until we were well out of town. Then we took shelter under a large pine tree. The rain was tapering off into a soggy mist, which, hopefully, would also foil any pursuit. Poor Flynn was soaked to the skin, and I wasn't that far off. Sieur Wraathmyr's fur coat looked damp, but inside it, he looked disgustingly dry.

"Where did that octopus come from?" Sieur Wraathmyr asked.

"It's a long story." I found a dry part of my kilt and tried to dry Snapperdog off. He was starting to shiver.

"I owe you thanks," Sieur Wraathmyr said, and then blew it by adding, "though I did not actually need your help."

I stared at him incredulously. "Are you fiking kidding me?"

Almost Daughter, don't be an imbecile! Tamp it down! You'll piss him off and lose him. He's too good to let go—

Shut up! Shut up or I'll turn you into fish bait!

Sieur Wraathmyr said loftily, "I could have busted out on my own later tonight, once the sheriff went home. I would have shifted, and then the cell would not have been able to hold me."

"Ayah, and ended up with a lynch mob on your tail! Well, I didn't bail you out for your own good, let me tell you. I know what's at stake here. Here's your dispatch. It was mixed in with my map. I know you are an express agent. If I were you, I'd quit standing there gaping like a broken window and get hot on your job. It's rather urgent."

I thrust the dispatch at him, and he took it, saying, "You read the dispatch?"

"It's in my mother's handwriting."

"It is a diplomatic communication!"

"Oh, ayah, well, sorry. Look, you don't have time to stand around and discuss this. The fate of Califa depends on its safe delivery and you are a wanted man. I'd get moving if I were you. Good luck! Come on, Flynn!"

I turned and marched away, out of the shelter and into the driving rain, hardly able to see for the tears—of anger, I swear—that had sprung to my eyes. *A good deed never goes unpunished,* Nini Mo said. I should have let Sieur Arrogance stay in his cozy little jail and take care of his own snobby self. Why had I even bothered? For Califa I had bothered. For him, no. He was free, and he had his dispatch back and I hoped I never saw him again. Octohands roared at me to go back, to beg Sieur Wraathmyr's pardon. I pried him off my shoulder and stuffed him back into the dispatch case, vowing to find a way to banish him once and for all.

"Where are you going?" Sieur Wraathmyr loomed over me.

"What the fike do you care? To jump off the nearest cliff! Leave me alone!"

"That's a stupid thing to do."

"No, a stupid thing is trying to help some arrogant snapperhead who doesn't need your help, and a stupider thing is falling for a stupid enchantment that makes you spill your guts to that stupid snapperhead, and to think you actually like him, and to think he likes you, too, and then kissing him, and then the enchantment wears off and he won't look you in the eye. How's that for stupidity? Leave me alone!"

Now the rain, not my tears, was blinding me. A Gramatica Curse boiled up out of my tum and I swallowed chokingly, but it was like trying to swallow lava, thick and burning, filling my mouth with viscous fire. I stumbled and almost fell, felt Sieur Wraathmyr's steadying hand on my arm, heard him say, "Spit, for Goddess' sake!"

A hankie appeared in front of my face. I spat out a horrible wad of black slime that left my mouth tasting like dog poo. I looked up to see Sieur Wraathmyr tossing the hankie over the cliff and into the water below. He pulled me into the sheltering lee of another tree, then shrugged off his jacket and pulled his checked shirt over his head. I dolefully noticed that his chest was just as muscularly grand as I remembered. Sieur Wraathmyr dried Flynn off with his shirttail, and then slipped the shirt over Flynn's head. Wrapping the sleeves around Flynn's tummy, he then tied them tightly, making a kind of shirt-coat. "That should help him a bit. It's wool, so it'll keep him warm even when it's wet."

"Thanks," I said.

He shrugged his jacket on. "So last night wasn't part of the enchantment? You really did tell me all that, and I told you as well?"

"Ayah," I said bitterly.

"I'm sorry," he said. "I was a snapperhead. You've saved my hide twice and I've not been very thankful for it."

"Just leave me alone."

"Come with me."

Now I looked at him. There was no sign of arrogance, only concern. "Why?"

"Because everyone will be looking for you and me both. It's best if we stick together and get as far away from Cambria as we can. I'm headed to Barbacoa. We'll be safe there."

Barbacoa is an island off the Califa coast; it's a pirate haven and offshore hideout, a real wide-awake place. Lots of iffy stuff goes through Barbacoa: smuggling, illegal high-stakes gambling, servitor slaving, and who knows what else. Buck often talks about cleaning the place out, but the Califa Navy has nowhere near the juice to tackle it. Now I wondered if her complaints were sincere. She was probably in league with them, too.

"I thought Barbacoa was a pirate hideout."

"It's a free port. Anyone can be there. Pirates or envoys or footloose lieutenants," he said, grinning. "There's a Kulani envoy there, waiting for this dispatch. So come with me, please, Nini?"

"I don't want to run into the Dainty Pirate again." Nor Udo the Flapdoodle Pirate, either, though I didn't say that.

"He's not there. Before I got busted, I was down at the docks, trying to get a ride over, and everyone was talking about the *Pato*. After the Dainty Pirate left the *Pato*, he sailed north, toward the City."

"And the *Pato* itself?" I asked, hardly wanting to know the answer.

"Sunk, I'm afraid. But don't worry, Nini. The pirates put the captain and crew into the other longboat before they scuttled the ship. They made it safely to Moros; they are fine. So please, come with me now, and as soon as the dispatch is delivered, we'll head to Arivaipa."

"How do you know I'm going to Arivaipa? You looked at my map!"

He grinned, and even with the swollen eye, it was a handsome grin. "Now we are even. Let us go together. I've been to Arivaipa before and I know the way. I can help you."

"Why would you go with me?"

"Why the fike not? Come on!" With the charm turned on, Sieur Wraathmyr seemed almost like a different person. No longer bearish and growly, but strangely appealing. The idea of traveling to Arivaipa with him was not an entirely unpleasant one.

"How will we get to Barbacoa?" I asked. "We're on the run. Who's going to take us over?"

"Oh, that's easy," he said. "We'll just steal a boat. It's no problem."

"No problem?"

"I've done far worse things than steal a boat, Nini."

"Why do you keep calling me Nini?"

He grinned. "I guess because the first time I ever saw

you, you were dressed as Nini Mo. The name fits you. Besides, didn't you tell me your real name was Nyana?"

"Ayah." I had told him that along with everything else.
I felt hot just thinking about how much I had blabbed.

"So, that's why." He paused, then said, "And Nini—I
do like you. I like you an awful lot."

TWENTY

A Ruckus.
Swimming. Barbacoa.

OUR HEARTFELT LITTLE CHAT was interrupted by a muffled explosion. At the sound, I almost jumped out of my skin and Snapperdog let out a yelp of surprise.

"What the fike was that?"

"I expect it was the jail," Sieur Wraathmyr said, heading down the path. I followed him. A fire bell began to ring.

"What do you mean?"

"On our way out, I threw some shotgun shells in the stove. I guess that'll keep them busy while we get the fike out of here."

"What about the sheriff and the deputy? We left them locked in the cells!" I said, horrified.

"They'll be fine, Nini," Sieur Wraathmyr said. "It's mostly just noise and smoke." He halted. The path had turned along the top of a cliff; below, we saw the harbor and the town. Thick black smoke was pouring from the direction of the jail and the wind carried with it the sound of bells and yelling. Clearly, the good townsfolk of Cambria were going to be too busy to be looking for us for a while. But Sieur Wraathmyr was scowling.

"What's wrong?"

"On a clear day, you can see Barbacoa from here. It's only about five miles offshore."

Today was not a clear day. Rain and mist blotted out the horizon and a stiff wind was blowing—*away* from Barbacoa.

"It would take ten men to row against the wind," Sieur Wraathmyr said.

"What are we going to do?"

"Oh, we've not escaped enchanters, bumpkin sheriffs, and Birdie agents—not to mention pirates—to be stopped by a little bit of wind."

"How? You are only one man, and I can't row at all. Neither can Flynn."

"I might be only one man now. But I can be stronger than ten men if need be. Come on."

I followed him through the woods a distance, along the cliff tops, and then we skittered down a narrow path and onto the beach. We were beyond the harbor now, and the waves here seemed terrifyingly large, flinging onto the beach with a thunderous roar and immense spray.

"Now what?" The wind blew my words away and he

didn't hear me. Sieur Wraathmyr was taking his furry coat off and rolling it up. When it became obvious to me that his jacket wasn't all he was taking off, I turned my attention to the horizon, which had turned a stripy pink. A few shafts of golden sunlight were spearing through the dark smudgy clouds. I heard his voice, but the boom of the surf drowned out his words.

"What?" I bawled without turning around.

He came up behind me, and I felt him lean down, felt his breath gust against my hair. "The wind is too strong for me to row against, and too strong for me to haul a boat. But I can swim it."

"Swim it?" It took me a moment to catch on, and when I did, I felt myself flush with fear—and something else. "You mean—"

"Ayah, as my other self."

"The waves are huge!"

"Once, I spent three weeks in a small boat with six other men and a pig. We rowed from Far Island to Keohe'le. Sometimes the waves were as tall as mountains. This is nothing. But we have to wait until the tide goes out; I can catch the current and that will help."

"When will that be?"

"An hour or so."

"It will be dark by then!"

"Then, you won't see how tall the waves are. Won't that make it easier?"

"But what about me and Flynn?"

"It will be no trouble. I can carry you and Flynn on my back. Wear my jacket—it's waterproof. I must leave you now. I—well—I don't like to change in front of people. I'll be back before the tide slackens."

"Wait a minute—" I turned around hastily and saw him holding up his furry jacket and his satchel. In the grayish pink light, his tattoos bisected him into fragments of a man: an arm, a leg, strips of chest. Most of his face was covered by his wind-whipped hair, but I got the sense that he was embarrassed—not of his skin, but of his werbearness.

I said awkwardly, "You won't, uh, I mean, as a bear, you won't go after me—"

"I will know you, Nini. You will be in no danger from me, I promise. I do not lose all my humanity. I can still think and reason; I know my friends. You will be safe. When we get to Barbacoa, go to the hotel. Get a suite there, the best they've got. Make sure you sign the register as T. N. Wraathmyr and Associates, Representatives for Madama Twanky's De-Lux Luxury Goods."

"What about the Wanted posters? What if they are on Barbacoa, too?"

"Everyone on Barbacoa is wanted. No one would dare try to claim a bounty there. Do you have any money?"

I nodded. I had a letter of credit, drawn on Buck's bank, and Poppy's cash roll. I didn't want to use the letter, of course, but cash is cash everywhere, and happily anonymous.

"Good. I must go. I need to eat before we begin, and I prefer to eat as my other self because I like my food raw." This was said somewhat defiantly, as though he was afraid it would disgust me. Udo always fusses over his steak being well done enough, but I like some food raw myself, so who cares?

"Um . . . didn't you already eat as your other self?" I asked.

He looked at me quizzically. He still had that streak of blood on his temple; I reached up with my thumb and smudged it away. His blackened eye did look awful, but there wasn't anything I could do about that.

"Madama Valdosta?" I prompted.

"What? Oh pigface, you thought I ate Madama Valdosta?" He laughed.

I said defensively, "Well, there was a lot of blood."

"That was mine, mostly," he said. "Madama Valdosta clipped me with a Gramatica Curse."

"You had blood on your teeth."

"Oh, ayah, well maybe I did nip her, but only in self-defense. Her blood was bitter—she tasted of death. The last time I saw Madama Valdosta, she was heading for the hills. Really, Nini, I did not eat her. I promise."

Did I believe him? He looked sincere. And hadn't Octohands bitten her? If Sieur Wraathmyr had eaten her, he would have been poisoned, too. Besides, why should I care if he had eaten Valdosta? The stupid sow deserved it.

"I'll be back," he said, but still he did not go. What was he waiting for? When I realized, my face turned hot. Our embrace was quick and awkward; his lips grazed my temple, and the top of my head banged his nose. His cheeks were scratchy. I took his coat and satchel, and he disappeared into the woods. The wind was chill, so I put the furry jacket on over my buckskin. The hem hung down to my knees and my hands were buried in the sleeves, but it was warm and smelled comfortably of apple pipeweed. A big piece of driftwood provided a bit of a windbreak, so I settled into its shelter to wait, holding my revolver in my lap, just in case.

The pounding waves receded into a windy twilight. Snapperdog got tired of chasing birds and plopped down on my lap. I was exhausted; I guess I dozed, for the next thing I knew, Flynn had raised his head, faintly growling. I felt Octohands squirming in my dispatch case but didn't fish him out. I was not in the mood to listen to his opinion of our current plan. The last of the light was gone, and the sand stretched before me, glimmering whitely in the windy darkness. A very large shape was loping toward me.

I climbed to my feet, put my hand on Flynn's head to quell him and also to give myself courage. Sieur Wraathmyr had said he would know us. Goddess, I hoped he was right. I'd like to say that I stood my ground bravely, but it would be fiking more accurate to say that I was rooted to the ground in fear as the bear ambled toward us. Flynn was vibrating under my hand, but he didn't move.

Even on all fours, the bear—Sieur Wraathmyr, I reminded myself—was almost as tall as I was. When he sat back on his hind legs, he towered over me. But he smelled of the salt-sea and the chill wind, and very faintly of apple pipeweed.

"Ave," I said. My voice sounded ridiculous and faint. The bear looked down at me, his head cocked. Then he dropped down again, and shived me in the chest with a moist nose, not so unlike Flynn's, except that Flynn's shivs don't almost knock me off my feet.

He opened his mouth—pigface, his tongue was longer than my hand—and made a low trilling growl. It was almost exactly the same noise Flynn makes when he wants to have a treat and his ears scratched. I fumbled under the furry coat and found two squares of a Madama Twanky's Black Magick chocolate bar in the pocket of my buckskin jacket. Sieur Wraathmyr took the chocolate with one enormous paw and a surprisingly dainty gesture and crammed it in his mouth.

"I only have one other bar of chocolate," I said. "You can have it when we get to Barbacoa. The tide's going out."

Sieur Wraathmyr made a sputtering noise and then turned, headed for the water. I hefted his satchel and followed him. The surf was not quite as high now, but it was still terrifying.

"Dare, win, or disappear," I said, but the wind whisked my words away. I slung the two bags over my shoulders, one to each side, and hung my boots around my neck. The two important documents—the map and the dispatch—were back in their oilcloth wrapper and tucked between my stays and my chemise, where I hoped they would remain dry. Sieur Wraathmyr flattened himself to the ground, ears twitching, and I took a deep breath.

Pretend he's a horse, I thought. *A very furry horse.* I went to his left side, reached as high as I could, and grabbed a handful of fur, then bent my left knee and swung up on his back.

Sieur Wraathmyr huffed at Flynn, who had retreated a few yards, staring skeptically at us. It look several seconds of urging before I could get Snapperdog to come over, and then I had to tempt him into jumping, with a nibblet of forbidden chocolate. Sieur Wraathmyr growled impatiently under me, but finally Flynn leaped up. I settled him before me, tying us together with my sash and then buttoning the furry jacket around him, so he was tucked snug inside, settled against my chest. He felt very bony and knobby. Sieur Wraathmyr didn't wait for me to signal. He took off toward the water line in a slow walk. His gait was smooth and comfortable, but it felt odd to look between small fuzzy bear ears instead of pointy horse ears.

And then a wave flung up and hit us full on.

Fiking pigface, the water was ice cold. I closed my eyes, tucked my head in, and clung to Sieur Wraathmyr, feeling Snapperdog shiver against me. But Sieur Wraathmyr was right; the jacket was waterproof, and from the waist up I was well insulated. From the waist down, my wool drawers, stockings, and kilt didn't provide much protection from the wet, although Sieur Wraathmyr's fur did help keep some of the chill away. He plowed on through the surf, and then I felt him launch onto a wave, felt the water pick us up, felt his muscles strain and pull beneath me as he began to swim.

The journey was a blur of waves, wet, cold, chill, darkness, and stark-raving fear. Sieur Wraathmyr swam steadily, strongly, without faltering, allowing the surge of the waves to lift us up and drop us down again. Sometimes I saw the night sky high above; sometimes nothing but the curve of the wave crested above our heads. I closed my eyes and clung to him, trying to keep my mind blank, trying to ignore the surging of the cinnamon rolls in my tum. If we made it to Barbacoa alive, I would never get anywhere near the ocean ever again—fike, Barbacoa was an island; I'd have to take a boat to get off it—but after that, never again.

Darkness, water, waves, up and down, up and down. I

lost all track of time. Had we been in the water an hour? A day? Forever? Once, I opened my eyes and saw a wall of water towering over us, reaching as high as the sky. I shut my eyes and crushed Flynn against me, cringing, waiting to feel the crush of water sweep us away. But instead, the wave bore us aloft, and then the next wave wasn't so high, nor the one after that, and soon the waves had calmed. Still Sieur Wraathmyr swam steadily on. When I opened my eyes again, I saw silver water and a scrim of silvery clouds above.

And then suddenly, it was over. Sieur Wraathmyr's feet scrabbled and caught and he was wading through the surf. He heaved himself out of the water, waddled a few yards, and then collapsed. My hands had frozen into stiff claws; it was a moment before I was able to let go of his fur. I fumbled at the buttons of his furry coat and untied Flynn, who catapulted down. I managed to sling my frozen leg over and then I slid to the ground in a cold wet heap. The ground heaved and swelled beneath me, and my cinnamon rolls were done. I leaned over, puking, feeling the blissful grit of sand beneath my hands, and swore I would never eat another cinnamon roll again. Ever.

A muzzle shived me. Sieur Wraathmyr sat on his haunches, flicking at his ears with a massive paw. Thanks to the furry jacket, my shirt was dry; I pulled my shirttail out, and when he bent his head, carefully dried his ears until they felt as soft as velvet. He hoisted himself up and shook himself like a dog, spraying water everywhere. My socks were also still dry; I pulled them on and then yanked my boots on.

We had landed on a small foggy beach that smelled strongly of fish and wet seaweed. A dock loomed out of the mist, and beyond that, I saw the shadow of buildings.

"Should I wait for you to change?" I asked.

He shook his enormous head.

"So I should go on to the hotel? And you'll meet me there later?"

He nodded, and then shived me one last time. I slid my arms around his head, and kissed his muzzle. "Thank you."

He licked my face, quickly, and then loped off into the darkness.

"Come on, Flynn. Let's get a room." I put the jacket back on and hefted our luggage.

As we neared the promenade, I heard the sound of squeaky wheels, and then a pedicab loomed out of the fog. The driver was insistent and we didn't need much persuading. Flynn and I settled back into the plushy velvet seat and the cab puttered off. Barbacoa did not look like a wide-awake place, but maybe that's because it was the middle of a blustery night. The *Califa Police Gazette* often reports on the lurid goings-on in Barbacoa; they made the lurid goings-on South of the Slot seem like a picnic. But tonight there was just wet mist, an occasional dim light, and, once, the cheerful jangle of distant music. It was a little bit disappointing, actually.

The cab pedaled up under a large blue silk awning, and a snooty doorman handed me out of the cab. I paid the cabbie out of Poppy's cash, then crossed the enormous lobby, Flynn trailing behind me. We passed a dark bar screened from the lobby by a long, open fireplace. Bright blue flames danced along the hearth's length. Just like the lobby, the bar was empty I was surprised the hotel was so fancy, but I guess pirates, outlaws, professional gamblers, and slavers have lots of money to spend.

The clerk at the front desk didn't seem the slightest bit concerned that I was damp and probably smelled of upchuck, or that I was accompanied by a muddy dog. As soon as I mentioned Sieur Wraathmyr's name, she was all smiles and upgraded us to a double suite. But before she called the bell girl to escort me to the room, she made me check my pistol, explaining that it was the house rule for all guests. I hated the thought of being unarmed on an island full of criminals, but then, they were unarmed, too, so I supposed that made us even. I handed over my gun belt, accepted the claim check, and followed the bell girl to the elevator. As we passed by the front doors, I saw that the fog outside was fading into pink dawn.

It had been a very long night.

TWENTY-ONE

Octohands's New Trick.
A Plan. Breakfast.

IN DAYLIGHT, THE VIEW outside my hotel window showed the sweeping vista of a natural bay harbor chock-a-block with ships; there must have been at least fifteen at anchor within the harbor, and more were visible just beyond the bay's mouth. Most flew no colors, a clear indication that they were outside the law. A few brazenly exhibited pirate flags, but I didn't see the Dainty Pirate's colors among them. Good. I wasn't eager to run into him, or Udo, again. Ever.

The streets of Barbacoa were now awake, but not widely so. The buildings were stolidly spruce, and the people moving briskly about did not look like murderers and thieves; they looked like people anywhere. But, then, what do a murderer and a thief look like, really? Their deeds set them apart, not their faces. Should I be surprised to find that the *Califa Police Gazette* had been slightly exaggerating? No, I should not.

Hours earlier, as soon as I had tipped the bell girl and the door closed behind her, I had dumped Octohands into the bathtub, kicked off my boots, and fallen onto the plushy bed, asleep almost instantly. Now I felt bleary but rested, a bit achy but ravenous, and ready to be clean.

The door to Sieur Wraathmyr's room was closed; by this, I assumed that he had come in after me and was sleeping. The tub was empty, but after a few seconds of searching I found Octohands wedged between the potty and the wall.

When I poked him to make sure he was still alive, he grabbed my finger with a tentacle.

Are you all right? I asked.

I'm fabulous, oh, you clever girl. What a coup!

What do you mean?

Now he owes us twice—he'll not be able to say no!

Will you just drop it?

You have no idea how important this is. Look at what happened with your dear mother—she almost left this family high and dry—

When I tried to pull my finger out of his grip, Octohands hung on stubbornly, still chattering on about duty, honor, and baby names. He didn't even let go when I carried him, dangling from my hand, into the bedroom. There I pried his grip off and dumped him in a heap of writhing tentacles into the trash basket, then covered its top with a towel weighted down with the room service menu.

Now I could get clean in private.

After my bath, I cracked Sieur Wraathmyr's door and saw only a tuft of curly hair sticking out from under the fluffy white duvet. I'd give him a little longer to sleep and then wake him. We had to get that dispatch delivered.

While I waited, I sat on the bed and unfolded my map, to look again at the flattened contours of Arivaipa Territory. I still wondered why Tiny Doom would hide out there. If I were hiding from the Birdies, I would have found Varanger not far enough.

They'll shoot you from the hip, out in old Arivaipa again. The words of the song ran through my head, which reminded me: Hadn't Hardhands spent time in Arivaipa, back during the Bronco Wars?

When I took the towel off the waste basket, Octohands sprang into the air, startling me. He soared by, and then swooped and swirled around the room in giant figure eights. Wonderful, now he could fly. He jetted around the room, tentacles trailing, sometimes briefly alighting on a piece of furniture and using his tentacles to creep about before launching back into the air.

Flynn leaped up, barking and snapping. Octohands soared out of his reach, skimming the ceiling. Flynn skittered after him, jumping up on the bed.

"Hey—stop it, you two!" I cried. "Flynn, get down! Off the furniture! Now!"

Octohands shot across the room and landed with a thump on the end of the bed. A tentacle unrolled and attached to my ankle. *That was fun!*

How did you figure out how to fly?

Oh, a little tiny teeny sigil. I've never been particularly good at sub-vocal Gramatica, but "where there's a Will, there's a way," as our darling Nini always said.

Can you change yourself back, then? Lift the Curse I put on you?

If I could have, I would have done so, long time past. But as Head of our House, your magick trumps mine. Anyway, I think I actually like this form. It's a nice change of pace. So is this hotel, after the dumps we've been staying in. I'm perishing of hunger. Let's order room service!

I was perishing of hunger, too. I found the room-service order slip, filled it out, and rang for the bell girl. After she'd taken the slip, and my laundry, too, I returned to the bed, where Octohands was creeping over the map. I let him snap a tentacle around my wrist.

What do you know about Arivaipa? I asked him.

Know about Arivaipa? Pigface, I lost two good years of my life there. It's a hellhole, that's what I know about Arivaipa. I wouldn't wish it on my worst enemy. They say if the Dæmon Choronzon owned Hell and Arivaipa both, he'd live in Hell and rent out Arivaipa.

Then why would Tiny Doom hide out there?

Goddess knows. She was always a contrary one, even as a child. I'm not the least bit surprised she's not dead. I was easily disposed of with an arrow to the throat, but it would take more than a Birdie knife to put that woman down. I'll bet ol' Tezcatlipoca ate her and then puked her right back up again. I am glad she's still alive, though. How is dear Sieur Wraathmyr today? Have you proposed yet?

Proposed what?

Don't be a nitwit. Proposed marriage, of course. You can't do better, I am sure of it—no family to interfere, and such a handsome—

Give it a rest! I'm not going to marry him.

You have to marry someone, or at least breed—

This was not a topic I wished to discuss further, and so I tried to shake off Octohands's grip, but those suckers were very sticky. He continued to babble on about ceremonies and marriage settlements, ignoring my attempts to pry him off. Thankfully, there was a knock on the door; our chow had arrived. I pried him free and answered. The bell girl had just left when there was another knock, this time at the adjoining door, and when I called, "Enter," in came Sieur Wraathmyr, wearing a comfy hotel robe, his hair wet and curling.

I yanked the sash on my own robe tighter and wished I had gotten dressed. Octohands was right; Sieur Wraathmyr was pretty magnificent. How had I ever thought otherwise? Udo and his overcurled hair and calculatedly square jaw didn't even begin to compare.

But I wasn't interested in marrying Sieur Wraathmyr. Or anyone else for that matter. My cheeks were getting hot. Fike Octohands and his suggestions. Sieur Wraath-myr didn't seem to notice my blush. He just poured my coffee—how did he know to add the correct amount of cream and sugar?—and outlined our plan.

"Last night, I stopped at the newspaper office and put in a notice that I had arrived, bearing with me Madama Twanky's spring pattern book and catalog. The Envoy will see the notice, know I've arrived, and contact me about placing an order." As he spoke, Sieur Wraathmyr kept glancing at Octohands, now stuffing himself with eggs and bacon, but he politely didn't ask me any questions about him. Udo would have been hard-pressed to leave it alone.

I said, "The clerk was very happy to hear you were back in town. Are you well-known here?"

"As well as anyone else. I've made some big sales on Barbacoa."

"Do outlaws buy Madama Twanky stuff? I'd think they just steal everything."

"I think most outlaws prefer to save their larceny for where it counts. Besides, this is Barbacoa—no one steals here. It's the most honest place in the world, I think, thanks to Cutaway's iron grip."

"Who is Cutaway?"

"You'll see. Come on, let's go downstairs and see if the Envoy has called for us yet."

"Can't we just go directly to her?"

"We have to play it cool, Nini. You never know who is watching. It's best if she comes to us. She knows I'm here for her, and she will come. You'll see. Don't worry, a few more hours won't matter. I had the bell girl check with the harbor master; the next ferry to Arivaipa leaves tomorrow morning. If you still want to go, that is."

"I do. But I can go alone," I said, although now, more than ever, I wanted him to go with me. Facing Arivaipa, facing Tiny Doom, was daunting. It would be wonderful to not have to do it alone.

"I said I would go. Unless you don't want me to. I've been there before. In fact, I just came from there."

"What do you mean?"

"I just carried a delivery from Arivaipa to the City—"

"To Buck?" I remembered that request for the chupa-cabra hunter from the commanding officer of Fort Sandy.

"I can't say; I'm sorry. Deliveries are confidential."

I didn't press him. I knew what the answer was. The dispatch from Arivaipa hadn't just happened to get mixed up with Buck's mail. Sieur Wraathmyr had delivered it to her secretly. The CO at Sandy must really be afraid of the chupacabra, to send his request via an express agent.

MY CLOTHES WERE not back from the laundry yet, but I had the shirt and drawers I had bought back in Cambria, wrinkled and damp, but clean. I got dressed and fixed my hair as best as I could, which would have to do. By the time I was done, Sieur Wraathmyr was ready to go downstairs. I left Flynn and Octohands lolling on the bed, both stuffed to the gills with room service. I took my dispatch case with me, but as a precaution, I tucked the map into one of my boots. I wasn't going to risk losing it again.

The front desk had a lot of messages for Sieur Wraathmyr, but none of them were from the Kulani Envoy. He collected the pile of cards and we went into the dining room "to see and be seen," as he put it.

The dining room was elegantly decorated in marble and gilt, and giant vases of orange and pink roses. Nowhere did I see any of the outlaw dissipation so oft described in the CPG. No raucous bar fights or screeching dancehall jills; no off-tune cow-bands. No one was hanging from the chandeliers or setting the waiters on fire. I've seen worse behavior at staff officer meetings.

"See the woman sitting at the table next to the painting of the ship?" Sieur Wraathmyr asked, when I whispered this observation at him.

I glanced over the rim of my coffee cup. A silver-haired woman in a simple black sheath dress sat alone, reading a newspaper and eating half a grapefruit.

"Ayah? What about her?"

"That's Cutaway Hargity. She owns most of the gambling along the west coast, both in Califa and Birdieland. Also, this hotel and everything else on the island. She's why everyone is so good. No one wants to get on her bad side."

"Why do they call her Cutaway?"

"Because she cuts away bits of people who cross her."

"She looks like a banker."

"She is a banker. And a businesswoman. An extremely ruthless banker and businesswoman. I heard that the Warlord once had a twenty million gambling debt to her."

"Twenty million divas?" I said, aghast. "How do you lose twenty million divas gambling?"

"By being a very poor euchre player. The Warlord's partner, a man named Merrick, refused to pay."

"The Warlord had a bodyguard named Merrick. He only had one hand—oh." I looked back at Cutaway Hargity. She had finished her grapefruit and was slathering her toast with butter.

Sieur Wraathmyr continued, "Remember that extra tribute tax a couple of years back, the one that was supposed to go to the Birdies? That's how the Warlord raised the money to cancel his debt. After Merrick, he was very motivated to honor his obligation."

I remembered that tax. It had prompted quite a few angry editorials in the papers—most of them aimed at the Birdies, not at the Warlord, who was seen as an innocent victim of their greed. Pretty clever, paying off your gambling bills by raising a tax that you can blame on your overlords, thus making them even more unpopular while you look like a martyr.

A yelp punctuated the hush of the room. We turned and saw two men scuffling at the buffet line. One appeared to be rubbing bacon in the face of the other. Judging from the screams, the bacon was very hot. Out of nowhere, two girls flanked the fighters. Suddenly the bacon-rubber was on the ground, moaning, as his victim screamed, "My face! My face!"

The bacon-rubber started to sit up and Bouncer One kicked him neatly in the head with a pink-toed boot. There was a sickening thud, and the bacon-rubber's head jerked back and he flopped over, suddenly very quiet. Bouncer Two grabbed the screaming man, threw a towel over his head, and steered him toward the kitchen. Bouncer One hoisted the bacon-rubber over her shoulder and hauled him away.

The whole incident had taken seconds.

"I beg your pardon, gentle guests." Cutaway stood beside her table. "It is very silly to fight over the last piece of bacon. There is always more bacon. I am sorry that your breakfast was disturbed. Champagne is on the house."

This announcement brought a smattering of applause and a shout of, "I'll take vino over bacon anytime!" Cutaway turned a quiet look in the shouter's direction and the applause abruptly stopped. Waiters began to distribute champagne glasses. Cutaway sat down and Sieur Wraathmyr continued, as though he'd never paused. "Over there, by the pillar, that man in the green and yellow ditto suit is the head of the Waco Slave Syndicate. And over there is the Bouncing Boy Terror himself, Springheel Jack—"

I turned my head so quickly that my neck cracked. Springheel Jack? Springheel Jack was dead, and his boots in the possession of . . . Oh, fike. That wasn't Springheel Jack at all.

It was Udo.

Wearing Springheel Jack's boots.

TWENTY-TWO

Jack Boots.
An Argument. Interruption.

NOT COPIES OF Springheel Jack's boots this time. But the Jack Boots themselves, in all their glittery, snaky glory.

Udo, that fiking idiotic fool! Hadn't he learned his lesson? The last time he'd put those boots on, they'd ensorcelled him. Springheel Jack's boots aren't just a fashion accessory; they *are* Springheel Jack. It's the Jack Boots that make the outlaw, not the other way around. They take over whatever poor snapperhead wears them, turning him into Springheel Jack.

And once they have their victim in their grip, they do not let go. Last time I'd only managed to get them to release Udo by promising that if they let him go, I'd find them another and much better snapperhead to ensorcel. I had broken my promise (is a promise to a pair of homicidal magickal boots really a promise?) and given the boots

257

back to Udo because he had sworn he would turn them in to the police and collect the bounty on Springheel Jack. Apparently I was not the only oath breaker around.

Speaking of which, I glanced around the room but saw neither the Dainty Pirate nor the Zu-Zu. Udo sashayed toward a table like he was Choronzon, Lord of All Creation. He was dressed head-to-toe in white—sumptuous, not funereal. Puffy white sack hose, white velvet doublet with white silk puffs on the enormous sleeves, frothy white lace at his cuffs and neck. He looked subdued but elegant. Of course, white was the perfect foil for the red sparkly boots with the snappy snake heads on the toes. They stood out like blood on snow.

"I heard that Springheel Jack had been killed in a shootout in the City, a year or so ago," Sieur Wraathmyr said. "I guess that rumor was wrong."

"No, it wasn't wrong," I answered. Udo sat down at his table. We were not the only ones looking in his direction. In fact, Cutaway Hargity was now gazing with sparkling-eyed interest at him.

"I gotta get out of here," I said. "Before he sees me."

"You know Springheel Jack?" Sieur Wraathmyr asked, surprised.

"That's not Springheel Jack. It's Udo Landaðon."

Or was it? From this distance, I couldn't read Udo's face well enough to tell if he was himself or if he had been subsumed into Jackness again. The outfit, though, screamed

Jack; the Jack Boots had much better taste than Udo himself did.

"He was at the Zu-Zu's party, don't you remember?" I said.

"Udo? You mean the idiotic courtier that dumped you? What is he doing in Springheel Jack's boots?"

"It's a long story, but I really don't want him to see me." Yet, if he looked toward our table, he'd see me for sure. Sieur Wraathmyr gestured, and we quickly changed seats. Now his bulk blocked me from Udo's view. But if Udo couldn't see me, I couldn't see him, either. I could, however, see Cutaway Hargity's table.

"Cutaway Hargity has just sent her card over to Udo," I said.

"Cutaway likes bright-eyed boys. Well, good luck to him. But let's get rid of him for the moment, shall we?"

Sieur Wraathmyr summoned a waiter, slipped him some money, and whispered something in his ear. The waiter nodded and went over to Udo's table. Suddenly Udo was leaving the room in a big hurry.

"What did you tell the waiter to say to him?"

"That he had an urgent package pickup at the Pacifica Mail office. That should keep him busy for a while. Ah, here we go."

Our chow arrived. Right behind the waiter with the food was another waiter with a card on a silver salver. The flood had begun.

It took us forever to eat breakfast; we were constantly interrupted by a stream of people. Sieur Wraathmyr produced a small notebook from one of his pockets and began to set up appointment times—he was going to have a busy afternoon. Apparently, so was I, for he introduced me as Vice President in Charge of Furbelows and Fripperies (what the fike is a furbelow?), and people seemed just as eager to see me.

Alas, I was not so eager to see them, for as each card arrived, Sieur Wraathmyr would, in a low voice, describe its owner.

". . . made a fortune in selling body parts . . ."

". . . sells elementals that she invokes and traps . . ."

". . . robbed sixteen different mule trains . . ."

But none of these rotters was the Kulani Envoy. Maybe she'd given up on Buck's response and returned to the islands, empty-handed. Maybe she was sick. Maybe she hadn't heard that Sieur Wraathmyr was in town. It seemed like everyone on Barbacoa had requested an appointment but her. Finally, when my bacon was gone, I was on my fifth cup of coffee, and my anxiety had built up to where I thought I might start screaming, another waiter appeared with yet another card.

Sieur Wraathmyr glanced at it and grinned widely. "At last. The Kulani Envoy begs us to wait upon her at her home, so that she might browse my sample case. This afternoon at one."

"Finally," I said with relief.

"Ayah so, finally." A heavy hand dropped on my shoulder and a familiar voice, dripping with nastiness, said, "Ave, Flora."

"Ave," I said warily, shrugging off his heavy hand. Was I addressing Udo or Springheel Jack? The glare, the hand on the hilt of his saber—very Jackish. But when he spoke again, the querulous accusatory tone was all Udo.

"We searched the *Pato* for you and never found you. We thought you'd perhaps fallen overboard, maybe drowned. I was pretty upset."

"Turnabout is fair play. Now you know how I felt," I answered.

"It's not a joking matter!"

"I'm not joking. Leave me alone, Udo."

"What are you doing here?" Udo demanded.

"She said to leave her alone," Sieur Wraathmyr said.

Udo sneered. "Who are you?"

"T. N. Wraathmyr, at your service, sieur." Sieur Wraathmyr waved his hand in a somewhat careless Courtesy. He didn't stand up.

"What does the T. N. stand for?" Udo demanded.

"T for Trouble and N for None of Your Business," Sieur Wraathmyr answered. He had picked his fork up and now spun it around his fingers as he stared flat-eyed at Udo.

Udo countered with, "T for Thief and N for Nobody

is more like it. I remember you now. The salesman, at the Zu's party. "

"What do you want, Udo?" I said hurriedly. Sieur Wraathmyr shifted his grasp on the fork; now he held it like a dagger. Udo curled his lips dismissively and turned back to me. "What are you doing?"

"Eating breakfast, Udo, or at least I was before you interrupted me."

"I mean, what are you doing on Barbacoa?"

"It's a free port, Udo. Anyone can be here."

"You'd better come with me, Flora."

"I don't think so, Udo. I'm busy."

"Not so busy, by the look of it. Your plate is empty. Come on, Flora."

"She is not a dog to come when you call her," Sieur Wraathmyr said, giving Udo a stone-cold look that would have rocked me back on my heels but that Udo received with a very Jackish sneer.

"I don't recall addressing you at all, sieur," he answered. "This is none of your business."

I protested, "Udo, stop it! You are being rude."

"I'll be even ruder if I have to be, to get you to come with me. Quit playing games, Flora."

Sieur Wraathmyr said softly, "You will excuse us, sieur, but we have appointments. If you wish to speak to Madama Romney, perhaps you should make an appointment as well."

Udo hissed, "I'll make an appointment to see you in the Abyss."

"Would you?" Sieur Wraathmyr said. He stood up.

"I'll send you there myself!"

"Name your place and your time."

"Stop it, you two!" I said as Udo and Sieur Wraathmyr glared at each other. Neither one looked at me. In the cheap romance novels, the heroine is always thrilled when her rivals fight. In real life, it was just horribly embarrassing. I was not the last piece of bacon.

Though we had kept our voices low, the furious tones had carried, and now everyone in the room was staring at us. Udo and Sieur Wraathmyr locked eyes, neither willing to give ground, and when I whacked them each on the arm, they didn't pay attention. The snake heads on the toes of the Jack Boots hissed and snapped, and Sieur Wraathmyr growled in response.

"Little boys," a new voice said. Cutaway Hargity was not much taller than me, but somehow she made the men look very small. "If you will fight, then go outside. We've had enough caterwauling for one day. Break apart or I shall cut you apart."

Like Udo, Cutaway wore a scabbard at her hip. His was empty. Hers held a very long pair of scissors. Now she rested her hand on their handle.

Udo and Sieur Wraathmyr broke away from their stare-down.

"I cry your pardon, madama," Sieur Wraathmyr said, sweeping into a bow.

Not to be outdone, Udo took off his hat and bowed so low that the fringe on his cravat almost touched the floor. "I beg your pardon, madama, for causing a disruption."

Cutaway answered, "How can I not grant you pardon, when you ask so prettily? But remember what I said earlier. There is no need to fight. There is always more." The sharp black eyes turned on me, appraised me, and found me obviously unappealing. "You are Tharyn's new associate?"

"Ayah, madama." I made my own Courtesy: Honored and Grateful for the Hospitality.

Cutaway's hair was silvery gray, but her face was curiously unlined, almost masklike. When she spoke, her eyebrows did not move. "Interesting. Madama *Romney*, yes?"

"Ayah." I did not like the way she was looking at me, like she saw the Gramatica inside of me. Her hand still rested on her scissors.

"*Very* interesting. I will look forward to speaking with you later. I have need of new furbelows, and hope that you will be able to instruct me on the latest fashion in Ticonderoga." She turned back to Sieur Wraathmyr. "Tharyn, you may come to my office sharply at five, with your catalogs and pattern book in hand."

"I will be honored, madama."

Now Cutaway narrowed in on Udo. "And you, dear

boy, may escort me back to my office and tell me the news on the high seas as we go."

Udo had no choice but to take Cutaway's arm and escort her away. Which he did, although not without one last sneer at Sieur Wraathmyr and me.

"Pigface, he's in for it now," Sieur Wraathmyr remarked, watching them walk away.

"What do you mean?" I could hear Udo telling Cutaway that he loved her taste in shoes. I couldn't help but think that Sieur Wraathmyr might be sullen sometimes, but he'd never stoop to such lap-doggery.

"Once Cutaway has 'em, they are done. Come on, we are going to be late for our appointment."

"Done? What does that mean?" I asked, following him from the dining room.

"Oh, I don't know exactly," Sieur Wraathmyr said vaguely. "But I've heard rumors that she keeps souvenirs."

TWENTY-THREE

Envoys.
Aunties. Ginger Ale.

THE KULANI ENVOY LIVED in a small house perched high above the town on a steep cliff face. From the street, the house was almost invisible behind brilliant purple bougainvillea, flowers so bright they hurt my eyes. The day had turned warm and the sky was sullen with clouds, the air heavy and wet. It looked like a storm.

Sieur Wraathmyr's words about the fate of Cutaway's conquests had rolled around in my head as we rode up the hill. Now, as we exited the donkey cab, I forced those uneasy thoughts into a dark corner of my mind and slammed the door on them. Udo's charms had saved his skin before, so surely they'd save it now, and, anyway, he had the Jack Boots to help him if there was trouble—and, anyway, what the fike did I care?

A Kulani boy in a red silk sarong answered Sieur

Wraathmyr's knock. Now I knew that Sieur Wraathmyr got his curly black hair and dark skin from his Kulani father, for the boy had the same coloring. But the boy's eyes were brown, not blue.

Sieur Wraathmyr gave the boy our greetings and he ushered us into a small foyer. The boy pointed at my feet, and I pulled my boots off. I think Sieur Wraathmyr must have left his boots on the *Pato,* because he'd been barefoot ever since. A small fountain sat to one side of the door, its water flowing into a footbath. Sieur Wraathmyr dipped each of his feet into the bath and then stepped on the towel the boy had laid down. I did the same, hopping ungracefully.

Our feet now clean, we followed the boy into a larger room, the walls made of panels of flat woven grass. The floor was glossy red wood, as polished as glass. There was no furniture, only a scattering of brightly colored pillows and a low table with a flat stove in its center.

The lady approaching us was wrapped in so many shawls that only her face was visible. She had a diamond pattern tattooed on each cheek and lines etched across her forehead. Her hair was white as snow, but under the tattoos, her dark skin was smooth and unlined.

Sieur Wraathmyr bowed deeply. "I give you greetings, madama."

"I give you greetings in return, nephew Keanu-enue'okalani!" the Envoy said, smiling.

Sieur Wraathmyr's suave smile disappeared. He looked surprised and discomfited.

The Envoy saw this reaction and said, "You do not remember me?"

"I am not sure," he said, uncertainly. "Are you my aunt Hauani?"

"I am her, exactly! You were a mere child when I last saw you, so many years ago. Many things have happened since then."

She swept Sieur Wraathmyr into an embrace; in his arms, she seemed small and doll-like. He still looked rather bewildered as she released him, and we followed her out onto the veranda, well shaded by pots of flowers and small trees. Here, cut off from the wind, the air felt gentle and warm, and the brilliant purple and pink of the geraniums and bougainvillea made up for the lead-colored sky above.

"You much resemble my brother," she said as we sat down on thin silk pillows. "He was such a handsome man. But you have your mother's eyes."

Sieur Wraathmyr remained silent, his face closed and wary.

"I cry your pardon, madama," I said. "But what did you say Sieur Wraathmyr's name was?"

"Keanuenue'okalani. It means 'Rainbow of Heaven' in our language."

"I left that name long ago," Sieur Wraathmyr said stiffly. "Today, my name is Tharyn Wraathmyr. I answer to no other."

"Keanonolo'kaloni," I tried unsuccessfully.

"No, Keanuenue'okalani!" The Envoy laughed at my mangled attempt at pronunciation. She said kindly, "Our long names are hard for any tongue that is not born to say them. When he was a boy, we called him Ke'anu."

"I am no longer a boy," Sieur Wraathmyr growled.

The Envoy's smile faded. "As you wish, Sieur Wraathmyr. Will you offer me your name, madama?"

"I cry your pardon," I said quickly. I glanced at Tharyn. Should I tell the Envoy my real name? Could I trust her? Did it matter?

He saved me from the decision. "This is my associate, Nyana Romney."

"Welcome, Madama Romney. Come, let me offer you refreshments. And then we shall have our business."

The boy brought three small green cups and a green china teapot shaped like a goldfish. The Envoy carefully poured the tea, then blew briefly over each cup before handing one to Tharyn and one to me. We drank the hot bitter liquid, which was oddly refreshing, considering the warm dampness of the day, and the Envoy asked us polite questions about our journey. Tharyn answered as briefly as possible, omitting the more sensational details. He sat hunched in his furry coat, radiating displeasure and impatience. The Envoy's attempts to draw him out proved totally futile, and eventually she gave up.

"On to our business, then. You have a delivery for me, sieur?"

"Ayah, so." He took the dispatch out of his furry jacket and offered it to her. She took it—the freedom of Califa on a piece of paper—and tucked it inside one of her shawls without reading it. "Thank you."

And that was it. Audience over. Delivery made.

I felt slightly disappointed, but then what did I expect to happen? Angels to trumpet and the sky to open up, raining roses? We were just messengers. Briefly, the fate of Califa had been in our hands, but now it was someone else's burden.

Tharyn bounded to his feet, hauling me up after him. The boy led us back to the house, but as I was fumbling to put my boots on, the Envoy asked Tharyn for a few words in private. He hesitated for a moment and then agreed.

Walking me to the door, he said, "I'll meet you back at the hotel."

"Are you sure? I can wait."

"I'm sure," he said abruptly. "Go on."

"Are you all right? You look upset."

"It was a surprise. I did not expect the Envoy to know

me. I do not know what she could say to me. She should not even know me. To the Kulanis, I am dead. A ghost."

"Maybe I should wait for you." I put my hand on his furry sleeve, but he shook it off.

"No, Nini," he said, a bit less growly. "Go back to the hotel. This has nothing to do with you."

"I don't mind—"

"Go," he said brusquely. Stung, I turned away. He had been so sweet recently that I had forgotten what a snapperhead he could be. I did not like the reminder at all. The donkey cab was waiting outside. I climbed in, glad I didn't have to make the sultry walk back to town.

Back at the hotel, as I crossed the lobby, I glanced over and saw a tall figure sitting at the bar, sparkly red boots hooked over the foot rail. Motivated by a weird surge of—guilt? sorrow? nostalgia?—I veered toward him. Udo was a snapperhead, but I couldn't let Cutaway get him. Or the Jack Boots, either. I had to try to talk some sense into him.

"Since when do you drink beer?" I asked, sitting next to him.

"It's not beer," he said. "It's ginger ale."

He waved his hand at the barkeep and ordered one for me. He waited to lift his glass until mine was in front of me.

We clinked.

"Cierra Califa," he said.

"Cierra Califa."

The ginger ale was fizzy and scorching hot. We sat in silence for a few minutes, sipping.

"I really thought you were dead," Udo said finally.

"Well, I thought you were dead, so we are even. It's a crappy feeling, ain't it?"

"The Dainty Pirate is really pissed. Thanks to your whip, he has to wear an eye patch."

"That's very piratical. He should thank me."

Udo laughed. "He does look pretty good in it."

We fell back into silence and finished our drinks. The bartender brought another round. Despite all Udo had done, all his snapperyness, now that I sat next to him I was reminded of how comfortable he was, how familiar. We'd been through a lot together. The thought that I might never have seen him again had been unbearable. Now that my anger had died down a bit, I had to admit I missed him.

"Why didn't you come with us, Flora? You always said you wanted to be a ranger, complained you never got to do anything. Here was your chance, and you wouldn't take it. I don't get that at all."

"I'm not a sack of corn to be tossed around. No one asked me. Buck didn't. The Dainty Pirate didn't. Buck didn't even trust me enough to tell me what was going on."

"I only found out when we were captured. You always complained Buck wasn't doing anything to save Califa, and now that she is, you're pissed about it."

"She could have told me," I said. "It matters to me as much as to anyone, maybe more."

"She was trying to protect you."

I slurped the last burning dregs of the ale. "Well, she can't. She should realize that and let me take care of myself. Where's the Zu Zu?"

"She went with the Dainty Pirate, up north. I think she has a crush on him."

"Sorry." I wasn't the slightest bit sorry, really.

"It's fine," Udo said. "She was just a distraction. A captain can't afford distractions, you know—"

"Captain?"

"Ayah. Dainty has promised me my own ship. It's not big, but it will be mine. I think I'll change the name, though. *El Pato de Oro* isn't really a suitable name for a pirate ship."

"That's Captain Ziyi's ship!" I protested. "The Dainty Pirate can't give it to you. And anyway, I thought the *Pato* was sunk."

"We spread that rumor around so the owner could collect insurance on it. See, Dainty ain't all that bad."

"It's still not right."

Udo gave me a scornful look. "This is war, Flora, in case you hadn't noticed. Or it will be soon. You can't be dainty in a war; didn't Nini Mo say that? But listen, that Wraathmyr fellow. He's shifty, don't you think? He needs a haircut and some moisturizer."

"Leave him out of this, Udo. He has nothing to do with you."

"I think you are being pretty foolish, Flora—"

"Foolish? Me? Are you fiking kidding, Udo? Look at your feet and tell me I am the foolish one." I gestured to his boots, sparkling and glittering. "After what happened before? The Jack Boots almost got you; they almost turned you into a killer, a thief. You barely escaped, and now here you are wearing them again."

"That was different. I was unprepared. And the Jack Boots and I have an agreement now. Unlike some people, they keep their word."

"What kind of agreement?"

"A private kind. Look, I know you think I'm an idiot and that I can't do anything right—"

"I never said that—"

"Oh, yes, you have, and even when you don't say so, you look it. See—you are doing it right now!"

"I'm only thinking of you!"

"No, you are thinking of yourself. You don't trust anyone to know what they are doing. I'm helping Califa and you are gallivanting around like this is some sort of game. Jumping ship like that, with some fellow you don't even know."

You don't know the half of it, Udo, I thought, *and don't think I'm going to tell you, either.* But I am willing to admit when I am wrong and I did so now.

"I was a total snapperhead. I know it," I admitted.

"You gotta grow up, Flora. There's a lot going on in the world, and not all of it centers around you. Think about someone other than yourself, for once."

"I said I was a fool—"

"Ayah, you say so, Flora, but you don't really believe it. You think you are smarter than everyone else."

I didn't have to listen to this. I had admitted my faults, and still that wasn't good enough for him. If he wanted me to crawl, well, he was in for disappointment. "Fine. Have fun with your pirates and your sparkly red boots. And if they turn you into a monster, don't come crawling to me."

"No fear of that!" Udo answered hotly.

I jumped off the barstool. I was so pissed that I wasn't paying attention to where I was going; all I knew was that I had to get out of there before I blew up. Blindly, I roared out of the bar, far away from a vain popinjay of a pirate.

"Hey!"

A man had run into me broadside, almost knocking me down.

"Lo siento." He caught my arm. I turned to tell him to watch where he was going, but he raised his hand and flicked his fingers toward my face. I saw a brief twinkle of

glittery dust, and then, before I could react otherwise, I had sucked it in. My muscles went weak and my knees gave out. I started to fall but the man caught me, and at his touch, my muscles stiffened again, but now they moved of their own accord.

"Come," he said, and I obediently followed him through the lobby, toward the elevator.

The clerk at the desk waved at me, calling my name, but when I tried to answer, my tongue lay in my mouth like a piece of dead meat. I tried to stop, tried to turn around, but my legs would not obey. Puppetlike, I followed the man into the elevator. The elevator door shut. He was standing behind me, so I could not see his face, but the hand that reached around to push the elevator button was long and narrow, and his fingernails were painted jade green.

Only Birdies paint their fingernails jade green.

I would have shrieked if I could, but I could only stand there, stock-still, as the elevator whirled upward. That glittery dust must have been Sonoran Zombie Powder, which paralyzes all who touch it. Udo had once used it to catch Springheel Jack, and I had used it to catch Springheel Udo. Now someone had used it to catch me.

At the sixth floor, the elevator shuddered to a halt and the cage door sprang open. I walked down the long hallway, hearing soft footsteps padding behind me. At room 65, the long, narrow hand unlocked the door, and I marched inside. The door shut behind us. I walked over to the chair by the dresser and sat down. My captor walked into my field of vision and crouched before me, smiling.

"Who are you?" the Birdie asked.

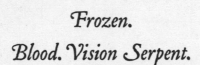

TWENTY-FOUR

Frozen.
Blood. Vision Serpent.

I HAD NEVER SEEN the face of an adult Birdie before. Birdie aristocrats wear masks of jade, leather, or gold. Everyone else obscures their features behind thick paint. The Birdie's silver mask dangled from his hand, and the face thus revealed was horrifying. The sides of his skull had been shaved and his warrior lock was long, stiff with blood, woven through with feathers, bones, and tufts of fur. His face was painted black, bisected with a yellow stripe across his eyes and the bridge of his nose. Golden thorns pierced his ears and his nasal septum, and his lower lip. His teeth, when he opened his mouth to speak, were stained red, the canines sharp.

The Birdie said, "You are traveling with Wraathmyr, the wer-bear. You were with him at Valdosta's." He paused to lick his lips. His voice was strangely familiar. When he spoke again, saying, "You helped the skinwalker escape me," I knew where I had heard him before.

He was Madama Valdosta's buddy at the lodge. The man who had set us up. "He belongs to the Lord of the Smoked Mirror, the skinwalker does. He has been marked. But you, you are very . . . familiar to me. Who are you?"

The Birdie licked his lips again. He needed to get some Madama Twanky's Lip Repair, I thought somewhat hysterically.

If they get you, said Nini Mo, *keep yer yip shut.* I tried to stay silent, but I could not. At the touch of his finger on my lips, my mouth opened. Luckily for me, the compulsion was simply to speak, not to tell the truth.

I croaked, "What skinwalker?"

"The boy," the Birdie said impatiently. "His scent is all over you."

"I don't know anything about any skinwalker."

The Birdie touched my lips again and I shut up. He raised a quizzing glass to his eye, peering at me through it. But he couldn't be looking at me, for the glass itself was black, completely opaque.

The Birdie let the quizzing glass drop on its chain, and stood up. His black shift was tufted with golden fur around the neck; his bare arms were covered in long scratches. Some were half-healed, still scabby; others were new enough to be stippled with red. He was either a magician or a priest—or both. But he wasn't a Flayed Priest; his skin appeared to be his own. Beneath my fear, another terror, even sharper, began to bloom.

He said, "I saw you in the mirror, while I was tracking the skinwalker. You are so familiar, and yet why? The Smoke drifts in your veins, twisting and turning, and yet you do not control it. Who are you?"

Now my fear shifted into hope. He didn't know exactly who I was; he was suspicious, that was all. If I could persuade him I was nobody, then maybe he'd let me go.

I whispered, "My name is Nyana Romney. I've been in the Current, it's true, but I'm not an adept."

The Birdie looked amused. "You call it the Current, as though it is something that can be channeled, controlled, or ridden. It is not a Current, it is a Smoke that drifts where it will; you cannot control it, only drift with it, go where it goes. I think you are lying to me."

"I am not," I protested. "I swear I'm not—"

"We shall see. Hush."

My protests choked and died. He stood staring at me, head slightly cocked. I recognized the look—it's the same one Flynn gets when he's trying to figure something out. Then he leaned closer, breathing deeply, and I realized, with a mental shudder, that he was smelling me. He pushed up my sleeve, turning my arm so my wrist was exposed. The cut I had made for the Blood Working was scabby, half-healed. He traced it with one green fingernail, and his touch made me cringe.

"You must be careful," he said. "You went too deep. You are lucky you didn't bleed out. And the cut is too long. Never use a razor."

Now he leaned so near that I would have choked if I could have. How could he smell me over the stench of himself? He absolutely reeked, of smoke, of rotting blood, of musky animal.

"Hmm . . ." he said. Briskly, he removed my dispatch case from my shoulder and carried it out of my view. I couldn't see him going through my gear, but I knew from his murmurs he wasn't impressed.

He came back to turn out my pockets. He found my toothbrush and a bar of chocolate; two unspent rounds and a casing from my last target practice; six divas; my collapsible drinking cup; Pow's soother. He picked up my right hand and raised it to his face—for one horrible moment, I thought he was going to kiss it, or bite it—but instead, he just sniffed at the cuff of my buckskin jacket. There was a stain on it, I remembered, very old and faint. I'd always assumed that Tiny Doom had trailed her sleeve through gravy or something, but by the way the Birdie was huffing at the leather, I had the sudden awful thought that the stain wasn't gravy at all.

"Where did you get this jacket?" the Birdie hissed, dropping my hand and wrenching my face toward him.

"I got it at a jobber," I babbled. "In Califa. It cost me twenty-two divas—"

His fingers squeezed my cheeks. "You lie. There is blood on this jacket and I would know its scent anywhere." He yanked the jacket off me and patted me down, running rough hands over my sides and front. He yanked off my right boot and then my left—and the map of my Working fell out.

Oh, fiking pigface Choronzon.

"What is this?"

"Nothing. A stupid thing. I was just fooling around with a Charm I'd found, a Locative Spell—"

He sniffed the map. "You have used blood. What did you seek? It is no small matter, a Blood Working."

"Uh, I was, uh, looking for, uh, my friend, Udo. He got taken by pirates, he was with the Infantina. I thought maybe I could, uh, do a Blood Working and find him, help rescue him—"

The Birdie opened the map and looked at it. He licked his lips again—pigface, if he did that one more time, I would scream. I said quickly, "It didn't work, 'cause he's here, I saw him. If you let me go, I'll show you—"

"*Callate,*" he said, and I was silent again.

Fike, he didn't believe me, but it didn't matter. The

map had no inscription on it, no *This Way to Tiny Doom,* nothing to give its purpose away. He would never get the truth out of me, no matter what he did. He could kill me and I would go to my grave with Tiny Doom's secret. Even if he found out who I was, I would never tell him about Tiny Doom. Never.

The Birdie picked up the quizzing glass—it must have been some sort of a scrying glass—and peered at the map through it. He moved out of my line of sight and I heard the sound of rustling, as though he was fishing around in a trunk or a drawer, or maybe a bag. And then, from some-where behind me, an order: "Sit down at the table."

I got up and walked over to a table and chair I hadn't known was there. A small brown bowl sat on the table; next to it lay a leather case. The Birdie sat down across from me and unrolled the leather case. Inside, small silver tools nestled in a chamois sleeve.

A bleeding kit. Buck hates bleeding and never allowed it to be done to us, not even when Idden had scarlet fever and the doctor said she'd die otherwise. I've never been bled before, and I certainly didn't want to be bled now, and not by this man, and not in this manner. But I was powerless to stop him.

"Give me your hand."

He placed an obsidian rod in my palm and closed my fingers around it. He trailed his fingernail up my inner arm and came to a stop in the crook of my elbow. He tied a black ribbon around my upper arm, tightly, and then flicked his finger at the veins until one stood out.

He selected a small silver box from the case: a scarificator. One side of the box is pierced with small holes; when a button is pressed, small blades spring out from the hole. It's a fast and easy way to get a lot of blood flowing.

"Clench your fist a few times," the Birdie ordered and, like a stupid puppet, I did. I tried to yank my arm out of his grip, squirm away, hit him, kick him, but no matter how much I struggled, I was trapped in my own skin. My writhing was imaginary; my body remained frozen and obedient.

The Birdie pressed the box to my skin. The spring made a popping noise as he thumbed the button; I felt a quick silvery pain. He removed the box from my arm, revealing four rows of little red dots. He lifted my arm and placed it in the notch of the bowl, which I now recognized as the polished brainpan of a skull. The dots grew, trembling, and then became trickles. The blood flowed down my arm like red ribbons unwinding into liquid red satin, pooling in the bottom of the bowl—which was, I realized, a well-polished skull cap. As the blood flowed, it seemed to take all the tension with it. My muscles, so tight and taut, loosened. My fear and revulsion began to vanish into a hazy warm lassitude.

A heavy formless feeling washed over me, as though

my body were dissolving into nothingness, my mind going gooey and soft. I heard the steady thump of my heartbeat, the tidal roar of the blood still in my veins. My head felt full of pressure, my brain too big for my skull. Everything seemed faraway and unreal. I watched calmly as the bowl slowly filled, and then the Birdie lifted my arm, pressed a wad of spider-silk to the little wounds, bound them up with a strip of cloth.

The Birdie laid my arm gently on the table and picked the bowl up. He angled it, swirling the blood within, gazing into its depths. Then he raised the bowl to his lips and drank deeply. I saw the length of his throat convulse as he swallowed. His lips, when he set the bowl down, were wet and red. He sighed and closed his eyes. Another pair of eyes was painted on his eyelids: golden eyes, the eyes of a jaguar. They stared at me, unblinkingly, glinting liquidly.

"Hotspur," the Birdie said. "I have tasted him before. No wonder you are familiar to me. He was a great fighter, a great warrior. To see him on the plinth, with the feather spear in his hand, was a fearsome sight. What a pity he broke. You are his daughter. But you taste of someone else, too."

He raised the bowl again to his lips and I heard the sound of his tongue licking the dregs. Putting the bowl down, he sighed contentedly, eyes still closed. I stared at him, my mind adrift and hazy; he seemed distant and unreal; I felt distant and unreal. Perhaps this was a dream, and soon I would awake, home in my own snug bed, Flynnie at my feet, and Poppy shouting, "The waffles are ready! Do you want syrup or jam?" while the delicious smell of fresh coffee drifted into the room, the sun slanting on the wall, the burr of voices in the kitchen below, Pow shouting happily, the sound of Mamma's bath running—

The Birdie opened his eyes.

"Haðraaða," he said softly. "Ah, I would know that taste anywhere. You are her child, Azota's child. He is your father, but she is your mother. And so I wonder what you are seeking with your own blood."

He took the map and crumpled it up, dropped it in the bowl, where now only a skim of blood remained. Light flashed at his fingertip and the paper exploded into a flare of fire, crackling and hot. The map burned quickly, a thick column of smoke rising up from the bowl, oily gray smoke that twisted and turned like a gauzy veil. The tendrils coiled around each other like a serpent, and then I began to think I actually saw a snake, diaphanous and scaly, floating in the air. The serpent's flat head hinged open, revealing a cavernous mouth and long sharp fangs, a wispy forked red tongue.

The serpent undulated out of my field of vision; I felt a gentle tickle on my ear, and then horrible awful pain, as though someone had hammered a spike through my brain. The pain echoed through my skull, turned my vision black, reverberated through my entire body, sucked all the air out of my lungs. Then it began to recede into something else, something far worse: a tiny squirmy tickle, a horrible itchy sensation of something slithering around inside my head. It was as though my brain was a little house, and each memory, each thought, each emotion a separate room. Now the serpent was slithering through those rooms, rifling through my thoughts, my dreams, my desires, my hopes and fears, looking for my memory of the Blood Working.

Eventually, it found it.

I felt the serpent slither out of my ear. I blinked away tears and saw the smoky serpent hovering before the Birdie. He opened his mouth, and the snake slithered inside. He swallowed. The map was gone, the blood bowl full of ashes.

"She is alive!" the Birdie said, and he sounded almost glad. "I do not know how this can be, for I killed her myself. But it is so."

He ordered me to lie down on the bed, and, of course, I did so. My limbs felt thick and heavy and my head was still spinning. He wrapped me in a blanket, tucking me in like a baby. I felt tired, oh so tired. I was lifted and carried, and then laid down again, this time on the floor. He rolled me over, and by the dust and darkness that suddenly enveloped me, I realized that he had pushed me under the bed.

I desperately wanted to slide into the darkness, to

disappear to a place where none of this was happening, but I forced myself to stay awake. The Birdie's feet walked through my field of vision. He had been wearing black boots; now his feet were bare. His toenails were also painted green and his feet were very long and worm-white. They disappeared under a fall of fabric, which he then kicked off. I heard a thump, and four black paws padded by me.

The Birdie had turned into a jaguar.

He wasn't just any Birdie. He was a nahual and a priest sacred to the Birdie god Tezcatlipoca, the harbinger of death. A skinwalker and a cannibal and a vampire.

And he knew where Tiny Doom was.

I closed my eyes and gave in to the darkness.

TWENTY-FIVE

Luggage.
Escape. Umbrella.

A BLAST OF cool air brought me out of blissful darkness, where there had been no Birdies, no stolen maps, no betrayals, no certain deaths. A hand fastened on my ankle and I was hauled out from under the bed. I opened my eyes; the room was dim, lamp-lit. I was dying of thirst.

"Sit up," the Birdie commanded.

Every muscle in my body screeched with pain.

"Drink."

The Birdie cradled my head, very tenderly, holding a cup to my lips as one would help a child to drink. The water drove an ice-cold spike through the fogginess of my brain. Although I could still not control my body, suddenly I could think more clearly. Probably not what the Birdie had in mind.

"Don't be afraid, muñeca," he said, stroking my forehead. "I promise you, when the time comes, there will be no fear, no pain."

Somehow this tender concern was worse than if he'd just put a knife to my throat. At least the knife was honest.

"I promised her that, and I held to my promise, though now I know she was faithless to me. Ah well, never mind. She'll be true, in the end."

The Birdie gently pushed me over and curled up my legs so my knees lay against my chest. He picked me up, and as my head lolled, I saw a large trunk sitting open in the middle of the room. He laid me inside it, on my side like a sleeping baby. He had put a pillow down and lined the bottom with a blanket—how kind.

He patted my head. "It will not be long. Just until we get off Barbacoa. I am sorry, but there is no other way. Sleep."

He could command my movements, but not that. I no longer felt the tiniest bit sleepy. He closed the trunk lid and I was plunged into darkness. I heard footsteps, a door opening, and then: "Here is my trunk. Be careful with it."

"Oh, no fear of that," the bellboy said cheerfully. "Which ship are you going on?"

"*Grazer.*"

"Oh, ayah, the ferry to Yuma. Going to Arivaipa, then? I got a sister in Arivaipa, a miner. Too hot for me, but she loves the dry!" As the bellboy chattered, the trunk tipped, sliding me against one side, and then began to roll, *bump, bump, bump.*

"I wonder, though, that the ferry will go, Your Grace," the bellboy continued. "It's starting to look nasty outside."

"The ferry will go," the Birdie said with confidence. "I am not concerned with a little bit of weather."

"A little bit of weather! More like a real howler," the chatty bellboy said. "Well, he who lives will see, eh?"

I heard the chime of an elevator. We bumped inside and then plunged downward. A door thumped open and we rolled through, jolted down several stairs, bruisingly, and then stopped. All around me I could hear the muffled sounds of people walking, people talking, the distant tinkle of music. I tried to scream, but I could not.

"I'll have the trunk loaded on your cab, Your Grace."

"Please do. I shall be there directly."

We rolled beyond the cheerful sound of help into a silence that was broken only by a tuneless whistle. The cart bumped down a short flight of stairs, bobbing my head against the top of the box. "Hey, Bob! I need a trunk loaded!"

This yell received no answer. The bellboy muttered under his breath and sat the trunk upright with a thud. Footsteps moved away.

Silence.

I thrashed and whipped my head around and kicked my legs and feet, and moved not an inch. Fiking hell. I had to get out of this trunk before it left the hotel. Once I was on the ferry, I was sunk. Even if I got loose, I'd be trapped with the Birdie, with no aid, no friends, nothing.

Oh, fiking pigface Califa.

I reminded myself I'd been in tight spots before. When I was trapped in Bilskinir's oubliette; when the kakodæmon attacked me and Tiny Doom; when I had to tell Buck I'd failed Secondary Maths. I'd been terrified, but never like this. Never to where I thought I might actually lose my mind with fear. How easy that would be, to give into the horror, to just lie back and let it happen. But if I let that happen, then I was as good as dead. And so was Tiny Doom.

Fear will kill you, said Nini Mo, *faster than any bullet.*

I closed my eyes and took a deep mental breath, imagined my chest inflating and then deflating, the air filling my lungs and leaving them again. I did this three times and, by the fourth, felt calmer and more in control.

The Sonoran Zombie Powder would wear off eventually, but when? If it didn't wear off in the next five minutes, it would be too late. And *too late is the same as never,* Nini Mo said. I had to get out of here now.

Maybe I could project my Anima outside my body, leave my meat and bones trapped behind, and let my mind drift away, escape into Elsewhere. I'd never projected before, but I knew the technique—could it hurt? I took another deep mental breath, trying to relax, trying to imagine myself light as a cloud. But no matter how hard I visualized myself floating free, I remained trapped in a cage of bone and flesh, motionless.

Fike.

If I could have spoken, I would have done a charm to unlock the trunk. Some adepts can subvocalize their Gramatica Commands; they don't need to speak the Words, just think them. But I'm not that good an adept, and I didn't dare try. At best, the Gramatica wouldn't do anything. At worst, it might blow the back of my skull off.

And then I thought of Pig.

I wasn't sure if Pig could get me out of the trunk, but I knew he could handle the Birdie. The Birdie might be a nahual, a wer-jaguar, and a blood-sucking cannibal, but Pig could handle him. Oh, Pig could handle him all right. Hadn't Pig handled a kakodæmon? Hadn't Pig handled a Quetzal? Pig would turn the Birdie into bird feed. Now that I was discovered, there was no reason to be coy with the Haðraaða magick.

The Invocation to summon Pig is almost laughably childish and requires no Gramatica, no funny gestures, no postures, or offerings. I know the Invocation works, because I'd tried it once before, summoning Pig from

Crackpot Hall to my room at the Barracks. He'd been slightly annoyed that there had been no actual enemy but had been solaced with ice cream. I wasn't sure if the Invocation would work without being spoken aloud, but I would try.

Pig, Pig, come to me. I need you to smite my Enemy.

Nothing happened.

Pig, Pig, come to me. I need you to smite my Enemy.

Nothing.

Fike. Maybe you did have to say the Invocation out loud.

Ayah, the rule: the third time is a charm.

Pig, Pig, come to me. I need you to smite my Enemy!

My every nerve was strung to bowline breaking point. The silence was as deep and empty as the ocean. It stretched on and on, forever and forever and forever— and then I heard a familiar sound, a wonderful sniffy snuffling sound, the kind of sound made by a wonderful sniffy snuffling dog.

Flynn!

I tried to call him, but no matter how much I strained, I remained immobile. Snapperdog whined and scratched at the trunk. Clearly he knew I was in there, but he wasn't doing anything helpful about it. My hope, momentarily alert, began to flicker out. Flynn wasn't a trained rescue dog. He wasn't going to run off and tell someone where I was. He wasn't going to open the trunk.

And the Invocation hadn't worked.

I was done.

Flynn barked sharply, and then the trunk lid began to rise up. I blinked against the light, and a shivy nose thrust itself into my face, slurping at me with a slimy pink tongue. I opened my eyes and saw Flynn leaning over me, front paws akimbo on the edge of the trunk. I welcomed the slime, welcomed the doggy breath.

A sticky tentacle brushed my cheek. *Are you all right?*

I'm paralyzed! He used Sonoran Zombie Powder on me!

I know. That's what took me so long. I had to get the antidote. Here. Another tentacle insinuated itself between my nerveless lips, smearing something bitter and gritty on my tongue.

Where'd you get it? I asked, swallowing the sour taste.

I picked it out of the Birdie's bag when he was paying his bill. People shouldn't leave their luggage unattended. There are a lot of unsavory characters out there.

My toes twitched. I could wiggle my toes, and even though they felt prickly and buzzy with sleep, no movement had ever felt better. My left foot jerked and then my right. And my fingers! I clenched my hands into fists. I bit down on my lip and the pain felt glorious.

Let's get the fike out of here before he comes back, Octohands ordered.

I sat up creakily, painfully, every muscle in my body stretching in agony. *How did you find me?*

I was bored in the room and decided to have a little look around.

Flynn was bored, too, so we went together, and we saw you follow the Birdie into his room. I squeezed under the door and saw the whole thing. We've been waiting for a hot moment ever since. Come on, move it.

I hoisted myself over the side of the steamer trunk. My legs were still prickly and weak, but with Octohands's urging, I managed to lock my knees and ignore the pain. Flynn jumped up on me, licking ecstatically.

Come on! Get your hinder rolling!

I wheezed, "I'm coming, I'm coming." My buckskin jacket, boots, and dispatch case had been wedged into the trunk at my feet. With nerveless fingers, I slung the jacket over my shoulders. My fingers were too numb to lace up my boots, so I just thrust my feet into them and left the tongues flapping.

Hurry up! Octohands launched off my shoulder and jetted ahead impatiently, tentacles trailing. I slung my dispatch case over my shoulder and followed him. What I would have given then for my pistol; fike Cutaway and her weapons policy.

The trunk was sitting on a loading dock; beyond the portico, I saw night and rain, a bright spike of lightning, the storm the bellboy had predicted. I toddled across the loading dock and in through the fire door, into a room full of luggage. By the opposite door, a stack of umbrellas leaned against the wall; I grabbed one on my way by. It wasn't much of a weapon against a wer-jaguar, but it was better than nothing. Buck had once killed a jaguar with a shovel; *It's not the weapon that counts,* Nini Mo said, *it's the Will.* I sure as fike had the Will. I staggered down a long, featureless white hallway brilliantly lit by white squares set into the ceiling.

Octohands settled back on my shoulder, coiling a tentacle around my neck. *Where are you going, girlie? We need to get out of here! Out is the other way! We can hide, go to ground until day. Night is the nahual's time—he can't change in the day.*

I have to stop him. He's going to go after Tiny Doom.

Let him go. She can handle him, I'll wager. And if she can't, well, you are the heir. You are who matters.

I can't let him get her. It will be all my fault!

Don't toy with old sweetness, my girl. You haven't the luxury, I tell you.

I stumbled through another set of doors, down a lavish hallway, past tall flower arrangements of orchids and calla lilies smelling to high heaven, past the silvery mirrors with their images of the wild-eyed girl with tentacles mixed into her hair, the prancing red dog following her. The hallway terminated at the elevator. I leaned on the umbrella and punched weakly at the call button.

What's your glorious plan, then? Octohands asked.

I'm going to let the Birdie have it.

Have what?

I pushed the call button again. And again. Where was the fiking elevator?

Everything. Every Curse I've been swallowing for the last six months. I turned you into an Octopus, and turned the Zu-Zu's hair green. Surely I can do something to blow him out of his tracks. If you don't want to help me, I can drop you off right here, Grampy.

With a loud *ping!* the elevator door sprang open and there stood Udo in all his glory, grinning like a fox.

"Udo!" I almost sobbed in relief. "Udo! Thank the Goddess—"

"Thank the Goddess, indeed," he said jovially. "It's my little pigeon. Just the dainty morsel I've been looking for. Faithless oath-breaker! How glad I am to see you. Let's chat, shall we, about what happens to people who try to cheat me."

Oh, fiking hell. Not Udo.

Springheel Jack.

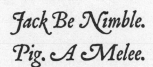

TWENTY-SIX

Jack Be Nimble. Pig. A Melee.

I TURNED TO RUN—or, rather, to toddle slowly—but Springheel Jack reached out with one long arm and, despite my feeble whacking with the umbrella, yanked me into the elevator and into his embrace. Flynn had barely squeezed in with us, when the door sprang closed and the elevator jerked into motion. Jack reached over my shoulder and hit the STOP button. With a squeal, the elevator ground to a halt.

"Let me go!" My struggle was feeble and his embrace was strong.

"Get down!" Jack pushed at the bouncy happy-to-see-him Flynn with one of the Jack Boots. The snakes' heads hissed and Flynn got down, looking confused. I didn't blame him. From the outside, Springheel Jack looked exactly like Udo.

"You look weak-kneed at my appearance." Jack took

the umbrella out of my stiff grip and tossed it away. He was grinning like a weasel with a rabbit in its sights.

"Let me go!"

"I would, but I think perhaps you would not be standing, and much as I love it when people grovel at my feet, in this case, I prefer the armful. You make quite an armful, darling."

I tried to kick his shin. My unlaced boot fell off. Jack just laughed.

I said, "I thought you and Udo had an understanding. You were going to share, or something. This doesn't sound like sharing to me."

"We do have an understanding. And Udo, unlike some people I could mention, keeps his part of the bargain. We take turns. I do with my turn what I will, and he does as he will with his turn, and this is my turn—*oof*—"

When Jack had grabbed me, Octohands launched off my shoulder into the air, where he swirled and jetted just above our heads. Now he dropped onto Jack's shoulder and snaked a tentacle around his neck. Jack gurgled in surprise and let go of me, reaching up to tear Octohands off. I slid to the floor in a muddled heap. But instead of yanking Octohands away, Jack let his hands fall, his face intent with concentration. Clearly Octohands was communicating; I could only imagine what he was saying.

I didn't bother to get up. Before, I would not have

considered Springheel Jack the lesser of two evils before, but compared to the Birdie, he seemed harmless. As long as Jack didn't kill me, I didn't care what he did; it couldn't be worse than what the Birdie had done. And I didn't think, with Udo in there somewhere, that he would kill me. Tears prickled at my eyes, but I blinked them away.

Octohands slackened his grip on Jack and waved a tentacle at me, perching on Jack's shoulder like a squishy parrot. Jack smiled and said, much more kindly, "Ah, now I understand. You should have said so earlier, girlie. Here, have a sippy. It will restore you."

He pressed a silver flask to my lips, and I had to drink or choke. The liquid was chocolatey and it burned as it went down my throat, but it also spread warmth and energy through my veins.

"Said what earlier?" I asked, bewildered by his sudden change of heart. My feet were no longer tingling, my muscles no longer ached. I hoisted myself up, leaning against the elevator wall.

Jack said, "That you were family. Hardhands has filled me in about your little trouble with Sieur Nahual. I shall let you off at your floor. You hightail it to your room, lock the door, and don't come out until it's all over. We'll take care of him, Hardhands and I—"

"What are you talking about, family? And you can't take on a nahual! Don't be a fool—he'll kill you, which means he'll kill Udo—"

"Leave it to us." Jack cut me off. He punched the STOP button again. The elevator began to move, but this time up, not down. "And if the improbable should occur and we should fail, take the boy and run. He's a handsome lad. Udo don't like him, but I think he'll do just dandy."

I grabbed at Jack's lapels, wadding the silk between my fists, and pulled his face down to mine, heedless of the sharp lace scratching at my face and the cravat pin threatening to put out my eye. "Udo! Are you in there? Come on—Udo—it's insane! He's going to get you killed! Udo! *Udo!*"

Jack tried to disentangle me from his coat; I twisted my grip and got a good lock on his queue. His hat fell off. We tussled; he was stronger than me, of course, but I was frantic and that gave me an advantage. I heard the elevator door hiss open, and as Jack tried to thrust me off, I clung to him even harder. Flynn danced around us, yipping happily. He thought we were playing.

"You . . . must . . . let . . . me . . . go, Flora!" he wheezed. I let myself fall into a dead weight, dragging him off balance. "You are the last one—if you die now, the Haðraaða family dies with you. Get off!"

He gave me one last push and I felt him slip through my grasp, felt my knees give way. He turned to face the open door. From the floor, I could see between Jack's planted legs. A cluster of feet were framed in the elevator doorway: a pair of purple court-shoes, a pair of rubber boots, a pair of brown open-toed sandals, and two white knobby feet with green toenails.

Flynn slunk up against me, and I put my hand on his head. The umbrella now within reach, I grabbed it, clutching it with sweaty, cold hands.

"Well," Jack said jovially. "Lookee here!

I heard the Birdie's voice. "Let the woman go."

"Naw, I do not think so, chickadee. She's mine!"

"This woman belongs to the Lord of the Smoked Mirror. You have no right to impede me."

"This is not Birdieland," Jack said. "This is Barbacoa. Who cares here what your glassy god wants? This woman is mine. We had a deal and she broke it. She owes me and I intend that she shall repay me. When I am done with her, you can have her then, if you should still want her."

"It is not wise to get on the wrong side of the Lord of the Smoked Mirror," the Birdie answered.

Jack was not impressed with the Lord of the Smoked Mirror and he said so, in a most uncomplimentary fashion. The people standing to either side of the Birdie began to slide backward, sideways, away. I didn't blame them one bit.

"Come with me, madama," the Birdie ordered, bypassing Jack altogether.

"Fike you!" I said, less afraid now that Jack's bulk was between us. "Your fiking powder wore off, and you can tell your Lord of the Smoked Mirror he can stuff it!"

Jack said, "She's mine and I'm not giving her up."

"You are a fool," the Birdie said.

"I've been called worse," Jack said. "But at least no one has ever called me *Birdie*!"

The elevator doors started to shut. The Birdie stuck a long hand between the closing panels. Jack brought the flat of his dagger down hard, and with a yelping swear, the Birdie yanked his arm back. Flynn barked, twisting in my grip. The elevator doors snapped shut.

"What floor are you on?" Jack asked, turning back to me.

"Four. Flynn! Shut up, get down—Jack, please—"

"Don't worry, Flora. We can handle ourselves. We'll be fine, really. You should see our flick o' the foot. Come on, Flynnie, shut it."

"Udo?" I squinted up hopefully. Jack looked exactly like Udo, so the only way to tell them apart was by expression and words. The glint in Jack's eye was no longer a cold, calculating stealie-boy glint. Now it was a crazy heroic glint. An Udo-glint.

Udo said, "I'm sorry I was such a snapperhead earlier, Flora, really, I am. You should have told me what was going on. I promise, we'll take care of this Birdie fellow."

"Udo, you can't. The guy is a nahual. He's a werjaguar. He'll eat you up—"

The elevator jolted to a halt. Udo said soothingly, "We are professionals. Don't worry."

"*You* are not a professional, Udo!"

The elevator doors opened.

"Jack is. Hardhands is. Oh, look, howdy, Pig."

I peered around Udo and saw Pig sitting serenely in the hallway. He looked jaunty and ready to go. Udo pulled me into an embrace and I flung my arms around his neck. The kiss was brief, but much improved from our last one. Then Udo pushed me and Flynn out of the elevator. I turned around, lunging back, but the elevator doors were already closing. Octohands had jetted out and scooped up Pig, and taken him back to Udo. Udo waved to me jauntily, Pig cradled in his arms.

"Udo! Wait!" I cried.

The doors closed and then reopened. My boot came flying out and almost hit me in the head.

"I'll want more of those kisses later, duckie!" Jack cried jovially, and then the doors closed again. I hammered on the call button to no avail. Fike! Those monumental moronic snapperheads! They were going to get Udo killed! I took a fast moment to put my boot back on and lace both up, then ran toward the stairs.

Fiking Udo, trying to play the hero. No doubt the Jack Boots could take care of themselves, but they didn't have Udo's best interest at heart. Udo could be killed, but the Jack Boots would live on. They'd find another host and resume their life of criminality. But Udo would be dead. True, they had Pig, which tipped the scales in their favor, but Pig was no guarantee of Udo's safety. People get killed in the crossfire all the time. Octohands's bite hadn't even killed Madama Valdosta; I doubted it would have any impact upon a nahual at all.

As I careened down the twisty staircase, Flynn bouncing along behind me, I let all my fear of the Birdie, my irritation at Udo, and my anger at Buck twist and roil and grow, until I felt the Gramatica begin to bubble and turn inside of me, my blood heating, my face flushing. Sieur Birdie was going to be in for a very hot moment when I caught up with him.

As I came to the third-floor landing, I began to hear— above the noise of the rain and wind the clang of steel— shouting, cursing, random screams of fear and excitement. A man came around the corner below me. He was running up the stairs as fast as he could, which wasn't very fast, as he was rather portly and the tails of his frock coat were long and draggy.

"... down there ..." He puffed. "Fight ... jaguar ... pig ... Jack—"

He pushed by and disappeared around the next turn of the stairwell. I held on to the railing and tried to pick up my pace.

On the second-floor landing, the noise of the ruckus was joined by the high-pitched yowling of a very large cat. Three risers down, I heard a loud bellow of pain, followed by a string of cutthroat curses that almost took the paint off the walls.

Flynn reached the fire door and jumped at it, barking hysterically. I was two steps away when I heard a metallic grinding noise, louder than the storm's howl. The walls seemed to ripple and twist. I lost my footing and fell down the last two stairs, landing at the bottom with a bright wrench of pain, my left leg twisted beneath me. Flynn let out a horrible wail. I staggered to my feet, ignoring the pain in my ankle, and hobbled to the fire door, then flung it open.

The lobby was a mess of busted furniture, busted walls, and shouting, crying hotel guests. The front doors were gone, smashed into glittering glass shards. A cold wind gusted through the gaping hole, driving rain into the lobby, soaking the carpet. Pink coldfire dripped from the ceiling.

In the middle of the wreckage, a figure lay facedown amid the splinters of a velvet sofa. I ran to him across the squelching carpet, kicking aside the dented spittoons, broken glass crunching beneath my feet. Udo's hair was sopped with blood, sticky with sweat, and when I pulled on his shoulders, his head flopped back in a sickeningly dead way. Distantly I heard someone screaming Udo's name and distantly realized it was me.

One of Cutaway's minions pulled me off of him; she

was saying something, but I couldn't hear her through my screaming. She shook my shoulders and shouted, "He's not dead, you stupid git!"

I went slack in her hands, and she pulled me to my feet, drew me away. Two more minions gently pulled Udo out of the wreckage and hoisted him between them. As they carried him away, his hair left a slick trail of blood on the ground. His hand dangled; there was something caught in his fingers—a scrap of pink plush.

All that was left of Pig.

TWENTY-SEVEN

An Unhappy Interview.
Regrets. Desperation.

THE MINION IGNORED my wails and frog-marched me out of the lobby, down a flight of stairs, and into a room where a voice said, "No, not there, she'll get blood on my good white sofa."

I was pushed into a chair, and there I huddled, crying bitterly, until a hankie appeared before my face. "Here, take this and blow your nose."

I took the hankie that Cutaway dangled before me. My fingers left red splotches on the fine white fabric. I blew my nose.

"Quit wailing," Cutaway said. "Your friend is not dead."

"He might be soon," I gasped.

"We all might be dead soon," Cutaway said. "But right now we are still alive. That's the important thing."

"If he dies, it will be my fault."

"If he dies, he'll be dead. It hardly matters then whose fault it is. Either way, he'll be a hero. Springheel Jack versus the Nahual. Of such stuff are legends made. I think that boy will enjoy being a hero."

I sniveled, "He's not really Springheel Jack. He's just Udo Landaðon. He stole the Jack Boots from the real Springheel Jack."

"As did the Springheel Jack before him. And the one before him, as well. It's how they all get started on their lives of crime, each Springheel Jack. Stealing the Jack Boots."

"Udo isn't a criminal," I protested.

"He will be by the time the Jack Boots are done. Perhaps you could explain to me why Springheel Jack and the Duque de Espejo y Ahumado were fighting it out in my lobby, Lieutenant Fyrdraaca?"

Somehow I was not surprised that Cutaway knew who I was.

"Who is the Duque de Whatever?" I asked.

"Espejo y Ahumado," Cutaway said impatiently. "Don't try to snow me, girlie. He is the high priest of Tezcatlipoca, the Lord of the Smoked Mirror."

"I never saw him before today! He tried to kidnap me! Udo—Jack—was only trying to protect me!"

"Kidnap you? Why would the Duque do that?"

"I don't know! He said he was going to offer me to his god, or something."

"That seems unlikely," Cutaway said. "The priests of the Smoked Mirror choose their offerings very carefully. They groom them, and tend them, and love them. They cry as they cut out their hearts. They don't have a habit of grabbing the first girl they see. What makes you so special?"

"I don't know."

"Hmmmm . . . Perhaps." I could tell she didn't believe me. "Lucky for you, I am not very curious. A famous criminal, assisted by a protection egregore, and a flying octopus have a knock-down drag-out ruckus in my lobby over a girl hiding behind a false name, who has arrived at my hotel in the company of a Pacifica express agent. Most people would be very curious. But I am not nosy by nature. All I care about is who is going to pay for the damages. And who will that be, I wonder? Should I send a bill to your mother, General Fyrdraaca?"

I grimaced at the thought. "Send your bill to the Duque Whosit. He started everything!"

"I would be happy to do just that. But he's gone. After your egregore exploded, Espejo, in his jaguar form, dashed out into the storm. I sent searchers after him; they report that he boarded a ship and sailed away on the wind. I suspect, in fact, that this storm is his doing. The Lord of the Smoked Mirror likes bad weather. So that just leaves you and my wrecked lobby, which is going to cost a fortune to renovate. What do you suggest I do?"

I had no suggestions. All I could think about was that Espejo was gone, gone after Tiny Doom. And he'd made sure that no one could immediately follow him.

As we were talking, Cutaway had sat down behind her desk. Now she reached for a cigarillo box, opened it, offered it to me. I took one and accepted her light. The tobacco smoke was smooth and tasted like cloves. It made me cough a bit, but it also steadied my nerves.

After taking a drag on her own cigarillo, Cutaway said, "Ah, now, another solution occurs to me. Like you, Sieur Wraathmyr is undercover, isn't he?"

"I don't know what you mean."

She smiled. "I think you do. You don't come across wer-bears every day. Right off the top of my head, I can think of two clients who would pay me well for him. One is always on the lookout for slaves to fight in his pits; the other supplies romance to open-minded people. I could easily get more than enough to pay for the damages to my hotel."

"Barbacoa is supposed to be a free port, madama. I would think that people would think twice about doing their business here if they had to worry about being kidnapped and sold into slavery."

"They only need worry if they don't pay their bills, Lieutenant. And I want them to be worried about that."

A knock at the door interrupted us. Cutaway called out an answer and a minion came in. They had a brief conversation in a language I did not know, and then the minion left. Cutaway turned back to me. "The surgeon is done. Your friend is all sewn up. He'll have a few scars—so dashing—but he'll live."

For some reason, this news, good as it was, set me to crying again. Cutaway ignored my sobbing and said, "Lucky for you, I do not care for Birdies. I particularly do not care for Birdies who show up on my island and break all my rules, and then do a runner without paying their hotel bill. So I think I shall send my request for payment to Espejo after all. But as for you, Lieutenant, I want you off my island as soon as this storm clears, you and your wer-friend both."

I blew my nose again on the soggy hankie. "I wasn't planning on sticking around. I'm going after Espejo."

"I would think that you would be pleased to see the last of him."

"I owe him for Udo," I said, and I did, too.

"Good luck with that. Happy travels, Lieutenant Fyrdraaca. Please do not come back to Barbacoa."

Cutaway gestured to the minion, who hauled me from my chair. We were almost out the door when Cutaway said, "He's got a good head start and once he hits the mainland, he can travel very fast on four legs. Nahuals are nocturnal. He can only change at night, but when he is in his jaguar form, he can move very quickly. I find it hard to believe that you will be able to outpace him."

"I'm going to try."

"Well. You might ask Sieur Wraathmyr for his help, then. If they need to, express agents can get around very quickly. Even more quickly than a jaguar. Goodbye, Lieutenant. My regards to your charming mother."

"Goodbye, madama," I said, making a Courtesy. "And thank you for your kindness."

"One person's kindness is another person's cruelty," Cutaway answered.

Udo was still asleep when I went in to see him. The left side of his face was muffled in a large white bandage that extended up to his hairline. When I picked up his hand, it was limp but warm. I kissed his forehead, just above the bandage. When I touched his hair, my fingers brushed something cold and sticky: a severed tentacle. I picked it up, but the snarky voice did not chime in my head. The Jack Boots sat at the foot of Udo's bed; the snake heads were lifeless, their eyes dull. Perhaps they had finally met their match.

The minions escorted me to my room and told me to stay there until the storm lifted; then they'd put me on the first boat to the mainland. The remnants of the room-service breakfast were still on the table. I took a stale muffin from the basket and sat on the bed, chewing and listening to the wind thump and howl. The windows had been shuttered, so the room was dark. It fit my mood.

Pig was gone; Octohands was gone. Hardhands was already dead, so he could hardly be killed again, but even a ghost can be destroyed, its Anima shredded, dissipated. Udo *had* almost been killed. And all because I was a moronic, snapperheaded idiot. I had been so prideful, so sure that I could make a difference, that I alone could save Califa by finding Tiny Doom. I had thought that Buck was powerless and cast-down, too weak to lift a hand against the Birdies, and here it turned out she was busy with a plan much better than mine. A plan she hadn't trusted me to share—and with good reason. If I'd known before, Goddess knows what I would have done to mess everything up. *Everyone has a talent,* Nini Mo said, and mine was clearly fiking things up bigtime. Now Espejo was heading directly toward Tiny Doom, and here I was, trapped on Barbacoa, unable to do a thing to warn her. I got up to get another muffin and noticed Tharyn's satchel laying on the bed. A new horror seized me.

Tharyn! Where was Tharyn? When Espejo had left me alone in his room—when he had turned to a jaguar— had he gone back to get Tharyn? Cutaway had spoken as though Tharyn was still alive, but maybe she didn't know. Maybe Tharyn was lying dead right now in some alley, shredded, clawed, rain falling on his empty face, his blank eyes. Maybe he was lying wounded in some ravine, the rain washing the blood out of his veins—these thoughts propelled me toward the door, which, when I opened it, was blocked by a minion.

"Go inside," she said.

"Tharyn Wraathmyr! Have you seen him?"

"Go inside."

"I have to look for him!"

"Inside," said the minion, and shut the door on me. When I tried the door again, it was locked. I pounded and shouted to no avail. The minion remained immovable and so did the door. I ran to the window; the rain was sheeting down, thunderously, an occasional flash of pink breaking through the darkness. At four floors up, it was too high to climb down, anyway.

I couldn't just do nothing, but there was nothing I could do. So I paced, and listened to the thunder and the rain, and chewed on my fingers, and cursed myself for being such an idiot as to drag everyone into this to begin with, and cried a bit at my own stupidity, and ate another muffin, and wished with all my heart I was back in Califa, sitting behind my desk, copying some ordnance return, blissfully ignorant, or changing Pow's diaper, anything but in this mess I was in now, getting everyone I cared about killed. Sometimes waves of terror would rush over me as I remembered the feeling of Espejo's serpent slithering through my brain, and then I would sit down on the bed and scream into my pillow until my jaw ached and my throat was raw. I was trapped, it was too late, it was over—

The door opened and there was Tharyn.

I jumped on him, sobbing hysterically. He caught me, lifting me up, making soothing noises, and said, "Hush. It's all right. It's all right."

"I thought you were dead! That he got you, like he almost got Udo!" I sobbed. He was soaking wet and he smelled of salt, but even his soggy embrace felt solid. Flynn jumped and bobbed around our legs, pawing at Tharyn. He pushed Flynn down gently, then carried me over to the settee.

"Stop crying, honey," he said soothingly.

"He almost got Udo! And he did get Pig and Octo-hands," I sniveled.

"Well, he didn't get me. Whoever he is. Maybe you should tell me what happened," Tharyn suggested.

I nodded and gulped, then told him.

When I was done, Tharyn said, "What an idiot I was! When we were on the road, I smelled cat but I didn't think anything of it. I should have been more on guard. I should have been more careful. But I was—well—I was distracted."

"Not as distracted as I was," I said bitterly.

He cursed again. "Fike it all! I left the Envoy's and needed a bit of a breather, so I went for a run . . ."

That explained the twigs in his hair. I blew my nose again on the now very soggy hankie. "It's just as well, Tharyn. He might have killed you. He almost killed Udo."

"He could have tried," Tharyn said. "I think I could have handled him. I am not a popinjay."

"Udo's not a popinjay, either! Well, he is, but he had help—pretty good help, too."

"Udo. I thought he dumped you," Tharyn said. "And you were very angry at him."

"He did. I mean, he kinda did. It was complicated."

"Yet you are upset that he was almost killed."

"We've been friends for years. Of course I am upset, and it was all my fault, too. But listen, Tharyn, Espejo knows about my mother, my real mother. He knows where she is. He's gone after her. But I'm stuck on this fiking island until the storm clears. He's got a big head start. He'll get there before me, and kill her. And it will be all my fault. I have to go after him. As quickly as possible. I have to get there first, warn her. Cutaway told me that express agents have a way to travel very quickly. What did she mean?"

"She said that, did she?" Tharyn said. He said something else in a language I didn't know. Kulani, perhaps, or maybe Varanger. It sounded like a curse.

"What did she mean?" I repeated. "I have to catch up with Espejo. I can't fly, nor can I translocate. It's way too far, and I'm not that good of a magician. I have to get there first and warn her! If you know a way to do it, a way I can beat Espejo, tell me, for Choronzon's sake, tell me!"

He didn't answer, just rocked back and forth, chewing his lip. Finally, when I was about to scream with impatience, he said, "I do know another way. But it's risky. Very risky."

"I don't care. I have to try. You have to try. You owe me three times. I have saved your life. And you owe me."

"I know it." Tharyn sighed. "By the Goddess, I know it."

TWENTY-EIGHT

Invocations.
Elsewhere. Bargains.

*H*AMISHA, THE BELL GIRL, promised she would take care of Flynn and then, when the storm was over, take him to the Pacifica Express office and get him passage back to Califa. I hated to leave him, but Tharyn said he could not go with us. So I kissed Flynn and left him curled up on the bed, Hamisha scratching his tum and feeding him chicken. He'd be safer at home, anyway.

I expected Cutaway's minions to stop me from leaving, but the guard outside our door was gone. The mess in the lobby was mostly cleaned up. Two minions were nailing boards over the broken windows, and the soggy carpet had been rolled up and carted away, revealing a sodden wood floor. As soon as we got out from under the hotel awning, the wind hit us, almost knocking me off my feet. Tharyn grabbed me and held on. Heads down, we fought our way across the drive and down the street. The rain felt as sharp as nails.

"Are you sure we can't do this inside?" I shouted.

"We need a crossroad! Come on. It's not far!"

We were the only ones out. The water on the street was ankle deep—or at least ankle deep on Tharyn. On me, it was more like knee-deep, a torrential river in which I struggled to stay upright. Above, the sky was a roiling leaden mess. A queer twilight had descended, a greenish gray light that made the town look underwater.

By the time we made it to the intersection, we were drenched. The cab shelter was small, but it did provide some protection. Tharyn put his satchel down on the bench and took a piece of paper out of his jacket. The wind had torn his hair from its queue, snarled it into a great tangle of curls, which made him look even more bearish than usual. I wanted to lay my head on his chest and close my eyes. Instead, I said, "I warn you, I won't get into a box. I've had enough of boxes for an eternity."

"No, nothing like that," Tharyn said. "Before we do this, I have to tell you, Nini, in all fairness, that I've only made an overnight delivery once, and it wasn't very a big package. You are a lot bigger. This is going to be very expensive."

"I don't care how expensive it is. The Bilskinir estate is fabulously rich. I can afford it. Though I'll have to write a postdated check—"

"The cost isn't in money. That would be too easy. If it were only money, everyone would use this method."

"What else can you pay with?"

"Each courier has their price."

"That other overnight. What did its sender pay?"

"A year off his life."

I thought Tharyn was joking, but he wasn't smiling.

"Are you serious?"

"Ayah. Are you willing to pay such a price?"

A year off my life. That was pretty steep. But if Espejo got Tiny Doom and then came back for me, I wouldn't have much life left, anyway. As if to underscore that point, a bolt of lightning cracked overhead and the walls of the shelter rattled.

"Ayah, ayah. I am willing. Let's get on with it. "

I took the address label he offered me. On it was written: *Poste restante, Fort Sandy, Arivaipa Territory.*

"What does 'poste restante' mean?" I asked.

"It means there's no actual address. The package goes to general delivery."

"Am I going to just show up at the post office in Fort Sandy?" I asked, horrified. If I materialized in the middle of the Fort Sandy post office, how in the fike would I explain that?

"No, of course not. This is just to get the order going. We'll discuss the actual delivery address with the courier. Actually, I don't think Fort Sandy even has a post office. It's the back end of beyond, Nini."

Tharyn took his jacket off and rolled it up. He'd never reclaimed the shirt he'd wrapped around Flynn and apparently he didn't have another. In the greenish-gray underwater light, the tattoos on his chest were inky black and seemed to undulate and waver.

Move forward, said Nini Mo, *and don't look back—even if you can hear the snapping of the wolves on your tail.*

I took Tharyn's outstretched hand and we stepped out into the storm. The driving rain stung my face like needles; I bent my head and tried to stay in the shelter of Tharyn's back, allowing him to pull me to the center of the intersection. It was slow going in the wind, but Tharyn was very strong, and eventually we made it. I wrapped my arms around him, buried my face in his chest, feeling the pound of rain on my back, his skin wet, slick, and warm beneath my cheek.

I couldn't hear his Invocation over the roar of the wind, the thunder of the rain, but I could hear it vibrating through his flesh. The hum started off low and slowly gained intensity until my tonsils quivered, my blood vibrated, my bones hummed in unison, and our voices blended and became one.

Distantly, I heard a howl and looked down to see a familiar red dog squirming between our legs: Flynn had somehow escaped the hotel and now added his voice to ours. The wind joined in, merging into one infinitely long note. I no longer felt the rain on my back, the cold whipping into my neck. No longer felt Tharyn pressed against me, the weight of my own body. My skull was ringing, until the noise was too big for bone to contain and I was sure that my head would split from the pressure, and then—

"All right! All right! Stop that caterwauling! I hear you! I hear you! Be quiet!"

The shout cut through like a hot knife in ice cream. The rain was gone, the wind gone. We stood in absolute silence. I raised my head and saw Tharyn looking over his shoulder, his face full of astonishment and dismay.

"Fike," he said. "Are you the courier?"

"None other," said Cutaway Hargity. She wore a crimson cocktail dress and held a champagne glass. She looked very irritated. The storm was gone. The sky above us was blue and as flat as paint, and the buildings looked almost one-dimensional, like stage scenery. We were Elsewhere.

"How can you be the courier?" I asked. Then I said to Tharyn, "I thought you told me that the courier was a dæmon."

"I am a dæmon. I am the Governor of Barbacoa, the denizen of this island," Cutaway said. "I have the contract for the Pacifica Mail and Freight. And I run various other business concerns on the side. You have a delivery for me?"

"I do, madama," Tharyn said. "A rush job. Very urgent."

"Where's the package?"

"Me. I am the package," I answered, and from the smile that curved across Cutaway's face, I had the feeling that she had known already. After all, hadn't she pointed me here to begin with? Why? I also had the feeling that I wouldn't like the answer.

"Hmmm," she said. "This is quite unusual. I have never transported a package so large before. Have you, Sieur Wraathmyr?"

"No, madama. But the circumstances are unusual."

"Maybe so. How many express packages have you sent?"

Tharyn glanced at me somewhat sheepishly before answering. "Only one, madama."

"Somehow that doesn't surprise me a bit. I know you know that transporting living creatures is explicitly forbidden. Surely you are familiar with the case of Tomas Bandicoot."

"I am," Tharyn said uncomfortably. "But that courier was new and inexperienced. Surely you, Madama Cutaway, would have no such problems."

"You do me great honor in saying so, but I am not so sure."

"What happened to Tomas Bandicoot? Who was Tomas Bandicoot?" I asked.

Tharyn answered, "He was an idiot who tried to have himself sent express from Porkopolis to Bexar on a dare. So he and some of his drunken pals stuffed him in a box and sent him off. The courier didn't know what was in the box; of course, the bill of lading said it was bricks or something. Anyway, the box got lost in transit."

"Did they ever find it?"

"Well, eventually, they found it. It was empty."

"Not entirely," Cutaway said, smiling.

"No, not entirely empty," Tharyn agreed. "After that, the Pacifica refused to ship humans, and also made a rule that express packages had to be accompanied by an agent at all times."

"But you are human. How come it's not dangerous for you?"

"He's a skinwalker," Cutaway said. "He's only part human. Skinwalkers—those born that way, that is—are all praterhuman-human hybrids. Didn't you know that?"

I had not known that. And now that I did, I wasn't sure how I felt about this knowledge. But I didn't have time to think about it.

"I told you it was not without risk, Nini," Tharyn said.

"And I said I didn't care. I'll take the chance. I doubt that Madama Hargity ever lost a package."

"I have not, actually," Cutaway said. "But if I do this, I jeopardize my contract with the Pacifica. It's a lucrative contract, not just Elsewhere, but in the Waking World as well. So it's going to cost you."

"It's fine. I'll pay. Whatever you want, I'll pay."

"Well, then, let us waste no more time. Thank you, Sieur Wraathmyr. I shall take it from here."

"But I'm the agent," Tharyn protested.

"I can't take you both," Cutaway said. "It's too much. Don't you trust me with your package?"

I looked at Tharyn in dismay. I had expected that he would go with me, and the thought had lent me a lot of courage. Now to find out I would have to go alone—this made my tum twist with fear. *Suck it up,* said Nini Mo, *before it sucks up you.*

I said, "I'll be fine, Tharyn. Madama Hargity said herself that she didn't wish to jeopardize her contract with the Pacifica. She'll take good care of me."

"Oh, yes, I shall. And I will tell you what. Since I'm obviously in a generous mood today, or I wouldn't even consider doing something so silly, you can bring the dog. I won't even charge you extra, just because he is so very sweet."

"Done." I turned to say goodbye to Tharyn.

But he was already gone. And so was the road, and the flat buildings, the blue sky. Flynn and I were following Cutaway down a short flight of marble steps, across a wide sidewalk slick with recent rain. All around us, buildings, gleaming silver and wet, rose like mountains above us, so tall they seemed to scrape the sky. Flashbulbs popped all around, voices shouting, *This way, Cutaway!* And *Where's Jaredo, Cutaway?* And *Cute dog!*

Cutaway ignored the catcalls. She had changed clothes; now she wore a black evening gown. The silk clung to her like shiny wet paint and trailed along behind her in a wispy train. But the scissors still dangled at her waist.

Ahead, a man in a black uniform and a peaked cap was holding open the door of a long, squat carriage. Cutaway ducked inside, and as I followed her, I saw that the carriage had no horses in front. Inside, two low seats faced each other. I sat down across from Cutaway.

Faces pressed against the windows, mouths open, but I couldn't hear what they were saying through the glass. Flynn jumped up next to Cutaway and peered out the window, drooling with excitement.

"Where to, madama?" the driver asked.

"Give me your address label," Cutaway commanded.

I handed it to her, and she glanced down at it. "Fort Sandy, Arivaipa, eh? That's a long way from here. And there's no Pacifica office in Fort Sandy. I'll have to take you all the way there myself. It's very inconvenient."

She said something to the driver in Gramatica, Words that I did not know. Here in Elsewhere, the Words had no spark. I sat my dispatch case at my feet and settled back for the ride.

328

With a hiss, a panel of glass glided up behind me, cutting us off from the driver. The coach began to move, so smoothly and silently that it took me a moment to realize that we were moving.

"What kind of a carriage is this?" I asked.

"It's a stretch Phaeton," Cutaway said. "Nice, isn't it? Such wonderful suspension. Rides like a dream. I can't understand why it never sold well."

"Where are we?"

Cutaway was fiddling under her seat; she produced a cut-glass bottle and two glasses, and sat them on the small table she folded down from the door. "On our way, Lieutenant Fyrdraaca, on our way. But before we get much further, let's discuss the matter of the price." She poured herself a drink and then offered a glass to me, but I shook my head.

"I told you I would pay whatever you asked."

"So you did. You are aware that this means I could ask for anything—your left ring finger, your favorite teddy bear, your life?"

"I'm not an idiot," I said. "I know what I agreed to. You can have any of those things, but you have to get me to Arivaipa first."

"No, I suppose you are not an idiot. Tempestuous and harebrained, but not an idiot. Lucky for you, I have no need for any extra fingers, I never cared much for teddy bears—"

"I don't have a favorite teddy bear, anyway."

"And I don't see what good your life would do me, it being so undeveloped and green, hardly ripe. And somewhat bitter. But you know who does want your life? Your Birdie friend. He seems to want it pretty badly, and to him, I'll bet it's worth a whole lot."

Here came the setup. The whole thing had been a trap. Cutaway was going to sell me out to the Birdies. No wonder she had refused to bring Tharyn with us. But I knew Cutaway wanted me to be afraid, that she was hoping I would be afraid and would show it. I was determined not to favor her. I said nonchalantly, "If you sell me out to Espejo, then you'll be breaking your contract with the Pacifica. Can Espejo pay you enough to make up for that?

"Oh, I'll just tell the Pacifica that the package was lost in transit. It does happen. And I dare say that your friend Sieur Wraathmyr will not want to admit what was in the package, for fear of his own position. They'll fire him if they realize what he's done."

"You are wrong." I wasn't sure if she was or not.

"Or perhaps I have already had my minions take ahold of Sieur Wraathmyr and am planning on selling him, too. Double my profit."

"Before, in your office, you said you'd let Tharyn go."

"I never said that. I only said I'd send the bill to Espejo and I wanted you off Barbacoa. But let's cut to the chase, Lieutenant Fyrdraaca. I'm a businessdæmon. I've got expenses to cover and employees to pay, and at the end of the year, I want to see lots of beautiful black numbers in my account books. I do not like red ink. Your petty human fighting has cost me a great deal and jeopardized my bottom line. I do not like to be in the red. Espejo can pay enough to balance my books again, at least get rid of the red ink, if not actually move back into a profit."

She continued, "However, lucky for you, I do realize that there is more to life than the bottom line. I've been Governor of Barbacoa for a long, long time. It's a rough place, and I've seen a lot of things. Now I find I'm bored. Barbacoa is wide-awake, but after a while, you've seen it all. Money can't buy everything."

"Then why were you threatening to sell me to Espejo if you don't care about the money?"

"I wasn't threatening," Cutaway said. "I was reminding you that I could. No, the money would be nice, but you have something else that would be nicer, I think."

Already I had learned that when someone smiles in just that way, whatever came next would involve something painful for me or happy for someone else. It was the same smile the head prefect at the Barracks used when she was telling someone to report to the Commandant for a flogging.

I said, resigned, "What do you want, Madama Hargity?"

"I want your love for Udo."

TWENTY-NINE

The Payment.
A Journey. Freezies.

THE PHAETON GLIDED ON through the night. I caught glimpses of rain-soaked streets and soggy figures, some huddling under big black umbrellas, as round and black as beetle carapaces. Once, the carriage crossed a long bridge, its lamp-lit struts arcing high above us; underneath was water, black as coffee, traced with the lights of ships. Off in the distance, city lights twinkled. After the bridge, there were no streets, no people, nothing but the road slipping by under our wheels, impossibly fast and impossibly smooth.

"I can't give you Udo," I said eventually. "He's not mine to give."

"Of course he's not. I want your love for Udo, Flora. Udo I can get for myself—should I decide I want him."

"Then why do you want it?"

"Because I see your love for him inside of you and it's shiny bright. I like shiny bright things."

"How can I give you my love for him?"

"Don't you worry about that. Do we have a deal? You give me your love for Udo and I'll get you to Arivaipa. As I said before, the dog rides for free. And I will not sell you out to the Birdies."

"And Tharyn?"

"May go his furry way unmolested by me. It's a generous offer, Flora. And after all, am I not asking for something you don't even really want? I heard you and Udo fighting in the bar. You said you didn't care if you never saw him again. Of course, that wasn't true at all, as the fit you threw in my office showed. But I can make it true."

Of course I had said hot things during our fight. I always said hot things. And Udo did, too, but we always regretted those things later and made up. Didn't we?

Cutaway continued, "And he doesn't love you, anyway. I saw him with the other one, the Zu-Zu. He's obviously crazy for her. Why waste your love on someone who doesn't want it? Give it to me, and you'll be free to find someone who will love you back."

"You mistake me, madama. I mean, I love Udo, but I don't *love* him."

"Don't you?" Cutaway said. "Well, then, all the easier for you. If you don't *love* him, then your love is easy to give up. You'll hardly miss it. And if Udo gets himself killed, you won't care a bit. How nice that will be, eh? How lucky for you that the price I ask hardly costs you a thing. If you want to love someone, there's always the bear. He's half in love with you already, and oh, what a chest he has. And I think you are not fully immune to his charms."

If I was honest, I had to admit that she was right. I was not fully immune to Tharyn's charms. He was solid where Udo was flighty, and sensible where Udo was flippery. He didn't chastise me or treat me like a child. He understood me in a way that Udo, brought up in a happy family, could not. We had a lot in common. When I was with him, I felt safe and secure. I liked him an awful lot. But I didn't love him.

Udo. As far back as I can remember, Udo has been constant. When dusty dirty Crackpot Hall, with Poppy screaming in the Eyrie, had been too much and I had gone on the bum, Udo had cheered me. And even when I couldn't be cheered up, he'd made me come stay with him at Case Tigger with his giant family of happily squabbling siblings and his three stable, loving parents. He had brought me back to life, even after I had drowned, so that I could save the Loliga. He had tried to rescue me from Espejo. He had lent me fifty divas when I ruined the teakettle making green hair dye (even though Buck had told me specifically not to make green hair dye in the teakettle), so I could replace it without Buck finding out. He had let me copy his maths homework when crazy Poppy had used mine as kindling. When he was captured by the pirates and I'd thought I would never see him again, my heart had felt pierced by a fiery needle. When I thought he might die of his injuries at Barbacoa, a part of me had felt that life without Udo was not worth living.

I did *love* him. I had just been too stupid and stuck-up and blind to see it. Oh, Flora, you fiking snapperhead!

But Tiny Doom. She had given me life, given me up, tried to protect me, and I had led Death directly to her. She was my mother. I had to save her. No matter what the cost.

Cutaway said, "Look, I'll even sweeten the deal, Flora. Not only shall I take your love for Udo, but I'll take away your memory of your love for Udo. You'll never even know you've lost something. Come, come—decide. We are wasting time here, and you told me before that you had no time to waste."

"You have to promise me you won't do anything to Udo."

"Of course I will not do anything to Udo. This is between you and me. Do we have a deal?"

I had no choice. I had to get to Fort Sandy and this was the only way to do it. And anyway, the sacrifice was all on my side. Anyone who almost gets you killed is someone you are better off without. Udo had the Zu-Zu. He had his sparkly red Jack Boots and his newly minted heroic stature and his pirate ship. He did not need me. He did not love me.

"Ayah, madama. We have a deal."

"Excellent."

At Cutaway's order, I pulled open my jacket, unbuttoned my bodice, and unsnapped the front of my stays. "Is this going to hurt?"

"Depends on your definition of hurt." Cutaway unsheathed her scissors. The blades were very long and looked very sharp. I didn't see how it wasn't going to hurt, but, well, *Grin and bear it,* Nini Mo said. I tried to grin, hoping that this would help me bear it.

"Hold still!" she ordered, and plunged the scissors through my chemise, into the middle of my chest. I shrieked, flailing, and she pushed me back onto the seat with one hand, saying, "Hold still!"

But there was no pain, just a strange tingly sensation. I quit thrashing, and looked down. Although Cutaway had sliced a large incision in my chest, there was no blood or guts. She stuck one hand into the gash and began to fiddle around ticklishly.

I giggled. "That feels really funny."

"Lucky you. Let's see, your love for Udo, where is it? I see your love for chocolate . . . Here's your love for dogs . . . Love for your little brother . . . It's got to be here somewhere. Ah, here it is, but it's very tangled."

"Tangled with what?"

She had pulled a thick skein of sparkling threads out of me, like a wad of tangled knitting. Now she picked through the threads, trying to unknot them. Some glittered redly, others were a sticky oily black. Some were gossamer and blue, others clear like ice.

"Oh, fear and desperation, desire and anger—you know, the usual things knotted up with love. What a mess! Hold still. This is going to be tricky." Now it wasn't so ticklish; I was beginning to feel a weird painful stretching, like my muscles were being overextended. "It's no use; I'm going to have to take it all. It's too bound up together."

Before I could protest, the scissors went *snip-snip*. The weird painful stretching feeling disappeared. Cutaway held the wad up, examining it, and then slipped the wad into her purse, out of which she produced a small sewing kit. Removing a very large curved needle threaded with red thread, she began to sew me up. That didn't hurt, either.

"Those are awfully big stitches. Am I going to have a scar?"

"Not that anyone will see. There you go. All done. Get some rest. We've a long way to go yet."

Cutaway yawned, snapped a facemask over her eyes, and lay back against the seat cushions. I pulled my clothes back together. I was exhausted, but too keyed up to sleep. Each mile we went took me further from Califa, away from Buck, and Pow, and Poppy, and Tharyn, away from Paimon and Valefor, away from everything and everyone I had ever known. I was alone now, truly alone. No, not entirely alone, a pesky wet nose reminded me; I scratched his ears gratefully. Whatever was to come, I would face it with Flynn. And that was, somehow, a big consolation.

Cutaway snored delicately. The gentle rocking and the muted roar of the carriage were lulling. *Conserve your energy and don't fret ahead,* Nini Mo said. I gave in to that lull and leaned my head against the cold glass. Eventually I fell asleep.

A LONG TIME later, I woke up to a slam and a slant of light. The driver was peering in through the open door. His skin was mint-green and he had one eye, right in the middle of his forehead.

Cutaway sat up, stretching.

"Are we there yet?" I asked.

In answer, she sang, "*The moon has riz, the moon has set, and here I iz in Elsewhere yet!* Alas, no. Not yet. This is Las Palmas."

The Phaeton had pulled up before a long, narrow building. Tall street lamps marked out a square of harsh white light; beyond that, darkness. A glowing green sign hung on the building: WIGGLY PIGGLY.

I left Flynn in the Phaeton; he leaned against the window and yapped mournfully as I walked away. Inside the Wiggly Piggly, loud music, heavy on the horns, was blaring. The air smelled of overfried pork. I followed Cutaway to a hallway at the back of the store, where two doors stood side by side. One had a sign with a silhouette of a cartoon bull with its legs crossed; the other had a cow in the same position.

"So cute," said Cutaway, and picked the door with the bull. While I waited for my turn, I examined the papers taped along the wall across from the bathroom. They looked like Wanted posters, but instead of bad drawings, each had a blurred ferrotype image on it.

MISSING: GOOD WILL. ON Saturday, August 22nd, LENA ERICKSON lost all her Good Will on the No. 19 Crosstown Bus when a Man Wearing a Black Cowboy Hat Tripped and Spilled Hot Coffee on her Cross Word Puzzle and then Cursed Her for Being in His Way. Ten Dollar Reward for Its Return. No Questions Asked.

MISSING: WILL TO LIVE. On the Sixteenth Germinal II, Philippe François Nazaire Fabre d'Églantine lost his Will to Live when He stood before the Hôtel Crillon and realized that Madam Revolution didn't care one wit about his calendar. No Reward. No Expectation of Return.

MISSING: WILL POWER: On the sixty-first day of their voyage in the ship FIREDRAGON, Sven Redsock did finally lose all his Will Power and drink the last of the mead, thus causing Hakon Dirtyhair to call him a PIG SWILLING SON OF A TROLL and Throw Him Overboard, thus making Sven the first Norse man to set foot on Markland. Pity the rest of him did not make it. Fifteen silver pieces REWARD so his Spirit May Go to Valhalla Whole.

"What are these posters about?" I asked Cutaway when she came out of the bathroom. She shrugged, fluffing her hair.

"People lose their Will. They want their Wills back again, but they can't find them, so they offer rewards. It's a waste of time. When your Will is gone, it's gone."

"I lost my Will once, and I got it back."

Cutaway smiled. "Did you, now? Hurry up, I'm dying of thirst."

The bathroom was black with grime, and smelled like mold. I managed to get in and out without touching anything but the floor. At the front of the store, our driver was sucking on a lollipop and holding two giant cups. "Do you want an orca bacon dog?" he asked Cutaway, gesturing toward the counter with one of the drinks. On the counter, a row of fat red cylinders were displayed in a glass-fronted silver case. Now I knew where the overfried meat smell was coming from.

"Goddess, no. You know I'm a vegetarian, Roger. Is that my freezie?"

"Ayah. Beetroot, just like you like."

"Thank you, Roger. Do you want a drink, Flora? The freezies here are excellent; that's why we always stop here. I recommend the beetroot salt and pepper, but the cucumber soy rhubarb is also lovely."

"I don't want anything, thank you," I said. I was hungry enough that the orca bacon dogs almost smelled good. But it seemed maybe not such a good idea to eat anything while I was with Cutaway. I've heard plenty of stories about witless people who eat the wrong thing at the wrong

340

time and end up enchanted or ensorcelled, and I'd already done both this year. Better hungry than sorry.

The slack-jawed clerk rang us up. Roger paid with an unfamiliar green bill, and then we went back to the Phaeton. Beyond the glare of the white lights, the blackness was beginning to fade to purplish pink. I was reassured. The darkness was just night. And night always ends.

The Phaeton roared through a thin pink dawn, which revealed the landscape as scrubby and flat, occasionally punctuated with a spindly tree or a weird iron sculpture, parts of which pistoned up and down. Cutaway had stuck little white stones into her ears and closed her eyes. Faint tinny music emanated, pulsing and droning. I slumped, with my head against the window, and watched the scrub go by, the trees slowly growing thicker until we were traveling through a forest, dark and dim. Sometimes I caught glimpses of animals, shadowy among the trees, like deer, only bigger and with sharp jagged antlers. I saw a red fox crushed by the side of the road; a huge black bird was dipping into the cavity of the fox's stomach, stringing out long skeins of gut with its beak. And once we passed a little yellow house with a girl in front of it; she waved as we passed by, but by the time I waved back, she and the little yellow house were long gone.

After several hours of the forest, the trees began to give way to muddy fields, patched with black-and-white cattle that watched our passage with bovine indifference.

Now the Phaeton was climbing up, the road twisting and turning around a rocky landscape. The trees and the fields disappeared and were replaced with high rocky cliffs, occasionally punctuated with roaring waterfalls, and, off in the distance, jagged granite mountains.

We climbed higher and higher, and below us I could see the road we had traveled over, gleaming like a silver snake in the barren gray-green landscape. Snow began to appear along the side of the road, first just a thin veil, and then piled high, so that the land looked smothered in a giant eiderdown. We passed through a brief tunnel, and when we popped out, we were surrounded by a gleaming expanse of glassy-white ice: a glacier. Dark fissures criss-crossed the rippling ice. I saw a gash of bright blue water far below, bounded by mountains.

"Where are we?" I asked Cutaway, but she didn't answer. Her eyes were still closed and now the tinny music was dirge-like, throbbing.

The Phaeton went through another tunnel and emerged into a sea of green tasseled corn, twelve feet tall or higher. The corn lasted the rest of the afternoon, and as a large round moon began to peek over the fringy tops, I began to get alarmed. Time works differently in Elsewhere, but I wasn't sure we actually *were* Elsewhere. In fact, I had no fiking idea where we were. But we'd been traveling all night and all day, with no sign of stopping and no indication that our destination was any closer. The whole point was a speedy delivery. This did not feel like a speedy delivery to me.

The fields of corn disappeared into the darkness, and the moonlight vanished as we began to pass lighted buildings, more and more until we were traveling through a city again, passing other Phaetons, people hurrying along the streets, glittering bright signs, brilliant shop windows. Then the lights, the people, the buildings began to thin again and we were back in a moonlight landscape of rolling hills.

And then we stopped.

Cutaway opened her eyes and pulled the white stones out of her ears. "I do love The Tygers of Wrath," she said. "Out you go."

The Phaeton's door opened. A blinding white light angled into the dark interior, so blinding I could not see beyond it. The light was accompanied by a blast of furnace-like air.

"Are we there?" I asked.

"We're here and this is as far as I go. Traffic report says there's a bit of a jam up ahead and I have to get back to the office. But first—I like you, Nini. You remind me of myself at your age. Espejo is not an adept, he's a priest, a very powerful nahual, probably the most powerful nahual alive. Or dead. Or whatever the fike he is. But he does have a pretty big weakness."

"Ayah?" I said warily.

"His power comes through Tezca and is rooted in darkness. Night is his time. At night he is almost invincible. He can't change into the god's totem animal during the day. And he can't stand the sun. It won't kill him outright, but it weakens him greatly. Makes him sluggish. Foolish."

"What does he do during the day, then?"

"Takes shelter. A house, a hotel, a hole in the ground. Anything to avoid the sun. And Arivaipa is a very sunny place. Come on, out you go. You are letting all the cool air out."

Roger stuck a clipboard in my face. "Sign this, please."

"What is it?"

"Delivery confirmation."

I took the pencil he offered and scrawled my signature at the bottom of the paper. Flynn had already jumped out of the Phaeton and vanished into the blazing white glare. I clambered out after him into blinding white sunlight, holding my hand up to my eyes, trying to see where I was. Then I felt the unmistakable feeling of a boot in my back. As I stumbled forward, I heard Cutaway say, "If you need anything else, Madama Haðraaða, let me know. It's a pleasure doing business with you. Please give my regards to Paimon."

I tried to catch myself but my hands grabbed at nothing. Air roared in my ears, and then I hit something hard in a blur of gravelly pain.

THIRTY

Stage Stop.
Hot. Captain Oset.

MY HEAD FELT as though it had been split in two and reassembled hastily, without matching up the seams. The slurpy pink tongue on my face was slimy, but at least it was wet. The rest of me felt shriveled and dry. Something hard and splintery was digging into my back. I thought I was alive, but I had felt alive before and been dead, so that feeling didn't signify much at all.

But if I was dead, then Flynn was dead, too, because, when I opened my eyes, there he sat, looking as eager as always. I gotta give Flynnie credit; he remains perky no matter what. He did not look like a dog that had gone on a very long coach ride through Elsewhere—or wherever the fike we had been. He looked like a dog who had just been for a long walk, with balls to chase, and who now anticipated beef stew for lunch. Darling Flynn.

"Oh, Flynnie!" I reached for him. I guess I wasn't as dry and shriveled as I thought, but I wasn't sure why I was crying. I was alive. Flynn was alive. And we were also, I discovered when I sat up, in the bottom of a well. This I deduced by the wreckage of the bucket under me. I doubted that the bottom of a well was poste restante, Fort Sandy, Arivaipa Territory. Obviously, Cutaway thought it would be a funny joke to drop me here instead.

"Har, har, you stupid snapperheaded witch," I said, and Flynn barked once, as though he agreed.

Well, as long as I was in Arivaipa, she could have her little joke. But I cursed her again when I realized I didn't have my dispatch case; it must have been left on the floor of the Phaeton. When I was ten, I had saved up four months of pocket money to buy that case from the Army-Navy store because it was just like the one Nini Mo always carried. The loss really stung. I still had the really important stuff in my pockets—my toothbrush, Poppy's cash roll, my match safe, Pow's soother, a knife—but that was small consolation for the loss of the case itself.

No point in crying over sour water, Nini Mo said. I focused on getting out of the well. Fortunately, I had recently conquered the Barracks' infamous climbing wall; compared to that, this looked easy, and was made even easier by the fact that no one was standing behind me, yelling curses. The walls of the well were knobby and rough, giving me handholds. I used my jacket and my garters to improvise a sling for Flynn. Then, with Flynn on my back, breathing heavily on my neck, I started climbing.

A long, bloody, bruised time later, I wiggled over the top and lay gasping in the dirt. My neck was wet with Flynn's drool, and the rest of me was bone dry. To say that it was hot was like saying that water is wet or snow is cold. It accurately described the temperature but did nothing to convey how hot it actually was. I could feel the heat of the rocks through my clothes; the air, as I gulped it in, seemed to scorch my throat. My head felt like it would split open and spill my brains on the ground, where they would fry. Flynn slithered out of the sling and went to lift his leg on a rock. I swear I heard the piss sizzling.

My hat was long gone, of course, but I did have my sunshades in my jacket pocket. I put them on and saw, above, a burning steel-blue sky; in the distance, jagged red mountains; in between, a prickly landscape of cacti, rocks, thorny mesquite trees, and more cacti, rocks, and mesquite. With a yelp, Flynn jerked back from the cacti he had been exploring, a tiny boll of spines sticking off his nose. It took five minutes of cursing (me) and growling (him) before I got them out.

"Be careful," I admonished Snapperdog, and he butted my knee gratefully.

The well sat by a burned-out adobe building. The soot on the melted walls and the flock of buzzards that drifted up from the interior confirmed that the fire had been recent. For a moment, I wondered if this was Fort Sandy after all, or the burned-out remains of Fort Sandy. Maybe Cutaway's joke wasn't a joke at all. But then I realized the ruins weren't expansive enough to be an army post. So which way was Fort Sandy? I walked to the middle of the rutted road. In one direction the road disappeared into a dusty haze. In the other it vanished into a stark mountain ridge.

I felt lightheaded, and Flynnie was panting hard, his drool dried up. We needed to get water soon. I vaguely remembered hearing from Buck's stories of her time in Arivaipa that the fat barrel-shaped cacti were full of water, but they were also full of spines. My knife would be no match.

The faint sound of singing drifted by on a hot waft of wind. After tying the sleeves of my jacket around my waist, I slung Snapperdog over my shoulder and followed the tune along the road, eastward, down into a wash and out again. The singing grew more distinct, and soon I could make out the words:

"... *seven girls are going to the graveyard, but only six of them are coming back ...*"

A woman sat in front of a sagging adobe building, grinding corn in a matate held between her knees. As I approached, she quit singing, stopped grinding. Without a word, she dashed into the building and returned a few seconds later, carrying a clay jug. The water tasted tangy with iron and slightly gritty, but it was wet and wonderful.

I lay Flynn down in the shade and poured water into his mouth until his tail began to wag again.

"Are you all right?" she asked, fanning Flynn with a cornhusk.

"Ayah, madama. Thank you. My horse took a scare with a rattler a ways back and dumped me, ran off. I'm afraid I'm a bit disoriented. Can you tell me where I am?"

"The Dos Rios stage stop."

"Where are the two rivers?"

She laughed. "Oh, they come when it rains."

"How far is it to Fort Sandy?"

"Ten miles to the south."

Fike Cutaway. Close but no cigar! Still, the stage stop was a lot closer to Fort Sandy than Barbacoa was.

"When is the next stage to Fort Sandy?"

"There ain't one, not for a few days, now. It was scheduled for tomorrow, but Taylor and his cowboys came in yesterday on their way from Calo Res, and they said Jefe, the stage driver, was in the pokey. Shot up Miner Pete for making cracks about his shirt. The magistrate is coming next week, so there won't be a stage until then, and after, too, maybe. Judge McAvoy is a hangy judge. She likes her law and order, and she don't approve of people who shoot up other people over fashion errors. I saw that shirt, it was mighty loud. Jefe don't have very good taste, but you daren't tell him so to his face. Anyway, I don't wager we'll see a stage anytime soon."

All that information was making me feel dizzy. Or maybe it was the sun. I sat down on a barrel and the stage lady refilled the clay jug for me.

"Here, now, take it easy. You look as fried as a hunka bacon. Where'd you come from?"

"Calo Res," I said after I'd emptied the jug. "My horse was startled by a rattler, dumped me, and ran off with all my gear. I guess I'm a bit bunged up."

"Here, sit in the shade and I'll get you something stronger than *agua*."

"I got to get on to Sandy. Can you hire me a horse?"

"Banditos cleared me out of horses last week, and got my cow, too. Burned my outbuildings. Here, drink this, but careful now."

I felt a bottle being pushed into my hands and raised it to my lips without opening my eyes. I almost gagged on the licorice flavor, but managed to swallow. The liquid burned a trail down my throat and into my stomach, but suddenly the pounding in my head eased up.

"What the fike was that?"

"Madama Twanky's Tum-O. Works on worms, headaches, and the Arivaipa polka. Here, you keep the bottle, I'm as healthy as a horse. Just don't drink it all, it'll kill you for sure."

"What's the Arivaipa polka?"

"It's them dance you do when you drink bad water and your tum starts to bubble. Come on inside, and I'll dish you up some beans. I made them last week, and they came out mighty tasty."

"I really have to get on to Sandy." I followed the stage lady into the adobe building; it was dark and cooler inside. Much cooler, and as my eyes adjusted to the shadows I saw why. A cage containing an ice elemental was suspended from one of the vigas. In Califa, caging elementals is against the law, but I guess we were a long way away from Califa now.

"You posted at Sandy?" the stage lady asked.

"How did you know I'm a soldier?" I asked, startled.

"You're wearing issue boots." The stage lady took a clay bowl from a niche in the wall and ladled beans out of the clay pot hanging over the fire. "I did a hitch myself, some time ago, and I know them boots well enough. You rest up and eat your beans. Captain Oset and the patrol from Sandy usually swing by here in the afternoon, on their way back to the post. You can join up with them then."

I didn't relish the idea of sitting around, but on the other hand, I relished less a ten-mile hike through the Arivaipa desert. And the throbbing in my head had receded but not vanished completely.

"Thank you." I took the bowl from the stage lady and sat at the rickety table. I wiped the greasy spoon off on my shirt and dipped it. The beans were soft as lard and so spicy I could hardly swallow them. Coughing, lips and tongue burning, I hastily guzzled the coffee the woman laughingly set in front of me.

"Everything is hot in Arivaipa," she advised, patting out a couple of tortillas and throwing them on the griddle. "What's your handle?"

"Captain Nyana Romney," I answered when I was through sputtering. "Enthusiastic Regiment."

"I'm Clara. Sometimes they call me Clara Que Sí! But mostly just Clara."

"Madama Clara, you said there's been no stage. Have you had any other travelers recently? Any strangers coming through?"

Shaking her head, Clara dropped the tortillas in my bowl. "No. We got banditos, but I know them. They ain't strangers."

I could feel the tortilla with my tongue but couldn't taste it. I wasn't sure if I would taste anything ever again. I gave the other tortilla to Flynn. But my headache seemed to have vanished now, conquered by the Madama Twanky's Tum-O and the chiles in the beans.

I said, "On the road, before I got dumped, I thought I saw jaguar tracks. I didn't know they had jaguars in Arivaipa."

"Oh, dear me, no," Clara said. "They got a chupa over at Sandy and of course we got coyotes and javelina, but I ain't never seen any cat tracks. A jaguar, you said. You mean a panther?"

"A large cat."

"I ain't heard of such a thing. After them banditos came through, La Bruja gave me a protection charm to throw around my whole spread. Ain't nothing triggered it so far. More beans?"

"No, thank you, madama."

The fact that Clara hadn't seen Espejo made me feel cautiously optimistic that he was still behind me. He may have floated away on the wings of the storm, but I had outpaced him. As long as I was ahead of him, I didn't care where he was. *Keep your eyes forward,* Nini Mo said. *Don't keep looking over your shoulder; it'll put a kink in your neck.*

So close now, it was galling to wait, but waiting was the only sensible thing to do. I hadn't come this far to end up dying of heat stroke. While I finished my tortillas, Clara pestered me with questions, which I answered as vaguely as possible. *Save your lies,* Nini Mo said, *for when you really need them.*

Eventually, to escape her, I went back out to the ramada. It was hot there, but at least it was quiet. Even in my shirtsleeves, the heat was baking me dry. The sky hung over the adobe like a blue-hot steel kettle, and the ground radiated heat, like an oven.

Somewhere out there, not very far away, was Tiny Doom. Soon I would meet her. It occurred to me that I probably wouldn't know her when I did. She wouldn't dare risk showing her own face for fear someone would recognize her. I quickly charged my sunshades with a Refraction Charm that would allow me to see through a Glamour. Now, when I met Tiny Doom, I would know her. That thought was both exhilarating and terrifying. The beans churned in my stomach; I took another swig of the Tum-O and soon felt a lot calmer.

It was hard to believe that I had left the City, what, only a week ago? Maybe less; I was a bit hazy about time. The City seemed a zillion miles away. By now Buck must have heard that I had disappeared. I wondered how she had taken the news. She would be pissed that I hadn't followed her orders. Of course, I was glad to have learned that she wasn't such a lap dog after all, but it still stung that she hadn't trusted me, even after our heart-to-heart. I did feel bad about Poppy—when this was all over, I'd send him a note letting him know I was all right.

And Tharyn. Funny that I could miss someone I had known for such a short time, and had liked even less time than that. But I did miss him. How quickly I'd become used to having him around. To trusting him. To not being alone.

But really, it was too hot to think, and so I did not. Just sat and waited.

Sometime in the afternoon—I'd forgotten to wind my watch, so it had stopped ages ago—a cloud of dust puffed up on the horizon. The cloud slowly got closer, and then resolved into a small group of mounted soldiers, approaching the stage stop at a slow trot.

The riders' coats were brown with dust, their faces hidden behind bandannas, their hat brims pulled low. They looked more like bandits than soldiers, and they were mounted on mules, not horses. With a jangle of tack, the patrol ambled to a halt before the stage stop and the lead rider shouted the dismount command. The troopers dismounted, drawing their panting mules over to the water trough; one private tossed his reins to another and began to pump. The mules brayed in anticipation. Two dogs, a shaggy poodle and a tiny terrier, weaved their way between the mules, pushing to be first at the water. At the sight of the soldier dogs, Flynn whined and pulled, but I held on to his collar as I scanned the dusty figures, looking for the boss. But none of the soldiers wore an officer's jacket or shoulder boards, or any other sign of rank.

So who was in charge? The soldier at the pump finished filling the trough, and with a cheerful "Hang on! Hang on! There's more than enough for everyone!" pushed out of the jostle.

"Captain Oset!" Clara offered her a clay jorum. She took it, saying, "I hope that's not water, Clara! I got too much of a thirst to waste on anything so bland."

The captain pulled her bandanna down; her blue eyes flashed in a sunburned, dust-encrusted face. She drained the jorum dry in one draft. I had loosened my grip on Flynn; now he leaped off the porch and began to sniff at her boots.

"Get back here, Flynn!" I said hastily. "Sorry, he thinks everyone is his friend."

"And I'll bet they are, charming boy." Captain Oset bent down and scratched Flynn's ears. He flopped over onto his back to make it easier for her to pet him.

"This is Captain Romney," Clara said helpfully. "She's been waiting on you, Bea."

"Oh, ayah?" Captain Oset stepped out of the glare of the sun, hand to her eyes, peering at me.

I took a deep breath and launched into a lie. "Ayah. I'm Nyana Romney, Enthusiastics Regiment. From the City. General Fyrdraaca sent me to deal with your chupacabra problem."

Captain Oset's brow furrowed, and I pressed the lie further. "Didn't you get the General's letter?" I was pretty sure there had been no letter; when I'd left Califa, Buck hadn't answered the request yet, and even if she had done so after I left, there was no way the response would have made it to Arivaipa yet.

"No."

"Well, I guess I outpaced it. Here are my orders." I retrieved my jacket from inside the stage stop and fished out the orders I'd forged in Barbacoa. All that slaving in Buck's office was finally paying off. I defied anyone—particularly a captain from some backwater post—to tell the difference between my rendition of Buck's signature and the real thing.

As she read the orders, I said, "I'm eager to get on to Fort Sandy. How soon can we leave?"

Captain Oset handed the orders back to me. "I'm mighty glad you've arrived, Captain. That damn chupa has been driving us all to distraction. In the last month, it's gotten half the post's herd, and this after it decimated most of the stock in the valley. We've done all we can to trap it, but it's a sneaky old thing and gets away every time. I think we'd kind of hoped that the General would send an entire company."

"Nope, just me. But I'm all you need. I'm the best in the business."

"How many chupas have you caught?"

"Well . . ." Here was the flaw in my plan. I had never actually seen a chupacabra, much less captured one. But I didn't intend to actually capture it; I planned on finding Tiny Doom and leaving before my skill as a hunter became an issue. "I have to say that chupacabras are not very much found in the City. But I've taken on criminals and deserters, and I'll wager I can handle a chupacabra."

"They are mighty hard to track," Captain Oset said. "We had our scout on it and she couldn't find diddly. La Bruja's good, too. When she ain't drunk, that is."

"Well, she didn't have Flynn," I said. "This dog is the best tracker in Califa. He could find a single snowflake in a snowstorm. He once tracked a pigeon on the fly from Pudding Pie to Barbary. That's sixty miles."

Captain Oset looked at Flynn skeptically. He didn't look much like a tracker, not with his tongue hanging out and his belly rolled up to the sky, paws flopped back.

I said hastily, "Don't let that soft look fool you. He's a killer when he's on the nose."

These lies seemed to satisfy Captain Oset. "Welcome to Arivaipa, Captain. You can get your gear and ride back to Sandy with us."

"She got dumped, Bea. Horse ran off with her gear." Clara had been standing at my elbow. "That's why she's been waiting for you."

"That's bad luck. At least your neck ain't broke. Well, we'll supply you, don't worry. It's a good thing we came by; we almost took the Lonesome Trail and bypassed this stage stop completely. We gotta rest and water, but we'll leave in an hour or so."

The Army in Arivaipa is not much; only four garrisons, roughly two hundred soldiers and fifteen officers in the whole territory. They are all from the Steelheart Regiment, which has the reputation of being the most harebrained and scattered regiment in the Army, which is why it had been languishing in Arivaipa all these years.

If the patrol was an example of the Steelhearts, then the reputation was pretty well deserved. A scruffier lot of soldiers I had never seen; they looked more like muleskinners than troopers. I didn't see a full uniform among them; most of them wore canvas jackets and canvas kilts, their legs covered with thick leather chaps. Each trooper carried a rifle slung over his or her back; several of the privates wore side arms as well, normally allowed to officers only. All carried enormous knives at their waists. It struck me as strangely amusing that all the outlaws I'd seen in Barbacoa had looked respectable and these soldiers looked like outlaws.

An hour later, we rode away in an orderly file, two by two. Captain Oset ordered one of the privates to stay behind and gave me his mule, a particularly mangy specimen named Evil Murdoch. Horses didn't last long in Arivaipa, she explained, which was why they rode mules, despite being a cavalry regiment. I'd never ridden a mule before; they are wonderfully strong as pack animals, tough as leather, but have a nasty reputation for being stubborn, irritable, and vengeful. Evil Murdoch didn't immediately pull any tricks, but he had an aura of *Just you wait and see* about him.

When I had been marching around the Barracks, toting a heavy rifle and a heavier pack, I had envied the older cadets who had progressed to mounts. Let the horse do the hard work while you sit in splendor. Better to be a bouncer than a strawfoot, the Army saying goes. Well, whoever said that had never bounced through Arivaipa on the back of a swayback mule. Evil Murdoch had a spine as bony as a fence post. Within fifteen minutes, my thighs were burning and my feet were going numb.

And it was hot. Pigface, was it hot. The heat was dry like a blast oven, evaporating every drop of sweat, sucking the moisture out of my mouth, my eyes, my skin. Clara had found me a beat-up old sombrero with a very wide brim; I followed the example of the others and pulled it low over my face, then pulled up the bandanna Clara had given me, in a vain attempt to filter out some of the dust.

I rode at the head of the file, next to Captain Oset, so we didn't have it as bad as those at the end. The file-closer must have been spitting gravel. The other soldier dogs didn't seem to mind the heat; they trotted along ahead of the file, alert and happy. But it was way too hot for Flynn; he rode across my pommel, draped in a piece of canvas provided by Clara.

Captain Oset was very chatty. As soon as she realized I was a greenhorn, she wasted no time describing Arivaipa's charms in detail. Arivaipa's charms were not in the least bit charming. Everything in Arivaipa, Captain Oset pointed out proudly, was trying to hurt you. The cacti scratched with nasty thorns; the rocks were as sharp as knives. If you stood too long in one place you were liable to end up swarmed with nasty black ants that stung like bees. The sun tried to fry you, sucking all the moisture out of your body, out of your soul. Buzzards and hawks wheeled overhead hopefully.

There were poisonous spiders, poisonous cacti, poisonous scorpions, poisonous snakes, poisonous lizards. There were mountain lions, wild bulls, wild horses, and javelina. There were outlaws, cattle rustlers, renegade broncos, miners gone crazy from the sun, and lone-wolf bandits, any of whom would kill you over a slice of bacon, a canteen of water—or a misguided remark about a shirt.

And, of course, there were the chupacabras.

What on earth had Tiny Doom been thinking to hide out in such a Goddess-forsaken place? If it had been me, I'd have picked someplace nice and distant—and civilized—like Porkopolis or even Ticonderoga.

"At least," said Captain Oset cheerfully, "we don't have to worry about any Broncos popping out from behind a mesquite bush and pulling our hair. They stay on their side of the Line now, and we stay on ours. Everyone's happy and it's a whole lot safer around here."

"Why are they called Broncos?" I asked.

"'Cause they are as wild as wild horses. They don't call themselves that, of course. They got their own name, Dithee. The People, I think it means. Oh, it was hot times in Arivaipa back in the day when the Broncos were on the ride. Before my time, of course. But you hear stories. Major Rucker was here back then; he'll tell you. Broncos behind every cactus, just waiting for a chance to put a bullet in your back. They are great warriors."

"But we beat them."

"Well, I don't know that we beat them, exactly. More like they just decided to retreat into the mountains."

"Why?"

She shrugged. "Who knows? They got a different way of thinking and they keep their own counsel. They ain't friendly to outsiders. Anyway, now we got peace. Of course, every once in a while, some miner hears a rumor about jade or gold on the other side of the Line and takes himself over for a look-see. Gets sent back in pieces, well barbecued. But otherwise, it's peace between us. Now in Arivaipa, it's the weather, and the banditos, and the chupas." She twisted in her saddle and shouted, "Hey, Nobby, blow dismount!" Then back to me: "We do forty-five on, fifteen off here, Captain, to save the mules."

As it turned out, walking through Arivaipa was worse than riding. Much worse. When the fifteen minutes were up and the bugler blew remount, I welcomed Evil Murdoch's razor spine.

The ten miles from the stage stop to Fort Sandy seemed like a hundred. Captain Oset kept a steady stream of conversation the entire way; I tried to listen, hoping to pick up some clue about Tiny Doom, but the words began to blur into a haze of dust. The hundred miles grew to a thousand. By the time we arrived, the sun would have worn me to a nub. Finally, finally, the sun slanted down behind the western mountains and the air began to cool.

To the east, huge black clouds began to build up over the mountains.

"We might get some rain, finally." Captain Oset pointed. "It's been over one hundred and fifty days now."

"One hundred and fifty days with no rain?" I said, incredulous.

"Ayah. When it's dry, it's dry, but when the rain comes, you never seen so much water in your life. It's all or nothing out here in Arivaipa. Hang on, Captain, I know it's rough, but we only got a mile or two to go."

A plum-colored dust was settling over the land, softening the harsh air and turning the mountains into silhouettes when we splashed across the Sandy River, muddy water barely coming up to our mules' fetlocks. On the other side, three brushy wickiups stood under a stand of scraggly cottonwood trees.

"That's not the fort, is it?" I asked Captain Oset. I had had another nip of the Tum-O and was beginning to feel a bit perkier. Now that we were so close, a nervous anticipation was beginning to stir inside of me.

She laughed. "Oh, no. That's just a Bronco camp."

"I thought all the Broncos lived across the Proclamation Line."

"Most of them do. These stayed on this side of the Line when it was drawn up. We ration them, of course, and generally they aren't much trouble."

A boy sat in the dirt in front of the wickiups, watching us ride by. He was wrapped in a red blanket and the top of his head was covered in a crust of mud.

"What's wrong with that kid?"

"Oh, Pecos? Nothing. That mud's keeping the sun off his bald head."

We rode past a low fence made of ocotillo ribs lashed together; inside, the enclosure was dotted with boards sunk upright into the rocky ground. The post cemetery. The boards were weathered and the sun had burned most of the inscriptions off. Two of the graves were fresh; miners, Captain Oset said, who had crossed the Line and been sent back in charred pieces.

We rode up a short incline and a yapping cloud of dogs dashed out of an arroyo, making the mules bray and dance. Evil Murdoch did a little soft-shoe, almost dislodging me, but somehow I managed to stay on, my thighs burning from the effort. Our soldier dogs ran to greet them and the reunited pack fell in behind our column. Flynn's ears pricked up, but he didn't bark in return, just looked down at the dogs from his superior position above them. Ahead, a flagpole stood in the middle of a barren, rocky ground. There, hanging limply, was the familiar purple of the Califa flag.

Fort Sandy, Arivaipa Territory.

THIRTY-ONE

Fort Sandy.
Drinks. Chupa!

ALL MILITARY POSTS HAVE the same layout, so I knew that the crumbly adobe buildings on the southern side of the rectangular parade ground were officers' quarters. The long, low building on the northern side was the enlisted barracks. There were no stables, only a corral, partially covered with a rough awning. Captain Oset detached, waving me to follow her, and we jogged across the parade ground toward the Commanding Officer's Office while the rest of the detail headed toward the corral.

"The stables burned down a few years ago, and we haven't had the troops to rebuild them," Captain Oset said. "I fear Sandy ain't the luxury you are probably used to, Captain. We got outdoor plumbing and our water is full of rust. Rope beds and mattresses made of cornhusks. But plenty of sunshine and fresh air. No, we ain't at a loss for the sunshine."

My heart was thumping, and I half expected to see Tiny Doom standing in a doorway or walking across the parade ground. But the only person I saw was a man in an officer's jacket coming out of the COO. He stood under the ramada and watched us ride up. A small fawn-colored dog with floppy ears sat next to him.

"Ave, Major Rucker. Hey there, Sally," Captain Oset said, reining in. So this was Fort Sandy's commanding officer, who had written to Buck asking for the chupacabra expert and then had given a year off his life to ensure its swift delivery. "Major Rucker, may I present Captain Nyana Romney, chupacabra hunter? Captain Romney, Major Powhatan Rucker."

She swung down easily from her mule; after saluting, I followed suit and almost fell on my face. My legs were so stiff, I couldn't bend my knees.

"Captain Romney got bucked earlier, Pow," Captain Oset said quickly, grabbing my arm and pulling me up. "She's real bunged up. She had a hard journey."

"Well, don't just stand there, then, come on inside where's it's cool and have a drink, Captain. We are mighty glad to see you," Major Rucker said.

He offered me his hand, and I shook it. His grip felt as dry and crackly as paper. The major was tall, and very, very thin. In fact, he looked deathly. His cheeks were sucked in, his eyes sunk deep into their sockets, his dark skin as taut as leather over the skeletal frame of his face. He wore a pair of sunshades with green lenses, and when he smiled, his teeth were very white.

Captain Oset and I followed Major Rucker into the office, out of the blast of the sun into a blast of ice-cold air. Sally followed closely at Major Rucker's heels, but Flynn refused to come inside, and so I left him sulking on the porch. The CO's office was dim, its windowshades drawn, but there was enough light to see the source of the arctic air: another ice elemental sat in a cage dangling from the ceiling. Apparently, the Articles of War didn't hold much sway at Fort Sandy.

I gave Major Rucker my forged orders. He took them without looking at them, then offered me a cigarillo that I refused and a glass of lemonade that I did not. The lemonade had bits of ice floating in it. I wondered where they got ice in the desert. Whatever the method, that was probably against regulations, too.

"We didn't expect you quite yet, but I am mighty glad to see you," Major Rucker said.

"I was able to travel very quickly."

"Indeed. Well, I know how important this is. I hope Buck is well? It's been a long time since I've seen her."

"You know General Fyrdraaca?" I asked uneasily.

"Oh, ayah. Many years ago we were stationed together. Here in Arivaipa, as a matter of fact. She went on to bigger and greater things, while I still remain." I recalled then that Major Rucker's first name was Powhatan, just like my little brother's. It's an odd name, not from the family. I wondered whether Buck had named Pow for him, and why. I'd never heard Buck mention him.

Major Rucker continued, "I am content. Not all of us crave excitement."

"It's exciting here, Pow," Oset protested. "We got floods, and chupas, and Broncos—how can you not call all that exciting?"

"True enough." Major Rucker laughed. He hadn't taken his sunshades off. "You are young, Bea—you like the fun. I was here when it was fun, and now I'm glad to be bored. I'm old and I just want my chair. Some people are good at pretending to be someone they are not. Not me."

At his words, a shiver of paranoia went down my spine. Major Rucker picked up my orders and began to read them. Captain Oset threw herself down on the rickety velvet fainting couch against one wall and closed her eyes. I waited, hoping he would be as taken in by my forgery as Captain Oset had been.

He was. He dropped the paper on his blotter and said, "You'll have to bunk in with Bea, but we can offer plenty of hot water. I'll let you wash up and then we'll meet and discuss your plan after lunch. You didn't happen to bring any newspapers with you, did you, Captain?"

"No, I'm sorry, sir."

Without moving, Captain Oset said, "They lost her luggage on the ferry, Pow. Dropped it overboard while they were unloading it. Then her horse got spooked by a rattler and she lost the rest of her gear. Like I said, she had a rough journey."

"Did you? Terrible luck," Major Rucker said, and again that little thrill of paranoia slid across me. "Pity. We haven't had a newspaper here in five months. We are way behind on news, and we could use a resupply of bog paper, too. Bea will show you where to bunk."

Groaning, Captain Oset got to her feet. "Come on."

Flynn was no longer waiting on the ramada; I heard barking and saw him running across the parade ground with the other soldier dogs. I didn't call him back; let him have some fun for a while, blow off some steam.

"Are there are lot of rattlesnakes around here?" I asked as Captain Oset and I went down the ramada steps.

"Don't worry about him," Captain Oset answered. "The dog pack is good at killing rattlers. And it's early in the season for rattlers, anyway. Not hot enough for them."

It seemed plenty hot to me. "How hot does it get?"

"Oh, this is just the beginning; it's barely done winter. Believe me, it's going to get pretty much hotter. You'll see."

I hoped I would be long gone before that.

The UOQ consisted of two rooms and a kitchen. The small parlor was crammed so full of an ornately carved suite (settee, two chairs, rocker, and parlor table) that there was barely room to move. It must have cost a fortune to ship that furniture from Califa. A large red lamp hung from the center of the low ceiling, and the scabby whitewashed walls were papered with the covers of beedle yellowbacks: *Broad Arrow Jack; Red-top Rev; Vigilante Prince; Nini Mo, Coyote Queen.* Behind the parlor was the bedroom, which contained two issue cots laid with hay-filled mattresses, two iron washstands, and a couple of chairs made out of old gunpowder barrels. Here the walls were draped in red velvet, and a plush red carpet lay underfoot.

The rooms were so cold that I could see my breath. I didn't see a cage, but when I put my hand on the corner stove, the metal felt like ice. I lifted one of the burner covers and peered inside; two baleful ice-white eyes stared up at me.

Captain Oset dug through a trunk and tossed me a wad of clean clothes. "Here, I'm a bit big for you, but La Bruja left some of her duds and I think you might be about her size. I'm sure she won't mind; she's been gone for several weeks, and who knows when she'll be back."

"Who's La Bruja?" I asked. I'd never seen garments so garish; this La Bruja had horrific taste. The shirt was a goddess-awful plaid: acid green, shocking pink, and a shade of orange that almost hurt my eyes. Compared to it, the kilt and weskit were sedate: bright purple. *Well, you'll wear it and like it,* Nini Mo said. At least the clothes were clean.

"Oh, she scouts for us sometimes," Oset answered.

"She's a bit of a tippler, but she knows this country well. I'll give your duds to Tio—he does the laundry. Your shirt is stiff enough to carry its own rifle. My striker can clean off your buckskin jacket. There's no loo, of course, but the bog is out back, and there's a pot under your bed. Pan, she's our striker, she'll set up the bath in the kitchen. Don't worry, there's curtains on the window. I gotta go make sure the kids get everything squared away at the corrals."

"Here, I'll go with you," I said quickly. I wanted nothing more than to sink into a tub and scrub the Arivaipa dirt off my skin, but Tiny Doom was here somewhere and the sooner I found her, the better. "The troopers come first."

Captain Oset gave me an approving glance and waved me to follow her. I didn't actually expect to find Tiny Doom hiding out among the troopers, but I thought I should cover all the possibilities. And it would give me a chance to look around and get my bearings.

Even though it was getting dark, I put my charged sunshades on. My heart thrummed with excitement, and my hands were shaking; I thrust them into my jacket pockets so Captain Oset wouldn't see. I had come so far, and now—any moment—I would finally meet her. But at the corral I didn't see anyone who could be Tiny Doom, only a passel of grizzled lifers and some sad-looking fresh fish, or new recruits.

Everyone on the post is required to attend Retreat,

giving me a perfect chance to spot Tiny Doom among the garrison. But as I stood next to Captain Oset, scanning the faces of the troopers arrayed before us, I didn't see anyone who could be her, not even Glamoured. I had thought the hard part would be over once I reached Fort Sandy, but now I realized how stupid that hope had been. If I could spot her, she wouldn't be very well hidden, would she?

Of course, if I couldn't find her, Espejo couldn't, either. Or, at least, I hoped he couldn't.

The last note of Taps drifted out into the purple sky. A small breeze was beginning to flutter. Captain Oset bawled dismissal and the troopers broke rank, wandering away toward the corral, the barracks, the sutler's store. A private bawled, "Chow time!" at the dog pack, which had been loitering in the shade of the COO during the ceremony, and the dogs surged out of the shadows and raced to his call, Flynn jostling happily among them.

"Come have a drink with me, Captain Romney," Major Rucker said. I could tell the difference between a request and an order, so I followed him across the parade ground and down a narrow rocky track. To the east, a pink gash of light flashed: lightning. The track ambled up and down several washes; we picked our way carefully through the darkness, heading toward flickering lamplight. We came to a small tented pavilion. Inside, a few rickety chairs were scattered on packed dirt. The bar was made of three boards balanced on barrels. A sad-looking man plucked aimlessly at a banjo in one corner.

We sat down on the rickety chairs and the barkeeper brought us two dirty glasses full of muddy liquor. Major Rucker held up his glass in a toast.

"Welcome to Arivaipa, Lieutenant Fyrdraaca."

I choked on the burning liquid. Major Rucker leaned over and pounded hard on my back and the bug juice dribbled out onto my front.

"How did you know?" I asked when I could speak again. I glanced over at the banjo player, but he didn't seem to be paying any attention to us. The barkeeper had vanished.

Rucker saw my glance and said, "Oh, don't worry about Jamon. He was a Redleg. Now he can't hear his own daddy calling him to dinner." He took another swig and continued, "I met you once before. I suppose you don't remember. You were just a baby. You had chubby cheeks and growly little teeth, and when I picked you up, you bit my shirt. Little wolf puppy, your mamma called you. Then you blew out your nappy all over my only white shirt."

"Sorry."

"I guess I've forgiven you after all this time, as long as you don't do it again. I'd say, 'My, how you've grown,' but that would be silly. Of course you've grown. That was almost sixteen years ago. But I have to say that I'm surprised Buck sent you. Very surprised."

He knew who I was, but he didn't realize my orders were forged. I could salvage this. I said quickly, "She needed someone she could trust."

"Well, that's understandable, but—no offense, Lieutenant—you are awfully young."

"She has a lot of faith in me."

"I am glad to hear it." The major slammed another shot down. "I have to say that I'm relieved that it will all be over soon. It's very tiring, you know. I fear I'm not the wild young colonial boy I once was. This sneaking around at night is beginning to wear on me. I am glad to give it up soon, and leave the goat-sucking to the professional goat-suckers."

"It must be tough work," I said cautiously. Had he just implied that the chupacabra was a hoax? Then why had he requested a chupacabra hunter?

"I never did like livestock," Major Rucker said dolefully. "And goats are the worst of all. Those horrible slitty eyes. Still, one must do what one must do. Duty, honor, et cetera. I am Buck's devoted servant."

"We are all Buck's devoted servants," I said. *Keep it meaningless,* said Nini Mo, *if you don't know the meaning.* Major Rucker hollered for another bottle, and the barkeep popped out of the back room, thumped another bottle on the table, and disappeared again.

Major Rucker poured us each another drink and slammed his down, then continued. "Those damn miners.

I think they know something is up; I swear, some of them can sniff out jade in their sleep. They keep creeping across the Line. We stop some. The Dithee get the rest, but each breach is an offense to them. I fear eventually it's going to mean trouble."

"The Dithee—you mean the Broncos?"

"Ayah. At some point they may grow annoyed enough by the incursions to call the treaty off. Or some miner will manage to make it back and tip the Birdics off about the jade."

Jade? What jade? It began to dawn on me that whatever was going on at Sandy was bigger than a chupacabra—a chupacabra that apparently did not exist.

"That would be very bad," I said, like I was completely clued in.

"Very bad indeed," Major Rucker said. "So you can see why I am eager to get things settled before everything blows up. One more incursion across the Line and we may well have lost them. There is a detail patrolling day and night, but those miners are sneaky. I don't know how much Buck told you about the Dithee—"

"She said you'd fill me in," I said quickly. I didn't know squat about the Broncos.

"There are five major clans of Dithee. They are interrelated, of course, but they each control their own territory. Although all the clans are equal in practice, some are stronger than others. There's no one leader of the whole tribe, but some clan leaders garner more respect. Tilithay is the leader of the Red Turtle clan. He's a good man, steady and wise, and very deliberate in his actions. He has a lot of clout and he is all for this treaty. Which is good for us, as the jade is in Red Turtle territory."

Suddenly, I understood. Jade. There was jade on the other side of the Line, in Bronco territory, and Buck was making a deal with them to get it. The chupacabra was code for jade. No wonder Major Rucker had been willing to give a year off his life to ensure the swift arrival of his dispatch.

Jade is probably the rarest stone there is, and incredibly valuable. But the biggest jade mines are in Birdieland, and so the Birdies have almost a total monopoly on it. They control the flow of jade, and with this control comes their power.

But what if they lost the monopoly? I thought back to my most hated and boring class at Sanctuary School: Economic Theory in Practice. If the market is flooded with a commodity, that commodity loses value. A country whose wealth and power is based on that commodity finds itself with too much of something that nobody wants because everyone already has it. That country's economy collapses. And often, too, so does its government. If Buck flooded the market with jade, the Birdie economy would turn into worthless mush. The Birdie empire would be forced to its knees.

Pigface, Buck had been busy not putting all her eggs

in one basket. Secret alliances with the Kulani Islands; secret alliances with the pirates; secret alliances with the Broncos—

But. But. But.

I realized something else. There was no chupacabra. Buck was not sending a chupacabra hunter. She was sending someone to strike a deal with the Broncos. And thanks to my lies, Major Rucker thought I was that person. Oh, fike.

I sat there, stone cold, while Major Rucker went on. "I've sent a message to Tilithay that you are here. I expect an answer quickly, and not soon enough for me. The sooner we can get all this settled, the better. Cierra Califa, eh. May she be free at last." He raised his glass, and I did the same, echoing his sentiment and wondering what the fike I was going to do now. I couldn't lie my way through a deal between Califa and the Broncos. There was too much at stake.

"Cierra Califa!" Major Rucker said, raising his glass again.

"Cierra Califa," I repeated automatically. My voice sounded a bit squeaky, but Major Rucker didn't notice— for barely had my words died away when Captain Oset burst into the tent. Behind her a private clutched his rifle nervously. For one horrible moment, I thought she was there to arrest me. Then she said, "Captain Romney, I guess you'd better come. The chupa just went through the remuda. It got the guard."

THIRTY-TWO

In Charge.
Sigils. The Line.

THE FENCE AT ONE END of the corral was busted down; something had spooked the mules so badly they had stampeded. A thick metallic tang overpowered the smell of manure and mule. In the middle of the corral, a pond of black liquid shimmered in the starlight; under lamplight, it shone crimson red. A dark lump lay in the center of this pool.

Trying very, very hard to look as though I had seen worse, I stepped forward cautiously as the bloody mud sucked at my boots. One of the privates helpfully dipped the lantern lower so I could see better. I had *not* seen worse, not even in my nightmares. I swallowed hard. An experienced chupa hunter would not upchuck in front of everyone.

"I got an arm over here!" a voice hollered.

Another voice called, "I found his boot. Oh, and his foot, too!"

I glanced at Major Rucker. He had pushed his hat back on his head, and the lamplight gleamed off his sunshades, turning them into shining little moons. He looked mighty unhappy. Flynn abandoned the dogs, who were yipping and growling on the far side of the corral, to huddle up against my legs as I petted him reassuringly.

"What happened?" Captain Oset asked the sergeant.

"Corporal of the Guard heard shooting, ran over, and found Private Hajo. Or what's left of him, that is."

"Where's the other guard?"

"Don't know, sir, but I got troopers out looking for him."

Major Rucker, with no trace of disgust, had been looking quite closely at the wreckage of the guard. Now he said, "I don't think the chupa did this."

"What else, then?" Captain Oset said. "I told you it was going to get a soldier one day, Pow." I guessed she was not in on the chupacabra ruse.

"I never heard of a chupacabra killing a human. Look, he's been ripped from limb to limb, and his throat torn out. And"—Major Rucker poked with his swagger stick—"he's been chewed on. Chupacabras don't chew their prey. They suck them."

"Nyana?" Captain Oset said to me. "What do you think?"

I didn't think a chupacabra had done this, either, and not just because I now knew there was no chupacabra.

Chupas may not chew on their victims, but jaguars sure do.

Before I could answer Oset, a corporal materialized out of the darkness in a bobbing circle of lantern light. "We found Mustadine. He's scared kiltless, but he's alive. He says he saw it and it weren't no chupa."

We followed the corporal around the corral to the hay yard, where a shivering private sat on a bale, clutching a bottle in shaking hands.

"Buck up, Mustie. It didn't get you," Major Rucker said kindly. "Tell me what happened."

"I knew I was on duty, sir, but I got the polka real bad, and sometimes you just gotta go," Mustadine said after another pull on the bottle. "I gave over to Pongo and he said he'd cover for me, and I ran to the bog, but it was oc-cupado. So I went looking for a nice bush, you know, and no cacti spines, and anyway, I found a spot, and I was get-ting down to the dance, when all of a sudden I heard a weird scratching sound. Well, of course I didn't move an inch, thinking maybe it were a coyote, but then I looked up and on the rock above me was the biggest cat I ever did see, as black as pitch."

Pigface. Espejo had caught up with me. Fike.

"A black cat?" Captain Oset said, scoffing. "You mean like a bobcat?"

"No, sir," Mustadine said. "I mean like a panther, a giant fiking panther."

"Language!" the sergeant said sharply.

"I cry your pardon, sir, but that cat was big. I saw a panther at the Califa City Zoo once, but this was bigger. And that one was all spotted, you know, yellow and gold. This was as black as Choronzon's nose. That cat scared the donk right out of me, begging your pardon, Captain, and I grabbed my rifle and shot at it, and it disappeared."

"Did you hit it?" I asked hopefully.

"I don't know, sir. It ran off, and I ran back here, right into the corporal who told me about Pongo."

Mustadine led us to the area of his makeshift bog. There, on the rock, we found some enormous dusty paw prints and a cholla with a tuft of black fur caught on it. A few feet away stood a saguaro cactus with a gaping hole in its middle.

Apparently Private Mustadine was a lousy shot. What a fiking pity.

"What shall we do?" Oset asked.

It took a second for me to realize she was talking to me. Everyone was looking at me expectantly, hopefully—Captain Oset, the corporal, the cluster of enlisteds behind them, even Major Rucker. I guess they figured, if I could take on a chupacabra, then I could get a jaguar, too.

So that was exactly what I would do. Turn the tables on Espejo. Hunt him down before he could hunt down Tiny Doom.

"The chupacabra can wait," I said. "Let's get this cat before he gets someone else."

"Too bad La Bruja isn't here," Captain Oset said. "She can track anything. When she's sober, that is."

"So can Flynn," I said. With a little help from a Locative Sigil, that is. "As soon as it gets light, we'll mount up and head after it."

Major Rucker looked skeptically at Flynn, but agreed. We left Captain Oset supervising the gathering up of poor Pongo and returned to the main post. A guard accompanied us, so Major Rucker couldn't question me further on my plan, for which I was grateful, as it didn't include him or the patrol.

"I'll order the patrol at first light," Major Rucker said, at the ramada of the UOQ.

"I'll be ready," I promised, thinking, *I'll already be gone.*

By showing his hand—or paw, that is—Espejo had done me a favor. It was possible that he was just trying to draw me out, but if it was a trap, it wasn't going to work. *Come up from behind,* Nini Mo said, *and put your knife to his throat.* Espejo could track me, but he didn't realize that I could track him. That's exactly what I would do. Get him before he had a chance to get Tiny Doom. Night was his time, Cutaway had said, and though she had cheated me, I believed her. During the day, he was weak. During the day, he had to hide from the sun. I would use this weakness to my advantage.

382

I sat a spittoon outside the bedroom door to act as an alarm when Captain Oset came back, then had another swig of Madama Twanky's. I settled down to create a Locative Sigil, using the tuft of fur from the cactus as my locus point. Locative Sigils are easy; they are one of the cornerstones of rangering, and before I had been forced to drop my Gramatica lessons, I had gotten pretty good at them. When the sigil was done, I took Captain Oset's sawed-off double-barreled shotgun off the gun rack and made sure it was clean. A carbine rifle would have longer range, but Captain Oset's was gone from the rack, and it was too late to go down to the Ordnance Stores and requisition one. But a shotgun is more powerful than a carbine and doesn't require any finesse. It would do just fine. Then I charged four shotgun shells with an Abacination Sigil. Let's see Espejo stand against that!

Just before dawn, I hot-footed it down to the corral and got Evil Murdoch saddled without encountering anyone other than the night corral guard, who did not dare stop me. By the time the sun crested the eastern mountains, I had left the post, Flynn trotting along beside me. The Locative Sigil was tucked away safely in the breast pocket of my buckskin jacket. Two nips of Tum-O had soothed my bubbly tummy and I felt cool and collected. The weight of Captain Oset's shotgun, now loaded with two of the sigil shells, hung comfortingly over my shoulder. The extra sigil shells, along with a few regular shells, were stashed in my other pockets. After running scared for so long, it felt good to act fearlessly.

I rode east, away from Sandy. As soon as the flagpole was out of view, I dismounted and called Flynn over. He sat at my bidding, tongue lolling. The sun was already baking away the dawn chill.

"Sorry, baby dog," I said, tying my lead rope to his collar. "I don't want you to take off without me." I took the sigil out of my pocket and fixed it to his collar, but as I activated it with a Command, Evil Murdoch strayed to the end of the reins to nibble on a mesquite tree. I jerked him away from the bush, which he didn't take kindly to and jerked back. He pulled one way, I pulled the other, and then the reins flew out of my hand. Evil Murdoch ambled away.

"Hey!" I made a grab for the reins and missed. Sensing my pursuit, Evil Murdoch picked up his pace. Dragging Flynn, I lunged at the saddle and came tantalizingly close to grabbing the right stirrup before Evil Murdoch lashed out with a back leg. I twisted away just in time. Murdoch gave another little kick, dust puffing in the air. He brayed derisively once—a mulish *fike you*—and then dashed into the river, back toward Fort Sandy.

Fike!

Flynn pulled at the lead, whining, and it was taking all my strength to hold on to him. The Locative Sigil was working, but I wouldn't be able to keep up with him on foot. I had no choice but to return to the post and get another mount. I strained to reel the lead in so I could take the charm off his collar. Snapperdog did nothing to help me, just quivered and pointed and let out a few anguished yelps. He wanted to go!

A voice hailed me. "There you are, Nini!"

I turned and saw Captain Oset, reining in at the head of a detail. Behind her, a mounted private held the reins of a very pissed-off-looking Evil Murdoch.

"He's a real clown, Murdoch is, Nini," Captain Oset said. "You should thump him good. It's the only way to get the message across. He'll dump you in a cholla bush if he gets the chance."

"He isn't going to get the chance." I took the reins from the private. "You are going to be a good boy, Murdoch, or you are going to be dog food. Your choice."

Murdoch rolled a large yellowish eye at me as if to say, *You think, puggie,* but he stood meekly as I remounted.

"Were you going to leave us behind?" Captain Oset said reproachfully.

"I'm sorry, Captain, but it's best if Flynn and I track the jaguar alone. It's very dangerous. No offense, but I need to focus on the hunt, not worry about bystanders." Needless to say, I did not want Captain Oset around when I ran down Espejo.

"I don't really feel very good about letting you go on alone," Captain Oset said. "Major Rucker—"

Evil Murdoch suddenly lashed out and bit at Oset's mule. The mule brayed angrily and snapped back. Murdoch bounced. I leaned backward, trying to keep my balance, and in doing so, dropped Flynn's lead rope. Like a shot, Flynn flew down the road, the lead trailing behind him.

With a bellow, Evil Murdoch took off after him as I fought to stay on his back. I regained my balance and sawed at the reins, but it was like cutting wood with cheese. He didn't slow down. Oset and the patrol were right behind me, whooping and hollering. Flynn showed no sign of stopping. The die was cast. For better or worse, we were on the hunt. When we caught up with Espejo, I'd just have to shoot first and then be surprised after that he was a man. The Abacination Sigils would be harder to explain, but I'd worry about that later.

As far as I knew, Flynn had never tracked anything in his life, but with the help of my sigil, he was like a bloodhound. He tore down the road and our mounts were hard-pressed to keep up. A mule at a fast clip is bouncy. My teeth rattled; my hinder jolted on Evil Murdoch's spiny spine. Down the road, down the wash, up the wash, up the ridge, over the ridge, down the ridge Flynn went, our detail bounding after him.

"That dog can run!" Captain Oset hollered.

"I told you he was a great tracker!" I hollered back.

"Señor Jaguar is going to wish he'd never been born!" Captain Oset crowed.

Ahead of us, Flynn's rope had gotten caught up on a cactus; he was struggling to free himself. I urged Murdoch forward, but with a writhing wrench, Flynn jerked free, leaving the rope tangled in the spines, and loped across a rocky riverbed. I followed, but Captain Oset shouted a halt.

"Why are you calling a halt?" I had pulled Evil Murdoch's nose around to confront her.

"That's the Line." Oset pointed. "We can't cross the Line."

I looked back at the riverbed. Flynn was already scrabbling down the rocky grade.

"It looks like a wash."

"Maybe so, but it's the Line."

"Do you want this jaguar or not?" I asked impatiently. "It killed one of your troopers. It could kill another."

"Of course I do, but we can't cross the Line," Oset repeated. "It's strictly against orders."

"You all don't seem too keen on orders out here," I answered. "You openly practice magick. You've got ice elementals and sigil lights. Now we've got a man-eater in our sights, and suddenly orders are all that matter?"

"Some rules are too important to break."

"You go back, then. I'm going forward."

"I can't let you do it, Captain," Oset said. Suddenly I was staring down the barrel of her revolver. "I will have to put you under arrest."

"If you want to shoot me, shoot me, but you are not putting me under arrest."

"Better to be under arrest than dead."

"I don't think so. But let's find out."

Oset was chewing on her lip, and by that I was pretty sure she wasn't going to shoot me. Her next words proved me right.

"Please consider this carefully," she pleaded.

The soldiers were staring at us avidly; it's always fun to watch officers threaten each other. I glanced at the Line; it looked like nothing, just a rocky wash. You could ride across it and not even realize you had done so. But it represented an agreement between the Broncos and Califa. Major Rucker had said one more incursion and the deal for the jade might be off.

Espejo was on the other side.

And there was a good chance Tiny Doom was as well.

It's not all about you, Flora. These words echoed in my brain, although I couldn't remember now who had said them. This was about more than just me. It was about the future of Califa, a future that I might never get a chance to share but that mattered more than anything else.

You aren't the center of the world, Flora, the voice said.

And neither was Tiny Doom. Not when Califa's freedom was at stake.

But Flynn, stupid Snapperdog with the sigil on his collar—I shouted at him to come back, but he had already reached the other side of the wash. The patrol set to hollering and calling: *Good dog, come back, sweet dog, happy boy, come back!* Captain Oset found some jerky in her pocket and waved it enticingly, to no avail. Snapperdog had crested the opposite edge, and in a few seconds he had vanished.

"He'll come back when he's hungry," Captain Oset said reassuringly. "I don't think the Broncos care about dogs crossing the Line. And if they find him first, well, they like dogs. I'm sure they'll take care of him."

"He won't come back," I said. "He's got a Locative Sigil on his collar. He won't stop until he's found the jaguar. He can't stand against a jaguar. He's as good as dead."

"Fike, I'm sorry, Nini," Captain Oset said, but so what her sorrow?

I shouted again, but my cry was pointless. Flynn was gone. Swallowed up by the brittle brilliant landscape.

Captain Oset ordered the detail back to the post, but when I clicked my reins, Evil Murdoch refused to budge. I hammered my heels against his sides and whacked at his head, but he just flicked his ears, dropped his nose, and stayed rooted to the ground.

"Go, you fiker! Go!" I shouted, and still he did not move.

Captain Oset drew around and jogged toward us, her swagger stick held at striking level. But before she reached him, Evil Murdoch bounced straight up into the air and gave a little kick. Suddenly I was lying on the ground. I rolled over, grit burning my hands, and saw Evil Murdoch bouncing across the wash, kicking joyfully. The troopers were shouting; a private jumped down to hoist me to my feet.

I wished I could have lain in the dust forever.

THIRTY-THREE

Waiting.
Rain. A Visitor.

DUTY GOES ON, despite your own personal sorrows. When we got back to Sandy, I discovered that an unfortunate side effect of impersonating an officer is that everyone expects you to act like one. All I wanted was to go back to the UOQ, curl up in a ball, and howl. Instead, I found myself assisting Captain Oset at sick-call, helping her hand out bandages to privates with hangnails and doses of calomel to corporals with the polka. After sick call came stable call, and after stable call I was ordered to supervise the completion of the forage returns. I had come a thousand miles and was stuck in the same old dull routine.

Only now, instead of worrying about my future, I was worrying about Flynn. He'd be safe until sundown, when Espejo crawled out of whatever hole he was hunkered down in. But the desert is full of dangers above and beyond a Birdie nahual. Rattlesnakes and thirst and javalinas and holes and Goddess-knows-what else. Flynn had heart, but he lacked the sense that would keep him from investigating a rattler or falling into a prairie-dog hole. Seeing my worry, Captain Oset tried to console me with stories of miraculous dogs who had miraculously survived floods, shipwrecks, avalanches.

"And, anyway," she said, "maybe Evil Murdoch stuck with him. I once saw a mule stomp a mountain lion to death."

I appreciated her effort, but somehow I didn't think Evil Murdoch would be much help to Flynn. Or to anyone.

Flynn had trusted me, had followed me willingly, and I had sent him to his death. I knew now I would never be a good officer. Nini Mo said that to win, an officer must sacrifice for that which she loves most—her soldiers. I didn't have the stomach for such sacrifices. I would have let Espejo live a thousand years if only Flynn were back with me.

After the forage returns were completed, Captain Oset tried to get me to help her with water call, but I played the shirker's card, pled a horrible headache, and so was dismissed back to the UOQ. I could not go one minute longer without bursting into howls of regret and sorrow. When had I last slept—really slept? It was so long ago, I couldn't even remember. But when I lay down, my nerves were like little wires, razor sharp and humming, and they would not let me rest. I took a big swig of the Tum-O and that did the trick, darkly.

When I awoke, hours later, the roof of the UOQ was groaning and moaning and a chill wind was worming its way in through the chinks around the doors and windows. Outside, it was dark. I had slept the afternoon away, slept through Retreat, slept through everything. Hard to believe that only a few hours ago I'd been sweltering. Now I felt as though I might freeze to death.

I put my buckskin jacket on and went into the parlor to close the dampers on the stove, cutting off the flow of cold air from the ice elemental. There was no firewood, no kindling, nothing to burn in the fireplace. I was wondering if Captain Oset would be really pissed if I burned her collection of old beedle novels, when I heard a soft scratching at the door.

Maybe it was Flynn? For a second, I felt so hopeful that I could have yelped. But Flynn would bark to be let in, not scratch. A jaguar, however . . . I crept over to the settee and took down Oset's shotgun from the gun rack. Snapped the breech and slid in two sigil shells. If it was Espejo, he was in for a fike of a surprise. As a series of sharp knocks rapped out the first few notes of "Califa's Glory," I raised the shotgun to my shoulder and hollered, "Enter!"

A small figure bundled in a blanket stood in the doorway; it pushed past me, unconcerned about the shotgun.

I recognized the Bronco boy I had seen by the river the day we had ridden into Sandy.

"Stop right there," I ordered as the figure behind him took a step toward me. "Don't make another move."

"It's fiking freezing out here," the figure complained.

I recognized her voice instantly.

She sounded exactly the same as when I had last seen her: one year for me, forty-four years for her. I let the barrel of the shotgun drop, and she came into the room and shut the door.

"Nice jacket," said Tiny Doom.

"Give me some chocolate, *por favor,*" the boy said.

"I don't have any more chocolate," I said.

"Then *damelo* that." He pointed to the pink ribband tied in the buttonhole of my jacket.

"Don't be rude, Pecos," Tiny Doom said to him, and then to me, "Although I have to say, I could use a bite of chocolate myself."

She wore a buckskin jacket almost identical to the one I was wearing, though hers was deep red and had beading on the shoulders. When she took off her hat, I saw she had hardly aged at all. Her curly red hair was gray at the temples and there was a deep line between her eyes. Otherwise, she looked almost as she had at fifteen.

Tiny Doom looked around the room. "Pigface, Oset has the worst taste in décor I've ever seen. And it must have cost her a fortune to ship this fiking crap out here, too."

"Who's the kid?" I asked, as the boy vanished into the kitchen. If he was looking for chow, I wished him luck. I'd already looked myself and found nothing but stale hard crackers and a jar of moldy pickles. Oset wasn't much of an eater.

"Pecos? Oh, he's a friend of mine. Keeps his eyes peeled when I cannot. Come on, let's sit a spell and chat."

Like a Sonoran Zombie, I sat. For weeks I had imagined what I would say when I saw her, and now I was struck into silence. But I couldn't take my eyes off her.

Tiny Doom threw herself down on Oset's red sofa and bounced once or twice. "Buck didn't send you, I'll wager. But you are here, and with some urgency. Why is that?"

"I came to warn you. Espejo, the nahual, is on your track. He knows you are alive, and he aims to kill you."

I hadn't exactly expected Tiny Doom to shriek with horror at this news, but I also hadn't expected her to laugh. But she did laugh. Long and loud. "Ah, dear Xava. Dear, dear Xava. I rather thought he'd catch up to me one day. Alas, today. He does have the worst timing."

"I will take care of the nahual," the Bronco boy said. He'd returned from the kitchen chewing on a hard cracker.

"Never mind about Espejo, Pecos. I'll deal with him,"

Tiny Doom said sharply. Then to me, she said, "But I am wondering how he found me. And how you found me, too. I was pretty well hidden."

"You can't hide from me," I said. "I did a Blood Working."

"Pigface. Well, no fiking wonder Espejo found me!" Tiny Doom said impatiently. "Why didn't you take out an advert in the newspaper? *Found: One long-lost dead traitor?*"

I protested, "I was very careful. No one discovered my Working. He caught me later and was suspicious of who I was, but I wouldn't tell him. So . . ." I realized I did not want to tell Tiny Doom what Espejo had done to me. I did not want to tell anyone. "Anyway, he found the map I used in the Working and figured it out."

"You weren't even supposed to know I was your mother," Tiny Doom said. "Buck swore she'd never tell you."

She had glossed over the danger from Espejo, moved right into accusation, and this irked me. I said sharply, "Buck didn't tell me. Lord Axacaya did—when he was getting ready to kill me so he could free the Loliga. Did you forget that? The Loliga hidden under the City? The one tearing the City apart? The one who could only be freed when the last Haðraaða was killed? Which happened to be me, not that I knew it at the time. But I sure found out later, when Axacaya put his knife to my throat."

"Fiking Axacaya," Tiny Doom said. "I should have

killed him when I had a chance. I'm sorry about the whole Loliga thing, but I guess I can't think of everything. And anyway, didn't I leave you a plan? And ain't you still alive and the City still standing? So obviously it all worked out in the end."

"Ayah, I'm still alive, and the City still stands. But I had to die to make it so. It was a great plan. The Ultimate Ranger Dare. How did you expect me to pull off that one?"

"You did, didn't you?" she said. "I knew when I first met you that you were a tough little biscuit. Anyway, we can hash it all out later. I don't have the time now. I've got important stuff going on."

"You mean the jade?"

"You are a nosy little thing, eh? Ayah, the jade. And if you've sussed that out, you understand how important it is. I can't afford to have a nahual sniffing around that. If word of the jade gets out to the Birdies, we are fiked. I need you to stay put, here, where you are safe, until we get all this settled, Flora."

"Nyana," I said. "You named me Nyana. Remember?"

Suddenly she did not look fifteen anymore, but sixty. She said softly, "So I did. Will you sit tight, Nyana? You'll be safe as long as you remain on the post. Right now he's after me. He won't come after you until he's got me, and he's not going to. I've got to draw him away from both you and the jade."

"I can help you. Let me help you."

"Thank you. It's best if I handle Espejo alone."

Pecos said something in Bronco through a mouthful of crackers, and Tiny Doom nodded in response. "We have to go. Will you do as I ask?"

"I suppose," I said mulishly.

"Thanks." She stood up and put her hat back on. She was leaving. All this way to find her, at so much cost, and this was all I got—a few short words and orders. What if Espejo got her before she got him? This would be all I'd ever have.

I leaped to my feet. "Wait! Wait!"

Tiny Doom halted at the door and turned back to look at me.

I said, "I'm sorry I left you behind. Really sorry."

For a moment she looked confused, and then she laughed. "Oh, you mean when we last met? When you left me behind for dear old ghoulish grandmamma to eat? Ah, don't worry about it. She didn't eat me; that honor was saved for someone else. And I'm sorry about the Loliga. I guess I should have planned ahead a bit better, but there was a lot going on."

"We must go," the boy said urgently, pulling on Tiny Doom's hand.

"I'm coming," she answered, but she didn't move. "Does your father know you are here?"

"No."

"Does he know I am here?"

I shook my head.

Her shoulders sagged in relief. "Thank the Goddess." She turned back to the door; the boy had already gone out.

"Wait!" I cried again. "You are going across the Line?"

"Ayah."

"My dog, Flynn. I tried to use him to track Espejo. He went across the Line. If you see him, or hear of him—he's a red dog, he's silly but really good, please—"

"I'll find him," she promised. "I'll find him."

The door banged shut behind her. I ran to the window and pushed aside the drape. Tiny Doom had already vanished into the night.

THIRTY-FOUR

Cows.
A Confession. Steak.

THE REST OF THE NIGHT, I paced the frigid room, growing more and more angry. Tiny Doom had abandoned my infant self, walked away, and never given me another thought. But she had still managed to ruin my life. Because of her, I had to hide in the shadows, I had to sneak and pretend. Because I hadn't known who I really was, Axacaya had been able to use me, manipulate me, make a fool out of me, and almost kill me.

I wasn't the only one she had almost destroyed. The Loliga had been her responsibility, and by ignoring this, she had put the entire City in jeopardy. Because of her poor judgment, Poppy had been imprisoned, tortured, crippled, and even now, though his body was free, his spirit remained in chains. Because of her, Flora Primera had been lost to the Birdies. Because of her, the War with the Birdies had been lost as well. Butcher was a good nickname for her; she left a trail of blood and corpses in her path. She lived, and yet so many of the people who had loved her, trusted her, followed her, were dead, broken, or worse.

I had come so far and risked so much, and she had spoken to me as though I were a child. She expected me to just sit back and wait for her to handle things. Well, fike that. Let Espejo have her. What did I care? For years I'd never even known she was alive, so why would it matter if now she was dead?

And so what if he then came after me? Let him try. He wouldn't find me so easy to compel this time. My blood burned with Gramatica; angry Words pounded in my head, choked my throat. Finally, I took a nip of the Tum-O to calm myself down, and I must have overdone it, because the next thing I knew, the striker was shaking my arm. I sat up and found myself on the overstuffed settee, neck stiff, fully dressed.

"Major Rucker wants to see you, sir," she said, offering me a coffee cup.

"Is there any milk?" I asked blearily. The coffee was burned.

"I cry your pardon, but the chupa ate the goat."

I'll bet he fiking did, I thought.

"Major Rucker said it was urgent, sir."

Urgent wasn't good. Rucker had either arranged the meeting to discuss the treaty with the Broncos—bad—or he had discovered that I was a fraud—worse. For a moment I considered scarpering, but I doubted I'd get far. Anyway, I'd come to the end of the line. My anger had died down into fatalism. Whatever was going to happen would happen. Let's get it over with.

"I'll be there directly." I went to wash up and change into another very loud shirt. This La Bruja person had very colorful taste. Her quarry must see her coming a mile away.

A RODEO WAS taking place on the parade ground. Cowboys on scrawny ponies were shouting and yawing at a scrimmage of irritated cows. On the sidelines, by the corral, a line of soldiers cheered the lively scene. Major Rucker and Captain Oset stood on the porch of the COQ, talking to a man in a cowboy hat. The little dog Sally sat at their feet. They broke off their conversation as we approached.

"Your servant, Major," I said, saluting. "Captain Oset."

"Ah, there you are, Captain Romney. I'm terribly sorry about your dog," Major Rucker said. "But he may still turn up. One of my pointers ran off and was gone a full week before he came home. It happens. Don't give up hope."

"Thank you, sir."

"Captain Romney, I'd like to introduce you to Sieur Taylor. He runs a ranch down south of here, has the beef contract for Sandy. He just brought in this month's allotment."

"Pleased to meet you, Captain Romney. Welcome to Arivaipa." Sieur Taylor was a big man, almost as big as Tharyn, but weightier. He wore high-heeled boots, fringy leather leggings, and a heavy black leather jacket over a red-and-white checked shirt. His grip, when he accepted my outstretched hand, was crushing. I tried to be crushing in return, but failed.

"The troopers will be glad to see the beef," Oset said. "They're tired of salt pork."

"Salt pork beats canned carrots," a lazy voice said. "I don't know how ya can live on canned carrots, Bea."

I saw that Taylor's bulk had been hiding someone lounging on a folding chair, smoking a vile-smelling cigarillo. For one heart-skipping moment the cigarillo made me think it was Tiny Doom; when I'd met her in Bilskinir's past, she'd smoked them incessantly. But I was wearing my Charmed sunshades. The woman had no Glamour and she didn't look a thing like Tiny Doom. She had dark hair, flat and straight, and even when she was sitting down, I could see that she was tall. I felt sour and angry again.

"Sorry, Bruja," Oset said, laughing. "I don't want animals eating me, so why should I eat them? Carrots do me well enough."

"Bea doesn't eat meat," Major Rucker said to me. "She takes a lot of ribbing for it, but she stands firm."

"It's the principle of the thing. I don't believe in killing things just to eat them."

"Good thing you ain't a Birdie, then. You gonna introduce us, Pow?" The woman rolled the cigarillo into the corner of her mouth and shot a spurt of tobacco juice over the side of the porch, narrowly missing the dog that lounged there in the shade. She had to be the grubbiest person I'd ever seen. Her skin was crusted with dirt, her buckskins were greasy, and her teeth, when she grinned, were greenish.

"I cry your pardon. Captain Romney, may I present La Bruja? She scouts for us sometimes. Other times she just eats our chow and drinks our bug juice."

"And mighty poor bug juice it is. They say ya kin tell a man by the quality of his likker. By them standards, Pow, ya ain't doing so well." La Bruja spat again, this time hitting the dog directly on the hinder. The dog jerked up and found another place to lie, out of range.

La Bruja took another swig from the tin cup she held; even from this distance and through the cigarillo smoke, I could smell the burn of alcohol. "I like yer shirt, Captain. Kinda flash, but pretty. Suits ya. Hope ya found the drawers that ditto."

"Oh, don't flush her, Bruja. You know you never wear anything but those ratty old buckskins." Oset laughed.

I said stiffly, "I cry your pardon. I'll have it laundered and returned to you as soon as possible."

"No fear, Captain. I don't get much call to wear my best shirt. Yer welcome to it."

The yipping from the parade ground increased, and we turned. A steer had busted out of the herd and was making a run in the direction of the mess tent, two cowboys tearing after it. Sieur Taylor's horse stood at the porch railing; he grabbed the reins, vaulted into the saddle, and tore after them, unspooling his lasso as he went. Captain Oset leaned over the railing, yelling encouragement.

"Come into my office, Captain, away from the noise," Major Rucker said.

Sally leading the way, I followed Major Rucker inside. The clerk was sleeping at his desk, head pillowed on his arms. Major Rucker didn't chivvy him, just went on by as though he hadn't even noticed.

"Close the door behind you and take a seat." Major Rucker sat behind his desk. He took a sip from the coffee mug on his blotter but didn't offer me anything, which I took to be a bad sign. I sat down in the chair across from his desk. Buck has a chair in that exact position; it's widely known as the hot seat.

Sally nudged my knee, and I rubbed her ears. She wasn't as cute as Flynn, but she did have pretty blue eyes. Oh, Flynn. My heart twanged again, and I blinked hard.

"I'm a wee bit confused," Major Rucker said. "I got a message this morning from Lieutenant Sabre, General Fyrdraaca's Adjutant General. He's arrived at the stage stop and now waits there for an escort. He said General Fyrdraaca sent him to take care of the chupacabra. And we both know what that really means."

Lieutenant Sabre was the envoy? Sick leave, my hinder. While Buck had given out that he was home languishing in his bed, he must have been on his way to Arivaipa. Once again I had been totally out of the loop. I couldn't muster up any bitterness over my exclusion, though. The only loop I deserved now was one that would hang me.

Major Rucker continued. "I admit that I am at a bit of a loss as to what to believe. His letter sounded genuine, but I saw your orders. They were quite obviously genuine. I'm riding out to meet him. You'd better come with me so we can straighten this out."

Know when to cash in your chips, Nini Mo said. It was time.

"My orders are a forgery, sir," I said. "I'm sorry. Lieutenant Sabre is the real envoy."

Major Rucker's face registered outsize astonishment. "A forgery? You are not the envoy?"

"I'm not."

"What's all this about, then? Why are you pretending to be the envoy?"

"I wasn't, sir. I was pretending to be the chupacabra hunter. I didn't realize at first it was a code."

"Why were you pretending to be the chupacabra hunter, Lieutenant Fyrdraaca?"

"I'm sorry. I can't say."

"Can't or won't?"

"Both," I said miserably. Major Rucker had been so kind to me and I had lied to him, and although I wanted to defend myself, I could not. And I didn't dare tell the truth, anyway. Tiny Doom's secret was not mine to share.

"Do you think this is some kind of a game? A lark? Do you understand what is at stake here?"

Oh, I understood all right. "I do, sir. I'm sorry, sir."

Major Rucker took another swig from his mug. "You understand that I will have to place you under arrest, pending an investigation, with the mind of preferring charges against you?"

"Yes, sir," I said even more miserably. The thought of my actions coming out into the open in a court-martial made me feel sick. But no one knew the reasons for my actions but me (and Tiny Doom) and if I refused to speak, they could not force me.

He said, "In the course of your deception, you've become privy to information that is absolutely vital to the security of Califa. Do I have your word that you will keep this strictly to yourself? I guess I don't have to tell you what would happen if the information were to get out."

"I swear, Major."

"I must meet Lieutenant Sabre and then accompany him to the parley with the Dithee. I have no time to discuss this further, but we will take it back up again when I return. During my absence, Captain Oset will take command. Do I have your word that you will confine yourself to your quarters until my return? I can order you to the guardhouse, but that would hardly be suitable to your rank."

"You have my word."

For a moment, I thought Major Rucker might say something else, but he dismissed me with no further comment. Outside, the rodeo was over and the cowboys were gone.

Back I went to the UOQ's velvety-cold parlor, feeling mighty cast down. I deserved to be court-martialed; I deserved to be cashiered. Maybe that would stop me from heading down the same primrose path Tiny Doom had taken. I couldn't bear the thought of just sitting there, waiting for Major Rucker to return, waiting for Espejo to find me, with nothing to do but consider my many failings. I reached for the Tum-O bottle, took a long swig, and collapsed onto my cot into a hazy warm darkness, where there was no failure, no blame, just fractured visions . . .

I SAT STIFFLY across from Cutaway, darkness endlessly sliding by the windows. She was wearing silvery sunshades; she took them off, and I saw Buck's face, eyes black and empty. *Trust me, Flora,* she said.

Flynn nudged my knee and I scratched his silky ears, rubbed his soft pink belly, his fur growing rough beneath my hands until it was as dry and coarse as hay, his body a sun-shriveled husk, eyes like dry marbles, lips pulled back over his teeth in a soundless snarl.

A blond man leaned over me and said, *I miss you so much, come back,* but before I could answer, Tharyn stood behind me, his hands on my waist, and said in a growly bear voice, *She doesn't miss you at all.*

The visions went on and on, round and round, dark dreamy fragments, voices calling in distant rooms, the roar of the sea, a dog barking, and then Oset said, *Come on, Nini, boots and saddles.* It took me a while to realize that I was not dreaming the words. *Come on, wake up!* I opened my eyes, groggily. I had taken too much Madama Twanky's; it had made me sluggish and slow. In the flickering lamp-light, I saw Oset sitting on her cot, pulling her boots on.

"What's going on?" I yawned. I had a splitting head-ache and my mouth felt gritty. "What time is it?"

"Message from Hooker's farm that they had a black cat nosing around their stables last night. I'm taking the patrol out to check up."

"I'm going with you."

"Of course. We have no time to waste."

She didn't mention I was breaking arrest, and so I didn't, either. I hurried, throwing my boots on, shrugging on my buckskin jacket. Water from the washbasin splashed some of the grog away. On the way out the door, I grabbed Oset's shotgun.

The moon had long since risen. It was almost full and its light made the night seem as bright as day. A small patrol had formed up in front of the corral, just four privates and Corporal Tzinga. The rest of the post was still and quiet. As we rode past the hog ranch, a mule and rider fell in with us. The rider's face was in shadow but her smell was already familiar.

"Nice night for a ride," La Bruja said cheerfully.

"We do not need company," Oset said stiffly. She held up her hand and the patrol jostled to a halt. "We are on official business."

"So am I, darlin'. Pow asked me to keep an eye on that cat myself. Not that he thinks yer no good, of course, Captain, but who can't use some help sometime?"

"We do not need your help," Oset answered.

"It's a free territory. You don' want me to ride wit' ya, alrighty, then. But I guess I'll ride, anyway." La Bruja turned her mule's head around and headed toward the back of the patrol.

Ignoring her, Captain Oset rode on. Corporal Tzinga gave the order to follow when it became apparent Oset was not going to. I looked over my shoulder and saw La Bruja now closing our file. Fiking great. Espejo would smell her a mile off and be warned. He must have tracked

Tiny Doom back across the Line and to the post. Fike. Why hadn't she covered her tracks better?

Hooker's farm was a few miles south of Fort Sandy. It was nothing much, an old adobe building surrounded by pumpkin fields. Sieur and Madama Hooker waited in front of the house, a knot of sullen kids huddled behind them. Sieur Hooker told us that early that night, they had been woken by the sound of their horse screaming. He and his wife had grabbed their rifles and run out to investigate; they'd seen the black cat clinging to the back of the shrieking horse and had fired at it and missed. The jaguar had run off into the night.

The horse lay, fly-covered, in the corral, its back a mass of raw meat, its throat torn out. In the lamplight, the blood shone luridly red. The horse was the family's only means of transporting their pumpkins to market; without it, they were ruined. Sieur Hooker told us this matter-of-factly, but his eyes were hard. The kids glared at us, and the smallest one hissed, as though this was somehow our fault.

"Did you see which way it went?" Oset asked.

"Toward Bexar Canyon," Hooker said. "That's where I'd go if I were a cat; there's plenty of shelter, and trees, and water in the spring."

"We will kill it," Oset promised.

"Won't do us any good now," Madama Hooker said. "But good luck to you, anyway."

"You put in a claim with the Army, Stevie," La Bruja said. She'd dismounted to inspect the remains of the horse, handing the reins of her mule to one of the troopers. Now she reclaimed the reins and stood by her mule's head, wobbling slightly. She was drunk.

"Can I do that?" Hooker asked.

"Sure enough. If the Army was doing its job, yer horse wouldn't be lying there chewed like a piece of shoe leather. Put in a claim; I'll wager they'll pay."

It look La Bruja two attempts to get back on her mule, and she only succeeded when Private Munds jumped off his own mount and gave her a leg up. She smelled so strongly of bug juice that I was surprised she could even stay in her saddle.

We rode on. Every once in a while, Captain Oset would hold up her hand in a halt-and-dismount, looking for a sign, and then, once she was sure we were on the right track, we'd ride on. The pale moonlight washed the desert out, softened it. To the north, the sky flashed pink and purple with distant lightning.

All my regrets and recriminations had vanished into one goal: tracking Espejo down. Night might be his time, but let's see how he handled a double-barreled shotgun blast of Abacination Sigils. I was primed. Every shadow, every movement of the night, could be Espejo. I was itching for the chance to blow him away.

At the next waterhole, we found a welter of paw prints

in the mud. About a mile further down the track, we found the scattered remains of a small animal. Clearly we were on the right track. La Bruja contributed nothing to the scout; she just sat on her mule, head nodding, and, every once in a while, took a pull from the canteen she'd hung on her pommel. Major Rucker's confidence in her was clearly misplaced.

At the edge of Bexar Canyon, Captain Oset called a halt. The moon was setting, and without it, it would be too dark to track; anyway, the canyon was narrow and jumbled with rocks, the perfect place for a cat—particularly one who was really a man—to plan an ambush. We were close. We had to be close. Come daylight, it was just a matter of finding Espejo's hidey-hole and flushing him out.

We made camp just inside the warren of rocks, where they could afford us some shelter if the storm made it to us. After we picketed the mules and fed them, I carried my saddle and bags to where Captain Oset had set up her gear. A private had dug a small fire pit and now began to heat coffee in a tin boiler. It smelled delicious.

"Go away," Captain Oset said to the private, appearing out of the darkness. He handed her a tin cup of coffee and, after saluting, went back to the trooper's camp, several yards away and hidden from ours by a large boulder.

"I am starving," Oset said. She dug a tin plate out of her saddlebag and withdrew an object wrapped in a gunnysack, which turned out to be a hunk of blackish meat. "Do you wish some?"

"No, thanks." I shuddered at the thought of eating meat that had been stuck in Oset's saddlebag for who knows how long.

She threw a chunk of meat onto the tin plate and shoved the plate into the fire. Normally Oset is chatty, but tonight she was quiet. That suited me just fine; I wasn't in the mood for talk. I chewed on a hard cracker and listened to the distant drum of thunder. The cracker tasted like sawdust. The steak was starting to sizzle, smelling deliciously of fat and char and meat, and it made my mouth water.

Oset put her gauntlet back on and pulled the tin plate out of the fire. When she cut into the steak, it oozed red. I swear I had never smelled anything so good before.

"Are you sure you do not want a taste?" She held a piece out to me, impaled on the end of her knife.

I couldn't resist.

It was, in fact, the best I had ever eaten, succulent and fatty, seasoned with a tang of wood ash and salt. She divided the rest of the steak in half and pushed the hot plate over to me. I chewed, enjoying the delicious fattiness of the meat, watching as she did the same.

And then I remembered the jibing on the front porch, La Bruja's comment about the canned carrots.

I put the plate down. The meat had left a nasty coating inside my mouth. A gulp of bitter coffee did not wash the taste away.

"I thought you did not eat meat, Bea," I said, glancing over to where Oset's shotgun leaned against my saddle.

Oset looked up from her plate, and for a second, her face was blank. Then she laughed. "Who does not eat meat? How silly."

Oset speared a large piece with her knife and shoved it into her mouth. Her cheeks were shining with grease. Her hands were pretty grubby, almost black around the nails and knuckles. And her left cuff was stiff with something that had dried black. I took another gulp of coffee. A vision had risen unbidden to my mind, a vision of the Birdie Ambassador's hands. The first time I had seen him, his hands had been blackish, not with dirt, but because the stolen skin he wore had been starting to decay.

Espejo was not a Flayed Priest.

But maybe he knew their mysteries.

My coffee cup was empty. Oset was still hacking at her meat. I said, "Bea, I know I still owe you that money from the poker game. As soon as I get back to the City, I'll send you a check."

"Oh, it's no worry." Oset shoved more meat into her mouth. "I know you are good for it."

"Thanks." I put the coffee cup down and folded my hands in my lap to hide their shaking. We had never played poker and I did not owe her any money. Another rumble of thunder rolled over us, louder this time. The storm was growing closer. Oset looked up from her plate, staring behind me, toward the mountains, and for a tiny second, her muddy brown eyes flashed jade green.

And I knew.

I knew.

THIRTY-FIVE

Tum-O.
Storm. Munds.

I SAT LIKE A STONE and watched Espejo tear at his meat. What kind of meat was it? Alas, I knew exactly what kind of meat Espejo ate. Burning acid began to fill my mouth, and I said thickly, "Excuse me—"

I grabbed the shotgun as I ran. I made it out of the circle of firelight before I puked, and puked, and puked, until my stomach muscles ached and my mouth felt scalded. I leaned against a boulder, the shotgun tucked into my shoulder, and wiped my mouth on my sleeve, then stuffed my fist in my mouth to keep from screaming.

Oset. Poor Oset. I should have told her—should have warned her—should never have left her in the dark, a sitting duck to Espejo. But it had never occurred to me that *she* was in danger. Espejo must have grabbed her back at the post, grabbed her and then—I felt sick. Her death was my fault. That was a cold, horrible realization, followed by another one: Here I was, out in the desert, with Espejo, at his mercy. All my brave thoughts about taking him down had died in the face of reality. Who had I been fooling? I was no match for him. He was a born killer and I was just some stupid snapperhead. I was only still alive because he hadn't yet decided to kill me.

It was taking all my nerve not to scarper into the night. But I could hear murmuring coming from the troopers' camp. If I ran, I'd leave them to Espejo, and he might just kill them all. Also, with Oset dead, the command had devolved to me. The troopers were now my responsibility. I couldn't abandon them.

I'd loaded the shotgun back at Sandy during mount-up. Now, seeking reassurance that I was still in the game, I broke it open and saw with soul-sucking horror that the barrels were empty. The gun was unloaded. I slapped my pockets for the extra shells and found they were gone as well. How the fike had Espejo managed that? As far as I recalled, the shotgun had never been out of my sight, had been tucked into the holster on Evil Murdoch's saddle since we'd left. Then I remembered the potty break at Hooker's farm. I'd left the shotgun in the holster while I visited the privy. The other shells must have fallen out while I was squatting.

Oh, pigface, mother of creation. I was dead, dead,

dead. Tiny Doom was dead; this was it. We were done, *punto final,* over, finished, capped—

Calm down. Calm down. Panicking won't solve a thing. Buck had once beaten a jaguar to death with a shovel. I had absolutely no faith in my ability to do the same with the now-useless gun. I bit down on my fist until I tasted blood, and then thought calmly, *I have what Nini Mo said is the greatest strategic advantage of all: the element of surprise.* I knew who he was, but he didn't know I knew.

I also had one giant Gramatica Curse up my sleeve, the Gramatica Curse to end all Gramatica Curses: the Oatmeal Word. That's not its real name, of course. It's actually the Adverbial form of the Gramatica Word *Convulse.* I call it the Oatmeal Word because the convulsions that it causes turn its target's internal organs into sludge— oatmeal-like sludge. I've spoken it twice: on one of Firemonkey's men when he interfered with my rescue of the Dainty Pirate, and on Lord Axacaya. Its effect on poor Herbert was catastrophic. Lord Axacaya managed to withstand it, but barely.

But Espejo was more powerful than Axacaya. At least now, in the night, he was. If I tried the Word and it didn't affect him, I would tip my hand. My advantage would be lost. He'd squash me like a bug. But it had to be getting close to dawn. Soon he would have to go to ground to escape the sun. He would not be able to call upon his god's power. If I could hold him off until then . . . but how?

"Are you all right?" Espejo called.

"I'm fine," I called back. I fumbled in my jacket pocket for the bottle of Tum-O. A nip would settle my belly and my nerves. As I lifted the bottle to my mouth, I remembered Clara's warning. *Don't drink it all, or it will kill you.* The bottle was three quarters full. *Always go with the sure thing,* Nini Mo said. Espejo might withstand a Gramatica Word, but poison?

Back at the fire, Oset had finished eating and was picking at her teeth with a knife.

No, not Oset. The illusion was so perfect that, for a moment, I wavered. Maybe I was wrong. Paranoid. Before I did anything rash, I had to be sure.

"Are you well?" Oset/Espejo asked, looking concerned.

"I'm fine, really. Look, when I get back to the City, Bea, do you want me to look up your sister? I can take letters to her."

"That would be good. I thank you."

"Remind me again where she lives. It was Laurel Street, right?"

"That is right. Laurel Street. You are very kind."

Oset didn't have a sister, only a brother, and he lived in Pudding Pie, Califa. I had heard all about him on the ride from the stage stop to Sandy. Thanks to Oset's chattiness,

I probably knew as much about her family as she did herself. Had known herself. *Oh, Oset.*

I said, "We're out of coffee. I'm going to see if the troopers have more."

The troopers fell silent as I approached their fire. They were eating salt pork and beans; no fresh meat for them. La Bruja had vanished. Wandered off to drink herself silly, I guessed.

"At ease," I said quickly. "Is there any coffee left?"

A private jumped to her feet and offered me their coffeepot. "We have a can of milk, too, Captain."

Her fellows gave her dirty looks, which were transferred to me when I accepted the can. Never take rations from a trooper, Poppy had told me, but I needed the milk to cut the taste of the medicine. I promised myself that I would buy them an entire case of canned milk when we got back to the post, but for now I had to endure the glares. I'm sure the troopers thought I was nothing but a troublesome shave tail, and they were right.

Back at the fire, Espejo was now picking at his fingernails with his knife. He leaned against Oset's saddle, oh-so-comfy, his blouse and weskit—Oset's blouse and weskit—unbuttoned. He looked more than a little smug. Clearly, he thought he had me. Fike him.

"More coffee?" I asked, refilling his tin cup. "I got a can of milk to fix it up just as you like it, Bea."

"Thank you," Espejo said. Oset drank her coffee black.

He dug her cigarillo case out of her saddlebag and lit up, the fiking bastard.

I forced my face into a smile and handed him the cup. I raised my own cup and said, "To the Warlord, long may he reign. And to the Goddess Califa, who gives us life."

"Ayah, so," he said faintly, then gulped his coffee. I pretended to sip at mine. I refilled his cup; he gulped that down and started in on a bag of jerky, chewing loudly. Fike; the Tum-O didn't seem to be working. I urged another cupful on him and he took it, but after one sip, he yawned so widely that I was surprised the stolen skin on his face didn't tear. Thank the Goddess it didn't; that would have been hideous.

"You look tired, Bea," I said. "You should get some shuteye."

"I am . . . tired." He slurred this. His chin was sinking down and his eyes were growing slitty.

"Then, lie down. I'll keep watch. Oh, you can be sure I'll keep watch. If I see any jaguars, I'll let you know. But somehow I don't think I'll be seeing any."

He forced his head up. "What do you mean?"

"You know fiking well what I mean."

"What are you talking about?" he said thickly.

"Turnabout is fair play, Espejo. You got me first last time, but it's my turn to get you."

He was trying to stand up, but his knees were weak.

The cup fell from his hand and rolled to the edge of the fire. He scrabbled at his revolver, but was too befuddled to grasp it.

"It's over, Espejo. I know you killed Captain Oset and took her skin—"

"You . . . are . . . crazy . . . Captain!" Thankfully, the wind was too high and his shout too weak; there was no way the corporal could have heard him. I stood over him, pulling the revolver from his holster, in case he summoned up the will to scream, and hissed, "You shouldn't have fiked with the Haðraaðas!"

Espejo's eyes rolled back in his head and he flopped forward like a busted doll, dangerously close to the fire. I didn't much care if he burned, but a charred corpse didn't fit my plan, so I suppressed my revulsion and gripped his shoulders to pull him away from the fire, then shoved him onto the bedroll. I knelt, puffing—he was heavy—and picked up his arm. His flesh was chill; his pulse was weak, but it was there. Fike. How long would it take this stuff to kill him?

The eastern horizon was hidden by the rise of boulders that surrounded the camp, but it seemed when I looked up that the dark wasn't quite as dark, the stars not as bright. Morning was not far off. But something else was not far off, either; distant thunder sounded, and a sudden gust of wind almost blew my hat off.

I called for Corporal Tzinga and he came at a run, cramming his hat on his head, rifle slung over his shoulder, two sleepy privates at his heels.

"Captain Oset is hurt," I said, standing up. "She went to piss and when she came back, said she had fallen, hit her head. She seemed all right at first—there wasn't any blood or even a bruise—but just a while ago she began to complain she was dizzy, and then she fainted."

"Did you try smelling salts? I have some—"

"She is out cold. The bang on her head must have been harder than she thought, and caused her some injury. We need to get her back to the post as quickly as possible."

"There's a storm coming, Captain. I don't think we can make it back before it hits." A roll of thunder punctuated Corporal Tzinga's words. The wind was growing stronger. "There are some caves further up the canyon, sir; we could shelter there. It don't take much water out here to flood the washes. We are best to be high and dry above them."

Pink lightning spiked the dark sky. Unhappy braying mixed with alarmed shouts came from the trooper's camp. The next clap of thunder shook the ground.

I said, "Let's move."

While the camps were struck and the gear hastily packed, I showed two privates how to make a sling out of a shelter, for Espejo. I would have left him behind to the storm, but that would be hard to explain to the troopers, who still thought he was Oset. The mules were kicking up a fuss. Every time the lightning flashed, they brayed and pranced, yanking at their pickets and bumping into each other, which would set off a chain reaction of biting and more braying. The troopers had a hard time getting them saddled; one private got kicked in the knee and collapsed, moaning.

"Are the caves big enough for the mules?" I asked Tzinga. Rain spattered my face, pattered on my hat.

"No, sir. Your pardon, sir, but if we let the mules loose, they'll take care of themselves. I never saw a drowned mule yet."

Before I left for the Barracks, Poppy had told me that the secret to being a good officer was knowing when to listen to your noncoms. I ordered Tzinga to let loose the mules, and to leave the saddles and tack. With Oset dead, I was personally responsible for the patrol's equipage, but fike it. I wasn't going to risk the troopers for a bunch of equipment. As the last mule was untied, a massive bolt of lightning split the sky. For a moment, the world was two-dimensional: stark black and white. The thunderclap that followed was almost deafening.

"Go!" I shouted, and we went, Corporal Tzinga leading the way and me at the rear. We scrambled through the narrow passageways between the boulders. The high rock walls offered some shelter from the wind, but they would be channels for the rain when it came, and anything caught in them would be in big trouble. Overhead, the sky had become a boiling black maelstrom. I hollered double-time, and the patrol broke into a shuffling run.

The cave, when we reached it, wasn't very deep, but it was on high ground. We squeezed in. Just in time, too, for the rain began to plummet down.

"Is that everyone?" I shouted to Corporal Tzinga.

He peered out into the dimness. "I think so—"

"Munds!" a trooper shouted in my ear. "He fell behind!"

"That damn Munds!" Corporal Tzinga said. "He never keeps up! I'll go back and get him."

"No, you keep the troopers together." I dashed into the deluge. The rain felt like hammer blows, almost knocking me to the ground. I staggered and managed to keep my footing as rocks and mud shifted beneath my feet. I found Munds lying on his face, a few yards down the trail, arms over his head. At first I thought he was dead, but when I bent over him and grabbed his shoulder, he quivered.

"Get up!" I shouted. He didn't, and so I gave him a good boot in the ribs—against regulations, but it got results, for he started and looked up at me through a mask of mud.

"That fiking mule broke my knee!"

"Get up!"

"Let me be! I don't care! I hate it here! I don't care!"

426

"Fike you, you'll care!" I shouted. "Get the fike up!" I grabbed at his sodden blouse and tugged; he struggled to his feet, and when I pulled him along with me, he came reluctantly, but he came.

The ground was slick, running with foamy water; somehow, we made it back up the slope. Lightning cracked above us. I jerked at Munds and pulled him sideways, scrabbling to find cover. Water foamed up around our knees; a tree branch whacked me in the shin and then was whisked away. Ahead, a dark shape loomed: I dragged Munds toward it, hoping it was the big cave. It wasn't, but it was shelter: a rocky overhang. When I pushed Munds underneath, he collapsed.

"I hate this place!" Munds yelped. He didn't seem grateful that I was saving his life.

"Shut up!" I wasn't in the mood to listen to whining.

"I wish you'd-a let me drown."

"Suck it up. And shut up. That's an order."

"My knee hurts."

"Your hinder is going to hurt when I kick it. Sit down."

Munds sniffed and plunked himself down, drew his knees up, and laid his head on them. My boots were squelching, my drawers were already chafing, and it was cold.

Rest while you can, Nini Mo said. Clearly we weren't going anywhere, so I, too, drew my knees up and lay my head on them, trying to stay warm. Surely Espejo would be dead by the time the storm was over. Then I'd regroup the patrol, get back to Fort Sandy, and try to send a message to Tiny Doom that it was over. She was safe. I was safe. I didn't feel safe, though. I just felt tired, as though I could sleep forever and never wake up.

For what seemed like a very long time, the storm howled, rain sheeting down like steel curtains, lightning bursting through the dark clouds like fireworks. But gradually, the thunder and lightning faded, leaving only the rain to pour down. I dozed a bit and woke up chilled but less wet, then dozed again. Munds sat silently, his head still pillowed on his knees. Eventually, I realized the rain was lessening. I stood up, my knees creaking, my feet as solid as blocks of wood, and peered out from the overhang. The torrent had softened to a patter, and the sky was slightly tinged with blue.

"Get up," I said. Munds raised his head and looked at me defiantly.

"You go, Captain. I'm staying here."

"Move." At the bite in my voice—pigface, I sounded just like Buck!—Munds staggered to his feet. Compared to the earlier deluge, the rain now felt almost gentle.

The ground was a muddy morass, churned into channels and littered with debris: rocks, broken branches, smashed cacti. Below us, the boulders where we'd camped were in a rushing river of foamy water, brown as baby shite and cluttered with uprooted bushes. A dead animal—a javelina, maybe—bobbed by. To the east, the sky was clearing, bisected by a gloriously iridescent rainbow. We clambered through the mud until we could see the mouth of the cave in the rocks above. A figure waved at us. Corporal Tzinga. He was yelling something.

I hauled myself up the last few feet and accepted Tzinga's outstretched hand for a boost onto the cave's lip. Two other troopers hauled Munds in after me. I leaned over, breathing heavily, and wiped the water from my eyes.

"Good news, Captain!" Tzinga said. "Captain Oset's awake."

THIRTY-SIX

Orders.
Drugged. Evil Murdoch.

TZINGA'S WORDS HIT ME like acid to the face. For a moment, I thought I might faint. I looked past him into the dimness of the cave. When my eyes adjusted, I saw Espejo, still wearing Oset's skin, sitting against the wall. He looked wet and muddy, but he was definitely alive.

"Corporal, disarm her," Espejo ordered.

Tzinga looked startled. "Sir?"

"Disarm her! She is under arrest! She tried to poison me!"

"Captain Romney said you fell and hit your head, Captain." Tzinga seemed mighty confused, and so did the other troopers, who were wide-eyed, brows furrowed.

"A lie!" Espejo said. "She poisoned me. She tried to kill me."

I said, "Corporal, you have to listen to me. He looks like Captain Oset, but he's not. He's a Birdie nahual. He killed Captain Oset, stole her skin. He's going to kill me and all of you as well, Corporal."

Espejo laughed weakly. "Don't listen to her! She's an imposter. She's not a captain; her name isn't even Romney. She's here under false orders. I order you to take her gun, Corporal."

"I know he looks like her, Corporal, but he's not! I swear to you on Califa's grave, you have to listen to me—" I said.

"If you do not take her gun and put her under arrest, I shall have you arrested, too, Corporal."

Tzinga looked agonizingly indecisive. He was in a tough spot, caught between two officers. But he had to follow the orders of the officer he thought was his superior. Behind him, the troopers were muttering uneasily, staring at the spectacle.

"Please, Captain," Tzinga said. "Just give me your side arm. I don't want to have to take it." He was two feet taller than me. He could take it easily. I unbuckled Oset's belt and tossed it toward Tzinga, who gave it to Espejo.

"Bind her hands!" Espejo ordered.

I took a step back. A Gramatica Word rolled sourly in my mouth, but I didn't dare spit it at Espejo—the cave was too small and Tzinga was in my line of fire.

I said, "I can prove what I say. Nahuals shun the sun. Step out of the cave, into daylight, if you dare—"

"I would be happy to prove your lie," Espejo said. "But

I am too weak to move from this spot, thanks to your poison. Corporal, obey me!"

"I'm sorry, Captain Romney," Tzinga said, pleadingly. I took another step back, and another—and ran into someone who said, "Advancin' in the opposite direction, darlin'?"

I could tell by the smell, a ripe combination of bug juice, sweat, and mud, that it was La Bruja. She took my arm in a not-so-friendly grip, and when I tried to shake free, the grip became squeezy.

Espejo ordered, "Corporal, bind her hands!"

Corporal Tzinga and a private moved toward me, but La Bruja forestalled them. "Oh, I got her. She ain't going nowhere. Looks like I am missin' a dance. Can I join the fun?"

"He's not Captain Oset," I told her. "He's a nahual who killed Oset, took her skin—"

"She's deranged," Espejo interrupted.

"She does sound kinda crazy, I'll admit," La Bruja answered.

"Let go of me." I twisted in her grasp. She just laughed and pinched my arm more tightly.

Espejo turned to Corporal Tzinga. "Corporal, take the troopers and go round up the mules."

Tzinga protested, "Sir, it's not right to leave you alone with Captain Romney, if she did try to kill you—"

"Oh, don't you worry, Tzinga," La Bruja said encouragingly. "I got madama here in good hand and will make sure everything is nice and fine. You better cross that wash while you can—the flood ain't over yet, not by a long shot."

"Obey me!" Espejo hissed to Tzinga. "And you may go as well, madama. I have no need of your services."

"No, I guess I'll stay. I got no place else to be and this is interestin'," La Bruja said cheerfully. Espejo gave her a withering look, but she didn't budge. Tzinga ordered the troopers to follow him, and they did, with many backward glances. We stood at the mouth of the cave, La Bruja firmly gripping my arm, and watched the troopers slip and slide down the hill in the warm flood of sunshine, dodging crushed cacti and torn bushes. They waded carefully through the still-foamy wash, then disappeared among the rocks on the other side.

"Did ya try to poison him?" La Bruja demanded, turning back to me.

"Ayah," I admitted. La Bruja had said *him,* not *her.* Did she believe me?

"This is Army business," Espejo said. "Leave us!"

She ignored him and asked me, "What with?"

"Madama Twanky's Tum-O."

"Cure ya or kill ya. Tum-O is nothin' but straight laudanum, with a little ginger to give it zing. Stop up yer bowels and send you to an endless sleep if you guzzle the whole bottle. So I gotta wonder." She turned to Espejo. "How is it that you drank it down and are fresh as a daisy?"

"The bottle must have been mostly empty," Espejo answered.

"It was almost full," I protested.

La Bruja said, "Now, a pophead could drink that bottle, have a little nap, and ask for more. But Oset, she wasn't no pophead. Dead set against the stuff, actually. Seems strange, then, to take such a big dose so easy. What do you say to that, *Captain?*"

"This is none of your concern," Espejo snapped.

"Yer peeling," La Bruja remarked.

Startled, Espejo put a hand to his head. The skin on the left side of Oset's face was beginning to sag, drawing the lip down into a snarl. He leaned over, clawing at his head, and the entire thing slid off in an awful slimy rush. I gurgled. Espejo straightened up, Oset's face dangling in his hand like a soggy discarded rag. His own face—his true face—was covered with a slick red bloody film, like a newborn baby.

"That is a relief," he said. "I do not know how the Flayed Priests stand it."

La Bruja gasped and dropped to her knees, yanking me painfully down with her. "Yer pardon, Great Lord!" she cried. "I didn't recognize yer before! I thought Captain Romney was plumb crazy! Fergive me!"

"You know me?" Espejo said in astonishment.

She had grabbed his slimy hand and was kissing it—yuck. She said as she slobbered, "Ayah, Your Grace. My ma, she was a Huitzil. I know I ain't turned out like much, but she brought me up to honor the Smoked Mirror. Once, she took me to the Harvest festival in Anahuatl City, and I saw ya give a hundred men to the Lord of the Smoked Mirror. I could never forgit the Duque de Espejo y Ahumado. I am yer servant!"

"You witch!" I hissed.

I didn't see the swing, only felt the sickening blow to the side of my head. I fell over in a heap, wheezing, and somewhere behind the tummy-turning pain was the thought that when I got my chance with La Bruja I wouldn't be squeamish, not at all. Through the ringing in my ears, I heard her say eagerly, "This girl ain't got no respect fer you, yer grace. Let me kill her for yer."

"Do not touch her!" Espejo said sharply.

"You kin bank on me!" La Bruja whined. I sat up dizzily, the world swooning about me. For a moment, there were two La Brujas groveling at two Espejos's feet. The blurred figures resolved down to the proper number, which were still two too many. Espejo pulled away from La Bruja and leaned over me, saying, "Are you hurt?"

"Fike you!" I spat, tasting blood through the bright pain in my mouth. I had bitten my tongue. "Don't touch me!"

"Don't yer flap at His Grace like that," La Bruja said sharply.

"Fike you, too!"

La Bruja made as though she was going to slap me again, and Espejo said swiftly, "This girl belongs to the Lord of the Smoked Mirror. If you truly honor him, you will obey me."

"This girl?" La Bruja said scornfully, "Why does the Lord of the Smoked Mirror want this girl? She sure ain't much. She's just a dirty Blackcoat, a soldier dog. And not a very good one, neither. She ain't hardly worthy of him."

"That is not for you to decide," Espejo said. "This girl's family belongs to the Lord of the Smoked Mirror. Until now, she and her mother have escaped his embrace. But I have found her now, and soon I shall find her mother. They will return to Ciudad Anahuatl to honor the Lord with their lives."

"Let me help you!" La Bruja said eagerly. "I kin find her mam—I'm a great tracker. An' I know everyone in this country. Who is she? I'll go out and get her, bring her to ya."

"She is hiding from me. I do not know her name here."

During this conversation, I had managed to leverage myself upright, despite the burning pain in my side. I noticed a little gleam in the darkness near the discarded blanket. I oh-so-slowly reached out and hooked the gleam in, pulled it toward me. It was an Army-issue fork: three-pronged and plenty sharp. I slid it up my sleeve, and just in time, for Espejo was kneeling before me. *Wait until the moment is hot before you strike,* Nini Mo said. This was not a hot moment.

La Bruja turned on me. "Do you know where she is? Tell us or I'll make you sad you kept yer trap shut!"

"I'm already sad you didn't fall off your mule and break your neck," I said. La Bruja raised her leg as though she was going to boot me, and I cringed in anticipation.

"Did I not tell you to leave her?" Espejo interjected, pushing La Bruja away. "I have other methods to know her mind. She can conceal nothing from me. If she knows where her mother is, I shall know, too."

He bent over me again. In the murk, his eyes gleamed goldly, flat and reflective. "Where is she, *muñeca?*"

"I don't know."

"Do not lie to me, *por favor.* You know that I can find out, whether you wish to tell me or not. I can take the information from you, but I allow you to give it to me. I am being kind. I know she came to see you. What did she tell you?"

"Fike you." The bravado was ruined by the quaver in my voice. He *could* take the knowledge from me, and I could not stop him. I had tried to forget what had happened in Barbacoa, but I could not, and the memory made me weak with fear. *Don't be a hero,* Nini Mo said. *Everyone breaks eventually. Save yourself the pain and give in.* I said, "She said she's going to kill you. And I should sit tight and let her."

"And then she left. Where did she go?"

"Across the Line. That's all I know."

"I followed that trail. It looped around and came back, and then disappeared. Tell me where she is!"

"I don't know," I said. "And that's the truth. With the Broncos, I guess. You are welcome to find them. I'm sure they'd be happy to roast you like a pumpkin—"

La Bruja shut me up with a sharp kick to the ribs. I flopped over and lay there, clutching my side and trying to distract myself from the pain by focusing on what I would do to her. Through my gasping, I noticed something else: Oset's gun belt. Espejo had tossed it aside, and now it lay ignored on the gravel.

Espejo had stood up threateningly when La Bruja kicked me, but before he could admonish her, she said quickly, "Across the Line? With the Broncos—listen—I've had some truck with them Broncos, camped with them from time to time, and I know their ways. There's a woman rides with them. She pretends to be a Bronco, but she ain't. She got red hair and I ain't never seen a Bronco with red hair. I know where they camp. I can show you. I'll wager you'll find her there, or else they'll know where she is."

That snapperheaded bitch. A Gramatica Curse hovered on my lips but I bit it back—for now. You could bet that when I was done with her, La Bruja was going to wish she'd never been born.

Espejo said, "We will go as you say. But we shall wait for nightfall."

"I can go on my own, bring her back to ya, Your Grace, so as not to waste any time. Take the girl with me—"

"No. We will wait. She cannot escape me now. It is only a matter of time."

"Well, then, let's settle in. Ya look pale, Lord. Need a little pick-me-up? I'll bet the girl tastes pretty sweet. I kin hold her for you, if you want."

"Leave her alone," Espejo said sharply, and La Bruja just laughed. She dug out a hip flask and offered it to Espejo, who shook his head with a grimace. I guess the Lord of the Smoked Mirror doesn't go much for mescal. I also rejected La Bruja's offer, but before Espejo could intercede, she forced the flask against my mouth. Despite my frantic head-shaking, a few foul drops got through my clenched lips and burned my mouth.

"Put the flask away!" Espejo said. "Show some restraint!"

La Bruja obeyed. I lay back in the dirt, my side throbbing, my jaw aching, thinking hateful, hateful thoughts about La Bruja, about Espejo—and waiting. The fork was tucked up in my sleeve. The Oatmeal Word lingered at the back of my palate. I was ready for the hot moment. I had to hit Espejo before nightfall, before he came into his full power. Espejo sat silent and still, his legs crossed, his hands folded on his knees, the painted golden eyes glittering. Next to him, La Bruja was crouched on her heels, braiding some strands of horsehair, humming tunelessly to herself. She was blocking my line of fire. I didn't think I could say the Word twice, so I sure as fike did not want to waste it on her. But maybe I could draw Espejo over to me.

"Your Grace," I said in a quavery voice. "Could I have some water—"

"We ain't got any water," La Bruja said swiftly, before Espejo could answer. "Shut yer trap and keep it shut, or I'll shut it fer yer."

"Go down to the wash and get her some water," Espejo ordered. Thank the Goddess! As soon as she was gone, I'd hit him hard, with all my might.

But instead of obeying, La Bruja stood up and said, "Here, I fergot I had a canteen. Drink."

Fike. I took the canteen from her and drank. The water tasted like ashes. The throbbing in my side was receding, but it was being replaced by a great wave of tiredness. I yawned so widely, I thought my skull might split.

"Ye ever been to Matapatos, Yer Grace?" La Bruja asked.

"No," Espejo answered.

"I was down there last year. There's this dama there named Loosey Lucia; she run the best rat fights in all of Arivaipa. She got a champion ratter, Teacup is his name. Oh, when that terrier is on a roll, he can bite fifty rats in five minutes, no trouble 'tall. His bite's sharper than an ungrateful child. Yer oughter go down there sometime. It's something to see. I won seventy-five divas and aim to take in more still. I'm saving up fer a new ditto suit . . ." On and on and on La Bruja went, yammering about poker games, and long-dead horses, and the Broncos she'd killed, and the drunks she'd had, and the hunts she'd been on, and the shirts she'd worn, and the BBQ she'd eaten, and the men she'd loved. Several times Espejo bid her shut up but she didn't remain silent long.

I tried to think of another plan, another way to get Espejo within my range, but my eyes were growing heavier and heavier and I could no longer hold my head up. My bones felt as though they were melting into jelly; my flesh was wooden, heavy. I closed my eyes, La Bruja's voice one long drone that carried me away to darkness.

I woke to a boot heel in the ribs. I sat up, groggily, head swimming, and said, "You drugged me."

"Naw," La Bruja said. "Ya just didn't like my stories. Come on." She yanked me to my feet and I stood shakily. My head felt as though it were full of wet sand. Outside, the bright glare was beginning to fade. Oh, pigface, fike. I had slept my advantage away. It was now or never.

Espejo was already standing. He said to me, "Can you walk?"

I started to say, *Fike you,* and bit the words back. "I think La Bruja broke one of my ribs," I said, twisting my voice into a whine. "It hurts to breathe."

He leaned over me. "Why did you not say so earlier?"

"Aw, she's malingering," La Bruja said. Espejo pushed her away.

I felt his ice-cold hands fumble at my side. I almost puked at the smell of him, so noxiously close. I mewed and whined, and eventually he hoisted me to my feet, an arm around my shoulder. I didn't have to pretend very hard to be wobbly.

"Let's leave her here," La Bruja said. "She'll only slow us down. I'll tie her tightly and we can come back later."

"No," Espejo said. He hoisted me up and half carried, half dragged me out of the cave. La Bruja was right behind us.

Outside, the sky was purple and yellow, dusk but not yet full dark. We skittered down the incline, rocks rolling under our feet. Below us, the wash was still flooded with rushing water, brown and foamy, seeded with broken tree limbs and drowned tumbleweeds. The steep grade was treacherous with uprooted plants, slick with mud. About a quarter of the way down, I went limp. Espejo sagged under my sudden weight, gripping hard as he tried to hold on to me. I flung my arms around his neck, almost choking from his foul breath on my face. I let my heels slide, felt his footing start to falter.

He grunted, fingers digging in, and said, "I won't let you fall."

The moment couldn't have been hotter if the air had been on fire.

"⟨glyphs⟩!" I spat. The Oatmeal Word seared my throat, scorched my lips. Glowing like molten glass, it hit Espejo square on the nose. He let out a gurgled yelp and dropped me. I hit the mud and skidded several painful feet before catching my boot heels and coming to a stop. Rolling over, I saw that Espejo had collapsed and was wiggling on the ground like piece of bacon in a frying pan. A blackish pink glow suffused his skin.

"Fike!" La Bruja shouted. I turned my head and saw her skidding down the incline toward me. Scrambling to my feet, I lunged at her, stumbling, and felt the fork sink in—I wasn't sure what part of her I'd hit, but her yelp sounded glorious. I got one good twist in before she shoved me away. Below, Espejo was still quivering, his back arching almost into a bow, his arms and legs stiffening like boards.

I skidded in the mud and clambered as fast as I could back toward the cave and Oset's gun. I tripped and a rock hammered a bright pain into my knee. I scrambled back to my feet. A horrible howl filled the air, reverberating off the canyon walls, curling up my spine.

I looked over my shoulder and saw La Bruja braced on the incline, a thin black rope looping lazily above her head. The horsehair she'd been braiding in the cave was now a lariat. Below her, a black jaguar crouched in the dust, tail whipping back and forth, puking up a roiling mess of blackish pink coldfire. The cat coughed and hacked, shaking its head, as the loop of La Bruja's rope whipped faster until it was a whistling blur. The jaguar looked up and sprang. The loop was moving so quickly I couldn't see if it caught the cat, but when La Bruja jerked the rope tight, the jaguar fell out of its leap into a tangled sprawl.

I didn't waste any more time; I scrambled the last few feet to the cave's mouth. Inside the cave, it was pitch-black. I fumbled through the darkness to where I remembered seeing Oset's gun belt. I almost screamed in relief when my groping hand felt leather. Oh, happy gun!

Outside, the dusk had darkened to night. The coldfire the jaguar had sicked up had spread to an uprooted bush, which now burned with an eerie blackish-pink light. The jaguar was still struggling at the end of La Bruja's rope, and she was having a hard time holding it. Her heels were dug in, but she was sliding.

"Come on, you snapperhead, come on!" she shouted. The jaguar writhed and sprang into the air, yanking the lariat out of her grip. La Bruja fell back and sat down hard in the mud. The jaguar surged up the hill toward her like a streak of black lightning, the lariat whipping behind it. La Bruja's moccasins weren't getting a grip in the mud. She fumbled at her waist, but I fired first.

In the dark, the moving cat was a hard target, and my shot went wide, exploding a harmless cactus. La Bruja was yelling something, but the gunshot had deafened me. I fired again, and the hammer snapped on an empty chamber. Fike.

The jaguar was barely a foot away from her when, with an echoing bray, Evil Murdoch exploded out of nowhere. Murdoch caught the cat by surprise, grabbing it by the neck and lifting it off the ground, tossing it like a toy. The jaguar twisted, paws lashing, and with a bray of pain, Murdoch let go. The jaguar was rolling when Murdoch lashed out with a hoof, caught the cat in its side. It flew through the air and landed in a cactus, shrieking.

During all this, La Bruja clambered to her feet and ran up the hill toward me, a very large unsheathed knife in her hand. I still couldn't hear her over the ringing in my ears. But I would be fiked if I stood there like a snapperhead and let her gut me.

"⟩⟨⟩⟨ ⟨⟩⟨⟩⟨ ⟨⟩⟨ ⟩⟨⟩⟨ ⟨!" I screamed. The Word tore what was left of my voice from me. Lucky for Tharyn he hadn't swallowed that Word at the ZuZu's ball. It ignited when it hit La Bruja, and she exploded into a ball of coldfire, lost her footing, and tumbled backward. The jaguar had torn himself loose from the cactus, but now La Bruja and the coldfire rolled into him, and he was enveloped by the blaze as well. The ringing in my ears was overlaid with a dull roar. A flash flood was filling the wash. I watched as the burning maelstrom bounced down the hillside. Then a wall of water burst through and washed La Bruja and the jaguar away.

THIRTY-SEVEN

Return.
In Command. A Reunion.

M Y KNEES WOULDN'T HOLD ME anymore, so I sat down on a rock by the mouth of the cave. I wished I had my canteen. My mouth tasted of oily blood, and my throat felt as though it had been cut to ribbands. It was too dark now to see the wash below, but I could hear the roar of the water. Plenty of water, but none to drink. Evil Murdoch ruffled my hair with his furry lip. There were some scratches and blood on his neck, but he otherwise seemed all right.

And then I thought I saw a dim pink spark in his eyes. "Pig?" My voice sounded like a dying accordion. Where had he come from? I hadn't summoned him. And yet he had still come. Tears pricked at my eyes. I scratched his nose in thanks. He *hee-hawed*, yellow teeth gleaming in the darkness, and then bounded away to nibble on an up-rooted mesquite bush.

Until the water in the wash went down, I was stuck. One of the privates had left his blouse lying in the back of the cave. I put it on and found a small bottle in the right pocket and, in the left, a tintype of a man holding a lacy baby in one arm and a bull terrier in the other. The bottle contained apple jack; it burned as it went down, but it also soothed the soreness. He had a hankie, too, relatively clean, which I used to wipe the mud off my face. I ejected the faulty round from Oset's revolver and reloaded, then sat back down on my rock and waited for the water to recede.

Somehow I fell asleep and when I awoke, stiff and tired, it was daylight again. Evil Murdoch was standing a few yards away, head drooping sleepily. When I sat up, he let out a bray that even I understood: *Let's get the fike out of here.* We made our way down to the edge of the wash. The water had gone down to a trickle. Evil Murdoch allowed me to clamber up on his spiny back, and then he picked his way slowly through the debris.

We rode through the bright morning, as new-scrubbed and blue as the first day of the world, and, about a quarter of mile or so down the track, came across the patrol's camp. The mules brayed out a welcome to Evil Murdoch and he *hee-haw*ed back, scattering the soldiers from their makeshift beds.

Sergeant Tzinga rushed toward me, asking anxiously, "Are you all right, Captain? Where's Captain Oset and La Bruja?"

"The jaguar attacked us," I said. "It went for La Bruja, and when Captain Oset tried to help her, they were all swept away in the wash."

It was obvious that Corporal Tzinga wasn't sure if he should believe me or not, and that my wild accusations regarding Captain Oset still weighed on him. But he didn't dare question my account. Rank does have its privileges.

We spent the rest of the morning wallowing along the wash, looking for some sign of La Bruja and Espejo. We found La Bruja's hat and one of her moccasins. We found tangled tack and soggy saddles; Private Pinto's knapsack, contents soaked; a busted tin oil lamp; a crate that contained a porcelain figurine of the Warlord, wrapped in straw and somehow unbroken. We found a dead javelina and a lot of brush. One of the mules was lodged up on the bank of the wash; the vultures were already on the job.

We piled up the soggy tack and covered it with a blanket, well weighed down with rocks. I wrote out a note identifying the gear as the property of the Army of Califa and pinned it to the blanket. When we got back to Sandy, I'd send a wagon to collect it all.

Hooker's farm had come through the storm. Madama Hooker gave us pumpkin soup and tortillas. When I told her what had happened to La Bruja and Captain Oset, she and the children were quite upset. I guess they'd been pretty neighborly with Oset, who'd often brought the kids candy.

"I can't believe the water didn't just throw La Bruja back up again," Madama Hooker said. "They weren't very friendly, water and her."

"Shush, Mamma," Sieur Hooker said. "It's not nice to say."

Madama Hooker said, "But at least we don't have to worry about that cat anymore."

I thought of that wall of water: brown with dirt, thick with debris. It would have been impossible for La Bruja or Espejo to survive the flood. But I would have liked to have seen the bodies, just to be sure.

Fort Sandy was a disaster. My first thought as we came up the hill, footsore and hungry, was that the entire post had been destroyed. The flagpole lay smashed on the parade ground. The roof of the QM depot had fallen in. The corral had blown away and the walls of one of the barracks had liquefied, turning the building into a melted muddy mess. Troopers should have been out cleaning up the mess, but there was no sign of industry. A private rushed across the parade ground and flung himself upon us in relief.

Apparently, Espejo's impersonation of Captain Oset had been only skin deep; he had ridden off the post without designating who was in command. Major Rucker hadn't yet returned from the treaty meeting with the Broncos. In the absence of obvious authority, discipline had broken down pretty quickly. A couple of troopers had released themselves from duty—that is, they'd scarpered.

Loud singing was coming from the sutler's store. The dog pack had gotten into the QM stores and eaten twenty pounds of fresh beef.

"Your orders?" the private said imploringly.

"Has there been any word from Major Rucker?"

"No, sir."

Corporal Tzinga said, "You're in charge, Captain Romney."

I was hard-pressed to swallow the almost hysterical laughter bubbling up in me. After all that had happened, now I was in command of Fort Sandy? The idea was ludicrous.

"Your orders, Captain?" the private asked anxiously.

"Organize some work squads, and get the colors flying."

Before, authority and duty had felt crushing. Now I was glad to have something to throw myself into. Tzinga and I went down to the sutler's store and found four drunken soldiers and several empty cases of beer. The guardhouse had made it through the storm just fine, and that's where the drunken warblers soon found themselves, in irons. Corporal Tzinga took a patrol out after the deserters, and these actions motivated the other shirkers to fall into line. Soon squads of industrious soldiers were, under my orders, getting the post put back to rights. By late afternoon, the colors of Califa were flying from a makeshift flagpole, most of the mules had been rounded up and corralled, the forage had been salvaged, and the troopers were sitting down to a hot meal. There was a lot of work left to do, but at least the animals and troopers were taken care of.

Just after Retreat, Tzinga came back with another deserter; he had found her, he told me, at the hog ranch, where a celebration was going on.

"Celebrating what?" I asked. And when he told me, I put him in charge and headed that direction immediately.

I heard the noise long before I could see the tent; the raucous sound of laughter mixed with hooting and the occasional *yippee*. The storm, which had almost destroyed Fort Sandy, somehow hadn't touched the hog ranch.

Inside, the tent was packed to its canvas walls with people: cowboys, miners, ranchers. Even the soldier dogs were there, weaving in and out of the standing-room-only crowd. Over the laughter, a voice was saying, "I had my knife in my teeth, and I was just waitin' for the right moment. Oh, ya can imagine how foul his breath was—"

A tall cowboy blocked my way and wouldn't move, even when I gave him a good push. He turned around, swearing, but when he saw the expression on my face, moved aside. There, sitting at a table covered with bottles, in all her grubby glory, was La Bruja. A dog was sprawled in her lap: a red dog with lovely caramel eyes and soft floppy ears.

"Flynn!" I shouted. Flynn's ears perked up and his

head swiveled. He flung himself out of La Bruja's lap in a scrabble of paws that upset the table. I caught him mid-jump and fell back under the weight of his wiggly joy. He licked my face, sprayed my boots, and I didn't care; I just squeezed him and kissed him and squeezed him some more. The crowd was laughing, but I didn't care about that, either. Oh, darling Flynnie, darling Flynnie.

"I guess that's yer dog." La Bruja joined the laughter. "Found him wandering around out in the scrub and then he followed me home. Hungry little bugger."

I covered Flynnie with kisses; I was never, ever going to let him go. But how the fike was La Bruja not dead? And . . . did that mean that Espejo wasn't dead, either? A cold wind blew through me.

La Bruja, still laughing, was saying, "Sorry about the roughhousing, Captain, but I knew ya could take it. Come on, now. Don't glare. I know I played it pretty strong, but I was on yer side all along."

"How are you still alive?" I demanded.

"Oh, the *agua* took one taste of me and spat me right back up! And that cat—pigface, he weren't nothing but a little kitten. No trouble 'tall!" She waved her bottle in the air and the crowd roared and clapped.

"He's dead, then."

La Bruja grinned. "Oh, I don't believe he'll be sneaking around anymore."

"Are you sure?"

"Oh, ayah, I'm sure." She pulled a buckskin pouch out of her shirt and upended it over her open palm: two long white things fell out. It took me a second to realize they were fangs. Jaguar fangs.

La Bruja threw her head back and let out a long, yipping ululation, and the crowd joined her, screaming and shouting and stamping their feet. The barkeep shouted, "Free rounds!" and that got an even bigger cheer.

"Well, now, no hard feelings, Captain." La Bruja smiled a mossy green smile. "I know I had ya goin' there for a bit, but I was only tryin' to get in a good hot moment. Here, I think you deserve these as much as I do. More, maybe!"

She tossed the pouch at me, and I awkwardly caught it. Someone pushed a glass toward me, and I felt hands pounding my back, congratulating me. I had no idea what La Bruja had told them I had done, but clearly she had made me look heroic, which was about as far from the truth as you can get. I drank the contents of the glass. It was shrub, so cold that it drove a spike of delicious pain between my eyes.

Suddenly the smell of the hog ranch was overwhelming: bug juice, hair oil, sweat, dirty leather, blood. I couldn't breathe; I was going to puke. Flynn at my heels, I made it out of the hog ranch just in time, and then goodbye shrub, goodbye.

I stood up, wiping my mouth on my sleeve, listening to the sound of revelry. Flynn nudged my knee and I bent down to clutch him.

"Come on, Flynnie. Let's get the fike out of here."

Dusk was coming down, and the trail back to the post was growing indistinct. I stumbled into a teddy bear cholla and swore. Just because there was no jaguar waiting to pounce didn't mean that Arivaipa was safe. Next to me, Flynn alerted, quivering, back and tail stiff. I put my hand on the butt of Oset's revolver; something big was coming down the trail. Something too big to be a man.

I smelled apple pipeweed and musty fur. I ran toward him, and he caught me up, almost smothering me in a furry embrace. I clutched him, and felt him change in my arms, fur turning slick, muscles and bones shrinking until I held a sweaty bare man.

"How did you get here?" I asked. The satchel hanging over his shoulder knocked me in the hip painfully, but I didn't care.

"I ran all the way!" he said breathlessly. That was the last thing he said for a long time. I didn't care now that I was grubby and tired; I didn't care that he was dusty and tired. All I cared about was that, at last, I wasn't alone.

THIRTY-EIGHT

Report.
An Offer. A Decision.

ALL I WANTED TO DO WAS lie down next to Tharyn and tell him everything. Instead, as soon as we were back on the post, I was sucked back into duty. I sent Tharyn and Flynn back to the UOQ to clean up and rest, hoping to join them as soon as Retreat was over. But after Retreat came the posting of the night guard, and then Tattoo; then I had damage reports to write. It was almost midnight before I could finally escape to Tharyn. Telling him everything took until dawn, and then, while he and Flynn could sleep the day away, I had to answer the Reveille bugle call. After that came roll call, then changing of the guard, then sick call, then inspection, then water call, and thus ran duty on and on and on, through the hot blue day.

There was no sign of Tiny Doom, but then I hardly expected that there would be. I was pretty sure I knew her game now. She'd scarpered, gotten as far away from Sandy,

Espejo, and me as she could. Well, this time I would not go looking for her.

Major Rucker returned from his parley with the Broncos late in the afternoon, alone. I guess Lieutenant Sabre had headed straight back to Califa as soon as the meeting was over. By then, Fort Sandy was in the best order I could make it. Actually, I rather thought it might have been in better shape than before; in some ways, the storm was almost an improvement. The major looked surprised to see me standing on the porch of the COQ; I told him that Captain Oset had been killed hunting the jaguar and that I had broken arrest to take command in the aftermath of the storm. Major Rucker ordered me back to my arrest, saying he would send for me later.

The UOQ was empty; Tharyn had left a note saying he'd gone to the hog ranch and taken Flynn with him. I lay down on the settee and tried to figure out what the fike I was going to tell Major Rucker. If I made a full and truthful report, I would be giving Tiny Doom away. My report would be sent up the chain of command and everyone along the way—officers, clerks, *everyone*—would know everything. A lie wouldn't work; there were too many witnesses. I was sick of lying, anyway. But I did not dare chance the truth.

Keep yer yip shut, said Nini Mo. So there was my plan. They could court-martial me, cashier me, whatever. I would keep my yip shut.

After Retreat, a private came and told me that Major Rucker was waiting for me in his office. I tramped across the parade ground—almost back to normal now—and found Major Rucker by his sideboard, fiddling with a bottle.

"Sit down, Lieutenant. Would you like a drink?"

"No, sir. I mean, yes, sir."

He handed me a glass of lemonade. Today, Major Rucker looked round-cheeked and bright-eyed—a vast difference from the desiccated man I had met on my initial arrival at Sandy. I decided I didn't want to know the reason why he was now so plump and fresh. *Sometimes it's better to be stupid but happy,* Nini Mo said.

"How did the meeting go, sir?" I asked.

"It was quite successful, I am happy to say. Lieutenant Sabre has already resumed his journey back to the City, carrying the good news."

"That's wonderful."

"It is good news." Major Rucker finished his lemonade and poured himself another. He sat down behind his desk, lit a cigarillo, and said, "The Goddess gives with one hand and takes away with another. Poor Bea. What a terrible tragedy. But it can happen to any of us at any time. I told her often to be more careful, to shake out her boots before she put them on. But she could be so impetuous, poor Bea, and sometimes she just didn't listen. I've already spoken to La Bruja, you see."

What the fike had La Bruja told him?

"When I first came out here, years back, one of the quartermaster sergeants got stung by a sangyn-backed scorpion. He picked up his hat and put it on without shaking it, and the scorpion stung him on the ear. The poison goes straight to the brain, you know, and there was nothing we could do but confine him to the guardhouse and watch him go mad. It was awful. He was convinced that his own hand was trying to strangle him. He died of blood loss when he tried to chew it off. Poor Oset. At least the madness did not take her that way."

Major Rucker leaned back in his chair, blew a little smoke ring. He stared at me, as though daring me to contradict him.

I was suddenly sure that he knew full well that Captain Oset hadn't been stung by a scorpion. I was suddenly sure that Major Rucker knew exactly what had happened at the cave, and why. He said he'd been stationed with Buck in Arivaipa, back in the day. Tiny Doom had been stationed there at the same time; he had to have known her, then. He knew her now, I was sure of it. But I wasn't quite sure enough to challenge him.

I said, "It was a tragedy. Poor Captain Oset. She was not herself at all."

"No," he agreed. "She was not. And this I will say in my official report. Captain Oset was a good officer and a fine woman. She didn't deserve such a death. But rarely do we get what we deserve, no?"

"Ayah." I was certain that I was about to get what I deserved, and welcomed that reckoning, too. Maybe it would help me feel better.

Major Rucker raised his glass in a toast. "A cup for the dead already and hurrah for the next to die." I echoed his toast and drank the last of the icy-cold lemonade.

Major Rucker said, "Now, about those other charges against you. In light of your actions in taking over Bea's command, I'm inclined to dismiss them. In fact, I'm inclined to forget about everything. Bea was the acting adjutant general, you know, and she was very way behind on her returns. I don't think she'd managed to complete the post returns for the last month or so . . ."

The post returns list every person present on a post, and their duties. Major Rucker was telling me that there was no official record I had ever been at Sandy.

". . . But we're getting caught up with the paperwork, and so I think, Lieutenant, perhaps you should be on your way as soon as possible? Get back on track; put this entire episode behind you. La Bruja's report is so thorough, I think it can stand for yours, as well. There's no need for you to add unnecessary details."

Now I knew he knew, and was covering for me. For Tiny Doom. But before I could confront him, he said quickly, "Sieur Taylor is running a herd out to Calo Res tomorrow. He's agreed to allow you to ride with him. You can catch the stage to Hassayumpa from there. No—" He raised his hand. "I think that closes this matter. As soon as we put it behind us all, the better we shall be. You are dismissed. Your arrest is lifted."

"Thank you, sir."

"You needn't thank me. Frankly, Lieutenant, it is Captain Oset's reputation I am considering, not yours. She deserves to be remembered as a hero, even if she didn't die like one. And I consider also your mother."

"My mother?" My heart jumped.

"Ayah. General *Fyrdraaca*. She does not need this kind of embarrassment right now. I take the prerogative of a senior officer to remind you that you have a sworn duty to put the interests of your country over your personal choices. When you break that oath, you damage not just yourself but your fellow soldiers as well. You broke confinement—you broke your word to me—you deliberately disobeyed my orders, and Goddess knows what other orders you ignored. You came here under false pretenses and put us all in danger. You deserve to be court-martialed—fike, if it were up to me, I'd cashier you and let you sit in the guardhouse for a couple of months before I sent you off with a bobtail.

"Captain Oset is dead. Nothing you do can ever change

that. You owe it to her to make her death meaningful. Do you understand?"

"Ayah, sir," I said miserably.

His tone softened a bit. "But you did well with your first command. You got the troopers home again safely, even if you did lose most of the gear—losses I am going to have to absorb personally, I'd like to say, since I don't want to tax Oset's estate. Her mother is elderly and will need all of Oset's pension. It was a tough situation even for a seasoned officer, and you haven't even graduated yet. And perhaps you are not solely responsible for Oset's death. Others bear some blame, including myself for not being more alert to the dangers. In the end, you did well. I think your mother would be proud. But, Lieutenant . . ."

"Yes, sir?"

"Please don't come back to Arivaipa anytime soon."

"Yes, sir."

Dismissed, I stood on the ramada for a moment, watching the colors flutter in the breeze. I should have felt relief—I had gotten away with everything—but I felt awful. Instead of letting me off the hook, Major Rucker had impaled me deeper upon it. I would prefer to be court-martialed, cashiered, sent to the guardhouse, maybe even shot. I did not deserve to get away with anything. Oset was still dead.

I would be glad to see the last of Fort Sandy, the last

of Arivaipa. Major Rucker had asked me not to return—he didn't need to make it an order. I had no desire to see Arivaipa again.

AT THE HOG ranch, the party was still in full swing. As I came through the door, a man in a blue sailor-collared shirt made a suggestion to me. I kicked him hard in the knee, which felt so satisfying that I did it again. The roisterers thought this was really amusing and yelled encouragement, but the gesture had made my bruised side throb, so I just left him.

At the bar, Flynn was sitting in a barrel chair, eating a steak off a china plate. Two tables over, Tharyn was playing euchre. From the scowls of the other players and the pile in front of him, I guessed he was winning. But when he saw me, he got up from the game and slipped his arm around my waist.

"Outside!" I hollered over the din. Flynn scrambled down from his chair and followed us.

"What happened? Is he going to court-martial you?" Tharyn asked as soon as we found a private spot near a saguaro.

"Nothing happened. La Bruja told him that Oset was stung by a scorpion and the poison made her crazy. That's the line he's sticking to, but he knows about Tiny Doom, I know it, Tharyn. He lectured me and told me to go home. He's going to cover up that I was ever here, and the only reason for him to do that is to cover for Tiny Doom."

"So what will you do?"

"I can't go home. I'm going to resign, I guess."

"And then what?"

"I don't know. I don't know."

"Will you go back to Barbacoa? Your friend has become the talk of the island, a great hero."

"Friend? What friend?"

"Your friend Udo Landaðon," he said warily.

I vaguely remembered going to school with an Udo Landaðon, but we had never been friends. He was a glass-gazing fop, and I hate glass-gazing fops. "I have no desire to see Barbacoa again. And any way, Cutaway told me not to come back."

"Then where will you go?"

"I don't know."

"You could come with me."

"You should get as far away from me as possible, Tharyn. I'm no good," I said dolefully.

"Nini, that's absurd."

"Oset's dead and it's my fault. I almost got Flynn killed, almost got you killed. I almost ruined Buck's revolution. She was right not to trust me. If I go back to Califa, I'll be a liability to her. Plus, if Espejo told the Birdies about me, about Tiny Doom, they could come after me. If I go back to the City, it would put my family in danger."

"You have to do something."

"Maybe I'll just shoot myself in the head," I said bitterly.

Tharyn grabbed my arm as I turned away, but I shook his grip off. I didn't want his comfort. I didn't want to be told that things would look different in the morning or that hope was free. All those happy optimistic words were nothing but fiking shite. You could be good and kind and still die, through no fault of your own. You could do what you thought was right and still cock everything up.

Tharyn grabbed my arm again, and this time his grip was like iron. "It's not a joke to talk about blowing your brains out, Nini."

"I'm sorry. I shouldn't have said it. Please leave me alone, Tharyn. I just really want to be left alone now."

He loosened his grip, but he didn't drop it. "Look, while we were in Barbacoa, I sent a letter to my boss. I told him about you, told him what a help you were to me, and how you saved my skin in Cambria."

"You must have been selective in your telling," I said, but he ignored the comment and said, "I got his response just before I left. He authorized me to offer you a job."

"A job?"

"Ayah. You'd have to start out at the bottom as my assistant, but it's a great opportunity, Nini. The Pacifica doesn't hire often, but when you are in, you are in—they'll take care of you forever. I've got a delivery to make to

Porkopolis—not an express package, but a regular over-land delivery. Come with me."

"Why would you want that? I'm a disaster."

"Oh, fiking hell, yes, you are. But I guess I have a taste for disasters, and you, darling Nini, do taste delicious."

His words were an unfortunate echo of Espejo's, and I couldn't stop a little shudder.

He continued, "You said you wanted to get away, to see the world, to travel. Here's your chance. Just think— Porkopolis! Their buildings are so tall, you can see them from miles away. We'll take the dirigible—"

"Can I think about it?"

"No. I can tell your thoughts are not very good ones. Just say yes, Nini. Please, say yes. If you resign, if you don't go back to Califa, what else will you do?"

He had a point. I had limited funds and not much experience doing anything useful. Express agenting was about as close to rangering as you could get these days. If I took the position, I would be Nyana Romney—I could say goodbye to Flora Fyrdraaca forever. No one would know or care who my family was. I would make my own way.

"What if I screw that up, too?"

"You won't. I have faith in you, Nini. Have some faith in yourself."

"Ayah, so. I'll go with you."

He whooped and lifted me up in a bear hug, and I

clung to him. Suddenly, I felt pretty good. Suddenly, I actually had something to look forward to.

And then, for the last time, I hoped, Flynn and I trudged back to the post, leaving Tharyn to finish fleecing the other gamblers. I had to do one more thing before I left Sandy for good. Since the celebration at the hog ranch, a little idea had been itching at the back of my brain, but I had been too tired and overwhelmed with duty to think about it. Now, with everything settled, I could barely think of anything else.

After the big storm, the river was flowing steadily, the water a silvery ribbon unwinding through the shadowy desert. A fresh breeze shivered the cottonwood trees, made the rustling of the leaves sound somewhat like rain. A small fire burned outside one of the wickiups; several Broncos sat around it, smoking and eating from a tin mess kettle. They fell silent as I approached.

"La Bruja?" I said.

A woman pointed toward the river. The Broncos went back to their chow, dismissing me. Flynn had already disappeared into the thicket of cottonwood trees; I heard him snuffling and scratching in the bushes. It took me a few minutes to find the pathway through the canebrake; it was narrow and overgrown, but it was there. I followed it, glad for the brightness of the starlight. The air smelled of moisture and lush greenery and of some sweet flower. It didn't take much water for the desert to bloom.

Ahead, Flynn yipped happily and a voice shushed him. The path became rocky, the bushes fell away to reeds, and then I felt sand underfoot. Flynn had waded out into the water and was splashing happily around a dark figure. Her clothes were piled on the sand, her gun belt sitting on top of the neat pile. A stenchy fog of cigarillo smoke hung in the air.

"Come fer a bath, Lieutenant," La Bruja said cheerfully. She sent a wave of water splashing over Snapperdog, who jumped in delight. "The water's chill, but fresh."

"Why didn't you tell me you were on my side?" I demanded.

She took another puff of the cigarillo. "I never did have the time, did I? Sorry about them kicks. I tried to make 'em look good, but not too tough. Get down, ya fiking dog!"

"I'm fine," I said shortly. "Is he really dead?"

"He's out of yer hair, and that's all that matters."

"Come here, Flynn!" Flynn slogged out of the water and plopped down at my feet, looking slightly put out. I patted his head and repeated, "Is he dead?"

La Bruja drawled, "He ain't gonna bother you again. That's a pretty man you got there, Tharyn is his name? How'd he get here, anyway? I didn't hear he was on the stage—"

"Cut the fiking crap!" I cried. Flynn's ears pricked up and he looked interested. "Am I that fiking stupid? Do you think I'm that fiking stupid?"

For a moment, she stared at me, and I glared back. Then she laughed, long and hard, huddling down in the water, her shoulders shaking so much that for a moment I thought she might be crying. Flynn looked at me quizzically, and I was suddenly unsure. Then she raised her head, wiped her face.

"Ah, fike. You aren't stupid, Flora. Far from it," Tiny Doom said.

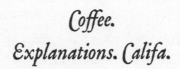

THIRTY-NINE

Coffee.
Explanations. Califa.

$\mathcal{T}$INY DOOM WADED OUT of the water, and I looked the other way as she dried off with a blanket. I put my sunshades on, but my Charm hadn't been strong enough to see through her Glamour in the daylight and certainly wasn't powerful enough to see through it at night. Tiny Doom was just a dark shadow. Silently, we went back down the path, past the Bronco fire. Their meal was done; one Bronco was chanting in a singsongy voice while the others listened. I couldn't tell if he was singing or just talking, telling a story, maybe. The smell of tobacco drifted through the air and for a moment my resolve wavered. I could walk away right now, go back to Tharyn, leave Arivaipa now.

But then I would never know the truth.

After the fresh air and the brilliant moonlight outside, the wickiup seemed close and stale. A small dented tin lantern hung from a branch, giving off a sallow yellow light. In the center of the hut, a coffeepot sat on the iron spider balanced over a heap of smoldering coals. There was no furniture; a battered Madama Twanky's Cream-o Crackers crate served as a table, and the saddle was a makeshift chair. A figure lay curled in a blanket near the fire: Pecos.

"Let's keep it low, so we don't wake up Pecos," Tiny Doom said. "Fike, I need some coffee."

"Is Pecos your kid?"

"Fike, no. He's just a friend of mine." She fished around in a woven basket and found two chipped cups. The coffee was thick as mud, and the condensed milk made it so sweet my teeth ached. She sat on the saddle and indicated that I should sit on the fur rug. I did not sit.

She took a gulp. "You know, this desert used to be at the bottom of the sea. Sometimes you find shells in the sand. Once I found the bones of a fish trapped in a rock. Are you all right?" She had lit one of those foul cigarillos, and in the close quarters of the wickiup it was very stenchy.

"Oh, ayah, I'm just dandy. My side hurts like fike, and I got an innocent woman killed, and my own mother lied to me, but otherwise I'm great."

"You've done your fair share of lying, Flora. So I don't see how you can bitch at me."

"Why did you have to lie to me?"

"I'm sorry. But I didn't know if I could trust you."

Well, I couldn't fault her there.

She continued, "And I thought it the best way to trap Espejo. I didn't want him to see me coming, and he didn't. But I'm sorry you got hurt in the process. And I'm awfully sorry about Captain Oset. She was in the wrong place at the wrong time. It's a shame, but there it is."

"Is he dead?"

Her silence was my answer, but I wanted to hear her say it.

"Tell me!" I hissed. The boy stirred a bit, and she patted his side reassuringly.

"No, he's not dead. But you needn't worry. He won't be a danger to you ever again. Or to anyone."

"Why didn't you kill him?"

"Because I don't want to piss off the Lord of the Smoked Mirror. Espejo is his boy. Ol' Tezcatlipoca gets mighty irked if anything happens to his boys. Espejo is nothing compared to the Smoked Mirror. But you never need fear he'll be any trouble to us again. How did you guess it was me? Even Espejo didn't catch me out."

"Your whole Bruja act is like something out of a Nini Mo novel. In fact, there was a La Bruja in a Nini Mo novel. *Nini Mo vs. the Arivaipa Tattler.*"

"It's a good thing for me Espejo only reads lofty literature," she said, laughing, but it wasn't funny.

I continued, "And you invoked Pig. Only a Haðraaða could invoke Pig."

"I was hoping you'd think he came on his own. And was I surprised when he showed up in the form of Evil Murdoch. What happened to Sieur Plushy Pig?"

"It's a long story," I said. "But, really, Flynn gave you away. I asked you to find Flynn and you did."

"Actually, Pecos had already found him. We were watching you at the Line when Flynn crossed, you know. Pecos followed him and caught him and took the sigil from him. It was a good sigil. Where'd you learn—"

"Never mind! None of that matters!" I said impatiently. "When you came to me that night, you said you had a plan. Was that your plan? To let me be the bait?"

"No, that wasn't my plan. My plan was to lure Espejo out into the open, track him while he thought he was tracking us. And at first, I thought we were doing just that. But when we camped for the night, Pecos caught up with me and told me that they'd found Oset's body, and then I knew he'd done the old switcheroo. Espejo isn't a Flayed Priest, but he's got enough mojo to pull off such a trick, at least for a while. By the time I got back to the camp, you'd already taken refuge in the cave. I had to wait until the storm was over before I could intercede."

"You should have told me what was going on."

"Maybe so. But I wasn't sure if you could keep your cool."

"Is that why you drugged me?"

"I'm sorry about that, honey. I didn't want you to do

anything, try to be helpful and just make things worse. Like your shotgun shells. It was a clever idea, but I fear such a sigil would have only pissed Espejo off and lost us our advantage."

"You took my shells? I thought Espejo did that."

"Naw, it was me. Advice: never leave your drink or your firearm unattended. But I underestimated you. You did excellently well. That poison trick was marvelous. If Espejo hadn't been a pophead, it would have worked. It was very good quick thinking. And that Curse was also superhelpful. Another second and he'd have had me."

"Everything I tried to do failed," I said dolefully.

"You saved us both," Tiny Doom said. "That's not a failure."

"I got Oset killed."

"Better her than you or me. If that sounds cold, well, the world is a cold place." Tiny Doom's cigarillo had burned down; she lit another and inhaled deeply. Death was nothing to her, I guess; she'd sent hundreds to their deaths, which is how she'd earned the nickname Butcher. But if she didn't care that Oset was dead, I did. And I would never let myself get hard enough not to.

I said, "I'm leaving tomorrow, you know. Were you just going to let me leave without finding out that you'd been nearby all along?"

"It seemed better that way," she said quietly.

I said hotly, "Well, I'm sorry! I screwed up, I know it,

and I led Espejo to you, just because I wanted to find you—more fool me! You didn't want me then and you don't want me now. Well, I don't want you, either!" She didn't stop me when I turned toward the door. She just sat there, smoking that cigarillo and twirling her coffee cup by its handle. She was going to let me go. I turned back. "You know, in Califa, they worship you. They have replaced the Goddess Califa with you. They think you will save them from the Birdies—"

"I barely saved myself from the Birdies," Tiny Doom interjected.

"But you did, didn't you? And now here you are, hiding from them like a coward! Your death almost killed Poppy. He's never been right since. He's ruined, and he ruined us, too, my entire family, and yet you were never even dead—it was all for nothing. How cruel can you be? Do you ever think of anyone other than yourself?"

"I thought of you, Flora. I thought of nothing but you. That's why I gave you away! I'm sorry that my choices dismay you, but I did the best I could at the time!"

"It wasn't good enough!"

She said furiously, "Well, fike you! I'd like to see you do better. It's fine for you to sit here now and tell me what I should have done. I hope you have no regrets later, that you do everything right the first time. But life isn't fiking like that, Flora. I'm sorry I couldn't be who you wanted me to be, but there it is. Take it or leave it."

I glared at her, and somehow it enraged me even more that she hadn't dropped the Glamour. She still stared at me with La Bruja's flat black eyes.

"Drop the Glamour! Just drop it! That joke is over and done with."

"It's not a Glamour," she said softly. "That form, that night of the storm, when you recognized me. That was the Glamour. This is my true face."

"What the fike are you talking about?"

She bowed her head, her voice muffled. "I'm sorry. I thought I was trying to spare you the truth, that you probably couldn't handle it, but maybe I was just sparing myself. Nini said, *Console your loss with vice, and pour vinegar on an open wound.*"

"Spare me the stupid sayings and just tell me the fiking truth!"

She lit another cigarillo and took several long draws, stalling, I guess. Finally, just as I was about to scream with impatience, she said, "I never thought they'd ever dare actually do anything to us—diplomatic immunity, blah, blah. I thought the Warlord would just cough up a ransom, we'd sign a peace treaty on their terms, then go home. Well, I was wrong. There was a trial, and we were found guilty of breaking all sorts of Birdie moral laws we'd never even heard of. I was too polluted to be given to any of the Birdie gods other than the Lord of the Smoked Mirror—he likes 'em bad, I guess. Hotspur was given to the Virreina, to fight as her champion. They'd already taken small Flora, Flora Primera. Poor Sorrel got thrown in with me, guilt by association, I guess.

"At first, I didn't actually care what happened to me. It seemed as good a time as any to get it all over with, and as good a way to die as any. When ole Tezca eats you, you are gone—no Cloakroom of the Abyss for you—and escaping Paimon sounded rather appealing. But then I realized I was pregnant. And suddenly I wanted to live. I wanted you to live. So Sorrel and I escaped. We had to leave Hotspur and Flora behind, but we escaped."

"How?"

She shook her head. "I'd rather not say. Some of the people who helped us are still around, and I don't want to compromise their safety. Anyway, Sorrel and I made to Arivaipa. But then I realized that Espejo was never going to let me go. As long as I lived—as long as you lived—he would be after us. As far as the Birdies are concerned, our entire family belongs to the Lord of the Smoked Mirror. As you have seen, Espejo is very tenacious when it comes to things he thinks are owed his master. So I came up with a plan. I guess you know what that was."

"Give me to Buck to raise as her own child."

"Ayah, so. I knew she could keep you hidden. I knew she would love you like her own. I knew she would keep you safe. And be a better mother to you than I could ever be. So we kept ahead of Espejo until you were born—"

I interrupted her. "Where was I born? Buck told me I was born by the side of the Shasta Road during the Trinity campaign, but obviously that wasn't true."

Tiny Doom laughed. "You were born in an encampment of the Red Turtle clan, up north, in the mountains. It was thanks to them that we were able to avoid Espejo for so long. I owe them an awful lot. Tezca may be pretty powerful, but he's no match for the power of the Dithee."

"So I was born in Arivaipa? I'm not even a Califan?"

"It's not where you are born that counts, it's how you live. I'd say you rate pretty high as a Califan, honey. Anyway, after I sent you to Buck, I gave myself up to Espejo, but first I made him promise to persuade the Virreina to allow Buck to ransom Hotspur. And he did. He's many things, dear Xava is, but he is a man of his word."

"But why did Major Sorrel give himself up, too? He was safe."

She sighed. "Oh, Sorrel. He was so honorable, sometimes he was downright idiotic. He had this idea that I should not face the plinth alone. I couldn't persuade or even order him out of that notion. Califa forgive me, but in the end, I was glad he was there, though it left his children fatherless."

"But you didn't die. Or you did die, and then you pulled the Ultimate Ranger Dare. You came back."

She shook her head. "He cut my heart out and ate it,

477

honey. There's no coming back from that. Even Nini Mo herself couldn't have managed that trick."

"You aren't a ghoul, are you, or a vampire?" I asked, afraid of the answer.

"No, yuck—Goddess, no. I am a revivifico. My Anima remains here, in the Waking World, but my body is gone. Consumed by Espejo. This body you see belonged to another. I have borrowed it, kept it sweet with a sigil. Soon it will decay and I shall have to borrow another. And then another and another. And so it goes."

A revivifico! My mother was a revivifico! I stared at Tiny Doom in horror. Revivificos aren't as ravenous as ghouls or mindless like zombies, but they are still animated corpses. Where did she get the bodies? I didn't want to know. Nini Mo was right. Ignorance is bliss. My hands were shaking. I clenched them so she would not see. I didn't want to give her the satisfaction of being proven right that I couldn't handle the truth, so I swallowed my horror and said, as airily as I could, "Well, at least you aren't a ravenous ghoul."

"Absolutely. There are advantages to this state. I don't need to sleep, I don't feel pain, and I don't need to eat." She laughed, but the sound was not mirthful.

"If you aren't really alive, then Espejo could not have killed you. You were never in any danger at all." This, more than anything else, enraged me. I had risked so much and for nothing. Nothing at all!

"Not true. Technically, the bodies I borrow are dead, so he can't kill them. But he could have destroyed my Anima, and then I would be done for permanently. And he certainly could have killed you. The danger was real enough."

"But it's over now. Espejo is taken care of. You have to come back to Califa."

She shook her head. "No. No."

"The people worship you. They'll rally to you. It's all well and good to have a blockade, and the jade stuff, but that's not the same as a leader. Rebellions need a leader, someone to rally around."

"Buck is the leader of the rebellion. And the return of Sylvanna Abenfarax is the rallying point."

"But she's been Birdie-ized!"

"No, she has not. She's made very nice to the Birdies so they would let her go home, but once she's there, they will find they have been mistaken about her. Badly mistaken. Listen, the woman they call Azota—she doesn't exist anymore. She's dead. I am not her. I am someone else entirely, Flora! Don't you understand?"

"Nyana! My name is Nyana! And I do understand. I understand that you are a coward!"

She sighed heavily, rubbed her face. "Nyana. I have done all I can for Califa. I have to let Buck do the rest—"

"You just don't want to face Poppy. You don't want to tell him you've been dead—alive—whatever the fike it is you are. You are a coward."

"Perhaps I am," Tiny Doom answered. "But what I do is my choice, not yours."

"And what about Axacaya? You said in the letter you left for me that you were coming for him. Where are those brave words now?"

"Oh, I have plans for Axacaya, but now is not the time for them. I can't go back to the City. But you should."

"Why should I?"

"You are the Head of the Haðraaða family. You are the focal point of Bilskinir House. Califa needs you. The City needs Bilskinir, needs our family's power. Getting rid of the Birdies isn't going to be easy. Buck will depend on you."

"Are you fiking me? Califa doesn't need my kind of help. I'm the last thing Buck needs," I said bitterly.

"You have fiked up plenty of this, it's true," Tiny Doom said. "But you've also stepped up and followed through when you had to. You saved the lives of those troopers and brought them home safely. You saved Tharyn's life not once, but twice. You stood against a nahual. Don't be so sorry for yourself, kid. Life sucks, you know; it's full of crap we don't want to do, but sometimes we have to suck it up and do it, anyway."

"Because it's my destiny?" I said bitterly. "Because I am a Haðraaða?"

"No. I can't afford to believe in destinies. If I believed my entire life and death had been ordained, I'd go insane.

Instead, I'd rather believe I made my own fate. Just as you will make yours. Go back because Califa needs girls with sand, and you, Nini, have a fikeload of sand."

Instead of soothing me, her words filled me with rage. How dare she tell me what to do? I hadn't come all this way and risked so much for her to lecture me. Let her stay in Arivaipa. Why the fike should I care? She had given birth to me, but that was all. In all other ways, she'd abandoned me. She couldn't tell me what to do now. She wasn't anything to me, just a moldering corpse. I didn't care what she did.

I sprang to my feet and ducked out of the wickiup. Tiny Doom called after me, but I ignored her. Flynn scrambled behind me. Tiny Doom could go to the fiking Abyss for all I cared. Tomorrow I would leave Fort Sandy and I would never look back. *You are either with us or against us,* Nini Mo said. Well, I was going to be neither. I was going to be far away from Califa and its problems.

At the parade ground, I stopped. The flagpole was empty. But in my imagination I saw the colors fluttering there: the blue and white regimental flag; the red and black insignia of the Warlord; the gorgeous purple flag of the Republic of Califa.

Califa. A wave of homesickness washed over me. I had been too frantic to think about Pow or Poppy or Paimon. Was Poppy still sober? Could Pow talk yet? I thought of Paimon alone in giant Bilskinir House, waiting for his family—for me—to return someday. The cozy clerks' office. Bilskinir's clean towels. Faithful Sieur Caballo. My annoying sister Idden. Buck.

If I went with Tharyn, it might be years before I saw Califa again. Pow would be grown. The rebellion would be over. Buck and Poppy would be old. Maybe even dead.

But how could I go back now? How could I explain to Buck what had happened? Why I'd run from the Dainty Pirate? Where I'd been all this time, and why? I couldn't reveal Tiny Doom's secret, and who knows how Buck would take my silence. Maybe she'd court-martial me. Worse, be disappointed in me. She had done so much for me, and see how I had repaid her?

And if I went back, I'd still be Flora Segunda. Always second to the lost Flora. I'd be trapped in family obligations, in duty and honor. I'd lose my chance to be my true self, Nyana, to have a job I'd earned, to be my own person, to see the world. And I'd lose Tharyn. I did not want to lose Tharyn.

"You know one of the things I miss most about Califa?" Tiny Doom asked quietly. She stood next to me, but I didn't turn to face her.

When I didn't answer, she said, "It's stupid, but I really miss the waffle dogs at Waffle Doggie Diner. We used to go there, late, after hours. It was always packed, so cheerful. You'd see the strangest people there and no one ever paid any attention to me. It was comforting. I am almost afraid to ask if it's still there."

"It's still there," I said. "Poppy and I ate there a week or so before I left."

"Do they still have pigeon-fat fries?"

"Ayah."

"And orca bacon burgers? They were Hotspur's favorite."

"That's what he had. With extra blue cheese."

"Ugh, disgusting." She shuddered and I shuddered with her, for she was right. Then she said, "I shouldn't lecture you. I haven't the right. I'm sorry. You must do as you think best. You are an adult now and can make your own decisions."

"All the decisions I make are wrong," I said bitterly.

"*Do the best you can,* Nini told me. *And let the chips fall where they may.* That Tharyn, do you like him?"

"Ayah, and he seems to like me, even though I'm hopeless."

"We are all hopeless in our hearts. I can see he does like you, very much. Go with him if you like. Enjoy him. Love him. Have adventures with him."

"What about Bilskinir, Paimon, the rebellion, the last Haðraaða, all that?"

"Aw, fike 'em. They got along without me, they'll get along without you. You have to follow your own Will. If it isn't your Will, don't force it. I forced it, and look where it got me. What do you want? What is your Will?"

When it's your true Will, you'll know it, Nini Mo said, *without having to think about it.*

I thought about it, and I still didn't know.

FORTY

Hassayumpa.
A Dilemma. A Delivery.

THARYN, FLYNN, and I left Fort Sandy the next morning, on borrowed horses, along with Sieur Taylor's cowboys. Before we mounted up, I paid a quick visit to the corral, where I fed Evil Murdoch half a pound of sugar and got spat on in thanks, then went to the post hospital, where I said goodbye to Munds. His shattered knee had earned him an early discharge, so he was in a pretty chippy mood; he thanked me profusely for saving his life.

As we rode off the post, I saw Major Rucker standing in the ramada of the COQ, Sally beside him. He waved, but I thought he wasn't as much saying goodbye as making sure that I left. No fear of that, Major Rucker. After we crossed the river, La Bruja jogged up on Evil Murdoch and fell in next to Sieur Taylor.

"Nice day for a ride, Taylor!" she hollered. Whatever the magick was that kept her going, it must pretty strong, for even now that I knew she was just a reanimated corpse, I would never have guessed. She was greasy, dirty, and her hair looked a rat's nest, but none of that awfulness was corpsey at all. Her current body must be fresh. Once again, I decided not to wonder where she got her supply. *Don't spit in your own well,* Nini Mo said.

"Nice day for a drunk, you mean," Taylor hollered back, but I knew now that the drunkenness was part of the act. La Bruja might look like a pickler, but Tiny Doom was always stone-cold sober.

Tiny Doom went all the way to Hassayumpa with us but never dropped her cover. That was just fine with me. For now, I knew all I wanted to know. Maybe someday I'd be ready for more.

We spent the night in Hassayumpa and caught the stage to Angeles the next morning. The cowboys rode off at first light, but the stage didn't go until midmorning, giving us time to lay in a hamper of chow at the café and for Tharyn to take an order from the general store. Tiny Doom had vanished into the saloon as soon we hit town and I hadn't seen her emerge, but when Tharyn and I got to the livery stable, she was already there. She traded insults with the stage driver as the freight was loaded, and I fed Evil Murdoch the last of my breakfast burrito. He didn't seem particularly appreciative, but he didn't try to bite me, either. I guess that's as grateful as a mule can be.

"I'm glad I'm not riding your spine all the way to Califa," I told him. He snorted mule goo all over me.

"Oh, ya leave ol' Murdoch alone," La Bruja said. "I'll fatten him up and when you come next, ya'll think yer riding on a featherbed."

"Major Rucker told me not to come back."

"Oh, Pow, don't mind him. Yer gonna work for the Pacifica now—we get mail sometimes, and send it, too. Speaking of which, can you deliver this letter for me when you get to Angeles?"

"Who told you I was going to work for the Pacifica?" I asked.

She grinned. "I hear things on the wind. Ain't I got the best hearing?"

"I've not been officially hired yet."

"Consider it a trial run, then."

I took her letter and slipped it into my jacket pocket. The other passengers were boarding the stage; Tharyn had already climbed inside. La Bruja kissed Flynn's nose and hoisted him up onto Tharyn's lap. She said something to Tharyn that I didn't quite catch, then turned back to me.

I was the only passenger left. The driver bawled at me and Tharyn leaned out the window, calling, "Come on, Nini!"

"Adios!" La Bruja said cheerfully.

"Adios!" I said.

"Come on, girlie! Git yer moving!" the stage driver bawled.

Tiny Doom smiled a mossy green smile and said in a low voice, "Don't fret, honey. There'll be time for us yet. *Dare, win, or disappear!*"

"We're leavin'!" the shotgun warned. I climbed into the stagecoach, and Tiny Doom slammed the door, then slapped the stairs up. With a jolt that threw me right into Tharyn's lap—squishing Flynn—the stage lumbered forward. By the time I got myself out of Tharyn's lap and leaned out the window, all I could see behind us was dust.

"What did she say to you?" I asked Tharyn.

"That she'd skin me alive and make my pelt into a coat if I let anything happen to you," Tharyn said, and laughed.

The trip to Angeles was grueling. Across the Sandlot Dry Drive—forty-five miles with no water—then through the Grivalda Pass, down into the Palma Valley, and eventually into Angeles. It took four days. The stage halted every few hours to change horses, take on passengers, drop off or pick up mail or freight, and give us a chance to piss and eat, but otherwise we bounced along, day and night.

The chow hamper stood Tharyn and Flynn well, but the rocking motion of the coach made me feel so pukey that I had to resort to the bottle of Tum-O I'd picked up in Hassayumpa. I spent most of the trip in a stupor, lulled by the heat and laudanum, buttressed from the worst of the jolts by Tharyn's furry bulk. If he'd been traveling alone, he would have reverted to his bear form and run the distance in half the time, so I knew the slow trip grated on him.

On the fourth afternoon, a cool breeze began to waft through the open window, and the dust was leavened with the smell of orange blossoms. The road smoothed out, and the mules put a spring in their steps. I rousted from my haze and looked out the window to see green rolling hills, festooned with grazing cattle, and long, low valleys filled with orange trees. We rounded a curve, and there on the horizon was a distant blue smudge of sea.

The stage had barely hit the outskirts of Angeles when a kid on a shaggy pony rode up alongside it, shouting that the Infanta Sylvanna's flotilla had arrived in the City. It had been escorted by three Kulani warships and the Dainty Pirate's flagship, and the Warlord had retired in her favor. As soon as we disembarked, I wobbled over to the news-hawk standing in front of the apothecary shop and bought a copy of the *Angeles Monitor,* so fresh the ink was still wet. On the front page was an engraving of the new Warlady and a copy of the speech she had made upon her arrival in the City.

Tharyn reading over my shoulder, I scanned the speech quickly. The new Warlady praised her father's wise rule, thanked General Fyrdraaca for her loyalty to the

City, expressed gratitude to the Virreina for providing her with such a fine education (did I detect a whiff of irony there?), and announced the formation of a new alliance between Califa and the Kulani Islands.

This was not exactly a declaration of separation from Birdie rule, but it was a start. Tiny Doom had been right. If the new Warlady was already making alliances with one of the Huitzil Empire's rivals, then she wasn't nearly as Birdie-ized as everyone had thought.

"The Virreina isn't going to like that one bit," Tharyn said as we headed toward the hotel. I glanced at him; he didn't look particularly happy about any of this exciting news. But he had had no stake in Califa's freedom. Nor, any longer, in Kulani matters.

I did.

But I wouldn't if I went with Tharyn to Porkopolis.

In the zocalo, a horn band was playing the Califa National Anthem over and over while people danced and sang, and a portable grog-shop did brisk business. The rousing choruses of "Cierra Califa!" gave me a twinge of nostalgia. *You cannot toy with old sweetness,* Nini Mo said. I swallowed the twinge down.

At the front desk of the Angeles Hotel, the clerk knew Tharyn, of course, and greeted him effusively. Tharyn introduced me as his new assistant, and after I signed the guest book, the clerk flipped it around and squinted at my name.

"Nyana Romney," he read. "Huh. I thought you might be someone else."

"Why is that?" I asked warily.

"Well, I got some mail here for a Flora Fyrdraaca, and I thought she might be you 'cause in both cases I was told that this here Flora Fyrdraaca is a young woman with red hair, and you are the only young woman with red hair I've seen in a long time."

Fike. Who would have left me mail at the Angeles Hotel? I was dying to know, but I wasn't sure I wanted to admit that I was Flora Fyrdraaca. The Dainty Pirate might be safely far away, but Buck could have noted me deserted by now, and put the guard on me.

"What kind of mail?" Tharyn asked.

"Luggage, Sieur Wraathmyr. A big trunk. And a letter."

Tharyn said smoothly, "Flora Fyrdraaca, did you say? I know her. She was in Cambria when last I was there. Look, I'm heading that way once I leave Angeles. Give the trunk over to me and the letter, too, and I'll be sure they are delivered." To my surprise, the clerk agreed to this suggestion. He rang for a bell girl, and while she fetched the trunk, he fetched the envelope from a mail cubby. I recognized the handwriting on the envelope even before he handed it to me: Buck.

The cold wind of guilty discovery blew through me, mixed with a dose of paranoia. How had Buck known I would be here? I glanced around, almost expecting to see her—or a provost marshal—hiding behind one of the potted plants, but the lobby was mostly empty. Judging from the roar, the rest of the guests were celebrating in the saloon. The bell girl appeared, wheeling a luggage cart, and there was my trunk, last seen aboard the *Pato de Oro,* so long ago! How the fike had it found its way here?

Well, no matter how, I was awfully glad to see it. I'd expended most of Poppy's mad money at the sutler's store in Sandy, replenishing my kit. I couldn't keep wasting divas on new pairs of drawers. Of course, I'd have no use for my uniforms anymore, but I could sell them and use the money to buy an outfit more suitable to an express agent.

The letter from Buck—briefly, I considered tearing the letter up and throwing it away. But no matter how much I might regret it later, I had to know what the letter said. I clutched it as we followed the bell girl upstairs, and my grip left sweaty marks on the paper. The bell girl showed us into the room, accepted Tharyn's tip, and left us alone.

"When I'm clean, I'm going to head down and book us passage to Porkopolis." Tharyn tossed his furry jacket and his satchel on one of the beds. Flynn took possession of the other, lying down with a happy sigh.

"That's a good idea," I said.

"The short route is north, through the Northwest Passage, but that means putting into Califa first."

"Is there another way?"

"Perhaps. I will see." He didn't ask me who the letter was from, and I did not offer the information. I sat on the bed until he went down the hallway to the bathroom, and then tore open the envelope.

The note was short and to the point, scrawled in Buck's own hand. It said:

Darling:

I heard what happened. They thought you drowned, but I have been to see your "friend" and I know you are still alive. I'm sorry, Flora. I should have trusted you. I'm sure you are thinking I'm pissed, and I was, but I'm not anymore. I just want you safe and home. We'll figure out what will happen next together. I've sent copies of this letter to every town along the coast, hoping that it will find its way to you eventually. If we are to succeed in our plans, I need your help. I love you very much.

—Mamma

P.S. No questions asked.

My "friend"? Fike. Buck had been to see Paimon. She's the Head of the House Fyrdraaca; he would owe her Courtesy and have to see her. What had he told her?

Surely he had been circumspect. Didn't he owe his loyalty to me? If he had told her everything about Tiny Doom and all I'd done . . . my blood turned to slushy ice at the thought. But then, if he had told her everything, surely she would not beg me to come home.

Tharyn reappeared, shiny clean. "Who is the letter from?"

"My mother," I said. "She wants me to come home."

"Oh." He put his furry jacket on, saying casually, "And will you go?"

"No. I've made up my mind," I said. "I'm going to Porkopolis."

"Good." He sounded relieved. "I'm off, then. I will meet you back here later, ayah?"

"Ayah."

At the door, he hesitated for a moment, but then just closed the door gently behind him.

I read the letter again. Need my help? Never before had Buck admitted that she needed me. What kind of help could I give her? No kind, for I would be far away in Porkopolis. Far away from all the fun.

I sat on the edge of the bed for a long time, staring at nothing, thinking of everything. Outside, the crowd had gotten tired of singing "Cierra Califa!" and had moved on to "Glorious Abenfarax." The room grew darker and warmer, and the delicious smell of toasting corn drifted in through the open window. And still I sat, Buck's words going round and round and round in my head, mixing with Tiny Doom's, in a bewildering chorus.

Come home, Buck said.

Do what you will, said Tiny Doom.

I need your help, Buck said.

They'll be fine without you, Tiny Doom said.

No questions asked, Buck said.

It's your life, Tiny Doom said.

The more I thought, the less clear things became. How can you want two things so badly that are complete opposites of one another?

Flynn had clambered up on the bed and fallen asleep, snoring faintly, his legs wiggling. Eventually, he woke up and nosed me hungrily. Thus rousted, I realized I was hungry, too, so went down the hall for a quick bath and then opened my trunk. My clothes were slightly damp and very wrinkly, but otherwise they were fine. There was mold growing on my dress wig; I pitched the entire wig case into the trash. The damp had not permeated the tin I kept my chocolate stash in. I did not open the case that contained the ferrotype of Buck, Pow, and Poppy. Instead, I ate two bars of Madama Twanky's Best Black Salted Cherry Crisps, gave Flynn a couple of jerky strips, and then dug Tiny Doom's envelope out of my dispatch case. Whatever I decided to do next, I had promised to deliver it, so I might as well get that job out of the way. It would be a welcome distraction.

When Tiny Doom had given me the envelope back in Hassayumpa, I hadn't looked at it too closely. Now I saw, irritated, that the label had no address on it, only a name and town: Madama Zarendeo, Angeles. Well, Angeles wasn't that big. Surely someone at the post office would know where Madama Zarendeo lived.

At the front desk, the clerk told me that the post office was closed by now. "But if you need to post something, there's a post box in the lobby."

"I'm looking for someone. She ordered something from Madama Twanky's new collection, but she forgot to put her address on the order," I said. "I thought maybe the post office might know where she lives." Tharyn wasn't the only one who could lie on his feet.

"What's her name?"

"Madama Zarendeo."

"Oh, you mean the Duquesa de Xipe Totec," the clerk said. "Look in the saloon."

"What? Who?"

"Ayah. She got here last week, and she's been sitting in the saloon ever since, waiting for someone, something, I dunno, you, maybe. Black hat, big sunshades, black coat. Saloon."

"There's some confusion. I'm looking for Madama Zarendeo, not the Duquesa de Xipe Totec."

"They're the same, madama. Zarendeo is her family

name. The Duquesa de Xipe Totec is her title. Look in the saloon."

What the fike is Tiny Doom playing? I wondered as I headed toward the saloon. If she wanted me to take a message to the Duquesa, why didn't she say so in the first place? Because I wouldn't have done it, that's why. What was the Duquesa doing in Angeles? My orders had been to meet her in Cuilihuacan, a hundred miles south of here, in Birdieland—before I'd abandoned those orders, that is. And why was Tiny Doom sending the Duquesa a message, anyway?

Then I caught myself. None of this was my concern. I was going to Porkopolis with Tharyn, and leaving intrigue, messages, and secret Birdie duquesas behind. Just find the Duquesa, hand over Tiny Doom's message, and forget about it. Job done, that's all.

The hotel saloon was full of people toasting Califa's new Warlady with punch and raucous cheering. I told Flynn to sit by the lobby door so he wouldn't get squashed, then pushed through the crowd. At the bar, a large man with a walrus mustachio swept me into a jubilant embrace. I applied my knee and he let me go, but not until after bestowing a very sloppy kiss on my neck. I did not see a woman in a black hat or big sunshades anywhere, but the crowd was so thick and I am so short that maybe I'd missed her. When my waving finally got the busy barkeep's attention, I shouted my question at him, and he pointed over his shoulder toward several secluded red leather booths at the back of the saloon.

The first booth contained a very spoony couple. The second hosted a poker game. And in the third sat a woman in a big black hat and black sunshades, who looked at me as I approached and said, "What do you want?" in a scowly voice.

"Are you Madama Zarendeo?"

"And so I am?" In the murk, I could just make out a glint of light reflecting on the lenses of her sunshades. She didn't seem to be dressed like a Birdie, but she was still hiding her face like one.

"I have a letter for you."

"I am she." She held out her hand and I gave her the letter. "Where do you come from?"

"Arivaipa Territory."

"Shall there be funds due on the delivery?"

"No, madama. Please, excuse me." Out of the corner of my eye, I noticed that Flynn had been hoisted up on the bar and was being offered a basin of what looked like beer by Sieur Walrus Mustachio. Beer makes Snapperdog burp; I hurried over to rescue him before he drank too much. To a chorus of disappointed shouts, I slung Flynn over my shoulder and headed toward the door, when a grip halted me. I turned, and there was the Duquesa at my back. She said something to me, but I couldn't hear over the din, and then Sieur Walrus Mustachio was pushing a glass toward me. I had to take it or risk liquid sloshing all over my front.

"To the Warlady!" he bawled, raising his own glass. This toast was echoed by those standing around us.

"To the Warlady!" I said, taking a cautious sip. The liquid was pure mescal and would have choked me, or killed me if I'd drunk it straight. As it was, once I swallowed, I wondered if I had just burned my throat out.

Sieur Walrus pushed a glass toward the Duquesa. She shook her head with a look of distaste.

"You will not drink to the Warlady?" Sieur Walrus demanded.

"I do not touch spirits."

"Ain't spirits, lady," the pipsqueak next to Sieur Walrus said. "It's pure cactus lightning! Califa's own glow!"

"I do not touch spirits," the Duquesa repeated.

"Drink to the Warlady's health!" Sieur Walrus demanded. His eyes had narrowed down into piggy little slits. *A drunk and a hair trigger,* said Nini Mo, *one and the same.*

"I shall toast in water, but I do not drink the alcohol," the Duquesa said.

"It ain't a toast until it's done in booze," Sieur Walrus said.

"She's a Birdie, Bob!" the pipsqueak said. "That's why she won't drink."

"A Birdie, huh?" Sieur Walrus's face grew darker. We

had caught the attention of the crowd around us, and it was an attention I did not care to have. The happy chatter was turning into a somewhat ominous muttering.

I said quickly, "Come on, madama, never mind him. He's drunk."

She said angrily, "So that I am a Huitzil? What matter does that make?"

"Your Virreina's a sow-backed hedger," Sieur Walrus said. "You eat our country alive, you Birdies, with your peck, peck, peck. I swear, I'd drill a hole in your liver and let the bile drip out—"

His hand dropped to his waist, but thank the Goddess he was soused, for his grip was a mere fumble and I was able to draw on him first. He ignored my draw until I shoved Oset's pistol right into his chunky ribs. Then he looked down at me, blearily, and I think he would have tried to bat the pistol away, except that he saw that I had already cocked.

"Leave the lady alone," I said. "Madama, if I were you, I'd go back to my room."

"I will not hide in my room like a coward," the Duquesa said indignantly. "It is a free country!"

"Not with you Birdies in charge, it ain't," the pipsqueak said. "You want tribute, we'll give you prisons and graves for your tribute! Fike your Virreina!"

The Duquesa raised her hand as though she was going

to pop the pipsqueak one, and at her motion, the crowd growled. With my free hand, I blocked her blow, and said to Sieur Walrus, "You and your friend, clear out of here, right now, before I drill a hole in *your* liver and see what comes out. Don't try me, I swear, or you'll find I'm as serious as hell in winter."

Sieur Walrus puddled a bit then; he wasn't drunk enough to chance a gun to the gut. But the pipsqueak said shrilly, "I say we make an example of her and send her back home again in pieces! Show the Birdies how we really feel!"

This suggestion was greeted with a few hearty cheers from the crowd, and now it seemed a good time to beat a hasty retreat. *It's a matter of seconds,* Nini Mo said, *from a friendly crowd to a bloodthirsty mob,* and I only had five bullets. I withdrew the poke from Sieur Walrus's paunch and, before the pipsqueak could say another word, buffaloed him with a mild Gramatica Curse. He folded like a stack of cards in a high wind, the high heels of his cowboy boots drumming amidst the peanut shells.

The crowd was suddenly very quiet. Now was the moment; they'd either draw back, or lunge and tear us apart. I realized I kinda didn't care which they did—in fact, I almost wished they'd lunge. I had a few more Curses to put to the test. But the barkeep killed the tension. He leaned over the bar and looked down at the pipsqueak, now drooling blood, and said to me, "That's a big enough mess tonight. Get you both out of here, before I call the sheriff. The rest of you, simmer down, or I'll shut the place down."

"My apologies," I said, and stuffed my last five divas in the tip jar and took the Duquesa's arm. The crowd parted for us and let us through.

"I should call the sheriff and have that man detained," the Duquesa said indignantly as we crossed into the lobby. No one from the bar followed. "At home, he would be whipped for his insolence."

"You are not at home, madama," I said. "And best remember that."

"I shall. I shall. You handled that well. I see why La Bruja speaks well of you. I shall be ready at first light."

"Thank you," I said automatically, and then, as her words sank in: "La Bruja? Ready for what?"

"To depart for the City, no?" the Duquesa said. "La Bruja recommended you quite well, and since my other escort never arrived, I shall rely on you. I know it is a long journey and perhaps it's best, considering this reaction, that I should go in disguise. I could dress as a dancer or perhaps a cigar girl—"

"I cry your pardon, madama," I said, interrupting her, since she didn't seem to have any intention of pausing long enough to take a breath. "I have no idea what you are talking about. I cannot escort you to the City. Do not mistake me, just because I bailed you out there—I'm not terribly fond of the Birdies either—"

"But La Bruja said you would! And how else shall I get there otherwise, with these ruffians besetting me? And I must arrive, else . . . well, I just must arrive. The Warlady counts upon me. La Bruja said I may count on you! She said you were a great ranger. Did you not bring me her letter?"

Now I was really pissed at Tiny Doom. She hadn't tried to persuade me to go back to the City, because she had planned to *trap* me into going, put me in a position where it was impossible to say no. Well, good luck to her, but no dice. Even if I did decide to return to the City, I wasn't going to escort the Huitzil Ambassador's wife there. Califa needed fewer Birdies, not more.

"I'm sorry, madama. I cannot help you," I said firmly. "No matter what La Bruja said. Please excuse me." Annoyingly, the Duquesa followed me, saying, "She said I could trust you completely. I shall pay you for your worry."

"Madama," I said firmly, turning to face her. From what seemed like a great roaring distance, I heard my breath catch roughly in my throat. The Duquesa had taken off her sunshades.

And she looked exactly like Buck.

No, not *exactly* like Buck: the green eyes were the same, and the shape of the chin, and the curve of the cheeks. Her hair, mostly hidden by the hat she still wore, seemed to be black. But the expression on her face was the clincher: annoyance mixed with irritation mixed with exasperation. How often had I seen that look on Buck's face?

The Duquesa de Xipe Totec was my long-lost sister, Flora Primera.

"Please help me, Madama Romney," Flora Primera said. "I really need to arrive to the City as soon as possible. It is urgent for the Warlady's plans."

Behind the Duquesa, Tharyn was coming through the hotel's front door. He saw me and waved, and with a twisting heart, I waved back. *When it's your true Will,* Nini Mo said, *you'll know it without having to think.* Now I didn't have to think at all.

I was going home.

Summation
Magickal Working No. 9

by
Nyana Georgiana Brakespeare Hadraada
or Tyrdraaca
Written in Sub-Rosa Ranger
Scriptive Code

It occurred to me a few days ago that I never got around to doing the summation of the Blood Working. I've been pretty busy, plus lacking paper and pen, not to mention time to suss out the code. Now, finally, I have a moment or two to reflect, and engraved stationery to reflect upon. So here's some reflection.

I guess the Working was a success, although not entirely in the way I had planned. I mean, yes, in that I tried to find Tiny Doom and I found her. If this were a sentimental weepie, I'd now write *And yet I found so much more, too* . . . Also, if this were a sentimental weepie, I'd list all the lessons I'd learned, and they'd be heartfelt and moving, and this paper would be damp with my tears, et cetera, very sickening.

Well, I did learn a lot of practical stuff. Don't put your bedroll on an anthill; never trust a fish; keep your shotgun when you go to the privy; rinse out your hankie immediately; a boot is an obvious hiding place, et cetera. As far as heartfelt and moving, well . . .

It's funny. For as long as I can remember, I have wished I wasn't a Fyrdraaca. If only I were someone else, I thought, I would be free of Poppy's crazy drunkenness, and Mamma's strict attention to duty, and Idden's stuck-upness. I wouldn't be the Second Flora anymore, I'd be able to follow my own Will, express my own desires, chart my own course. I thought if I wasn't a Fyrdraaca, I'd be free.

Thanks to the Working, I now realize that being a Fyrdraaca isn't so horrible after all. My family may be full of wild craziness, but they are loyal to a fault, and will stick up for each other. Dealing with them all these years taught me a few things that turned out to be superhelpful. It's like Nini Mo said, *They may be snapperheads, but they are* my *snapperheads.* I may not be a full Fyrdraaca by blood, but I sure am by temperament. And maybe that's not such a bad thing.

I watch the Duquesa de Xipe Totec, who is a full Fyrdraaca by blood, but not by temperament, and I think how lucky I was to grow up with a family at all. Doña Ana, the Duquesa's duenna, told me that the Duquesa was raised by the priestesses of Xochiquetzal. She lived in a barracks with forty other girls. Having recently spent some time in a Barracks, I would not have wanted to grow up in one.

When I was a kid, I had imagined that one day I would find Flora Primera, rescue her from the Birdies, and bring her home. Her disappearance was the shadow that loomed over our family, the reason Poppy drank, Mamma worked like a servitor, and Idden was sour. I was just a replacement for her, not nearly as good as the real thing. I had believed her return would make us all happy. Later, I had realized that there was probably no point in looking for Flora Primera, that surely the Birdies had killed her, sacrificed her to one of their bloody gods. Otherwise, Mamma would have ransomed her, like she did Poppy, long ago. But they did not sacrifice her. Here she is, when I least expected her.

I'm sure La Bruja knew all along who the Duquesa really is, and that's why she sent me to her. Devious, but obvious. I asked the Duquesa how she knew La Bruja and she said vaguely, "Oh, she rescued me from the Broncos long ago" and then she started in on what color petticoat she should wear, and I couldn't get any more out of her on the subject. I couldn't tell if she knew that La Bruja wasn't La Bruja at all. I don't dare ask.

I wonder if the Birdie Ambassador knows who the Duquesa really is, and that's the true reason he asked me to escort her back to Califa. He was rubbing it in, showing Mamma his power. *I can take your child and make her mine.* Well, if he thought that, fike him, because she might act Birdie on the outside, but she's a Fyrdraaca on the inside. She'll always be. You can't change that, no matter what. Blood will win out.

I've definitely learned *that* lesson.

Anyway, the summation. I'm supposed to consider what I would do differently next time. Fike! Maybe everything? If I had to do the Working all over again, I wouldn't do it.

Don't look a gift mule in the mouth, Nini Mo said. She was right. If I'd left well enough alone, Captain Oset would be alive. I never would have met Tharyn, or La Bruja, or found out what I could do in a pinch. But Captain Oset would still be alive. I thought I was so fiking clever, and so fiking in control, and so fiking sure of myself. Actually, I was none of those things and so Captain Oset is dead. Nothing I ever do will change that. I don't know what else to say to that. I'm sorry, of course, horribly awfully terribly sorry. But that hardly does Captain Oset any good, does it?

Tharyn was really irked when I told him I wasn't going to Porkopolis with him. I tried to explain why, but he wouldn't listen. He just seized up into arrogant coldness, told me to have a nice trip, and stalked away. I didn't chase after him, even though I wanted to, because, why bother? I had ditched him, and no explanation softens that.

Also, I was rather irked, too. Of course I want to go to Porkopolis; of course I want to join the Pacifica Express.

But I have to go home first. I had poured my heart out to him, told him all my secret desires, and if, after all that, he couldn't understand, well then, fike him. I have enough people in my life who don't understand me. The last thing I need is one more.

We saw Tharyn on the boat to Barbacoa; he refused to speak to me and spent the trip huddled by the goat pens, staring out at the ocean and looking broody. Flora Primera was quite taken with this broodiness and tried to sweet on him several times, but he gave her the high hat, too. That's probably just as well. She is a married lady, even if she doesn't act like it. She flirts with everyone, and they all think she is so darling, they smile and give her everything she wants. I can't begrudge her too much; it must be small consolation for being married to the awful, raw Duque de Xipe Totec. She's his third wife, Doña Ana told me, and not the Conde's mother, which was quite a relief to me, as I hated like fike to think of Birdie blood entering the Tyrdraaca line, even if that line is only half mine. Also, the Conde is a brat and I don't want to be the aunt of a brat.

The Duquesa is actually pretty silly, but in a cute way, so it's hard to hold that against her. She keeps mentioning that she's the Warlady's best friend and that the Warlady relies on her in all things, and she keeps dropping hints that the Warlady's plans cannot succeed without her assistance, but I find that hard to believe. Perhaps the Warlady's hairdressing plans need the Duquesa's assistance, but I can hardly see her giving any useful political advice.

The Duquesa's still calling me Madama Romney, and I haven't dissuaded her of the name. I can't tell if she knows her true heritage or not. She certainly acts like a Birdie, but she's been with them since she was six, so I guess by now she wouldn't know how to act any other way. The minute she sets foot on City soil, everyone is going to know who she really is if she doesn't keep her face covered. Doña Ana keeps telling her to put her veil back on, but she refuses. I'm surprised someone hasn't recognized her yet. It's creepy how much she looks like Mamma, but then she giggles a very silly giggle that blows the resemblance. Mamma's been a lot of things, but she's never been silly.

When we got to Barbacoa, Cutaway met us at the dock, full of sweeping smiles and lavish Courtesies. *Oh, Your Grace, welcome to my little island,* she said, *and Madama Romney, how nice to see you again, I see your trip was a success! Congratulations!* No mention of the fact that she told me never to come back; I guess the Duquesa's glory canceled out my sins. I would have loved nothing more than to flick my foot right into that supercilious smile, but I dared not, of course. It's her island. Yet Haðraaðas have very long memories. She can bet her silver-handled scissors that I am not done with her yet.

Now we are installed in the fanciest suite in the Barbacoa Hotel. Flynn got his own room with his own valet, which he totally deserves after all he's been through. This morning I got lost trying to find the bathroom—shades of Crackpot Hall and its shifting rooms, but here, everything is fancy and clean, not old and moldering. The towels are the size of bed sheets and thick as horse blankets. When Tharyn and I had stayed here before, our towels were average-sized and rather thin. Well, we weren't Birdie aristocrats. I doubt if the Duquesa could have survived a smaller towel.

Oh, ayah, and guess what I found hanging in the closet of my room? My dispatch case. Completely intact, everything as I left it. And guess what was sitting on the bed?

Pig, as pink and inscrutable as ever. I have to say I like him much better as a plushy pig than as a mule. He's much huggier and less prone to spitting.

Tharyn didn't check in at the hotel; I don't know where he's staying. I guess he's consoling his loss with vice somewhere, pouring vinegar on his open wound. What a snapperhead! Why did I let down my guard? I was so much happier when I hated him.

We came to Barbacoa because we couldn't get a ship directly to the City. The Warlady has ordered the Gate closed, they say, and Kulani warships gathered right outside. No one is sure when the Birdies will answer the new Warlady, or how, but waiting is making people nervous. No ships in Angeles were willing to leave port until they knew what was going on, but I did find a schooner heading to Barbacoa and got us passage on that. I figured that once in Barbacoa, we'd find someone to take us to the City. Surely pirates would not worry about Birdie warships.

But we've been here a week now, with no luck. I hit every ship in the harbor and offered each a fantastic amount of money, and no one would take us. Not too long ago I never wanted to think about seeing the City again. Now I can't wait to get there. It's very frustrating to be sitting here—even with giant plush towels—and know all the excitement is very far away.

But then, earlier today, the weirdest thing happened. I'd gone down to the concierge to see if she'd had any luck getting us a ship north, but she hadn't. There's a new rumor now: that the Birdie Navy is on its way to force open the Gate. A fishing boat came in early this morning and said they'd talked to another fishing boat from Qeuca Bay and that this boat had seen the flotilla sailing up the coast. No one will leave the Barbacoa harbor until they know whether this rumor is true. Cowards! And they call themselves pirates and privateers! By the time the Birdie Navy got to Angeles, a fast schooner could be in the City already, and surely they would open the Gate once they knew who we were.

Anyway, so I went to the lobby bar to tell the Duquesa we were still stuck. I found her sitting on a velvet sofa, ringed by admirers vying to buy her drinks and popcorn snacks. I recognized some of these admirers from my previous visit to Barbacoa, and to a one they were a lot of murderous rum-gunning racketeers, slavers, and thieves. But they sure thought she was cute. And she was, too, with her fluttering fan and the little dimple in her chin when she smiles. Even I find it hard to resist her.

I extracted her from her rapscallion admirers and we went into one of the private saloons, where I broke the bad news. The Duquesa wasn't happy. She said, "This is ridiculous. We have to get to Califa. We are running out of time." She stamped her feet; she was wearing purple court shoes with tiny red heels and big silver buckles. They were the sweetest shoes I'd ever seen.

"I'm doing the best I can, Your Grace."

The Duquesa snapped her fan open and shut, once, twice, irritated. All the sweetness had drained out of her face, and now, suddenly, she looked like Poppy. "La Bruja said I could trust you. She said you are on our side. You are not trying to hinder my passage, are you?"

"I want to get back to the City as much as you do, Your Grace," I told her. "It's not my fault that all the outlaws here are cowards."

Before she could answer, a voice said, "I believe, madamas, that I may be able to help you."

A settee stood with its back to us. While we were talking, Flynn had disappeared behind it. Now we turned and saw a vision rising from the settee's depths, a vision in black and purple: purple frockcoat with black frogging; black weskit with purple embroidery; purple trunk hose worn over black cannions and stockings. The vision's broad chest was bisected with a gold embossed leather buckler; he was well armed with both cutlass and pistol. Topping off this confectionary outfit—or bottoming it, I suppose—was a pair of red sparkly high-heeled boots, each toe tipped with a hissing snake's head. The boots were hideous, but otherwise, he was absolutely the most glorious young man I had ever seen. Flynn was frisking ecstatically at his feet.

As the Duquesa and I stared slack-jawed, the Glorious Man bent low in a Courtesy: Abasing Myself Before Incomparable Beauty. The Duquesa's fan snapped open again, and the dimple reappeared.

The Glorious Man said grandly, "Allow me to introduce myself. I am Udo Moxley Landaðon, captain of the *Pato de Oro*."

I had known an Udo Landaðon back at Sanctuary School, but that Udo was a silly flippergidget, and scrawny to boot. This man was none of those things, and most particularly not scrawny. But he did seem strangely familiar. Flynn shived Captain Landaðon's glorious leg and he bent down to scratch Flynn's ears.

"You are the one they call El Calavera," Flora Primera said. "The Rake. The pirate."

"Pirate is a strong word, madama. I sail under a letter

of marque signed by the Warlady herself. I believe that makes me a patriot, not a privateer," Captain Landaðon answered. He said that he had overheard our conversation and wanted to offer his services. He would be delighted to take us to the City; in fact, he said, he had business there anyway, so it was no trouble, which gave him great sorrow, for he would like nothing more than to go to great trouble on the behalf of two such elegant and refined ladies.

I had to admit that even though Captain Landaðon was laying it on a bit thick, after Tharyn's recent snooti-ness it was nice to meet someone with such exquisite manners. Of course, we accepted his kind offer and went with him to the bar, where we celebrated our newfound association with champagne. The Duquesa giggled and was charming, but Captain Landaðon kept looking at me sidelong, in a blush-making way that I didn't mind at all. It somehow seemed as though I had always known him.

While we were sitting in the bar, Tharyn came in, but as soon as he saw me with Captain Landaðon and the Duquesa, he turned and stomped out again. This time I did run after him, but by the time I got to the lobby, he was gone.

So now we have passage to Califa. We are leaving as soon as the winds pick up, which Captain Landaðon—El Calavera—anticipates will be tomorrow. In two days, we could be home. I wonder if Pow is walking or talking yet. I wonder what Poppy will say when he sees the Duquesa.

I wonder if Mamma is really going to ask me no questions. I hope Valefor isn't too mad when he finds out I was the reason he was banished. I hope Idden will understand I've been places and done things, too, and will treat me accordingly. And I hope Mamma will understand that I am not the second Flora anymore.

Ayah, so—the weird thing that happened . . . Meeting Captain Landaðon wasn't the weird thing. The weird thing happened as we were leaving the bar. He walked us to the elevator and kissed the Duquesa's hand, promised her he would send for her luggage first thing in the morning. Then he bent over my hand—who would have thought a kiss on the hand could be so tingly—and as he did so, I saw something crimson wiggling in the curls cascading down his shoulder. It took me a second to realize it was a tentacle waving at me.

It was Octohands. Dear, darling, Octohands. Alive!

Before I had a chance to exclaim, Captain Landaðon straightened up and the tentacle disappeared. It seemed best to be discreet, so I acted as though I hadn't seen anything unusual. But you can bet, as soon as we are on board the *Pato,* I will get Captain Landaðon alone and find out how he hooked up with Octohands. And then get Octohands alone and find out how the fike he survived the fight with Espejo. That old snapperhead. I should have known no Birdie nahual was going to take down a Haðraaða.

So.

For a long time I've felt pretty full of despair and darkness. Now I actually feel pretty good. *Hope is free,* Nini Mo said, and I've got a lot of hope. I know we have a long way to go before Califa is free, before I can tell the world who I really am and claim my rights as the Head of the House Haðraaða. All my problems are not magickally solved. But right now I feel pretty fiking good about the coming fight. I know who I really am, and I know who my friends are, and that's what counts.

Which sounds totally sentimental and sickeningly heartfelt, but just happens to be abso-fiking-lutely true.

She who lives will see.